An avid reader from childhood, Paula J. Beavan grew up on a small property in the Hunter Valley, riding horses, mustering cattle and listening to the tales of local farriers, cattlemen and farmers. Her love of the land and its history together with a curiosity about the challenges faced by the pioneering women of the region led her to seek out stories of the area's early European settlers. Serendipitously, she discovered a family connection to William Harpur, local landowner and one of Australia's early surveyors. Inspired by this connection, she delved deeper to discover that when William Harpur lost his sight, his wife Catherine managed their Hunter River property—a perfect illustration of the women she writes about.

Daughter
of the
Hunter Valley

Paula J. Beavan

mira

First Published 2021
First Australian Paperback Edition 2021
ISBN 9781867221449

Daughter of the Hunter Valley
© 2021 by Paula J. Beavan
Australian Copyright 2021
New Zealand Copyright 2021

This is a work of fiction. Names, characters, places, and incidents are either the product of the author's imagination or are used fictitiously, and any resemblance to actual persons, living or dead, business establishments, events, or locales is entirely coincidental.

Published by
Mira
An imprint of Harlequin Enterprises (Australia) Pty Limited (ABN 47 001 180 918), a subsidiary of HarperCollins Publishers Australia Pty Limited (ABN 36 009 913 517)
Level 13, 201 Elizabeth St
SYDNEY NSW 2000
AUSTRALIA

® and TM (apart from those relating to FSC®) are trademarks of Harlequin Enterprises (Australia) Pty Limited or its corporate affiliates. Trademarks indicated with ® are registered in Australia, New Zealand and in other countries.

A catalogue record for this book is available from the National Library of Australia
www.librariesaustralia.nla.gov.au

Printed and bound in Australia by McPherson's Printing Group

For Dave, always.

Prepare thy work without, and make it fit for thyself in the field;
And afterwards build thine house

Proverbs 24:27 KJV

One

Friday, 16 December 1831—extremely hot

Madeleine Barker-Trent shielded her eyes against the sun and pulled at her loosely tied stays. The heat was unbearable. Peering over the heads of the twelve yoked bullocks, she sighed. How much further could it be? The bullock driver walked beside the team, patrolling up and down and constantly observing the slow-moving oxen.

'Mr O'Brien?' Maddy called over the sound of the creaking wheels.

His shoulders stiffened; his own sigh was loud in the sudden silence of the bush. The oxen lumbered on, but he waited until she drew level. His blue eyes met hers: eyes that were, she noted, startlingly bright in the leathered darkness of his face.

'Bout five miles,' he muttered and turned his attention back to the bullocks.

'But you said five—' Maddy began, but the snaking stockwhip swirled and cracked, echoing through the bush, and cut her off mid-sentence. She frowned—had she misunderstood? She was certain he'd said it was only five miles when she'd asked earlier.

Five miles from Papa. A tingle of apprehension ran up the back of her neck and lifted the hair on her scalp. Why hadn't he been at the docks to meet the ship, or even at Green Hills? Her stomach tightened and she prayed he had not suffered overly at the terrible news in her letter. Oh Mama, I wish you were here. She blinked back the tears.

A blast of raucous laughter echoed from the trees. Maddy swayed alarmingly, almost toppling from her precarious position on the hard bench seat as the dray lurched over the uneven track. Peering around, she searched the forest for the source of the mocking laughter. It had stopped as suddenly as it had begun. Two large-beaked birds sat side by side on a branch, watching as the dray rolled by. The twin lines of cattle showed no sign of being disturbed by the laughter, but went on dragging their burden through deep ruts of dried mud. Spinning around on the narrow seat she saw Mr O'Brien also was unbothered, and he had to have heard it. His concentration remained locked on the beasts.

One of the birds opened a vicious-looking beak and, with head tipped back, repeated the laughing call. Another unseen bird answered in the distance. Maddy scanned the trees for more of the creatures but saw only the dust and scrub. The surrounding forest was tone on tone of grey and olive green, looming threateningly above her. The open grasslands and fields of ripening wheat had been left behind as the bullocks wove along the trail, taking her further from what small measure of civilisation she'd seen since leaving Sydney on the overnight steamer to Greenhills.

'Get up there, Sweety,' Mr O'Brien cajoled, as one of the team paused to tug a clump of dry grass that sprang from the side of the trail. His gentleness with the oxen was incongruous, but she had noted the way the animals responded to his kindness.

'Have you been in New South Wales long, Mr O'Brien?' The glance he sent her told her she'd made some kind of faux pas.

'I'm sorry,' she apologised hurriedly, wishing she could recall her words.

The driver waited as the dray rolled on, and when he was once more beside her, he strode along next to the wagon. ''Tis of no matter, miss. I came a freeman, but some folks round here don't take kindly to sharing history they'd sooner forget.'

Maddy swallowed, duly chastised by his quiet words.

Mr O'Brien sent an assessing glance over the track ahead before calling out once more to the yoked pair at the lead. Ahead the road was little more than twin ruts running through the thick scrub. Maddy wiped a rivulet of sweat from the corner of her eye and, extricating the bonnet from her head, flapped it before her face. She had been hoping to find a modicum of relief but was disappointed. Teeth clashing, she clutched the side of the seat as the dray lurched through yet another deep hole, her entire body rigid in the effort to stay put. Her stomach churned as she anticipated the reunion with Papa. It should have been a joyous time, but it would be bittersweet without Mama. A sob swelled in her chest— the discomfort of the hard seat and the strange noises of the forest were forgotten as her thoughts, bouncing almost as much as her bottom, ran over the last bittersweet days she'd had with Mama and imagined how Papa must have felt on receiving her letter. That she and Papa had not been with Mama at the end would forever be a source of distress for Maddy; she wiped an errant tear from her cheek and straightened.

After what seemed hours, Mr O'Brien turned the lead pair of bullocks off the road and into the bush. It was a moment before Maddy could distinguish the track they followed.

'Here we are, lass,' the bullock driver said cheerfully, and Maddy had the sense he was happy to be rid of her.

Her stomach fluttered and tears threatened once again, but she forced a wobbly smile which soon slipped away. There was no discernible difference from the bush they'd been travelling through all morning, though in the distance she heard a dog barking.

'Ah, where are we?' This couldn't be right. She swung her head from side to side, searching for the homestead Papa had described in his letters.

'Why, we're at Shelby, yer pa's place.'

'Mr O'Brien, there must be a mistake.' She stared around in dismay.

'No mistake, missy.' He did not look at her.

The twin strips of dust widened into a clearing flanked by four lopsided slab structures the same colour as the grey bark of the nearby trees. This wasn't right. It couldn't be.

'No!' She stood up on the cart, only to have it lurch once more, sending her thudding back down onto the seat, adding another bruise to her already tortured backside. The sight that lay before her was as depressing as it was ramshackle.

Then Maddy breathed out, relieved. This was the working farmyard—the homestead would be situated elsewhere. A cloud of beige dust obliterated the scene as the bullock team drew to a halt at Mr O'Brien's command. On her right she saw timber yards barely fit to contain the horses therein. She swallowed around the lump in her throat, not giving way to the threatening sob. Instead she examined the horses: the furthest yard held a grey and a scruffy brown horse with the solid stance of a draught horse; in the next she saw a small roan mare; and the yard situated closest to her had a higher fence from within which a lean black beauty stared indignantly out at her, ears pricked and nostrils flared. She immediately knew this would be her father's mount. Papa's fondness for fine horseflesh hadn't been left in England. She smiled, twisting on the seat to peer around. But where was the house?

'Mr O'Brien, my father wrote of a grand house. Can you take me to it, please?'

'I don't know about a house,' he said, still not looking up. 'This is all there is.'

'Mr O'Brien ...' she began, but he seemed not to hear.

Maddy watched in dismay as he pulled her trunks from atop the supplies he was taking further up the Hunter Valley to Patrick's Plains and deposited them on the ground beside the large wheel. He reached up and wrapped his gnarled fingers around her waist and lifted her down.

Speechless, she stood beside her luggage.

He unfurled the stockwhip and called to the oxen.

'Good day, missy.' He nodded in her general direction before turning his attention back to the team. 'Gee up, Sparkle.'

'Wait, Mr O'Brien,' Maddy called, taking several halting steps after the dray. She wanted to climb back on the wagon, to run away from this place. After a few yards she stopped.

'Mr O'Brien, please wait.' Her stomach sank as the bullocks leaned into the stocks and as one began to walk, obedient to Mr O'Brien's cracking whip, they turned a tight loop and pulled the heavy-laden wagon around and away. For some reason the beasts moved with a speed she was certain they'd not managed when she was on the dray.

She knew the man must have been able to hear her, but the only indication he gave was the slightest hesitation between strides, and soon he and the wagon had disappeared around the bend.

Maddy turned back to see a tall honey-haired woman had appeared and was watching her with a somewhat less than welcoming expression. Beyond the woman, a leggy black dog strained at the end of a chain. Straightening her shoulders, Maddy approached her.

'Ah, good morning, I am Madeleine Barker-Trent and I would like to see my father. Can you direct me, please?'

'Aye, miss, he'll be happy to see you,' she said in a distinctive West Coast accent, and her blue eyes flicked over Maddy before dropping away to examine the patch of dirt at her feet. Relief coursed through Maddy; she prayed her presence would bring him some consolation.

'Thank you, ah, Mrs ...'

For a moment the woman continued to stare at the ground, but then she lifted her head, her expression somewhat defiant. 'Rose McMahon,' she said, and she dragged a half-naked child with dark gold curls and large grey eyes from behind her skirts. 'And this is Luke, my son.'

'I, er—' Maddy faltered. 'Where is my father? Where can I find him?' She rubbed her throbbing temple.

'Robbie, er, I mean Mr Barker-Trent is in the field,' Mrs McMahon said, her face pinkening as she returned her attention to the dust.

Maddy stiffened at the woman's use of her father's Christian name. 'And where will I find the field?'

'Down by the river.' A small frown furrowed the woman's brow as she met Maddy's eyes. The connection was fleeting; almost immediately her glance flicked away.

'Best wait here though, you don't want to be going down there, miss—there's been a lot of snakes around.'

'Snakes?' Maddy swallowed. Then her chin came up; she'd travelled from the other side of the globe alone—the possibility of encountering a snake would not deter her. At the far side of the clearing, she saw a break in the trees and glanced back at Mrs McMahon. 'That way?'

The woman shrugged, then nodded.

'Thank you.'

Maddy lifted the hem of her skirt and started in the direction indicated, for once grateful for the darkness of the fabric as each step she took kicked up a cloud of powdery dust. The trail led her down the hill, and Maddy prayed it would take her to Papa. She tossed a glance over her shoulder and saw the woman and the little boy had disappeared. Feeling suddenly bereft at their absence, Maddy paused and swallowed hard; she straightened her shoulders once more and with her chin held high she continued down the track.

The forest floor was a tangle of rocks and branches and Maddy stepped carefully over the tufts of spiky grass that grew in the space between the dusty wheel ruts. She'd barely gone a hundred yards before she heard rustling nearby. Maddy froze. A snake? Her heartbeat thundered in her ears as she strained to see what had made the noise. When she neither saw nor heard anything more and her heart resumed beating something close to its usual rhythm, Maddy continued. The track wound down the hillside and the going became harder as the incline became steeper. She came to a fork in the path and heard another scuffling in the brush. She jumped and pitched sideways on the uneven ground. One foot landed in a deep wheel rut and she fell hard on her hip, scraping the skin from the palm she thrust out to break her fall. The largest ant she'd ever seen stood on hind legs, red and angry, waving nippers in an aggressive warning. Scuttling backwards, she dragged her skirts in the dirt as she scrambled away from it, hardly noticing the small stones and twigs beneath her hands.

Through the sparse canopy of leaves, the sun beat down on her head and she realised she'd left her bonnet on the dray: it was well on the way to Patrick's Plains by now. As she got to her feet Maddy contemplated which direction to take. To the left the wheel ruts were deep, and the gradient easier, while the other track seemed not so well used. She followed the more obvious path and silently cursed her unsuitable footwear.

The forest thinned and through a gap in the trees she saw a beautiful valley and distant mountain range. Her heart leaped when she saw the neatly fenced fields on the far side of the river. Looking back up the track, she frowned—the farmyard was quite a distance from the fields. But as she took in the view, wondering again about the house, she knew Papa would have chosen the ridge for the aspect.

To the left, past the last of the standing timber, was a large sloping field terraced with rows of hilled plants she thought were potatoes; beyond it was an expanse of open grasslands dotted with sheep. Directly below her, the river, a brown ribbon, looped across the wide valley floor, sweeping close to the base of the escarpment, from which it was separated by a narrow strip of green. She imagined Mama seeing this with her and Maddy's step faltered. What would she have made of it? She recalled the haphazard state of the farmyard on the ridge and realised the neatly fenced fields she could see on the other side of the river were on someone else's estates. She closed her eyes for a moment before continuing, hobbling a little and skidding on a patch of loose gravel, down the hill to find Papa.

The trees closed in around the track again before it levelled out and as she stepped out into glaring sunshine, it took her a moment to notice the men working in the centre of a field of reddish-brown ploughed earth. The cawing of a crow drew her attention and she recognised the ribbon-leafed maize plants on her right growing in the narrow field between the escarpment and river. The plantings were at various stages of growth; with glimpses of gold ripening ears visible in the furthest plot, and she felt a momentary pang of familiarity and longing for the fields near her Wiltshire home.

Her attention returned to the men and she searched for Papa in the line of dust-covered workers but couldn't distinguish him as they moved forwards, digging into large sacks slung over their shoulders, bending to press seed into the soil, stepping onwards and repeating the procedure. Only two of the men were clean shaven, and neither looked like Papa. Where was he? Maddy's gaze scoured their profiles, trying to identify him. She tried to visualise the miniature portrait her mother's locket contained. None of these men appeared anything like the man of her memories, but it had been almost six years since she'd seen her father.

The man closest to her sported bright red mutton-chop whiskers and strings of faded red hair hung from beneath his battered hat. A younger man, clean shaven and tanned, worked beside him, then another two bearded men, and a skinny youth on the far side also bereft of whiskers. One of the men, whose clothing was somewhat worse for wear, stood to stretch and noticed Maddy at the side of the field. Even from a distance she didn't think he seemed particularly friendly. His face, wide beneath a low brow, had a hard expression; his thin lips twisted as he stared at her across the field. His failure to resume his work alerted the others, and one by one they all paused and stared. In the centre of the group, one of the men, who was a little taller than the others, jerked with recognition, and she knew this must be Papa. He'd changed so much in the intervening years he was almost unrecognisable. She started across the field towards them.

She noted the shape of his wide-set eyes, so similar to her own; the rest of his features were hidden by whiskers growing high on his cheekbones. He gaped at her. He seemed much thinner than she remembered; the father of her memory had a youthful fullness of feature where this man was lined, almost gaunt. A stillness stretched for several heartbeats before he broke rank and stumbled across the uneven ground. His halting gait gained momentum until he was running towards her, his arms outstretched.

'Papa,' Maddy cried as she started forwards.

'Maddy,' he sobbed as he ran. They met halfway across the hot dry ground and Maddy was enveloped in her father's arms.

'Why weren't you—' Maddy began.

Pushing away from her, he peered into her face, as if he didn't believe she was really there. His gaze narrowed as he took in the black gown she wore. He frowned and looked past her shoulder. 'Where is your mother?' His hands gripped her arms painfully.

'Mama?' she said, dumbfounded. What did he mean? 'Didn't you receive my letter?'

'When you didn't arrive on the *Asia* ...' His words trailed off and he pulled her close once more. 'It doesn't matter, you're here now.'

The tight control she'd kept on her emotions crumbled as his strong arms were wrapped around her; safe in his embrace, the last vestige of her composure gave way and she melted into him. With her face pressed into his broad chest and her arms tight around him, at long last she found a place of comfort in which to grieve. Sobs wracked her body and he held her tight. Eventually her tears abated until only the occasional hiccough and sniffle remained. She became aware of the steady beat of his heart beneath her ear; his work-roughened hands rubbed her back as they stood in the middle of the field.

Remembering they had an audience, Maddy looked around to see the men had resumed their work and, other than an occasional curious glance, were allowing their master his privacy. Maddy watched them through watery eyes until her vision cleared sufficiently to meet the gaze of the one man who watched her. Some unreadable emotion twisted his features for a moment, but when one of his co-workers spoke to him he resumed his work without comment. She glanced away from him to find herself being observed by the younger man, who offered a small smile.

'Maddy, what happened? Where is your mother?' Papa said, dragging her attention back to him.

She pushed away to stare up into his face. 'But Papa, I wrote, I sent a letter to you—Mama was so ill, she could not travel. Did you not receive it?'

'Is she up at the hut?' His dark grey eyes followed the track towards the farmyard. 'I must go to her.'

Maddy opened her mouth to answer him, but nothing came out. She saw his joy leak away as he stared down at her once more. She struggled to find the words to tell him the terrible truth.

'She … died, Papa. She was taken with a fever and did not recover.'

She searched his face for understanding, but he stepped back from her, letting his arms fall to his sides. For several long and agonising moments they surveyed one another. Then his gaze ran down over her black dress and his mouth twisted.

'I sent a letter …' Maddy lifted shaking arms; like a child needing reassurance, she reached for him. His expression grew stony, as hard as chiselled granite. Without a word he turned and lurched away, staggering like a drunkard over the broken earth.

'Papa?' Maddy sank down on the hot dry soil and watched him head towards the river. Her chest ached as despair enveloped her. Trying to stem the flood of tears, she murmured, 'I sent a letter.' She stared at the empty river bank for a long while.

'Excuse me, Miss Barker-Trent.'

Maddy lifted her head to see the clean-shaven young man stood a few feet away, and after a moment he stepped closer and, reaching down, took hold of her hand and helped her to her feet. When she was upright she searched the field once more. There was no sign of Papa.

'Your father—'

Maddy looked up into the man's tanned face and saw his blue eyes were filled with pity.

'I'm sure he will be along soon: he just needs a little time. He's been disconsolate. To have his worst fears confirmed ...'

Maddy nodded.

The man offered his arm. 'Let me walk you back up to the huts.'

With one last look for Papa, Maddy put her hand on his wrist. His skin was warm; she felt the soft down of the golden hairs beneath her fingertips and jerked away.

'I apologise, I should introduce myself,' he said. 'I am Daniel Coulter, overseer here at Shelby. I work for your father.'

Maddy stumbled again as she turned back towards the river, but there was no sign of Papa. With a sigh, she replaced her hand on Mr Coulter's arm and allowed him to guide her back to the track. 'Papa will be along shortly.' Her voice cracked as she blinked back the tears that flooded her already stinging eyes.

'I expect you are right.'

At the top of the trail they slowed, and Maddy took in the disappointing array of the ramshackle farmyard again. 'In his letters my father spoke of a homestead.'

'Yes,' Mr Coulter said, and hope flared within her, 'he certainly has a wonderful vision for the house.'

'Where is it? I asked Mr O'Brien the bullock driver, but he said there was no house.'

'No, well, it's not finished.' There was something in the way he spoke that caused her to glance around at him. He didn't meet her eyes, and after clearing his throat he continued, 'The kitchen is almost done, along with the storeroom and scullery, but when you and your mother didn't arrive, he lost momentum.'

Maddy's heart pounded with relief. There was a house, only it wasn't finished. 'Can you show me?' She strode on, invigorated by the thought of seeing the house, even if it was only partially completed.

'Yes, I suppose so, though there isn't much to see. Are you sure you wouldn't like to wait for your father?'

'Please—I have come so far with an image of what I would find, and I am longing to see it.'

He led her past the shacks and horse yards to a narrow foot path which took them to a clearing at the edge of the escarpment. A stone structure stood forlorn, without a roof, door, or windows, and seemed more a ruin than newly constructed to Maddy. Beyond it were mounds of earth where foundations had been dug. Turning to face Mr Coulter, Maddy's mouth gaped in disbelief: she had no words.

'It's important to establish the farm first. To ensure there is a supply of food. Your father was fortunate when George Lester was sent to Shelby; he's a mason, and men with such skills aren't common amongst assigned labour.'

She nodded, barely taking in his words. She looked away from the sorry sight before her, the view blurring as tears filled her eyes. None of it made sense. Papa had been here for years. After several seconds she blinked and nodded. Taking in the river, rolling fields and distant hills, she could see at least why Papa had planned to build their home on the top of the cliff.

'The view will be spectacular.' She could hear that her voice was flat, emotionless.

Mr Coulter nodded but said nothing.

Glancing at the building site once more, Maddy pressed her lips into a determined line before heading back to the farmyard.

'Miss Barker-Trent,' he said, and she paused to glance back at him. 'You didn't travel all this way alone, surely. Where is your maid, or companion?'

Maddy hesitated before explaining, 'I'm afraid my maid changed her mind on the day we were due to leave. But I did not travel alone, as there was a kindly matron on board the *Bussorah Merchant*, a Mrs Macleod. She and her husband were heading to their son's property south of Sydney. They generously chaperoned me and saw me aboard the *Sophia Jane* when we arrived in the colony.' She twisted to glance back at the house site and sighed, 'I thought perhaps Papa would have engaged someone suitable for my arrival.' Even as she spoke, she remembered Papa had not received her letter.

'I see.' Mr Coulter seemed at a loss.

Maddy nodded, pushing aside the threatening wave of desolation, and continued walking. 'I shall settle in while I wait for Papa.'

Two

Saturday, 17 December 1831—*warm and sunny*

A melodic yodel rent the veil of slumber. Maddy blinked away oblivion and for a moment forgot where she was. A tear ran down her face into her ear and she lay still upon the bed as she recalled her reunion with Papa. Tears tangled her lashes and made her eyes gummy and hard to open, but when she forced them apart, she was greeted by a soft pink glow that could only be sunrise squeezing through the gap around the edges of the badly fitted door. Had she slept all night?

Pulling the quilt up beneath her chin she snuggled down, drawing comfort from the smell of Papa that lingered in the bed-clothes. Her head throbbed and she squinted around, taking in the odd shapes of boxes, chests and trunks stacked along the walls, and recalled the turmoil of the previous day. Maddy leaned over the side of the high bed, half expecting her father to be asleep on a pallet on the floor. But there was no sign of him. Why had he walked away and left her?

She was still dressed in the previous day's travelling clothes, with only her shoes removed. In the evening, Maddy had heard the men return from the fields, the murmur of conversation and the clank and clatter as they prepared a meal. Mr Coulter's offer of a bowl of stew from beyond the closed door had been refused. Certain Papa would soon return, she waited in the hot little room. Eventually exhaustion had overcome her, and, unable to remove her dress on her own, she'd lain down on the bed and fallen asleep in seconds. At some point she'd grown cold and climbed beneath the covers.

Despite the cool morning air, Maddy was sticky and uncomfortable. She ran her tongue over her teeth; her mouth was so dry she could barely swallow. She searched for a pitcher of water and saw a small desk and chair nestled between the trunks and chests. The top was littered with papers and journals, amid which she saw a tin jug with a cup beside it. She climbed down from the bed and was relieved to find the jug half full of water. She poured a cup and gulped it down. Maddy consumed three cupfuls and emptied the jug before her thirst was mostly quenched.

Papa was probably preparing the men for the day's work. After all he had an estate to run. There was no time to waste, so she'd change out of the clothes she'd slept in and ready herself for her first day at Shelby. Her trunk was by the door where Mr Coulter had carried it in the day before. Maddy unbuckled the straps with determined fingers and dug past gowns dyed black when Mama had died to the dark green one she longed to wear. Mama had had several serviceable gowns made for each of them, suitable for what Papa had described as their *pioneering life*. In other circumstances it would be perfect for the first day of her new life alongside Papa, but observing the buttons, she realised she would be utterly unable to manage alone and smoothed it back down into the trunk. Instead she stood and straightened the gown she'd slept in, and bit her lip, staring down at the impossible gowns. She'd have to ask Papa to help her find her a maid, and in the meantime he would have to assist her. Whoever designed ladies' clothes hadn't taken into account what one could do without anyone to take care of the buttons.

As she struggled to replace her shoes amid the layers of petticoats, she heard the murmur of male conversation outside and hurried to complete her ablutions. Using Papa's small shaving mirror, she peered at her reflection. Red puffy eyes stared out of a wan face set in a riot of untidy brown hair. Maddy drew in a fortifying breath, found her brush in the trunk and braided her hair into a knot, then then twisted the fortuitously natural curls at her temples into ringlets with quick fingers. Once she'd seen Papa, all would be well. They would talk, and together they could grieve.

She pulled open the door to a beautiful cool morning and squared her shoulders. It was the first day of her new life in a new land. Across the clearing three of the men she'd seen the day before were gathered around a small fire. They looked somehow less disreputable, and she realised they'd shaven. There was no sign of Papa or Mr Coulter. Casting a quick glance around she saw the stallion and the draught horses were there but not the roan mare. Papa's abrupt leaving was understandable given the news she had brought, but she didn't know what to make of his continued absence. Where was he?

Pulling the door closed, Maddy crossed to join the men she'd seen working in the fields; all silently watched her approach. The red-haired man and the hard-eyed one held steaming cups in their hands, while a younger lad with dark curly hair was crouched, the black dog beside him, adding sticks to a fire over which a tin canister was suspended on a metal tripod. Steam rose from a cup balanced on one of the blackened stones that ringed the fire pit. The aromas of tea and wood smoke made her mouth water.

A joyous cacophony filled the air of the small clearing. Above her she saw a flickering silver cloud as a flock of sunlit birds crossed the open sky momentarily before disappearing beyond the treetops. Awed at the sight, she paused, watching the blue expanse and listening to the receding screech as the birds followed the river along the valley. A delighted smile on her face, she continued towards the men, but it quickly faded as she met the cold blue gaze of the man who'd watched her the previous day. He was hatless and his hair was sandy brown and shaggy, and something in his expression perturbed her. She looked away.

'Good morning,' she said, her voice overly bright with forced cheerfulness. The lad glanced up for a moment before he silently resumed staring at the ground.

'Morning, Miss Barker-Trent.' The red-haired man stepped forwards, a frown creasing his brow even while a tentative smile revealed deep lines around his eyes and slightly crooked teeth. 'Er, I'm Phillip Hardy.' He gave the young man a nudge with the toe of his boot; the boy sprang to his feet, a deep red staining his cheeks. 'And this is Charlie O'Connell.'

The boy nodded, bent and picked up his cup and took a sip, glancing over the rim before his eyes flicked away from her. Maddy almost missed the fleeting frown on Mr Hardy's ruddy face as he studied the other man. 'And this is George Lester.'

'Morning, miss,' Lester said, his voice gravelly, as if rusty from lack of use.

Maddy nodded and smiled. 'My father—do you know where he is?'

As her gaze went from one man to the next, all refused to look at her. What was wrong?

'No, miss, we ain't seen no one yet besides Mr Coulter, and he rode out earlier, down to Tillington,' Mr Hardy said after a moment.

'Well, never mind, I'm sure he will be along shortly,' Maddy said, wondering where Tillington was. Mr Hardy nodded and opened his mouth to say something more but seemed to change his mind, because he closed it again. An awkward silence lengthened. Maddy, not quite sure whether these men were assigned labourers, though it was likely they were, had no notion how to break it.

The aroma of tea wafted her way on a puff of breeze and saliva filled her mouth again. 'Could I trouble you for a drop of your tea?' The words were out of her mouth before she knew it.

At her request both Mr Hardy and young Charlie peered into their cups and then tossed the remaining tea onto the dusty ground. Maddy frowned, unsure what to do or say. Mr Hardy stepped forwards and plucked the tea from the fire and she realised they had emptied their cups for her to use. George Lester's stare was somewhat sullen and she wondered why he seemed to have taken such a dislike to her.

'Oh no!' she exclaimed, jerking her attention back to the others, 'I didn't mean … I will get my cup.' Flustered she hurried back to the hut for the tin cup she'd used earlier and returned, holding it out to Mr Hardy. He tipped the dark liquid into the cup and then poured a splash into his own.

'Thank you,' Maddy said. 'Is there any milk?'

'No, miss, the cow went dry,' Mr Hardy replied.

'Oh.' She nodded knowledgeably, though she really knew almost nothing about farm animals.

'We took her down to Tillington, to Mr Garrick's bull,' Charlie said, before his face transformed into a brilliant shade of scarlet.

'Ah well, that's good.' Maddy wasn't sure what else to say, so she took a sip of tea. It was strong and bitter, but she drank it with barely a grimace. When she finished, George Lester was staring at her, his eyes full of something she could not read but which made her uncomfortable. Was it dislike?

'What were you sowing in the field yesterday when I arrived?' Even as she spoke she wished she hadn't. Heat crept up her neck. The mention of yesterday brought back the memory of Papa's rejection, witnessed by these men.

'Mr Hardy.' The voice came from behind and held a note of panicked distress.

Maddy turned to see Mrs McMahon emerge from the scrub beyond the horse yards.

Mr Hardy stepped up beside Maddy. 'What is it, Rose, what's happened?'

'It's Robbie,' she panted, her eyes large, 'he's dead.'

Comprehension came slowly, but as Mrs McMahon's words penetrated, Maddy realised she meant Papa. Maddy's vision swam and she began to sink towards the ground. Mr Hardy gripped her arm and managed to keep her from falling.

No. She'd only just arrived. They were going to make a new life. Together. Maddy shook her head as if to clear away the confusion of her racing thoughts. 'There must be a mistake.' Her voice sounded as if it came from far away. Maddy turned her head from Mrs McMahon to Mr Hardy and back to the woman.

Mrs McMahon's face crumpled, and a sob escaped her.

'What does she mean?' Maddy shakily asked Mr Hardy.

His features seemed to run together as her vision swam.

'Where is he, Rose?' Mr Hardy asked.

'Down at the river,' Mrs McMahon panted, still breathless after her run up the hill.

Maddy stared at her, took in the features distorted by anguish. Everything had slowed down; nothing was real. It couldn't be true. It had to be a mistake.

'Charlie, take a horse and go to Tillington. Tell them what's happened.'

Charlie ran to do as Mr Hardy bid him and Maddy watched on, unable to take in what was happening.

'Come on, missy, let's get you back to the hut—you should sit down.'

Maddy sagged and he grabbed her arm once more. 'Lester, help me here, man.' Mr Hardy turned around, taking Maddy with him. 'Lester?'

'He's gone,' Mrs McMahon said.

'Where is Papa?' Maddy tried to pull away from Mr Hardy. She had to see for herself. 'I want to see him. Where is he?'

'Nay, lass, you best wait here. We'll take care of your pa.'

Mr Hardy helped Maddy to the hut where she sat on the edge of the bed but refused to lie down.

It wasn't real. It couldn't be. Any moment Papa would stride in and announce it had merely been a misunderstanding. Maddy could hear someone weeping and lifted a hand to feel her own face. It was dry. She had no tears; she could not cry.

'Miss Barker-Trent.' The voice was familiar.

Maddy looked up. 'Mr Coulter?'

'Yes, I met Charlie on the road. He has continued to Tillington, and I hope Mrs Garrick will return with him shortly.'

'Is it true?'

He stood silhouetted in the doorway, but she saw the way his shoulders sagged and knew it must be. The ache in her chest swelled until it burst out in a terrible wail that echoed in the confines of the hut.

Maddy lay curled on her father's bed for a long time. Her throat burned with the effort to breathe; it was as if something had stolen the air from around her.

It wasn't *true*. She tried to sit up. She had to see for herself. The woman had made a mistake. Rising from the bed, she clutched the corner of the desk, and even as she made her way to the door, deep inside she knew it was true. Fear was a physical barrier and Maddy stumbled back to the bed to lie and stare once more at the rough-hewn beams with dry aching eyes.

After what seemed to be hours but could have been minutes, she became conscious of voices outside. Her senses had slowed so she didn't comprehend the sound of the door opening but turned away from the bright glare of sunshine that flooded in through the doorway.

'Madeleine?' It was a woman's voice. 'I'm Susannah Garrick.'

Maddy turned her head enough to see the silhouette of a woman standing close beside the bed, another figure behind her. She squinted against the glare. 'Mr Coulter?' Maddy rasped, cleared her throat and started again. 'Mr Coulter, what …?'

She heard the sound of movement and a murmured conversation. She swallowed, suddenly unable to participate in this unwanted reality. Daniel Coulter joined Susannah Garrick at the bedside. Beyond them, she saw the silhouette of another man standing outside the open door. Mrs Garrick stepped back to allow Mr Coulter access and she bumped into a trunk.

'I'm sorry,' Maddy croaked, 'I need to tidy the hut.'

'Nonsense, my dear, don't worry about such things,' Mrs Garrick said kindly.

Maddy's gaze returned to Mr Coulter. Solemn-faced, he met her glance. Maddy licked her dry lips and felt a cup pressed into her hand. She took a grateful sip of cool water.

'What happened to Papa?'

Mr Coulter's eyes flicked away and he turned his head, as if seeking guidance from the woman. Maddy curled up tighter; she squeezed her knees to her chest as the tears finally came with great raw-throated sobs.

'Darling girl, come here.'

A gentle hand touched Maddy's shoulder and she turned into the soft embrace. She clung to the woman, this neighbour, this stranger. It didn't matter that Maddy didn't know her: nothing mattered. In Mrs Garrick's arms, she cried for Papa. For Mama. For herself.

Eventually her sobs eased until only the occasional hiccough lingered. Mrs Garrick's gown was damp beneath her cheek. Maddy shifted a little and pulled away from her.

'I'm sorry.'

'My dear, there's no cause for apologies.' Mrs Garrick's voice was kind and gentle.

Maddy wiggled out of her embrace and sat, noticing gratefully that Mr Coulter had left the hut. Her hair hung in a tangle around her face, and Mrs Garrick smoothed it back with a gentle hand before removing what remained of the pins. She found the brush Maddy had left on Papa's desk earlier and began to brush Maddy's hair. It seemed so long since Maddy had hurriedly prepared herself for the day—How long? It was important to know—And then it wasn't.

'I'm sorry,' Maddy said again.

'Please, dear, there is no need.'

'But your dress ...' The image of Mrs McMahon's distraught face flashed through Maddy's mind and she could not finish the sentence. There was no order to her thoughts; shapeless, they wandered and jerked just out of her reach.

'It shall dry: don't give it another thought.' Mrs Garrick stepped around to face her and examine her handiwork. Her kind smile of encouragement reminded Maddy of her mama and tears welled once more. She searched for something to focus on and drew in a shuddering breath.

'Do you know what time it is?' she asked Mrs Garrick. A small ripple of memory spread through her as she recalled feeling the same way when learning Mama had died. She'd not been with her mother at the last either.

'It must be midmorning,' Mrs Garrick said. And for a moment, lost in memories of Mama's illness, Maddy was confused.

'How can it be?' she asked, almost having forgotten the original question. Maddy grasped Mrs Garrick's hand, holding onto her as if she too might leave, and looked up into the sweet face. Her smile was understanding and the older woman waited quietly until Maddy's grip slackened. Easing away, Mrs Garrick propped open the window hatch. Light flooded the crowded space, revealing the confusion of luggage and unpacked crates, a saddle and various other unidentifiable items.

Maddy recalled the foundations. What had happened to the house? Why had Papa written to them as if it were already built? His letters were full of vivid description. Maddy's temples throbbed. How had he described everything in such detail? Nothing made sense. It had all been a lie. But why?

The buzz of whirring insects stopped abruptly, highlighting the absence of noise so far from civilisation.

'Perhaps a hot drink?' Mrs Garrick suggested. Maddy realised she was shivering. She peered at her stockinged toes poking from beneath the hem of the awful black gown and wondered what had happened to her shoes. She had no recollection of removing them. Feeling as if she needed to hold her bones together, she wrapped her arms tight around her knees.

Through the window she heard the jangle of harness and muted conversation, and she saw Mr Hardy and Mr Coulter walking behind a cart pulled by the grey gelding under the gentle guidance of young Charlie. Behind them was another man, and she assumed it was he she'd seen earlier silhouetted in the doorway.

Maddy's blood turned to ice as the cart drew level to reveal a bare foot hanging over the tailboard. Without intending to move, she was off the bed, past Mrs Garrick, and through the door, barely registering the sticks and pebbles beneath her stockinged feet. The sight of her father's lifeless body wrung another wail from her. His clothes were sodden, and his boots and one stocking were missing. Where were his boots? Maddy clung to the timber boards as she took in her father's face: a clammy swollen facsimile of her beloved papa, grey, waterlogged and distorted, with his discoloured eyes visible through puffy slits.

Horror-struck, Maddy saw an inch-long black ant crawl across his brow. She brushed it away, and when she saw another she plucked it from his skin. Had they bitten him with those nasty pincers? She crushed it, barely aware of the insect's jaws working on the pad of her thumb until she felt a painful sting. Maddy yelped and flicked the crushed carcass away.

The image of the lifeless shell that had yesterday been her father was harrowing, but she could not look away. Instead she reached out and took his hand but quickly dropped it again. Damp, cold and limp, it felt foreign and wrong. This wasn't Papa. Papa was excited and full of dreams. He was not this puffy and clammy thing. Her hand fluttered above him, wanting to touch him but reluctant to handle the waterlogged husk. She rubbed her throbbing thumb against her thigh and began to sway; tears blurred his face.

The blackness crept up slowly at first, framing her vision as she stared down into his face. A piece of reed clung to his cheek and she reached out to remove it. Her vision shrank to a pinpoint until all she could see was the limp ribbon of foliage on the skin stretched over his cheekbone. And the darkness was complete.

Three

Tuesday, 20 December 1831—hot dry winds

It seemed to Maddy as if she'd been in bed for weeks rather than days: everything since Papa's death was a blur, one day barely discernible from the next. The doctor had been unable to identify the cause of the illness that had overtaken her—he said it could not be explained by grief, as she had experienced fever and a rash—and put it down to an ailment contracted on the journey from England. She pushed herself up on the pillow and winced as her hand took her weight, still painful and swollen after the ant had stung her thumb.

This morning the room that had seemed unbearably hot when she'd been in the grip of the fever was now cool, and flopping onto her back, she stared up at the ceiling. She was eighteen years old and alone, more than a quarter year's journey from all that was familiar and safe.

The door opened a crack and Mrs Brown, called Cookie by the Garrick family, peered in. 'I see you are awake.' Her black button eyes were almost lost in the rosy plumpness of her smiling face.

Maddy returned her smile and nodded. The cook set a tray on a small table and bustled over to the bed. Almost as round as she was tall, the cook was a kind but opinionated woman who loved nothing more than a good gossip and had taken to delivering her breakfast each day. Maddy found she anticipated seeing her as she recovered from the fever—her visits had broken the boredom of the sick room.

'You're looking much better this morning.' She beamed down at Maddy.

'I'm feeling much better, Mrs Brown, thanks to your wonderful cooking.'

'Now you can call me Cookie, same as the rest of the family,' she said, her eyes twinkling.

'Thank you, Cookie.' Maddy lifted her arms and allowed the cook to straighten the bedclothes around her. 'Have there been any interesting visitors today?'

'Only old Molly Hunt: she was here to see the master at the crack of dawn. That woman is always bothering Mr Garrick, complaining how some of the folk about treat the assigned servants.'

'Doesn't Mr Garrick treat his workers well?' The words were out before Maddy considered the inappropriateness of discussing the master of the house with the cook.

'Oh he does, missy, he does. But if a lass is no better than she oughta be, he's no choice but to send her back to Parramatta.' Maddie leaned forwards for her pillows to be plumped as Cookie continued indiscretely, 'And that Mrs Hunt, she comes here to have a word with the master about it.'

Maddy wasn't sure if Cookie would have said more about this Molly Hunt or not, but before she could pursue the topic, Mrs Garrick swept in and picked up the tray.

'Good morning, Maddy,' Mrs Garrick said.

Maddy replied in kind and blinked back sudden tears. Despite the kindness of the Garricks, she was alone, and so far from everything familiar.

'Mr Garrick was looking for you, Cookie,' Mrs Garrick said. 'I think he's after some of your scones.'

'Very good, Mrs G,' Cookie said, and, with a plump-cheeked smile at Maddy, added, 'You make sure you eat it all, lass,' and left the room.

Mrs Garrick placed the tray on her knees, and with a flourish she plucked an embroidered napkin from the tray and laid it across Maddy's lap. Coddled egg with strips of hot buttered toast were arranged invitingly, and, for the first time since Papa's death, Maddy felt something akin to hunger stir her belly.

With a deft crack Mrs Garrick removed the top of the egg and handed her the spoon. 'Now eat up. If you don't eat it all I shall find myself subjected to one of Cookie's stern looks.'

Maddy smiled, picked up a soldier of toast and dipped it into the soft gooey yolk. Her mouth watered in anticipation. The egg and toast were better than she imagined but even so she couldn't manage to finish them.

'Come now,' Mrs Garrick began, encouraging Maddy to eat more, but she was saved from the gentle urging by Tida, the Garricks' four-year-old daughter. The middle child between two boys, Tida was a mix of busy little mama and wild tomboy. She had a mop of soft chestnut curls and dark eyes like her mother's, eyes that contained a determined gleam as she peered into the room.

'Tida, I told you to wait outside until Miss Barker-Trent had finished her breakfast.' Mrs Garrick removed the tray from Maddy's lap.

'Oh Mama, don't scold me. I couldn't wait another minute.' She scrunched her little nose and gave Maddy an assessing glance before entering the room. 'I thought you would be finished.'

Maddy suppressed a smile.

'Tida, where are your manners?' Mrs Garrick's voice was stern, but there was amusement underlying the reprimand. Young Tida had visited Maddy on several occasions, much to her mother's dismay, but Maddy was grateful. The sweet and precocious child had been a welcome distraction during her recovery.

'I'm sorry, Miss Barker-Trent,' Tida said, her tone not contrite in the least; nor was the gleam of interest dimmed. 'But are you yet well?' She stood, plump legs set firmly apart, fists resting on her hips. 'Papa said I was not to bother you until you were well. Are you well?'

Maddy's amused smile brought a scowl to Tida's face. In order not to offend her further, she schooled her features and assured her as seriously as she was able, 'I am far better than I was.'

'But are you well enough to be bothered?'

'I think so,' Maddy said solemnly.

'Good, because me and Edwin want to pick the peaches. Can you come and help?'

Maddy hadn't met the child's brother Edwin, who according to Cookie was a serious and quiet lad; his father's miniature in appearance, he shadowed Mr Garrick wherever and whenever he was permitted.

'Edwin and I,' Mrs Garrick corrected.

Tida turned her intense stare towards her mother and said, 'You can come too.'

Maddy met Mrs Garrick's eyes over Tida's head and lifted a brow in question. Not that she needed permission to leave her bed, but she didn't wish to encourage Tida to mutiny.

Mrs Garrick nodded.

The temptation of leaving the confines of the room and breathing in fresh air and sunshine was all at once appealing. 'If you allow me a little time to wash and dress, I will meet you outside.'

Tida nodded solemnly before she spun on the heel of her small boot and raced from the room.

'Edwin, she's coming,' she yelled as soon as she was through the door, 'just as soon as she's dressed.'

'Tida!' Mrs Garrick followed her out, taking the tray with her. 'I've warned you before about screeching like a shrew.'

The smile faded from Maddy's lips as mother and daughter left the room. She'd promised to help pick the peaches, but it meant she must rise, and in an instant she wished she hadn't agreed. Still, a promise was a promise. She swung her legs off the bed and hesitated. Her trunk had been unpacked, so she crossed to the armoire. Before she could turn the key, the bedroom door opened to admit a neatly dressed servant.

'Good morning, Miss Barker-Trent, I'm Beth. Mrs Garrick sent me to help you dress.' Slightly built, with a narrow face and mousy blonde hair pulled back tight beneath a mobcap, she hovered near the doorway.

'Oh yes, thank you, Beth.' Maddy returned to sit on the edge of the bed and allow the maid access. Though she had considerably improved since the first days of her stay at Tillington when her legs had shaken with the effort of crossing the room, the thought of going outside was a little daunting. Still, she couldn't lie in bed forever; no matter how tempting the thought.

'Mrs Garrick said you're to go for a stroll in the garden.' She rifled through the black gowns hanging in the armoire. 'Let's get you into this nice one with the lace collar.' Beth pulled out the dress she'd worn the day she arrived.

Maddy shook her head. 'No!' she snapped. 'No, not that one, please choose another,' she continued in a gentler tone.

'Yes, of course, miss,' Beth agreed readily, though Maddy knew she'd shocked her with the abrupt refusal. As it was, she had hardly ceased imagining Papa's distorted face, and the thought of wearing the dress was distressing. She would give it away. Mrs Garrick would know someone suitable. Someone Maddy would never see wearing it.

'This one is nice.' Beth held up another of the black gowns. She nodded but longed to return to the oblivion of sleep. Nevertheless Beth soon had her out of her nightgown and into her shift and petticoats.

'It's a fine dress, miss,' Beth said as she helped her step into the gown, 'though you are so thin, it could do with a tuck or two.'

Maddy tugged at the sagging bodice and shrugged: it hardly mattered.

She recalled the plans she and Mama had made for their journey, and their imaginings of what they would see. Despite knowing her mother was weak, they continued to prepare to go. But Maddy's visit to say goodbye to a childhood friend had proved devastating—it was during her absence that Mama had developed a fever and had passed away within two days.

The room Maddy occupied was on the western side of the main house and accessed from a flagged anteroom that opened directly onto the courtyard. A large covered veranda with a walkway curtained the gravelled courtyard, shading the servants' wing and kitchens. The house at Tillington wasn't complete but the shape of it was evident, with its good-sized courtyard nestled between the rear wings of a single-storey U-shaped building. The western wing housed the kitchen, servants' rooms and stores; the eastern side was unfinished, with Mr Garrick's office the only completed room. This had been described by Tida on one of her visits, when she'd apparently been scolded for getting under the feet of the men trying to build foundations for an additional two bedrooms. Maddy paused for a moment and was pleased to match the reality to everything Tida had told her. The child had been remarkably accurate.

Stepping through a small gate at the corner of the kitchen Maddy found the children waiting. Edwin was much as Maddy had imagined, stout with plump cheeks, pale hair and soulful dark eyes. He stood holding a basket and waiting patiently, a stark contrast to his bouncing sister.

After days spent inside the sun was blinding. Maddy stepped from beneath the protection of the wide veranda, wishing she'd remembered a bonnet. Tida grabbed her hand and dragged her along a path behind the kitchen. On a small rise above the house was the stable block, and Maddy saw a tall man leaning on a rail talking to a young girl. For a moment she thought it was Mr Coulter but soon realised the man near the stables was much taller than the Shelby overseer. When the man looked up and saw her watching them, he straightened and said something to the girl.

'Miss Barker-Trent,' Tida said, drawing her attention from the pair.

'Yes, Tida?'

'It's this way,' Tida said, taking Maddy's hand and drawing her along a well-worn path.

As they rounded the corner, Maddy realised how inappropriate mourning black was in the midsummer heat of New South Wales. Sweat trickled between her shoulder blades and peppered her face.

'Miss Barker-Trent,' Tida began and then hesitated, squinting up at Maddy. 'Can I call you Miss Madeleine?' she finished, her small face serious.

'No.' Maddy struggled to appear austere.

Tida dropped her hand.

'I insist you call me Maddy.' For the first time since Mama had taken ill Maddy laughed aloud when Tida's face went from disappointment to joy in an instant. She took Maddy's hand once more and skipped towards the gate, explaining about the cursed birds who would steal all the peaches if they didn't get to them first.

'Tida,'—Edwin's tone was stern—'Mama will paddle your behind if she hears you say that.'

'Say what?' Tida asked, a picture of innocence.

'Tida,' Maddy began.

'Oh, very well,' she sighed, 'but Cookie calls them that all the time.'

'Well she shouldn't,' Edwin said before Maddy had a chance to comment.

She let the matter go and was led around the rear of the kitchen to a large kitchen garden. It was fenced with woven saplings, which Maddy assumed were meant to keep out the livestock.

Two men worked beneath the blistering sun, sweat saturating the backs of their calico tunics as they turned over rich black soil for a new garden bed.

Once through the gate Tida ran past them to the far side of the enclosure, where several fruit trees grew just inside the fence line. The men glanced over and stared curiously at Maddy.

'Maddy, hurry,' Tida called.

Maddy waved her on and waited while Edwin closed the gate before they joined the little girl.

'Papa says we must only pick the ripe ones.' Tida proceeded to stand on her toes to pull at the nearest barely coloured peach.

'Perhaps this one over here.' Maddy directed her to a riper specimen within easy reach.

The sound of jingling harness and the steady clop of an approaching horse caught Maddy's attention as she stretched for a higher peach. With the sun-warmed fruit still in her hand she turned to look up into the smiling blue eyes of Daniel Coulter.

'Good day, Miss Barker-Trent.'

'Mr Coulter.' Maddy nodded politely, but her stomach flipped, and she felt unaccountably nervous.

'Daniel, Maddy is out of bed at last,' Tida exclaimed.

'So I see.' He grinned and swept an assessing glance from the top of Maddy's head to the slippers peeping from beneath her skirts. 'Are you fully recovered?'

Maddy stared up into his tanned face and felt a blush begin to heat her neck. She nodded and quickly bent to place the peach in the basket. She'd bruised the tender flesh with suddenly clumsy fingers. What was the matter with her? Perhaps the fever had addled her brain. She rubbed at the still hot welt on her thumb and averted her gaze from the handsome overseer.

'May I have a ride please, Daniel?' Tida's question broke through Maddy's confusion.

'I don't know—' Maddy began to say.

'It's my turn, Tida.' Edwin raced after his sister, leaping across the garden to wrestle with her at the gate. The peaches were forgotten as they tussled to be the first through.

Daniel laughed and Maddy couldn't help admiring the dimple that flashed beside his mouth. He nudged the mare with his heel and wheeled the horse around to meet the children. Left behind, Maddy picked up the basket containing only three peaches and followed. Her heart skipped as she recalled the amused smile they'd shared. The children were still squabbling at the gate and Maddy wondered if she should refer to their mother for permission.

She was saved from making a decision when Mrs Garrick came around the corner with baby George perched on her hip. Maddy had only seen the infant once when the children's maid had been holding him as she hurried to remove a curious Tida from the sick room.

'Mama,' Tida whined, 'Edwin says it's his turn and it isn't.'

'Mama, it is my turn.' Edwin stared up at Daniel for confirmation.

'Children, if you can't behave, neither of you shall have a ride on Baby.'

Baby?

'But …' Tida began to argue then abruptly snapped her lips closed.

'Edwin is first, but only if Daniel has time.' Mrs Garrick frowned at her daughter. 'And if you behave, Daniel might permit you a small ride too. Only once around the house, mind.'

'I'm sure I have time for one lap,' Daniel said and tossed Maddy a conspiratorial grin. 'Perhaps we can allow Tida first go,' and seeing Edwin's expression become mutinous, he added 'as I need afterwards to ride down and check the river levels, and you can come with me.'

Edwin's face lit up and Tida squeaked in protest.

'A splendid idea, Daniel. Say thank you, Tida,' said Mrs Garrick.

Tida scowled and sent her mother a defiant glare before capitulating, as she undoubtedly knew she'd end up with no ride at all if she wasn't careful.

With a gleeful wave, Tida, along with the riding party, moved away from the garden gate. Maddy paused to take in the well-ordered establishment. Straight fences; a long avenue of tall sapling beech trees that would one day be magnificent; whitewashed buildings; fields and gardens all neat and well-tended. It was everything Papa had described in his letters.

Later that day Maddy was sitting in the shelter of the courtyard watching the children playing in the shade when she heard a carriage coming down the avenue of beech trees. Edwin looked up from where he was scratching in the gravel and frowned. The lack of warning when visitors called seemed to be the norm at Tillington.

'It's the Everettes,' he said, his tone flat.

'Oh.' Tida paused, her family of peg dollies momentarily forgotten. She was unexpectedly unexcited by the visitors. Instead of rushing to the gate in welcome, she picked up her dolls and placed them carefully in the basket.

'Ah, the Everettes.' Mrs Garrick came out of the house. Carefully closing the door behind her, she strode to the gate. 'Come, Edwin, Tida. Say good morning, and then you can go and find Nanny Ann.'

'Oh, Mama, do we have to?'

'Tida!' It was the first time Maddy had heard Mrs Garrick snap at one of her children.

'Yes, Mama,' Tida said, her large eyes wide.

A petite blonde woman drove a four-seat buggy with an ease borne of practice, bringing the leggy bay in the shafts to a smooth halt at the gate. Beside her sat an older plump woman with a sweet countenance, who scrutinised them from her perch on the buggy. On the rear seat rode two girls who were perhaps a little younger than Maddy. Both were blonde, but there the similarities ended. The thinner and, Maddy thought, elder of the two, alighted first, and immediately moved to assist the older woman. Maddy recognised the tall man who appeared from the direction of the stables to take hold of the horse, from earlier.

'Thank you, Bowman,' the young blonde woman smiled down at the groom, who, as soon as the women were all safely clear, led the horse away.

'Mrs Everette, Catherine,' Mrs Garrick greeted the older women, 'this is an unexpected pleasure.'

If Maddy hadn't witnessed her reaction earlier, she would not have known Mrs Garrick was anything but truly delighted to see them. The mistress of Tillington turned and ushered her children forwards.

'Say hello, Edwin.' She put a guiding hand between his shoulder blades.

'Good morning, Mrs Everette, Mrs Catherine.' He nodded solemnly before addressing the girls. 'Miss Belle,' he said to the taller plain girl, and to the prettier girl, 'Miss Amelia.' Maddy noticed a slight pinking on the back of his neck. Tida stepped up beside her brother and parroted his greetings.

'Now run in and ask Mrs Brown to send tea for six into the drawing room, please.'

Both children needed no second bidding and made good their escape. Maddy wondered what could be so distasteful about the visitors to have the children running for cover.

'So, this is the girl then, is it?' The older woman's cold voice didn't match her soft, plump features, though her disapproval was obvious in the pursed set of the small mouth.

'Mrs Everette, this is Miss Madeleine Barker-Trent.' Mrs Garrick's voice was courteous. 'Maddy, this is Mrs Everette the Elder, and Mrs Catherine Everette of Cragside; Catherine is our neighbour on the other side.' She offered Maddy an encouraging smile before continuing, 'And Isabelle and Amelia are visiting from England.'

'How lovely to meet you at last.' The younger of the girls sprang forwards, her hand outstretched and her eyes sparkling. 'I'm Amelia,' she said. 'May I call you Madeleine?' The words bubbled and her blue eyes shone with enthusiasm.

Beyond Amelia's prattle Maddy heard the old woman's comment: 'Madeleine? What kind of name is that?'

'Please, Mother Everette,' came from Mrs Catherine Everette.

'My mother named me for a friend of hers, a Madeleine Dupéré,' Maddy explained, directing her words to Amelia. The old woman snorted derisively but, ignoring her, Maddy resolutely kept her attention on the young women. 'I am delighted to meet you, Amelia, but please call me Maddy.'

Amelia's eyes sparkled mischievously as she turned and dragged her sister towards Maddy. 'This is Isabelle, or Belle for short.'

Belle scowled, first at her sister, then at Maddy.

'Hello, Belle, or would you prefer I call you Isabelle?' The girl's expression was so uninviting that Maddy was unsure if the shortening of her name was for family only.

'Belle will do,' she said, though she sent her sister a glare, her lips twisted as if she'd been tricked into eating a lemon.

'A misnomer if ever there was one,' the elder Mrs Everette muttered loudly. Maddy was sure it was deliberate and risked a glance at Mrs Garrick, whose face bore a small frown that revealed she was of the same opinion.

'Mother Everette insisted we come, and the girls took no persuasion at all.' The younger Mrs Everette's voice was soft, with a hint of a Scottish burr. She stepped forwards and smiled, holding out her hands to Maddy. 'I would have come sooner but heard that you have been ill,' she said, her heart-shaped face full of compassion. 'It's lovely to meet you, Miss Barker-Trent. My husband sends his condolences. He is unwell himself, or he should have liked to have joined us.'

'Thank you, and please call me Maddy.' Maddy liked the soft-spoken woman immediately.

With the introductions made, the party went inside, Mrs Everette the Elder preceding them through the dark hall, past the open door to what Maddy saw was the dining room, and straight into the drawing room. It was obvious she'd been there before as she crossed to sit in the wingback chair usually favoured by Mr Garrick, while Mrs Garrick and Mrs Everette sat together on the settee. Amelia, Belle and Maddy made themselves comfortable at a small round card table near the glass-panelled doors that opened up onto a wide front veranda.

'Well, young lady, what do you have to say for yourself?'

Maddy blinked and looked to Mrs Garrick for guidance, but her hostess merely smiled and nodded. 'I'm not sure what you mean, Mrs Everette.'

'I want to know what you intend to do now.'

Maddy felt pinned by her penetrating glare.

'Mother Everette, the poor lass has just lost her papa,' the younger Mrs Everette said with a hint of reproach. The door opened to admit Beth carrying the tea, much to Maddy's relief.

'Tell us, Mrs Everette, how are you finding life at Cragside?' Mrs Garrick took advantage of the arrival of the tea to redirect the conversation.

'Dreadful,' the elder woman spat. 'I've arrived to find my son's children permitted to associate with criminals.'

Maddy glanced around to see Belle and Amelia sipping their tea, their faces the picture of blank passivity. The younger Mrs Everette's expression was resigned.

'The heat is not to be borne,' she continued, 'ye'd not find such abominable heat in Scotland.'

'It does take time to acclimatise,' agreed Mrs Garrick.

'I'm sure it does a soul no good at all to be so hot. My health has suffered greatly since my arrival.' She did her best to model her plump features into a semblance of ill health and failed. 'If it weren't for the fact that all my children see fit to live at the ends of the earth, I would return home on the next available ship.'

Maddy wondered uncharitably whether they'd moved to the ends of the earth to escape her.

'Catherine, how are Douglass and the children?' Mrs Garrick, balancing her cup and saucer gracefully, turned a little on the settee to look at the younger woman.

'Quite well. Young Francis struggles with the heat, but babes do tend to suffer in temperatures such as we've experienced of late.'

'You fuss far too much over the child.'

'Yes, Mother Everette, so you have told me.'

'He is hardly a babe,' the old woman continued, intent of having the last word on the matter. She then proceeded to share her views on the weather, the state of the roads, and convicts.

'Maddy.' Mrs Garrick took advantage of a break in the diatribe as Mrs Everette the Elder paused for a sip of tea. No doubt she was parched after such a heated monologue. 'Why don't you take Belle and Amelia for a stroll across the lawn. Perhaps you will be fortunate and find a cooling breeze.'

Maddy placed the still half-full cup in the saucer and stood. She was more than happy to take the advice.

The three girls exited via the doors, crossed the front veranda and stepped onto a gentle slope of open ground. Beyond the lawn several rows of vines separated the homestead from the Hunter River. As they walked past the rows of newly planted vines, she recalled Cookie telling her how Mr Garrick nurtured the vines with particular care. He had lost his first planting almost entirely the previous year and was determined to succeed this time.

Maddy glanced back at the house, admiring the low sturdy shape and shingled roof. She wondered what had happened at Shelby, for the Garricks had only been in the Hunter Valley a few years longer than Papa. She hoped Papa had drawn plans of the house he'd described in such detail. He must have, she assured herself: though he was undoubtedly a dreamer, surely his letters hadn't been entirely fantastical.

'Miss Barker-Trent.' Belle initiated a conversation with her for the first time since their introduction.

Maddy blinked at her challenging tone. 'Yes, Miss Everette?' She smiled at Belle, despite her misgivings.

'The talk of the valley is that a … woman lives on your property?'

Maddy stared at her. Something in Belle's tone made her wary.

'Oh, Belle, don't be so stuffy,' Amelia chided before Maddy could formulate a reply.

'Well, Miss Everette, I met a woman called Mrs McMahon on my first day.' A flash of Rose McMahon's devastated features as she told them what she'd found flooded Maddy's mind. 'I didn't spend much time there: as you know, my papa drowned the day I arrived.' Annoyance sharpened Maddy's words; no one had mentioned anything about Mrs McMahon living at Shelby. What was Belle implying? 'I've had no opportunity to get to know her.'

'Know her?' Belle's words dripped disdain. 'One does not get to know that sort.'

'I find most people are as good or as bad as they are treated.'

'She isn't someone gentlefolk associate with.'

Maddy's mouth dropped open. Myriad caustic replies to Belle's statement rushed to her lips.

'Stop it, Belle, we have so much to talk about without you striving to start an argument. You mustn't mind her.' Amelia leaned in to murmur, 'She quite had her heart set on Mr Coulter. Now you've arrived and any hope she had is quite dashed.'

Maddy felt heat flood her face, and she saw Belle was in much the same state. Belle muttered something Maddy didn't catch, but thankfully, nothing more was said on the subject.

Most of the land between the house and the river was cleared and much of it under cultivation at Tillington. They followed a tree-lined track to a small clearing by the river bank. Maddy had been told by Tida it was often used by the family and neighbours for picnics.

'Maddy, we recently met your overseer, Mr Coulter—he is related to Mrs Garrick, isn't he?' Amelia plucked a leaf from an overhanging branch. Was he? She had thought he was merely an overseer. The sudden change of topic was every bit as bewildering as her sister's acerbic remarks had been.

'Amelia, can you think of nothing but men?' Belle snapped.

'Can you—' Amelia spun towards her sister quivering with indignation, and Maddy realised she was spoiling for a fight.

'Oh look,' Maddy exclaimed. Beyond Amelia's shoulder she saw three elegant black swans gliding on the water. Their necks curved in graceful lines as they sailed by with delightful dignity.

'I have read of them,' Belle said, and sounded pleased for the first time since she'd arrived, 'though this is the first I've seen.'

They stood and watched the glossy black birds with bright red beaks until they passed out of sight around a bend.

Amelia sighed heavily, making it clear her interest in the native fauna had dissipated. 'I wish more interesting gentlemen would visit Aunt Catherine's,' she said, turning away from the river.

'Plenty of gentlemen drop by on their way to Patrick's Plains,' said Belle.

'None that are interesting,' Amelia said. 'Nor as handsome as Mr Coulter. Oh Maddy, you are lucky.' She shot her sister a sidelong glance.

This comment rankled. How could she be considered lucky? Both her parents were dead, and Amelia thought only of Mr Coulter.

'What is so fascinating about Mr Coulter?' Maddy asked her.

'Oh, he is so handsome, he has such lovely blue eyes.'

Maddy shook her head and forced a laugh. She didn't want to discuss Daniel Coulter with Amelia, and certainly not his lovely blue eyes.

'Amelia, you are being silly. It's inappropriate to discuss a gentleman in such a fashion.'

She smiled at Maddy. 'Does he not remind you of Mr Wickham in *Pride and Prejudice*?'

'Mr Wickham is a beast,' Belle said.

'Yes, but he was so romantic, and Mr Coulter is exactly like him.'

'You can't possibly know that!'

'He is in my imagination,' Amelia said, looking at her sister coquettishly.

Maddy hadn't read the novel, so offered no comment. But she thought it odd that Belle knew exactly who Amelia spoke of in spite of her protests.

'Belle, you're too stuffy. A girl can confide in her friend, can she not?' said Amelia. With that Amelia took Maddy's arm and tucked it beneath her own.

'I must admit there's quite the excellent social set here—far better than we expected,' Amelia told her in a confiding tone too low for her sister to hear.

Before Maddy could respond a movement caught her eye. Her entire body went rigid and she gasped. The very thing she dreaded most lay on the ground behind Amelia, head raised slightly and forked tongue flickering as it tasted the air. Amelia started at Maddy's small cry and glanced around to see the snake.

An ear-splitting scream rent the air and it seemed even the snake reacted to Amelia's shriek, for it changed direction and began to slither towards the river. Belle spun to look and leaped behind Maddy in a single bound. Later they were to marvel at the distance of her leap, but at the time Maddy's attention was solely on the wavering black line of the serpent.

Amelia's scream brought Daniel Coulter, along with two farmhands, at a run. The workers carried a shovel and a hoe respectively and quickly dispatched the poor creature, who'd done nothing in the slightest to harm them. Maddy wondered if Mr Coulter had been all day at Tillington.

'He was a big 'un,' said the man who'd removed the snake's head with the shovel, 'easy six feet.'

'Indeed,' Mr Coulter agreed.

Maddy couldn't turn away from the twisting coils as it undulated, headless, on the sloping grass.

'Are you unharmed?' Mr Coulter addressed his question to Maddy, who nodded.

'Oh, Mr Coulter,' Amelia said, her voice shaking as she began to crumple. Mr Coulter had no choice but to catch her as she sank towards the ground in a suspiciously dramatic faint.

'Miss Everette,' he said, 'we'd better get you to the house.'

Belle frowned at her sister's behaviour, and Maddy glanced at Amelia in time to see a slight curve to her lips, which Maddy thought was quite out of place on the face of someone who'd fainted. A wave of anger swept over her. Mr Coulter was Shelby's overseer. What was he still doing at Tillington? Shouldn't he be about his duties? She fumed but said nothing as she followed them back to the house.

Four

Thursday, 22 December 1831—extremely hot with dry winds

Hesitating at the door, Maddy drew in a deep breath. She glanced over her shoulder at the five men who stood watching her from across the yard: Mr Garrick, Mr Coulter, George Lester, Phil Hardy and young Charlie. She wondered what they were thinking. Regardless of how she felt, or what anyone thought, it was time to take stock of her circumstances.

Though Mr Coulter and the three convicts had stayed on at Shelby during her absence, there was a forlorn, abandoned feel to the place. There was no sign of Mrs McMahon or her child. What had become of them? Maddy turned back to the hut, placed her hand on the latch and, lifting her chin, opened the door. It was five days since she'd last seen this room, and a swirl of dust motes played in the beams of sunlight as she stepped inside. This was the place her father had called home for over four years. She crossed to the desk, and she imagined him sitting there, writing by candlelight. Penning the letters Mama and she had read with such eagerness in the comfort of their Wiltshire home. Letters full of exciting news of their new estate. He'd written little of the flora and less of the fauna. Nothing of the dust, or the heat, or the hardships. Why hadn't he mentioned the strange beauty of the olive-hued countryside? The colourful birds and unusual wildlife. Instead he'd sent endless descriptions of a non-existent house.

Not for the first time, Maddy pondered what he could have thought to gain by describing Shelby in such glowing detail, when it was so obviously untrue. Had he thought Mama would not have come if the house wasn't ready? Her throat constricted, and she wasn't sure if it was grief or anger that filled her. Perhaps a mixture of the two. Maddy's eyes smarted with tears as she recalled his face when she'd arrived—*so haggard*—and then his devastation when he'd realised Mama hadn't come with her. For the thousandth time she relived that moment. A sob escaped her. How could he leave her there alone?

Knuckling away a fresh well of tears Maddy drew in a deep breath. She needed to collect Papa's journals and ledgers, and, hopefully, any plans he'd recorded for the property. She didn't want to do it but knew she must.

'Be strong,' she said aloud and sat down at the desk. The central drawer contained the letters from Mama. Beneath them was a leather-bound journal. She pulled it from beneath several loose pages. Papa had never been organised, and the more she saw of Shelby, the more she wondered at Mama's agreeing that he go ahead and prepare a place for them. It had always been Mama who'd possessed sufficient good sense for them both, but something was definitely amiss.

Gathering everything that seemed pertinent to the running of the estate she put it into the satchel Mr Garrick had loaned her, gave the room a final look and sighed. Sooner rather than later she would have to sort out the hut, but not today. She left, closing the door firmly behind her.

Before returning to Tillington Maddy wanted to visit Papa's grave and say goodbye. Due to the heat, the men had needed to bury him immediately. She crossed to the buggy and put the satchel on the seat. Her heart was a hard lump in her chest as she walked silently beside Mr Garrick to the barely started foundation trenches. He indicated a small offshoot track and, without a word, Maddy turned and followed it. Near the edge of the escarpment she saw a mound of overturned soil through the trees. A rough-hewn cross marked the place where Papa had been laid to rest. She'd been in the grip of a fever when they'd buried him, but her dreams had been plagued by images of his body being lowered into the hard dry ground. Dreams and memories mingled into a distressing kaleidoscope when she thought of Mama's coffin lying beneath the dark damp soil of Wiltshire.

'We'll make a headstone for yer pa,' Phil Hardy said, his words gruff, then he cleared his throat. Maddy nodded. She couldn't tear her eyes from the cross, that symbol of Christ's sacrifice. A solitary tear slipped over her lashes and tracked down her cheek to drip from her chin. She longed to go back in time, to speak to Papa once more, to explain what had happened. If only she could have told him all that she'd written to him in the letter. The letter he'd never received. She wanted just one more moment. Maddy was aware of the soft shuffling of feet as the men moved away. She glanced down to see the black dog standing beside her.

'Betty, come away,' Phil Hardy called, and the dog slunk off. Maddy turned back to the grave.

'Why did you do this?' Though she spoke the words aloud, Maddy wasn't sure if she was talking about his death or the lies. 'What do I do now?'

Of course. There was no earthly response, and yet she heard his words as if they'd been spoken aloud. *Stay: realise my dream.* Looking away from the cross, she lifted tear-filled eyes to the hills beyond the wide valley and wondered where she belonged; was it with Papa, in this place of heat and dust, or with Mama, in the soft air and fertile soil of England? Both had a strong grip on her.

Evenings spent listening to Papa's vision for a life in New South Wales and Mama's indulgent encouragement seemed to speak the loudest. Had both her parents lived, it would have been Mama who would have made those dreams reality. Mama had been the practical one, and with her good sense she'd have taken on the challenge and guided Papa to success. She would have completed what he had begun, and it would have been wonderful. Mama had exuded excitement and enthusiasm, but these had been tempered by good sense and grit. If she'd been able, she'd have rolled up her sleeves and worked alongside Papa. Maddy didn't know if she had enough of her mother's pluck to achieve their dream, but she knew she must try.

With her resolve consisting mostly of ignorance and a tiny speck of hope, Maddy returned to the farmyard where Mr Garrick and Mr Coulter waited for her.

'The men are planting tobacco in the north field. If you are finished here, I'll head down to join them,' Daniel told Mr Garrick.

Maddy bristled. Shouldn't he be consulting her when it came to the property? *Of which you know nothing at all*, she reminded herself.

'I have Papa's journal and ledgers, and I think it's time for me to acquaint myself with the situation here at Shelby.' Neither man replied so she elaborated, 'I need to know how things stand financially.' She climbed into the buggy.

'We can take a look when we get home,' Mr Garrick agreed as he joined her, and added, glancing over at Mr Coulter, 'Daniel, we shall see you Sunday for lunch.'

'Of course.' Mr Coulter smiled and nodded politely at Maddy. 'Miss Barker-Trent, Alex.' His mare spun on her hock and he cantered her across the clearing and disappeared down the track.

'Mr Garrick?' Maddy began as he turned the horse towards the road.

'Yes?'

'Amelia Everette said that Mr Coulter is related to Mrs Garrick.'

'Not related: Daniel's sister Charlotte is a dear friend of Susannah's.'

'Why then is he working at Shelby?' Although Maddy didn't understand much about how things worked in the colony, it made no sense for Mr Coulter to work for her father when he could be working with Mr Garrick.

'Daniel had originally come to Tillington, but we agreed he could be a great help to your father, and so it was arranged for him to work at Shelby for a time.'

'I see.' Maddy was beginning to see all too clearly. The silence stretched as she considered her next step in light of what she'd learned. Would Mr Coulter wish to move on now that Papa was gone? She supposed everyone would expect her to sell Shelby and return to England.

'Do you intend to sell?' Mr Garrick asked, confirming her thoughts. 'If so, I can assist with the arrangements.'

'Thank you, but I have no intention of selling Shelby. I mean to see Papa's dream through to completion.' The words were out before Maddy knew she was going to say them, but once ignited, they fanned a flame. Both her parents had dreamed of this life; it had charmed them from afar, and now she was here, it held her heart too. Maddy would build the house and establish the farm. She would do it.

Maddy waited, expecting Mr Garrick to object, but to her surprise, he did not. He was silent for a few moments, and she turned on the seat to face him. His fair hair receded from an intelligent brow, and neatly shaped sideburns framed his kindly face. Papa had been fortunate to have such neighbours as the Garricks. Maddy didn't like to think what would have become of him had they not been close by.

'Well, Maddy,' he said eventually, 'it's difficult to run such a holding with convict labour, even more so for a woman.' He gave her an assessing look. 'But it is not impossible. A good many women run things in place of their husbands. Susannah keeps everything ticking along whenever I'm away from Tillington.'

Gratitude swelled in the shrivelled husk of her heart, pumping it with life once more. 'Oh, Mr Garrick, thank you, I'd expected you to try to convince me otherwise. To tell me that it was implausible.'

'Your papa was fortunate when Daniel agreed to work for him as not many convicts have farming experience, and even the majority of free settlers were originally city dwellers.' He clicked the mare up when she arched her neck to peer at something in the shrubs beside the road. 'You are a man down—' He stopped abruptly, realising too late what he'd been about to say.

'With Papa dead,' Maddy completed the sentence for him, her voice bleak. She drew in a wobbly breath. 'I understand. And I know I will need guidance in so many aspects of life here. I hope I may come to you for instruction?'

He smiled. 'Of course, you must.'

'I admit I'd not expected you to be so agreeable.'

'Perhaps you'd prefer me to be disagreeable?'

Maddy shook her head and smiled. She might not succeed, but she would do her utmost to fulfil the promise she'd made to her parents.

'I have Papa's ledgers. I shall study them and, if you don't mind, I will consult you on my findings?'

He nodded. 'That will be as good a way to start as any.'

Sunday, 25 December 1831—hot but no wind

Christmas Day dawned clear and dry, with the promise of a pleasant if somewhat warm day. The dining room was decorated with as many flowers and sprigs of greenery as the children and Maddy could find after her return from Shelby. There'd been no time to even open the account books before Tida and Edwin had informed her of the task they'd been set.

The smell of Cookie's roast goose wafted in through the opened windows and intensified the festive mood as Mrs Garrick and Maddy laid the table.

Maddy shared a family recipe for sage and onion sauce as an accompaniment for the goose and was duly sent into the garden to pick the sage. She smiled as she recalled the hours she'd spent in the kitchen watching Mrs Watters; she'd spent a lot of time in the servants' domain. The dew was still on the ground in the shade of the house, and Maddy paused for a moment to lift her face to the sun; what a contrast to previous Christmas mornings. There was a small window of time in which she could enjoy the warmth before it became hot enough to blister. All too soon it would reach its zenith and scorch all it lighted upon. Mrs Garrick had clucked disapprovingly at the freckles that already covered her nose. Maddy loved to feel the sun's heat on her skin and refused to wear a bonnet except during the hottest part of the day.

'Good morning, Miss Barker-Trent.'

Maddy jumped at the sound of Mr Coulter's voice and slapped a hand over her wildly thudding heart. The peppery aroma of the freshly picked sage filled her nostrils as she crushed the velvety leaves against the bodice of her gown. 'Oh, Mr Coulter, you gave me a start, I didn't hear you approach.'

'I apologise, Miss Barker-Trent, I hadn't intended to frighten you. Mrs Garrick insisted I join the family for lunch.'

'No need to apologise, Mr Coulter, nor explain. I'm afraid you caught me daydreaming, a character flaw, according to my nurse. She warned it would one day be my downfall. She was quite correct: it has caused me difficulty on more than one occasion.' Maddy realised she was prattling and stopped speaking abruptly. His blue eyes shone and she saw a hint of a dimple when he smiled at her kindly. Warmth rose in her cheeks.

'I can't help but wonder what kind of adventures your imaginations have taken you on.' His teeth flashed white in his tanned face and she felt as if the air had been sucked from her lungs as the dimple played hide-and-seek to the left of his smiling mouth.

'I doubt you would find my silly stories of any interest.' She hid her heated face by bending down to pick another unnecessary sprig of sage. In her flustered state she dropped the small garni and bent to retrieve it. Maddy's head bumped against something solid. Mr Coulter had also bent down to pick up her small harvest.

'Oh, I'm sorry.' She jerked up only to clash foreheads once again.

'There.' His strong fingers wrapped around her elbow, searing the skin through the thin fabric of her sleeve. 'Are you all right?' he asked.

Maddy rocked back. Her vision was a little blurred from the knock, though she saw clearly enough that concern had etched fine lines around his eyes as he peered at her. Maddy nodded and blinked several times.

Forcing herself to look away from his handsome face, she said, 'Yes, I'm fine, thank you.' And holding up the crushed leaves she continued, 'I must take these into Mrs Brown, so she can make the ...' For the life of her, Maddy couldn't remember what the herbs were for. She started towards the house, stumbling a little in her haste to get away from him. With burning cheeks, she scurried out the garden gate.

'Happy Christmas, Miss Barker-Trent.'

Her heart leaped again and she hesitated, glancing back at him. 'I, er, thank you, and Happy Christmas to you too, Mr Coulter.'

The timbre of his voice did something odd to her stomach and made her heart beat such a crazy tattoo she could barely hear herself speak. Head down she unlatched the gate and hurried back to the safety of the house.

The roast goose and accompanying sauce were perfect, despite the sorry state of the herbs she'd delivered to the kitchen. Though the Garricks were warm and welcoming, Maddy couldn't help feeling out of place. A sudden pang of longing for her own small family clenched her heart. Snatches of memories came unbidden as she ate: the entire household, servants included, had always come together for the midday meal. Her parents cuddled close as Maddy tore the wrappings from gifts of dried fruit and nuts, while her own small token for them, a badly executed sampler or the like, was laid aside as they watched her. Maddy experienced a pang of guilt as she recalled feeling an outsider to their closeness and pushed it away. They were gone, and it grieved her there would be no new memories. It was up to her now: she would be the one to make a new life. Recalling the ceremony with which Papa had presented gifts to each of the servants, Maddy was determined to do the same at Shelby. She would ask Mr Garrick what would be suitable. Perhaps some new clothes?

The noise and bustle of the Garrick table was at odds with her recollections and she pushed the melancholy thoughts away. Maddy grew painfully aware of Daniel Coulter seated opposite, of the sound of his voice, his laughter, the ease with which he talked to Tida and Edwin and made young George shriek with delight as he swung the babe high in the air. When the family moved towards the drawing room, Maddy hesitated at the door, not wishing to intrude.

'Maddy, where are you going?' Tida demanded as Maddy started to leave.

'I'm afraid I have no gifts—'

'Nonsense, come in,' Mrs Garrick interrupted. Maddy did as she was told, settling reluctantly on a small stool near the fireplace. Instead of a crackling fire, Mrs Garrick had set a large urn of greenery with native ferns and aromatic eucalyptus leaves in the grate. It filled the room with a delightful fresh fragrance.

Maddy watched on as the family exchanged gifts, smiling at the children's delight and trying not to feel an interloper when Tida came and stood before her; in her hands she held a package she'd obviously wrapped herself. She handed over the gift and, before Maddy could begin to open it, suddenly snatched it back and with urgent fingers swiftly dealt with the unwrapping herself.

'Tida, no!' Mrs Garrick chastised.

'It's fine,' Maddy reassured her, 'I appreciate her help.' A length of delicate cream lace fell from the scrunched folds. A proud smile spread over Tida's face as she stood straight-backed, her chest puffed out with pleasure. Maddy pulled her close and hugged her, tears prickling her eyes.

'Oh, Tida, how lovely. You are a clever girl to give me such a beautiful gift.' Maddy hugged her again and dropped a kiss on her smooth brow.

Edwin stepped forwards with a larger parcel and nudged Tida out of his way. He took the prime present-opening position at Maddy's knee and handed her his gift. Maddy unwrapped the parcel and gazed down at a small leather-bound journal.

'So you can write down your thoughts.' His big brown eyes were solemn, while Maddy's filled with tears once more.

'Thank you, Edwin, I shall treasure it always.' She pulled him to her, and he allowed her to hug him for a moment before pushing her away. She glanced up to see Daniel Coulter staring at her, a strangely serious expression on his face.

'Papa said you would need a journal,' Edwin continued, and she dragged her attention back to the boy.

'Indeed, and I am certain I shall use it every day.'

'Mine next,' Daniel said.

Maddy's breath caught as she saw the small wooden box balanced on Daniel's open palm. Hesitantly she reached out to take his gift before pulling her hand away.

'Oh no, I couldn't—I have nothing in return.'

'Please,' he insisted, stepping closer, 'take it, it's only a trifle.'

She took the box and opened it. Inside was a small polished stone, a beautiful deep grey teardrop shot with bands of creamy white.

'Oh,' Maddy sighed, 'it's exquisite.' Picking it up she ran a finger over the smooth cool surface and smiled up at him. It was only a stone, and yet it was lovely and a thoughtful gift. She knew she would treasure it always.

'Daniel, I have a letter for you,' Mrs Garrick said, and there was something odd about her tone. She handed over a folded piece of paper. 'My instructions were to give it to you on Christmas Day.'

'Thank you,' he said, his face suddenly sober. It was a moment before his lips curved into a forced smile and he scrutinised the note and excused himself. The brightness of the day seemed to go with him, and Maddy's bubble of joy deflated—what could have so distressed Daniel? The pleasure of the family lunch and the special gifts seemed a little less enjoyable than it had moments before.

Maddy had little time to contemplate her mercurial emotions, for the sound of lively conversation came from the entry hall only moments after Daniel had left via the French doors. She recognised one voice as Amelia Everette's but not the low-toned murmur of the answering male one. Mr Garrick rose from his seat and pulled open the door to reveal three visitors standing in the hall.

'Happy Christmas,' sing-songed Amelia prettily as she entered the drawing room.

'Miss Amelia, Miss Belle.' Mr Garrick smiled and stepped back to allow Belle and the man with them to enter.

'Mr Garrick, this is Mr Douglass Hobson,' Amelia said.

'Mr Garrick,'—the newcomer nodded and with a quick glance around the room, he smiled—'sorry to intrude on your celebrations. Miss Everette assured us you would not mind.'

'Not at all; I am pleased to meet you, Mr Hobson,' Mr Garrick said, his voice warm and genuine.

Mr Hobson nodded politely. 'Please, call me Chase, everyone does.'

'Chase?' Mrs Garrick asked.

'Mr Hobson—Chase—allow me to introduce my wife, Mrs Garrick.' His voice had a definite hint of amusement, then as he turned to Maddy she saw his eyes were shining.

Mr Hobson turned to Mrs Garrick seated on the chaise and crossed the room to bow low over her hand.

'And this is Miss Barker-Trent,' Mr Garrick continued when the younger man had straightened.

'When Mr Hobson told us he'd not met you, Maddy, well we had to come, didn't we?' Amelia grabbed the young man's elbow and hauled him forwards.

Chase Hobson's features were marred by a small frown at Amelia's manhandling, but his face lit with pleasure as they met

Maddy's. 'Miss Barker-Trent,'—he left Amelia's clutches and crossed the room to take her hand in his—'I've heard much about you.'

Unsure how to answer she merely smiled and nodded. Maddy wasn't sure that she liked being the topic of local conversation, though it was hardly surprising, given the circumstances.

'We've not heard of you, however, so please come and sit,' Mr Garrick said, and Maddy flashed him a grateful look. 'Tell us about yourself.'

'I am late of London, sir. My father served in the Napoleonic wars, was in the Peninsular with Mr Everette's elder brother.'

'Mr Hobson has come to make his fortune in the colonies,' Amelia told them proudly, her face gleaming with excitement.

'Mr and Mrs Everette have kindly made room for me for a day or so. They're already quite full, what with Mrs Everette the Elder, and the young ladies.' He took in the fine furnishings in the room. Maddy wondered if he was angling for an invitation to stay at Tillington.

'Where are you intending to settle?' Mr Garrick asked.

'I'm not sure. I have seen a little of the countryside, but I've heard much of the land west of Patrick's Plains. I intend to spend some time at Merton, with the Ogilvies. Mr Everette has drafted an introduction for me.'

'Ogilvie is a good man. He'll see you right. His knowledge of the area is capital.'

Maddy was thankful for Mr Garrick having neatly diverted Chase Hudson's attention. She was tired and wished the trio would soon leave. Belle was listening to the men's conversation avidly while Amelia chatted with Mrs Garrick. The door opened and Mr Coulter re-entered, looking as if his letter hadn't contained good news. The sight of him sent Maddy's pulse racing. He greeted the Misses Everette first, and Amelia sent him a coy glance from beneath her lashes. Maddy berated herself for feeling relieved when Daniel seemed to be oblivious to Amelia's attentions; she had no time for such things. But still she was glad when he crossed to join the men. Maddy sighed and noticed Belle's frown. Warmth rose in her cheeks as she realised her sigh must have been louder than she'd realised. Maddy smiled ruefully at her and received a scowl in return. What had she done to deserve the other girl's dislike? Perhaps it was Amelia's flirtatious manner that irked Belle, and nothing to do with Maddy at all.

Daniel had not so much as glanced in Maddy's direction since he'd returned. What had his letter said? And who was it from? It was hard to reconcile his stony facade with the new friend who'd given her a beautiful polished stone.

As Maddy sat with the women she found her attention straying to observe Daniel's interaction with Chase Hobson. If Daniel's stance was anything to go by, he had quickly taken a dislike to Mr Hobson. She wondered what the newcomer had said to upset the usually amiable overseer. Amelia's titter broke into her contemplations and she was forced to pay attention to the women's conversation. Having no wish to be teased or scowled at by these sisters, Maddy tried to focus on Amelia's prattle.

She heard her name mentioned by Mr Hobson and looked over in time to see Daniel's narrowed eyes and creased brow. Again she wondered what had been said.

Five

Friday, 30 December 1831—pleasant, with a southerly breeze

It was several days after Christmas before Mr Garrick and Maddy had an opportunity to go over Shelby's ledgers together. She'd made several attempts to make sense of the figures; it was embarrassingly obvious that her father hadn't a head for business. Maddy had learned to keep accounts at her grandpapa's knee, the family mill having been her playground when her mama had been poorly. She watched Mr Garrick's frown deepen as he scanned the entries, and she knew her conclusions were accurate. Shelby was ailing.

'This makes no sense,' Maddy said, waving a hand over the figures. 'Papa sold Grandpapa's mill. There should have been more than sufficient funds available.'

'I suggest we draft a letter to the bank in Sydney, in the meantime—'

'In the meantime I have enough to carry on with,' Maddy cut him off with a smile, sensing he intended to offer her a loan. Thankfully that would not be necessary, she was not without means thanks to her mother's careful planning.

Together they made a list of chores Maddy would attend to and instructions for Daniel and the men. She had written pages of notes in the journal Edwin had given her for Christmas, and now believed she possessed a rudimentary idea of what was required to run the estate. A calendar of crop rotations and work priorities was discussed. All of which Papa should have begun or at least planned, though Maddy had found no evidence of it. She cringed when she considered Papa's obvious lack of preparations. He should never have come without Mama. She was grateful to have Daniel at Shelby, for however long he could remain.

'You have a good man in Daniel Coulter. He'll see you right in most matters.'

Had Mr Garrick read her mind again?

'Papa relied heavily on Mama when it came to keeping accounts,' Maddy told him, unaccountably defensive, as he'd said nothing negative about Papa or the state of Shelby.

'It's a very important part of running a business, and a farm is a business.' He closed the ledger. 'You must keep an eye on the finances—they are as crucial as planting and harvesting.'

Maddy nodded her agreement and paused, determined to ask the question that had been niggling her since Christmas Day when Daniel had received his letter and his attitude towards her had changed so abruptly.

'Yes?' Mr Garrick said, looking at her quizzically.

'Oh, please pardon me.' Heat rushed to Maddy's face; she stared at the pile of books on his desk. 'I was wondering whether perhaps Mr Coulter might not wish to continue at Shelby with Papa gone?'

'I think that's something you should discuss with Daniel. But I see no reason to believe he's unhappy there.'

Maddy didn't want to ask Daniel. She'd seen little of him since Christmas and whenever they had crossed paths he'd seemed somewhat distant. More than once she'd seen him leaving Tillington without having made any attempt to see her. Maddy was beginning to think he was avoiding her. She let the matter drop when Mr Garrick moved on to address the arrangements for their upcoming visit to Sydney. Maddy had several matters in need of attention there and was glad of Mr and Mrs Garrick's willingness to accompany her.

The persistent barking of a dog drew their attention and Maddy followed Mr Garrick out of his office onto a small porch on the eastern side of the house. A tall man clad totally in black and riding a leggy grey was halfway along the drive and cantering steadily towards the homestead.

'It's Mr Hawkins,' Mr Garrick said as they stood in the shade. They'd been working longer than she'd realised. It had been midmorning when they started on the books, only pausing to consume the light luncheon Cookie had sent in. Now she emerged to find the sun was well into the west and casting a long shadow over the ground.

'Mr Hawkins is the local chaplain,' Mr Garrick said.

Maddy nodded, watching the man as his horse drew to a halt a few yards from where she and Mr Garrick waited.

'Garrick,' Mr Hawkins said as he stepped down from the saddle. No sooner had his foot hit the ground than a boy from the stables appeared and took the reins of his horse. As he stripped off his riding gloves Maddy took in the dark thick brows, a perfect match for the thick sweep of hair over his forehead and brushing the collar of his coat; deep grooves bracketed a wide mouth and his dark eyes glinted with religious fervour—or perhaps it was amusement.

'John.' Mr Garrick smiled. Mr Hawkins turned his gaze from her and lifted a dark brow inquiringly. Mr Garrick urged Maddy forwards. 'This is Miss Barker-Trent, our newest neighbour.'

The reverend's pleasant features realigned into a sombre cast as he bowed his head. 'Miss Barker-Trent, I heard of your recent loss. A terrible thing to happen. I have been out of the valley, or I would have called sooner.' Years of Papa's ravings had made Maddy wary of the clergy, but Mr Hawkins struck her as quite amiable. Mama had never been vocal about her opinions, but she had often quoted scripture and read Maddy stories from the Bible. Instinct told Maddy that Mr Hawkins was not like the men of religion Papa had so detested.

'Thank you.'

'I knew well your father's opinion of the church, but if you would like me to say a few words …'

Maddy swallowed, not sure how to respond in a way that wouldn't offend him. 'Your offer is most kind, Mr Hawkins.'

'But perhaps not?' One thick black brow lifted but there was no censure in his expression. 'I know your father was not a believer.'

Maddy bristled at that. Papa had been a believer; he'd believed in God, and our Lord Jesus, just not in the contrived piety of religious orders.

'Ah, I see I have offended you.' His expressive face was a picture of dismay.

'No,' Maddy said, not wishing to have him belabour an apology, for she had the feeling he was a good man, despite his religiosity. 'Though, I feel I must clarify, Papa did believe in God and the Bible, just not the church.'

There was a moment of uncomfortable silence and immediately Maddy wished to fill it with her own apology. She resisted. Papa's beliefs had been his own, and he'd never hidden them.

'Let's go inside—I'm sure Mrs Garrick will be delighted to see you, John,' Mr Garrick said.

'Yes,' Mr Hawkins said, his expression still kind as he glanced at Maddy, and she saw he'd taken no offence at her words. 'After you, Miss Barker-Trent.'

'Thank you, Mr Hawkins.' Maddy smiled at him.

The men went off to find Mrs Garrick while Maddy returned to Mr Garrick's study to tidy away Shelby's ledgers. More than a little flustered, she considered Mr Hawkins as she carried the journals back to her room. Was she mistaken in blindly following her father's lead in distrusting the clergy? After all, she'd no reason to do so personally. And Mama had not agreed: she'd not liked it when Papa had ranted on the subject.

Maddy sat the books on the small writing desk. She surveyed the pile and thought she must speak to Daniel soon. She needed to know what he and Papa had discussed regarding plans for the farm in the coming months. Had she left it too long to take up her responsibilities? Her conversations with Mr Garrick had only served to accentuate her lack of knowledge. Maddy knew nothing about farming practices, nothing of planting, and even less of pigs, cattle and sheep.

Was she foolish to believe she could attempt such an undertaking? Maddy pushed down the traitorous thought and, with a slightly shaky hand, smoothed her unruly hair. Pausing to look out the window above the desk she realised she could see Shelby. Tillington was situated east of Shelby, and due to the sweep of the river, she was able to follow the ridge line to the escarpment where one day the house Papa had imagined would be visible. For a moment she imagined the two-storey building dominating the view, flanked by manicured lawns and a prosperous farm. Maddy determined she would make her parents' dream a reality. There was nothing for her to return to in England. Shelby was her home now. The sooner she set the wheels in motion, the sooner Shelby would be all that Papa had described. And perhaps then she would sleep; and only then could she rid herself of guilt and regrets. Her father's face when he'd realised the truth about Mama flashed before her and tears threatened. She closed her eyes and sent a silent promise to Mama and Papa; she would do it—she would build Shelby for them.

After checking her reflection in the small mirror on the bureau, she pinched some colour into her pale cheeks. Meeting her eyes in the glass, she saw fear there. Swallowing hard, she squared her shoulders. It would be well, it had to be.

Remembering the tea, Maddy straightened her skirts and hurried from the room.

Although she'd spent long hours thinking about staying on in New South Wales, it wasn't until that moment that she truly committed to the decision. With Daniel by her side, Maddy knew they could do it. If he would stay on at Shelby ... She gulped: he had to stay. With Daniel she had someone to help with the assigned labour—someone familiar with the day-to-day running of Shelby. She ignored the odd fluttering in her chest as she recalled his handsome face and kind blue eyes. Pressing the palms of her hands to suddenly hot cheeks, Maddy paused in the hall for a moment. What was wrong with her? When her heart had resumed a normal rhythm, she continued and headed to the drawing room, where she could hear Mr Hawkins talking with the Garricks.

'I wonder how long it will be before they begin to line up?' she heard Mr Hawkins say as she opened the door.

'Ah, here she is. Maddy, please do come in.' Mrs Garrick greeted her warmly and shot a frown in the reverend's direction. That they were discussing her was obvious. Not that she needed it confirmed, having assumed her situation and next moves would be the topic of more than one conversation in the valley. Maddy considered asking him how long before what or who lined up but refrained.

'Tea?' Mrs Garrick offered.

'Please.' Maddy smiled.

Once seated and balancing her delicate porcelain cup on its saucer, she looked first at Mrs Garrick and then the men. An awkward silence followed, and Maddy wondered exactly what she'd interrupted. The usual polite topics of conversation didn't apply, for Reverend Hawkins would hardly enquire about her impressions of the colony, or if she'd been enjoying herself thus far. Nor would he ask if she intended to stay or sell Shelby. Maddy had spoken of her plans with Mr Garrick alone, and he would not break her confidence. Besides, until now she hadn't fully determined she was going to stay.

'I dare say you've not had much opportunity to meet many of the good folk of the valley.'

'No,' Maddy said, 'though the Everette ladies have called twice. Mr Everette's nieces called on Christmas Day and brought Mr Hobson to visit.'

Mr Hawkins frowned. 'Hobson?' he asked Mr Garrick.

'Yes, the Misses Everette stopped by after lunch. Along with a Mr Hobson, or Chase as he likes to be called, who was staying at Cragside for a day or two before heading out to see Ogilvie at Merton. I think he said he'd been invited to stay at Dalwood on his return journey. He's quite interested in George Wyndham's stud horses.'

'Chase,' Mrs Garrick said half musingly, 'we didn't find out the significance of that, did we?'

'I didn't think to ask,' Maddy said. She'd not been terribly interested at the time, and still wasn't.

'I bypassed Cragside,' Mr Hawkins said, 'and came straight here.' He gave Mr Garrick a meaningful look. Mr Garrick's sage nod gave Maddy the impression that neither he nor Mr Hawkins was overly enamoured of Mrs Everette the Elder. She hid a smile in her teacup.

Silence once more filled the room. Something was not being said. But what?

'I take it there will be an inquiry into Mr Barker-Trent's death?' Mr Hawkins asked.

She jerked, staring first at him, then at the Garricks in turn, until she settled on Mr Garrick.

'Why?' she asked.

'I'm sorry, my dear,' he said, 'but all deaths that occur in unusual circumstances are investigated.' He sighed. 'There is nothing to be concerned about, and nothing for you to do.'

'I see.' Her mind raced. 'Will this inquiry be conducted locally, or in Sydney?'

'I imagine it will be in Sydney,' Mr Hawkins said, then looked at Mr Garrick for confirmation.

'I would say so.'

'When will it be held?' Maddy asked.

'In the new year, I expect,' Mr Hawkins said, again turning to Mr Garrick, who nodded his agreement.

'Will Mrs McMahon and I need to be present?'

'Mrs McMahon?' Mr Hawkins frowned. 'Private McMahon's widow?'

'No,' Mr Garrick said, addressing Maddy's question rather than Mr Hawkins's, 'but there's no need for you to concern yourself.'

'But how can there be an inquiry if those concerned, the witnesses, are not present to give evidence?'

'Perhaps they will need to send a constable from Newcastle,' Mrs Garrick said, 'to interview the convicts.'

'I suppose I should attend,' Maddy said, not sure if she wanted to relive the dreadful moments. 'I have other business to attend to in Sydney, so perhaps I should make my plans to align with the inquiry.'

'There's no need,' Mrs Garrick said, her brow wrinkling with concern.

'Business?' Mr Hawkins asked.

'Yes, I need to see the bank and send notice to Papa's solicitors for probate.' There was no point in delaying, sooner or later, she would need to take hold of the reins of her future for herself.

'Surely you could allow Mr Garrick to make the necessary arrangements,' said Mrs Garrick in a kindly tone.

Maddy wondered why Mr Garrick hadn't told his wife of her intentions. Did he expect her to change her mind? 'I must begin somewhere,' she said.

'Begin what?' Mrs Garrick and Mr Hawkins asked in unison.

After a quick glance at Mr Garrick, who merely lifted a brow, Maddy met her eyes. 'I intend to keep Shelby, to establish the property myself.'

'Keep?' Mr Hawkins looked as if she'd suddenly began to speak in a foreign language.

Maddy nodded.

'Of course, you must stay here with us,' Mrs Garrick said.

'Thank you for your kind offer, but I shall return to Shelby as soon as possible.' Her discussions with Mr Garrick had laid the foundation, and Maddy knew what she must do. 'First, I shall go to Sydney and make the necessary arrangements.'

Mr Hawkins's mouth worked, but no sound came from him.

'Maddy and I have discussed her options, and it seems she is not of a mind to sell,' said Mr Garrick.

'I see,' said Mr Hawkins, but Maddy wasn't sure what it was he saw.

Mrs Garrick, however, was more than a little taken aback.

'My dear Maddy, I insist, you must stay with us.'

'Mrs Garrick, I truly appreciate your generosity, and thank you, but I cannot accept your kind offer. I have discussed the running of Shelby in detail with Mr Garrick, and I believe it's imperative I start as I mean to go on. Papa was not an absentee landowner, and neither shall I be.' Having stated her intentions aloud, Maddy knew in an instant she'd made the right decision. 'The completion of the kitchen is the priority, and when it is ready, I shall move back in.'

'But my dear, you cannot,' Mrs Garrick said, 'it wouldn't be appropriate for you to stay there unaccompanied.'

'Oh, I shan't be on my own: I intend to secure the services of a companion maid.'

Six

Monday, 16 January 1832—warm but pleasant

The small caravan consisted of three wagons, all laden with grain
for the steamer to Sydney; the first two belonged to Mr Garrick,
and, though a much smaller load, the third was Shelby's own.
Maddy tugged her shawl closer about her shoulders—the early
morning air was crisp with wisps of mist still hovering over the
river below. Her decision to accompany Shelby's harvest to the
docks at Green Hills had elicited several concerned comments
from both Mr and Mrs Garrick as well as Daniel Coulter, but
Maddy was determined to learn everything she could about
farming life. Since she had decided to stay, the spark of purpose
within her had grown into a conflagration. With the harvest
in and a letter from the Bank of New South Wales confirming the bank would stand a loan until probate was granted. Just
why Papa had failed to invest in Shelby would likely remain yet
another mystery, but it was of great relief to know she was not
destitute. Having the matter of finance settled, Maddy requested
the men concentrate on finishing the kitchen in preparation for
her moving to Shelby.

She was intent too on choosing a horse for herself at the sale-yard and had insisted on travelling on the wagon in order to make the journey home riding her new horse. When Phil Hardy shifted on the seat as the dray rocked through a deep rut on the road, flinching away when his shoulder touched hers, a prickle of guilt itched along her spine. It was one thing to obey only her own sensibilities, but another entirely to make those in her care uncomfortable. Maddy thought perhaps she should have taken up Mrs Garrick's offer of the buggy, but she ignored her misgivings and resolved to find a horse she could ride home. Papa's stallion had been sold to Mr Garrick, the beast being too much for her to handle, but on Mr Garrick's insistence, she had retained breeding rights, and with this in mind she intended to purchase a mare.

Ahead Mr Garrick and Mr Coulter rode side by side try-ing to have a conversation, but the stallion was spooky and was constantly prancing sideways, eyes flashing at dangers mostly imagined. Mr Coulter's roan mare took little notice of the antics of the other horse and plodded stolidly on, though her ears twitched with each bump. With its tail aloft and eyes rolling, the stallion was not giving Mr Garrick an easy ride. Papa may not have known much about farming, Maddy thought, but he was an excellent judge of horseflesh and could outride anyone, anywhere.

Mr Coulter turned in the saddle and tossed her a conspiratorial grin. She realised he knew Papa had handled the colt with ease. Something fluttered in her middle, and heat flooded her cheeks as she returned his smile and tugged the brim of her bonnet lower on her brow. She couldn't allow herself to be distracted, Maddy reminded herself, as there was much at stake and there was no place for romantic notions in her plan.

'Miss Barker-Trent, I, er ...' Mr Hardy began.

'Yes, Mr Hardy?' Maddy turned to look at him.

He swallowed. 'I, er. That is, we were wondering if it was true.' He kept his attention on the rumps of the horses between the shafts.

'If what is true?'

He flicked a quick glance at Maddy before returning his attention to the road ahead before his eyes finally met hers again.

'There's talk you are going to keep Shelby, even stay on yourself.'

She realised she should have shared her plans with the men at Shelby, though she'd spoken to no one other than the Garricks and Mr Hawkins; she wondered how he had heard.

'Yes, it's true, I intend to continue with Papa's plans.' She assumed Mr Garrick had discussed the matter with Daniel Coulter, but Maddy saw now she should have done so herself.

Phil Hardy beamed. 'That's good, miss,' he said, and he clicked his tongue to gee up the horses.

'It was kind of Mr Garrick to lend help with the harvest,' Maddy said, twisting around to admire the plump sacks of maize stencilled with SHELBY. Pleasure and misgiving warred within her; had she been imprudent to accompany the men? Both Mr Garrick and Mr Coulter had tried to explain the docks were the domain of some rough fellows, yet she'd insisted. Maddy straightened on the seat: if she was going to stay, it was up to her to learn everything. And she must not take too much assistance from her new friends, despite their well-meant offers. She turned her attention to the track ahead. It was her first journey back to the docks at Greenhills since she had arrived and she noted most of the fields south of the river were cleared and under cultivation, while the opposite side was untouched forest.

The forlorn lowing of cattle alerted them they were almost at their destination only minutes before the smell of livestock and manure reached her. Maddy squinted and in the distance saw a cloud of dust rising into the air, marking the yards where livestock and produce waited to be transported by ship to Sydney.

'We're almost there, Miss Barker-Trent.'

'Please, Phil, perhaps you could call me Miss Maddy? Miss Barker-Trent is such a mouthful.' She smiled at his slack-jawed shock. 'You don't mind if I call you Phil, do you?'

'Er, no Miss Ba—ah Miss Maddy: you can call me Phil,' he said, grinning. His smile faded quickly. 'But perhaps it'd be best if I don't do it in company. You know, it might not sit well with some folk. A lady being too familiar like, with convicts.' A deep red stained his throat.

Maddy swallowed, knowing he was right. 'Yes of course, I understand.' Her own face was burning—she realised she should not have asked.

She chewed the inside of her lip, wanting to say something more, but what was there to say? Her parents had treated servants like an extension of the family and Maddy wasn't sure how to feel about what he'd said. She didn't want to upset him, but part of her rebelled against the accepted conventions.

She was soon distracted by the hubbub and clamour of the docks. No sooner had the dray stopped than several men appeared and began dragging the sacks from the wagon bed, hoisting the Shelby-stamped grain over their shoulders.

While Daniel, Phil and the Tillington men took care of unloading the grain, Mr Garrick and Maddy wove their way between other arriving wagons. With her skirts lifted clear of all manner of muck, she followed Mr Garrick to the far side of the sloping field where several sturdy timber yards held a dozen or so horses. A bald-faced chestnut caught Maddy's eye as they approached, and she knew instantly this was the horse she wanted. She crossed and lifted her hand for it to sniff.

'I like this one,' she said, liking its soft eye and wrinkled brow.

'You were going to purchase a mare. That one would be an excellent choice,' Mr Garrick advised, pointing at a neat bay filly in the next yard.

Maddy shook her head and rubbed a gloved hand beneath the gelding's copper-coloured mane.

'A mare would be dual purpose, and this filly would give you a fine foal or two.'

She turned to Mr Garrick, knowing his advice to be sound, but Maddy was determined this was the horse she wanted.

'I see your point, Mr Garrick, but I feel the gelding will suit me well, so I'll stick with Red here. However, when the accommodations are complete, we will have the horse yards extended and then I will consider purchasing a suitable mare.' She rubbed the white blaze between the horse's eyes with her knuckles. Its ears flopped and lids closed with pleasure. Maddy smiled as Mr Garrick opened his mouth to argue, then closed it again, resigned.

'Who do I see?' she asked. 'And I'll need to purchase a saddle.'

Maddy's decision was proven sound as the horse tied to the wagon followed along steadily, though her desire to ride him back to Shelby had been foiled by her inability to purchase a suitable saddle. Instead Mr Garrick had ordered one made and elicited a promise for it to be delivered to Shelby by the month's end. She twisted on the seat and considered the horse: she could buy a mare later; for now she was satisfied to have purchased a reliable mount for a fair price.

Seven

Wednesday, 25 January 1832—cloudy

Maddy stepped off the paddle steamer and onto the dock in Sydney Cove. While waiting for Mr Garrick to secure transport to their accommodation at the Australian Hotel she took in the bustle of disembarking passengers. Barefoot men in ragged britches bounced across a plank between the dock and ship, bags of grain balanced over their shoulders. Beside her Mrs Garrick also peered into the hubbub.

'I wonder where Alex has disappeared to?'

Mr Garrick had been gone for quite a while, and Mrs Garrick and Maddy stood beside their luggage as the crowded dock slowly emptied of passengers.

'Ah, there he is.' Mrs Garrick nodded, and Maddy looked around to see Mr Garrick speaking to a ruddy-faced balding man. 'That's Mr Atkinson, an acquaintance of your Papa,' Mrs Garrick said.

Maddy nodded, recalling mention of Mr Atkinson and his family in Papa's letters. He'd admired Atkinson's daughters— they were educated in the sciences and, according to Papa, were interesting and knowledgeable. She remembered thinking she would like to meet them and hoped to have an opportunity. Before Maddy could pursue the topic, a small hand-pushed cart stopped beside them, and a burly man, dressed in worn canvas trousers and tunic, began loading the luggage onto it.

'To the Australian?' he said to Mrs Garrick.

'Yes, please.' She turned to Maddy and smiled. 'It's not far, so we can walk. But mind the manure.'

They set off in the wake of the cart and luggage but had hardly gone more than a dozen paces before Mr Garrick caught them up.

'Susannah, I ran into James Atkinson,' he said.

'I saw you speaking with him.' Mrs Garrick nodded and continued after the man and his cart.

'Atkinson has invited us to a reception tonight.'

'Tonight?' Mrs Garrick didn't seem overly pleased.

'Yes, it's an opportunity for Maddy to meet some people her own age. Several of Atkinson's daughters shall be there, and a few others.'

'I see,' Mrs Garrick said. Maddy watched her, wondering what had caused the change in her countenance.

Maddy's room at the Australian Hotel was clean and comfortable and situated next to Mr and Mrs Garrick's suite. She was at the window, watching the activity on the street below, when a gentle knock sounded. She crossed and opened the door to Mrs Garrick.

'Mrs Garrick.' Maddy smiled but wondered why she'd come for her so soon. They'd parted only moments before.

'Maddy, I wanted to check if you are feeling up to attending dinner at the Atkinsons' tonight? If you feel it is too soon after the loss of your dear Papa ...'

Maddy considered it for a moment; she hadn't been expecting to go anywhere but was excited at the prospect of a social event. 'I look forward to it,' she said. 'It will be a pleasure to meet people of whom Papa thought highly.'

'Very well,' Mrs Garrick said after a long moment. She turned to go, then hesitated and turned back. 'You mustn't mind Mrs Atkinson,' she said quietly. 'She has a plethora of unmarried daughters and takes the arrival of any eligible young lady in the colony not only as competition for them but as a personal slight.'

Mr Garrick first helped his wife from the carriage he'd hired to take them from the hotel to the Atkinsons' home. Taking his hand, Maddy stepped down to see a grand sandstone house with a wide veranda across the front. It was much as she'd imagined Shelby House should have looked if it existed. They were whisked in through an imposing entrance and straight to the drawing room. A short apple-shaped lady with ringleted pale red hair bustled into the room. She was dressed in a high-necked gown of soft pink, complete with enormous sleeves finished in a delicate lace cuff. The gown was a little the worse for wear, and Maddy thought it would be better suited for someone much younger than the middle-aged matron. Mrs Atkinson beamed; her raisin eyes twinkled above rosy cheeks as she thrust her plump beringed fingers at Mrs Garrick. Maddy wondered if she'd misunderstood Mrs Garrick's warning.

'Susannah,' Mrs Atkinson cried, 'Such a delight to see you. So fortunate James ran into Alex.' She turned in Maddy's direction before Mrs Garrick could respond, her expression changing dramatically. 'And this must be your charge.' She tottered towards Maddy; her eyes gleamed with a less welcoming light.

'Mrs Atkinson.' Maddy nodded. She felt herself examined closely as she took in the older woman's calculating countenance.

Without warning her expression dissolved and, almost before Maddy could take it in, Mrs Atkinson began to gush.

'We were so terribly sorry to hear of your misfortune—first your mama, and then your poor papa. Both dead.' She pressed a plump fist against her trembling lips, her eyes brimming. Maddy realised these people had cared for Papa, and tears filled her own eyes. Yet Maddy had so little knowledge of his time here other than what had been in his letters. Letters that had so little foundation in truth. She shook her head and felt a tear trickle down her cheek.

'Mama, why didn't you tell me the Garricks had arrived?'

Maddy quickly brushed away the tears and turned to see a short slim orange-haired girl standing in the doorway, sporting an impish grin and an elaborate hairstyle. She turned her direct stare to Maddy. 'Miss Barker-Trent, I swear you are the most talked-about gal in the colony.' With several quick strides, she swept Maddy into a tight embrace. 'And it is lovely to meet you.' She released her as suddenly and turned back to Mrs Garrick.

'Henrietta,' Mrs Garrick said, smiling.

'Mrs Garrick, it's wonderful you are here. I was sorry to have missed you last time you visited.' She glanced around, her expression puzzled. 'Where is young George? Surely you haven't left him alone in the wilderness?'

'Not alone, Henny,' Mrs Garrick said, a smile playing at the corner of her lips.

'It's such a shame—I love to draw babies.'

'Henrietta,' Mrs Atkinson said, her voice sharp, 'do behave, and where is Lizzy?'

'I'll take Miss Barker-Trent upstairs,' Henrietta said, ignoring her mother. She grabbed Maddy's hand and dragged her to the door. Maddy had no choice but to allow herself to be towed down the hall in the wake of such a whirlwind.

'Do you like books?' Henrietta didn't wait for Maddy's reply but released her hand and charged up the stairs, leaving her to follow. They entered a cluttered parlour crammed with bookshelves, comfortable-looking chairs and a large desk; it was a room suitable for both reading and study. The desk situated near the window was crowded with papers and chunks of charcoal. Henrietta examined Maddy closely, waiting for a reply.

'Yes, ah, yes.'

'As do we, Miss Barker-Trent.' Her pale blue eyes were intense.

'Please, call me Maddy,' Maddy said, at a loss as to how to relate to such a fierce passion.

'Then you shall call me Henny, as Henrietta is too much, and Miss Atkinson is overly formal.' She spun on her heel and flung herself into a wingback chair. 'Maddy, are you interested in embroidery?'

Maddy stared down at her: what had embroidery to do with anything at all? 'I'm afraid my attempts have been described as dismal,' she admitted, recalling her brief acquaintance with a governess, and that worthy's deep despair over her lack of skills 'suitable for a lady'.

Henny's face lit up as she sat forwards, her face aglow with happiness. 'Oh good! I knew the moment I saw you we were bound to be kindred souls.' She sprang to her feet, clasped Maddy's hands in hers, and peered at her again. 'I do like you, Miss Madeleine Barker-Trent, and I know we shall be great friends.'

'I believe you are correct, Miss Henrietta Atkinson.' Maddy was swept up in the other girl's enthusiasm and returned her grin.

'Papa says you inherited a property on the Hunter River,' she said, waving Maddy towards an adjacent chair and flopping back down into her own. Her energetic bursts of movement were quite startling, but Maddy admired her enthusiasm.

'Yes, I suppose I did,' Maddy said as she sat down. It was one thing to make the decision to stay while at Tillington, but another entirely to hear it from the lips of someone she'd only met. A strange elation filled her.

'What are you going to do? I imagine you have suitors lining up to beg your hand.'

Maddy's breath caught in her chest. It wasn't the question, but the supposition that she would wish to marry that Maddy found disquieting.

She was saved from answering when Henny continued, 'Or do you intend to sell and return to England?'

'I am going to manage the estate myself,' Maddy told her. There, she'd said it.

Henny's eyes widened, and her expression changed from inquiry to delight. 'You are? That is wonderful. Good for you.'

'You approve?'

'Of course! I don't think any gal should be stifled by the dictates of a man, be it husband, father, brother,'—she cocked a brow and hesitated before continuing—'or even a neighbour. Lizzy says she shall never marry, and I doubt I shall either. Much to Mama's distress. I should like to draw you,' she said, changing the subject without warning, and she frowned as she scrutinised Maddy's features.

'Oh.'

Henny straightened abruptly, and with another lightning change of topic, she said, 'You'll find the house terribly crowded at the moment, as my sister Georgiana and her husband have returned from India. They and their children are staying here until they arrange suitable lodgings.' She paused. 'However, they shall not be joining us for dinner.' Her tone indicated she was pleased about that. 'I hear the sound of male voices; come, we must return.'

Maddy was surprised to see the drawing room was full of people. Where had they all come from? She hadn't expected such a crowd and fought the impulse to retreat back up the stairs. Glancing around she found Henny had disappeared, leaving her to scan those gathered, searching for a familiar face. Through the open doors she saw the sky was pinkening and recognised the silhouette of Mr Garrick. Maddy paused only long enough to plan a route through the crowd when her egress was thwarted by a drawling male voice.

'Miss Atkinson, you must introduce us to Miss Barker-Trent.'

Maddy rotated cautiously to see an auburn-haired young woman in her mid-twenties, and two young men: one tall and fair, elegant in dress and feature and wearing a friendly smile, and the other shorter but very handsome, with dark hair and eyes, and a square jaw which was greatly emphasised by his chiselled side whiskers.

'Maddy, here you are.' Henny stepped around her sister to take Maddy's hand. 'I see you have met Messrs Middleton and Platt.'

Lizzy, for Maddy assumed the woman was the learned Miss Atkinson, spared her a cursory glance, her expression austere. She couldn't tell if Lizzy's disapproval was directed at her, the gentlemen, or Henny.

'We've not been introduced,' the dark-eyed man said, his tone droll, almost uninterested. His gaze flicked over Maddy and, in spite of his good looks, she did not like him. A painful lump formed in Maddy's throat and a sudden and sharp longing for Mama strangled her.

'Maddy, this is my sister, Lizzy, and Mr Alexander Middleton.' She nodded at the taller and fairer of the two men.

'Miss Atkinson, Mr Middleton,' Maddy said, returning his welcoming smile.

'And Mr Francis Platt,' Henny continued; her tone had grown noticeably expressionless.

'Mr Platt.'

He nodded in Maddy's direction, but his eyes barely alighted on her before once again scanning the room.

'I was sorry to hear of your poor father's fate,' Alex Middleton said.

'Thank you.' Before she could say more, Mr Atkinson clapped his hands loudly to draw everyone's attention and announced that soup would soon be served.

Mrs Atkinson led the way and moved to the head of the table, and her husband to the foot. Maddy hung back to see where she should sit and noticed Lizzy turn away. Why did it seem as if she thought Maddy was not quite to her taste?

'Come along, Maddy, you can sit beside me, and we shall let everyone else find a place for themselves.' Henny pulled out a seat near the middle. Mr Platt took the place one removed from her; while Lizzy and Mr Middleton sat, side by side, opposite the seat left vacant. Maddy assumed it had been left for her. Mr Garrick was on Mrs Atkinson's right, and Mrs Garrick was at the far end adjacent to Mr Atkinson. There were two more men she'd yet to meet and another girl with colouring similar to Mrs Atkinson's; Maddy thought she was likely another of Henny's sisters. She inhaled deeply and sat down between Mr Platt and Henny. Hopefully Mrs Atkinson would monopolise him and Maddy would be spared having to converse with such a proud gentleman.

Henny whispered the names of the other guests as each sat down. Opposite Mrs Garrick was James Macleay—'He and his brother George are the Colonial Secretary's sons. They're up from Brownlow, their farm located south of Sydney.'

'Rosa,' Henny pointed out her sister beside Alex Middleton, 'has her sights set on one of the Macleay boys.' Maddy gaped at her. Henny grinned before continuing. 'And you mustn't mind Lizzy: she's frightfully smart and would much rather be in her room studying a specimen in her insect collection,' Henny said, and Maddy watched Lizzy Atkinson straighten the cutlery beside her plate, ignoring Alex Middleton, who it seemed she didn't want to encourage, for Maddy was certain he desired to engage Lizzy in conversation. Opposite Mr Garrick was Francis Platt; then Maddy; with George Macleay between Henny and Mrs Garrick. Her head swam with all the names and she was certain she could never remember everyone.

As Mrs Atkinson served the soup, Maddy saw her cast more than one disapproving glance in her direction.

'Take no mind of Mama,' Henny said in a whisper, 'she's just annoyed I've upset the seating arrangements. For you, rather than I, are seated beside Francis Platt.' She beamed, 'You, my dear Miss Barker-Trent, are competition.'

Before Maddy could fully comprehend Henny's remark, Francis Platt turned towards her. 'I too was sorry to hear of your father's accident. A fine chap.' He scrutinised her face. 'I've heard great things about the Hunter region, and I intend to make it my business to visit in the coming months. Perhaps I will inspect the property when I do.'

It wasn't a request to visit but a declaration. The muscles in Maddy's shoulders tightened; why did this man want to visit Shelby? She glanced around and saw more than one set of eyes on her. Heat rushed to her face. She shot Henny a look but saw her new friend was speaking across the table to Lizzy.

Did Mr Platt intend to stake his claim? Maddy bristled with annoyance: Shelby was hers, and it would stay thus. She clenched her jaw against the retort she longed to deliver to the all-too-obvious Mr Francis Platt. Shelby had for so long been the focus of her parents' dreams, and she would not let it go without a fight. She picked up her spoon and resolved to never, ever, hand Shelby to a man.

$\mathcal{E}ight$

Saturday, 28 January 1832—cool and cloudy

The high stone wall surrounding the Parramatta Women's Factory filled Maddy with a sense of foreboding as she stared out the carriage window. Until that first sighting, she hadn't truly considered the possible consequences of her next decision. The women housed within those walls were convicted felons, and her choice would affect both herself and the woman she chose. The short time she'd been in New South Wales she'd been sheltered from the reality of the colony's true function. New South Wales was a penal colony: a place of punishment.

Mr Garrick alighted from the coach and helped her down. The journey from Sydney had been uneventful and quiet, as Mr Garrick read London newspapers almost six months old. Maddy's thoughts had been as wispy as the clouds flitting across the sky as she stared out the window, taking in the passing wilderness interspersed with small farm holdings. She considered the previous day's events. The inquiry had ruled Papa's death an accidental drowning, but there remained deep inside her the fear he'd taken his own life: that he'd been unwilling to exist without

Mama by his side. There was nothing she could do about what had happened, but Maddy was determined to do everything she could to make secure the future of Shelby.

They entered the complex through a large gate and were quickly ushered into a receiving room by the matron—a tall angular woman who shot Maddy a disapproving scowl and treated Mr Garrick to an ingratiating simper. A number of neatly dressed women, each with a piece of sewing, were seated along a wall, lined up for perusal. Maddy's stomach squirmed, and heat rose in her face. They were being treated like cattle at the market. She wanted to run away. Perhaps she should have advertised for a companion, or at the very least allowed Mr Garrick to find someone suitable … Maddy lifted her chin: she could not disgrace herself. She'd insisted on accompanying Mr Garrick, and so she would see the matter through. No matter how distasteful she found it.

Most of the women were young, but there were a few older, and all had their eyes trained on Mr Garrick. Mr Garrick and the matron paused by the door to conduct a hushed conversation while Maddy preceded them into the room. As she approached the first woman, Maddy became aware that their attention had shifted focus and they were watching her, sewing forgotten in their laps. Maddy smiled nervously but received only expectant stares in return until almost as one they turned to the door: several men had entered the room. Henny had told her it was common practice for single free men to find wives from the newly transported women. Maddy noted the eager stares the men were given and realised these women might not be entirely unhappy with the prospect. Her attention was caught by a girl halfway along the room, the only one not looking at the men, but who had continued to watch Maddy make her way down the room.

Though she was seated, the girl was tall and seemed strong, and Maddy thought she had an intelligent face. Somehow, despite the girl's presence there among the convicts, Maddy knew instinctively she was a decent sort. As Maddy approached her, the girl dipped her chin and lowered her eyes.

'Good morning,' Maddy said and asked the girl her name.

'Jane, miss, it's Jane Brooks.'

'Brooks,' the matron snapped, 'do be silent.'

Maddy was gratified when Jane neither cowered nor flinched but rather grinned ruefully.

'Oh, aye, 'tis sorry I am, Mrs Gordon,' Jane said and then frowned. 'Ma always did say I talk too much.'

'Enough,' Mrs Gordon snapped. The woman turned back to Mr Garrick. 'Brooks is sentenced to seven years for stealing.'

Jane's smile slid away, and she lowered her gaze to stare at the floor. Colour crept up from her collar. The hair prickled on the back of Maddy's neck. Why did the beastly woman have to speak so loudly?

'Jane, would you like to come to the Hunter River and be my companion?' Maddy asked.

Jane's head lifted and she looked into Maddy's face, a wide smile revealing both her agreement and slightly crooked teeth. 'Oh yes, miss, I'd like that fine.'

Once again every eye in the room was upon them, but Maddy ignored them all and returned Jane's smile.

'Mr Garrick, I am finished here. Jane Brooks is my choice.' Maddy took Jane's hand in her own and drew the girl to her feet.

'So I see,' Mr Garrick said, his words tinged with dry amusement.

'There are protocols to be followed before taking a convict for assignment,' Mrs Gordon said with an indignant sniff.

Maddy met the young girl's eyes, 'Come along, Jane Brooks, we have protocols to follow.'

Tuesday, 31 January 1832—pleasant and cool

'Push,' Maddy said, tugging at the mattress jammed in the doorway.

'I am pushing, Miss Maddy,' Jane said, grunting with the effort to shove the mattress out the narrow door of Papa's cabin.

As the hut wasn't large enough for both Jane and Maddy, they were moving into the almost finished kitchen. She'd taken Mr and Mrs Garrick's advice and both she and Jane had remained at Tillington until the cooker had been installed. They would be camping in the kitchen until the two smaller adjacent rooms were completed, for Maddy was determined they should not impose upon the Garricks for even one more night if she could help it. Maddy was convinced she and Jane would have their new accommodations ready for habitation at Shelby and be moved in by sunset. A shiver of excitement ran through Maddy: at last she was to truly be in residence on her own property.

'Then push a little harder,' Maddy instructed through gritted teeth as she gave the ticking a savage pull.

'Argh!' Jane bellowed, and the mattress shot through the narrow doorway. Maddy stumbled backwards, the bedding moving faster towards her than she was able to retreat. Unable to escape, she landed flat on her back, with a ticking mattress and Jane on top of her. Maddy gasped for breath only to drag in a mouthful of powder-fine dust. Over the roaring in her ears, and the pain in her oxygen-deprived lungs, she heard muffled giggles as Jane shook with fits of laughter. Maddy writhed, trying to get out from beneath the pile, pushing against the weight that stopped her drawing in sufficient air.

'Oh Miss, I'm sorry,' Jane said between gasps of laughter as she rolled off the mattress. Relieved of the suffocating weight, Maddy drew in as much of the warm morning air as possible.

'Miss Maddy, are you all right?' Jane's tone was suddenly concerned. The mattress was lifted, and Maddy closed her eyes against the rolling billow of dust Jane set off by dropping the bedding onto the ground beside her.

'Yes,' Maddy gasped, pushing up onto her elbows.

'Well, what have we here?'

Maddy groaned, closing her eyes again. Of course Daniel Coulter would happen along to find her rolling in the dirt.

'Good morning, Mr Coulter. Miss Maddy and I were just trying to get this damnable mattress out the door, and it was like birthing a bairn.'

Daniel's eyes twinkled as he looked down at Maddy and, after a moment, he reached out a hand to help her up. Maddy took his offered hand, ignoring the tingles running from her fingertips to her stomach. Amusement lit up his tanned face. With his sweat-soaked hat held in his other hand and his hair plastered to his forehead, Maddy thought he was never so handsome.

'Why didn't you wait for myself or Mr Hardy to move the furniture to the kitchen?'

'Because you have plenty to do in the fields, and Jane and I are quite capable.' Maddy heard her priggish tone and heat flooded her cheeks once again. As if it wasn't bad enough to be found gasping like a landed fish, she had to snipe at the poor man when all he'd done was offer to help.

'Very well.' He frowned. 'Then I should return to my chores.' He turned and started towards the stores.

Remorse flooded through her. 'Daniel,' Maddy said to his retreating back and froze. She swallowed. She'd called him by his Christian name. 'I mean Mr Coulter.' Her face burned painfully.

She thought she must look like she was about to explode. Daniel paused but didn't look around.

'Jane and I are fine with the majority of the hut's contents, but perhaps we could use a little help later, when the men are finished in the field. I'd not wish to take them from their work.'

He turned and smiled. 'How about I help you get that mattress over to your new quarters, and the men and I can help with the rest before tea?'

'Thank you.' She kept her smile directed at the dusty ground, not daring to lift her tomato-coloured face for him to see.

'Oh, that'd be grand,' Jane joined in enthusiastically. Maddy started, dragging her gaze back to her; she'd entirely forgotten Jane's presence, so in Daniel Coulter's thrall was she. Maddy picked up one end of the mattress, leaving Daniel to walk backwards along the narrow trail to the kitchen. He smiled and instructed her to leave it to him, and he promptly stood the mattress on one end, gripped each side and walked off, handling the task easily.

The kitchen was only a few hundred yards from the huts and the farmyard, but it was a world away in design and construction. The sandstone, cut from a small quarry at the northernmost corner of Shelby, looked strong and permanent when compared with the slab huts; and the clean lines of the shingle roof made Maddy's heart ache for Papa. Every accomplishment and each advancement felt like a mark against him, and yet she knew that she was only doing what he and Mama would have done. Still, it saddened her they would never see it.

A narrow veranda ran around the three sides of the building, which would one day be connected to the house. Maddy stood on the northern side of the kitchen and took in the view across the foundation trenches, imagining the vista from the house. Daniel had manoeuvred the mattress through the doorway without fuss and she realised it had been far easier for him carrying it on his own. She didn't follow him in but walked around the foundations to a gap in the trees to take in the view, tracing the uneven line of the distant mountains against the summer blue sky, and consider all there was yet to do.

'It's a beautiful spot,' Daniel said from behind her.

'Yes.'

'There's a few who criticised your pa for building so far from the farming land.'

'More than a few, I'd imagine,' Maddy said, her tone dry.

'Most folk build their homestead close to the work.'

'Papa wasn't always the most practical man.' For a moment she lowered her usual shield of protectiveness. How like Papa to choose the most illogical site to build. But the view far outweighed his lack of sense, and Maddy was grateful for it.

'Indeed, but he certainly knew what he wanted, and he often got it,' Daniel said, his words tinged with a kind of wry indulgence.

Maddy laughed; it was certainly true enough. 'I know most people think I'm mad to attempt this.'

'Yes,' he agreed.

'Do you?' she asked.

'Not mad,' he said at last, and she released the breath trapped in her lungs. 'Stubborn: that's the word I'd use.'

'Stubborn?' Should she feel offended?

'Out here stubborn is the only thing that will see you through,' he said and stepped closer to peer past her shoulder, squinting into the glare. Maddy turned back to the rolling fields and valley below. After a long moment he continued, 'It's a tough land. It's harder, dryer and hotter than anything we're used to. I don't know if your pa would have made it work, but there's steel in your spine that will keep you trying long after you could have, perhaps should have, given up. And that's the kind of person this country needs.'

Gratitude spread through Maddy like warm honey and she smiled up at him. For a moment their eyes met and held, then they both turned back to the view.

'Well, as nice as the view is, it won't help Jane and me move in by nightfall.'

'Nightfall?'

'Yes,'—she turned and started walking back towards the farmyard—'is there a problem?'

'Ah no. I just hadn't realised you intended to … That is, do you intend to stay here tonight?'

'Yes, I have imposed on the Garricks long enough.'

Their new premises consisted of three adjoining rooms; the centre room would eventually be the private quarters for a cook. However, when its roof was completed, it would be Maddy's room. There was sufficient space for a bed, desk, and eventually the pile of trunks still to come from the hut. She would go through them one day, but for now they could stay where they were.

The third room, and furthest from the kitchen, which was eventually to be the dry store, would serve as Jane's bedroom, though she would have to share the space with some of the supplies. Phil was building Jane a bed and there would be room enough for a small desk and chair. Jane had cried when she saw it, never before having had a room to herself.

Maddy stood in the doorway to the kitchen and admired the wingback chairs papa had kept stored in with sacks of seed potatoes, now positioned beside a west-facing window; the large pine table kindly loaned to her by Mrs Garrick until the house was built and she could have her parents' furniture shipped; and the

new and immense black range. Maddy's bed and a pallet for Jane
had been placed by the north wall, where they would be comfortable enough until the other rooms were completed.

Maddy moved to the edge of the veranda and paused to watch
a flock of squawking pink and grey galahs; their colours were
muted against the pale rose sky. The trees dripped ribbons of bark
to reveal fresh lime and creamy green trunks in the fading light.
The sun was nearly set, and darkness would soon fall upon the
valley; the air was still and calm. The sound of the men preparing
their evening meal over the fire in the farmyard drifted through
the trees, and in their own little cottage, Jane was busy burning
mutton chops.

A wave of anxiety hit Maddy. How could she have thought
she was capable of running a property such as Shelby? She had no
experience or knowledge of farming practices. Everything was
unfamiliar and the enormity of what she'd taken on felt like a
smothering blanket, weighing her down. Tears filled her eyes and
she longed for the time before New South Wales had ever been
mentioned. Maddy recalled sitting by the fire with Mama and
Papa, tentatively sipping spiced wine and knowing what the mor-
row would bring.

The murmur of voices reached her through the panic: Phil's
Yorkshire drawl and Daniel's low tones. Though she couldn't discern the words, she knew they would be discussing plans for the
coming days. Maddy knuckled away the tears. She was not alone.
Drawing in a fortifying breath she turned back to the lamplit cottage and smiled at Jane as she entered.

'The bread smells lovely,' Maddy said.

'Oh, aye, but I've burned the chops a bit,' she said, frowning
as she lifted the charred meat with a fork and examined it closely.

'Well, never mind, I'm sure it will be fine.'

Nine

Sunday, 5 February 1832—beautiful weather, fine easterly breezes. Tremendous squall blew up in afternoon.

The morning sky was streaked with pink and the air pleasantly cool after a week of hot dry winds. Maddy stood with a cup of tea beyond the house foundations, admiring the view while she considered the coming day.

'Morning,' Daniel said from behind her; although she'd been expecting him, a jolt of awareness had her blood thrumming. He'd happened upon her there the first morning after she and Jane had taken up residence at Shelby, and now each morning they met to discuss the coming day.

'Good morning,' Maddy said, tossing a quick smile over her shoulder, hoping he wouldn't notice her heightened colour. He held a tin mug of tea in one hand and his hat in the other. She lifted her own cup, only to notice with disappointment it was empty.

'We've a good selection of timber cut for the barn, so I thought I'd head over to Tillington this morning and arrange a day to stand the frame with Mr Garrick.'

'Very good—I should like to see him myself, and Mrs Garrick. She has offered us a few chickens.'

'Do you want me to get the men onto building an enclosure? There are wild dogs about, and there's talk some have had trouble with the local Wonnarua tribe helping themselves to livestock.'

'I see. I hadn't thought of that.' Although Maddy knew it was the way of things, she was a little uncomfortable with the realisation the valley had belonged to others before the Empire had taken possession. According to the men, Shelby had never been bothered by the local tribe—she could only assume there wasn't enough there to be bothered with.

There was so much Maddy needed to learn; there were things she'd taken for granted in England that now needed careful consideration and a different approach.

'Lester is at the quarry with Joseph, and Charlie and the twins are finishing off the fence for the new sheep paddock, and there isn't anything so pressing Phil and Joey can't knock together a hutch for some chickens. No doubt we'll all enjoy the eggs.'

Shelby had been granted a further four men on assignment: twin brothers Patrick and Michael Hickey, Joseph O'Brien, and young Joseph Mahony, whom they called Joey. All four had come from Ireland convicted of Whiteboy crimes. So far they seemed a genial and compliant lot. All the servants assigned to Shelby were remarkable for their good behaviour, even Lester, she thought grudgingly. Though he only spoke to her when she asked him a direct question, he'd caused her no trouble, and Maddy was grateful for it. Lester's attitude towards her wasn't exactly friendly, but when she'd presented him and the others with new clothes, boots and a hat, he'd seemed a little less sullen for a moment. She blinked and dragged her attention back to Daniel and the chickens.

Maddy took in his damp combed hair, his strong smoothly shaven jaw. 'Yes, that would be wonderful, thank you. What time do you intend to leave?'

'After breakfast,' he said, tossing the last dregs of his tea onto the ground. The drops of her tea sat atop dusty soil that seemed to repel moisture. Maddy shook her head and smiled wistfully as she looked over the valley below: this was why Papa had planned to build up here, not for the quality of the soil.

'Unless you—' Daniel said when she didn't respond immediately.

'No, after breakfast is fine,' she said, realising he'd misread her expression.

'You needn't go at all. I can organise the chickens while I'm there.'

'I want to go,' she said. 'I'd like to visit with Mrs Garrick and see the children. And I haven't ridden my horse enough.' And I want to ride with you.

He nodded, but for some reason he seemed reluctant. 'I'll have your horse ready.'

'Thank you. Are the new men settling in?'

'Aye,' he said, frowning and taking a moment to consider her question, 'they seem to be a good lot, and Phil is an excellent supervisor.'

'Very well. I shall see you at around nine?'

'Yes—do you want one of the boys to come, to carry the chickens back?'

She considered this for a moment. Charlie could drive the wagon over, but it was a waste of his time. 'I think we should be able to manage a few chickens between us. If Phil and Joey are going to be building the hutch they will already be down two men.'

He smiled and nodded before turning away. 'I shall be ready at nine.'

She watched him until he rounded the bend through the scrub and disappeared. There was still much clearing to be done, but the fields came first, and leaving the scrubby trees gave her and Jane a bit of privacy, shielded them from the direct view of the men.

'Morning, Miss Maddy,' Jane said as Maddy entered the heat of the kitchen.

'Good morning, Jane.' Maddy saw the Bible open on the table, Jane's finger on the page as she attempted to read the text. Maddy had begun teaching her to read on their first night at Shelby, and she was to be found practising at every opportunity, laboriously spelling and sounding out every label or scrap of print she came across.

'Mick shot one of those wallabies yesterday, so I'm going to try stewing some of the meat up. We still have a lot of turnips,' she said. Maddy took this to mean that she'd use the turnips in the stew. Maddy closed the book and placed it on the shelf and out of range of the mess from Jane's cooking.

'Good—I've not tried wallaby meat before, have you?'

'No, but Mr Phil says it's not bad. Just needs plenty of salt and fat, as it's a bit lean.'

Maddy grinned: Phil's not-so-secret ingredient for anything was salt.

Neither Maddy nor Jane were very good cooks, but they were learning. Jane, after several dismal baking attempts, which had ranged from totally blackened outside with raw in the centre, to perfectly golden outside and still raw dough in the centre, could now turn out a decent loaf of bread consistently enough that she'd taken on the chore of baking for everyone at Shelby. Daniel said that her bread, though sometimes a little burned, was a great improvement on the salty damper Phil made in the coals.

'I am going to Tillington today to bring back a few chickens. What are you doing after you finish baking?'

'There's the washing and there's plenty of mending.'

Maddy smiled, as there was indeed always plenty of mending.

'Very good. I don't think I'll be gone more than a few hours, and I'll ask Mrs Garrick if she has a good recipe for the wallaby stew.'

Jane and Maddy had settled quickly into a routine of domestic duties, and Maddy was thankful to have acquired such a hardworking and diligent maid. She didn't have to supervise or instruct her, nor ever rebuke her. In fact, Jane knew more about their duties than Maddy did. Maddy's life in England hadn't required her to know much of anything useful. Other than managing the accounts she'd learned very little that would be of any help to her in New South Wales. She was sure that in time Mama would have instructed her on running a house. If only there'd been time.

Maddy's horse was saddled and tied to the post alongside an elegant bay horse she didn't recognise.

'Morning, missy,' Phil said.

'Miss Barker-Trent,' Daniel said with unusual formality.

She frowned, searching for an explanation for both the strange horse and Daniel's suddenly stiff expression.

'Good morning, Mr Coulter, Phil.' She smiled a little warily. 'Whose horse is this?'

'A Mr Platt's. I'm surprised you didn't see him. He headed up the path to the house only minutes before you got here,' Phil said. Maddy frowned as she tried to place the name. When it came to her she wasn't reassured, remembering the haughty young man she'd met at dinner with the Atkinsons. She looked at Daniel, whose face was carefully devoid of expression. Maddy scowled— it was hardly her fault the man had turned up.

Maddy spun to look at the track leading to the house and found it empty. 'No, I didn't come across him. Are you sure he went towards the house?'

'Well, I didn't watch him, but he said he intended to,' said Phil.

'Did he say what he wanted?' Maddy turned to Daniel.

'Not to me—just tossed the reins to young Paddy and asked him where his mistress was.'

'I see,' she said, but she didn't. 'Well, I don't suppose I can just leave him here.'

'Er, here he comes,' Phil murmured, nodding at the track.

Perhaps he'd needed the privy and didn't wish to mention it. They stood and watched as he strode along the dusty path, slapping a crop against the polished leather of his long boots, the tails of his coat flapping behind him as he approached, looking like he should be in Hyde Park rather than the wilds of New South Wales.

'Ah, Miss Barker-Trent, there you are!' He said it as if she'd been the one who'd wandered off.

'Indeed, Mr Platt. An unexpected pleasure,' she said, certain it was not. She'd not been impressed with his observations of the colony at the Atkinsons'.

'The girl said you were down here.'

'Yes, and here I am.' Maddy glanced around at Daniel and Phil. 'This is Mr Coulter, overseer of Shelby, and Mr Hardy, work supervisor, and this is Mr Francis Platt, lately of England.'

Phil muttered, 'Aren't we all?' and Maddy's lips twitched.

'The idea came upon me to travel to the area via the new road through Wollombi, and I thought to pay you a visit,' he said, ignoring the introductions.

'I see,' Maddy said, feeling less cordial towards him by the second. 'I'm afraid Mr Coulter and I are about to ride over to Tillington and are unable to entertain you at the moment. However, I'm sure Mr Hardy could find you a cup of tea should you like a small refreshment.'

'I shall ride along,' he announced, not waiting to be invited. 'A lady such as yourself shouldn't traverse the wilderness alone.

A chap I met along the road near Wollombi said there were bushrangers about.'

'That's not necessary,' Maddy said, bristling. 'I've Mr Coulter with me and would therefore hardly be alone.' How dare he dismiss Daniel so. As to bushrangers? She'd heard nothing on that score. 'I'd not wish to take you out of your way. Where are you heading? To Patrick's Plains?'

He was momentarily taken aback by her refusal, and more so by the question. Had he thought to stay at Shelby? Surely not.

'I've a mind to stop in at Oswald and see Mr Harpur; he was an acquaintance of my father.'

'Then you've come too far and missed the turnoff to Oswald,' said Daniel, his tone anything but friendly. He turned to Maddy. 'We'd best be off.'

'I'll ride along anyway as I should like to visit Garrick whilst in the area,' Mr Platt said, once again ignoring Daniel.

There was no polite alternative but to acquiesce. Maddy forced a smile and took Red to the mounting block. 'Very well, shall we go?'

Her horse was restless beneath her and Maddy forced herself to relax lest her annoyance with Mr Platt was conveyed to Red via her tight hold on the reins. She'd intended to take advantage of the ride to Tillington to discuss plans for Shelby with Daniel, but the opportunity was gone and instead they had Mr Platt.

The day promised to be warm as the sun climbed higher into the wide blue sky, and Maddy was glad for once she'd not forgotten her bonnet.

On the road, her knee began to ache with constant bumping from the interloper's mount, as it tended to prance sideways and spook every few yards. Her aversion to the man grew by the second. She glanced around to find Daniel further behind than she'd expected and sent him an imploring look. *Please save me from this tedious man.* She was sure Daniel pretended not to notice her silent plea for intervention.

'How long have you been in the colony?' she asked, dragging her attention back to the visitor.

'I've just told you, I arrived three months ago.'

'Oh, I'm sorry,' Maddy said and scrambled for an excuse for her rudeness, 'I didn't realise you meant that's when you'd arrived from England.' She stopped, recalling he'd said something about having stayed for a while in the Canary Islands. Better to cease before she made it all the more obvious she'd hardly been listening to a word he said. Well, the man had been postulating since they'd set off from Shelby, and she wasn't in the least interested. In fact, all Maddy wanted was for him to leave her alone.

'After exploring Sydney and Parramatta, I visited the Kangaroo Valley, having been told of the beauty of the place, though I couldn't see it. In fact, all there was to see was miles of impenetrable scrubland. I find this area much more to my liking.'

Wonderful.

'I've not seen much other than this small part of the valley, and Sydney. I find the bush has its own attractions. You just have to look closely; it isn't blatant in its beauty as is the English countryside. It whispers, inviting you to come nearer.' Maddy smiled, realising what she said was true, though she'd not consciously considered it prior to that moment, but as she gazed around, taking in the tiny yellow flowers amid the needles of a spiky and otherwise nondescript shrub, and the delicate soft pink of the new growth on a sapling, she realised she'd grown to love the treasures of the bush.

'I can't say I'd noticed,' he said, frowning at her.

'Are you intending to settle here, Mr Platt?'

'I've not decided; I met a whaling captain in Sydney, and he told me of the adventures to be had in New Zealand, so if nothing impresses me here, I'll venture across the way.'

His manner irritated Maddy in a way disproportionate to his words, though they were offensive enough. One could only hope he would take his sneering top lip and embark for New Zealand without delay.

'I know little of New Zealand.' Nothing, more like. Of course, she'd heard of the islands a little to the south east, but that was all.

'According to the chap I met in Sydney, the hunting is remarkable, but the natives there are murderous savages. Far more than the drunken lazy creatures to be found hereabouts.'

Maddy glanced over, her dislike of the man growing with every word he uttered. Was the promise of battling murderous savages a siren call to him? She squashed a caustic retort and instead asked, 'Is there a British settlement?'

'I believe there are several unofficial towns sprung up, but there is still much left to explore.'

'It sounds dangerous.'

'Oh, it is,' he said enthusiastically.

Thankfully, there was no need for a response, for they had come to the end of the road and turned into the avenue of beech trees. The barking of dogs heralded their arrival, and Maddy saw movement in the distance.

The estate lay on a soft slope a few hundred yards from the river, with neat whitewashed outbuildings and flourishing gardens. Once again, Maddy lamented the sorry state of Shelby. There was so much to do, and she experienced a momentary lack of confidence. If Papa couldn't manage Shelby, why did she think she could?

'This is Tillington,' she said as they drew in the horses and admired the view. Daniel caught up, and, by his stony expression,

Maddy thought he seemed as happy to see their companion as she felt. At least he'd not been forced to endure Mr Platt's tiresome boasting.

They rode on three abreast down the lane and it was only a moment before they were met by Bowman, the head groom, and one of the stable boys. Maddy looked across the fields and saw two teams of ploughs working the ground, while a small party of men toiled in the tobacco. Mr Garrick and Mr Harris, the latter being Tillington's overseer, stood waiting for them on the porch outside Mr Garrick's office.

'Good day, Maddy.' Mr Garrick smiled warmly at her before turning his attention to the men. 'Daniel.' His smile remained intact until it fell upon Francis Platt, where it faltered fractionally. 'Ah, Mr Platt, I see you've made good your promise to visit.' Maddy was glad to see her mentor was not overly taken with Mr Platt either.

'Indeed, Mr Garrick, though I deem it more reconnaissance than visit,' he said, stepping down from the saddle and tossing Bowman his reins with hardly a glance. Maddy slipped her foot from the stirrup, unhooked her leg from the saddle head and slid to the ground. The last thing she wanted was to have Mr Platt lift her down. She'd sensed his proprietorial attitude towards her and silently vowed that if she was the focus of his reconnaissance, she intended to be found wanting.

Maddy watched as Daniel handed his horse over to the stable boy, taking a moment to speak to the lad and tousle the boy's mop of red hair. When she held out her reins for Bowman, the man was looking past the corner of the house and didn't notice at first. Maddy followed the line of his gaze and caught a glimpse of Beth peeking from behind the kitchen gate.

'Mr Bowman?' Maddy said, smiling at the distracted groom. He jumped and with a quick and articulate, 'My apologies, Miss

Barker-Trent.' He took her horse along with Mr Platt's mount and led them away to the stables. Beth watched him go, her face a mask of longing. Maddy wondered how many of the Tillington maids were smitten with the handsome groom.

Thankfully Mr Platt remained at Tillington when Daniel and Maddy rode back to Shelby. She was pleased to be relieved of the gentleman. Mrs Garrick's generous gift of a dozen chickens had been too many to carry and it was decided to send Charlie the following day with the cart. Maddy was content to ride home, unhindered by chickens and Mr Platt; she daydreamed of the splendid farm Shelby would be one day in the future. One year. As they rode, the silence between herself and Daniel stretched. Was he ignoring her?

'I didn't know anything about Mr Platt coming to the Hunter Valley,' Maddy blurted.

Daniel shook his head, confused. 'I didn't think you had.'

'I have no interest in him or any other man. Shelby is mine, and I intend to keep it that way.'

'I see,' he said, peering at her face for a long moment before he nodded and turned his attention to the road before them once more.

Maddy cringed: where she'd intended to make matters better between herself and Daniel, she'd only managed to widen the chasm.

'That looks ominous,' Daniel said, breaking the silence. There was no birdsong, Maddy realised, or chirping insects either, now she listened carefully. A low bank of clouds raced towards them from the west. There was an odd greenish tint to the mass and, even as she watched it approach, sheets of lightning glowed from within the clouds. The air tingled and the sharp smell of eucalypts filled the air.

Beneath her Red began to dance, his head high, his muscles tensed.

'Can we make it home?' she asked.

Daniel frowned, reining in his horse as it jigged about, muscles bunched and ready for flight. 'We can try,' he said, shouting as a sudden and tremendous rush of wind buffeted them. With that said, he jammed his heels into Baby's sides and galloped for home. Red needed no urging to take off after them, soon eating up the gap between them with his long stride.

They'd barely gone a hundred yards when the heavens opened. The wind-driven horizontal rain battered them and Maddy's riding habit was plastered to her. Her bonnet was whipped from her head and swept away. She couldn't see a thing as torrents of water and her hair, now wrapped in stringy ropes about her face, obscured all vision. Red and Baby galloped towards the tree line, racing neck and neck along the rough track. A fleeting fear of a stumble popped into Maddy's thoughts but was soon lost to the need to hang on. Both horses were blowing with fear and fatigue by the time they reached the farmyard, and no sooner had Maddy and Daniel flopped to the ground did the rain stop and wind drop. Daniel had fared a little better than she but had kept his hat by shoving it into the open neck of his shirt. His face was slick with rain, his hair plastered to his head, as were his clothes to his body, with the exception of the misshapen bulge where his hat was stuffed. He looked at her, and she at him. His lips twitched with humour. Maddy giggled. And then they were doubled with laughter born of relief and exhilaration; the mad ride home through the storm seemed to have broken the tension between them.

The mood was soon shattered as Phil came puffing up the track from the maize field. He too was soaked and his expression despairing. 'It's flattened, the whole blessed lot,' he panted, 'sorry,' he said to Maddy, after a few harsh breaths.

'What's flattened?' she asked, ignoring his language.

'The maize: it's all lying over. The boys and I watched the lot go over in the storm. There was nothing we could do about it.'

'No, of course you couldn't,' she said, her heart sinking.

'Was anyone hurt?' Daniel asked, and Maddy was ashamed she'd not thought to ask.

'No, we sheltered under the cart,' Phil said.

'Where are the boys now?' Daniel asked.

'They're trying to stand it back up, but I doubt it will work.'

'You're probably right, but we must try.' Daniel turned to Maddy. 'Can you see to the horses? I'll go and see what can be done.'

She nodded and took the reins of his horse and watched as the wet and bedraggled men strode across the yard. Daniel pulled his hat free of his shirt and gave it a few hard thwacks against his leg, sending droplets glittering in the sunshine, before ramming it onto his wet hair.

Maddy quickly unsaddled the horses, propped the tack in the store to dry, and after giving both horses a quick rub down and a scoop of corn, she hurried to the kitchen to check on Jane and the building, hoping there was no damage to the place. The trenches were brimming, but that seemed to be the extent of it. Jane had closed the small windows and thankfully the storm had hit the western, and narrowest, side of the structure. Jane's eyes grew as big as saucers when she saw the sorry state Maddy was in, but before Jane could speak, Maddy beckoned to her.

'The maize has been flattened and the men are trying to stand it back up; come along, we will have to help.'

Jane didn't hesitate or ask any questions.

'You haven't left anything to burn, have you?' Maddy asked as they sloshed along the track. There was no point to her changing her dress as her riding habit was already soaked and muddy. Jane was dry, but soon the hem of her skirt was twisting around her legs as they half ran, half slid down the muddy track to the fields.

'No, miss, I'd just moved the pot off the heat when you came in.'

'Good.' Maddy nodded distractedly, her mind racing through the ramifications should they lose the crop. 'That's good.'

Uprooted and bent, much of the field of maize, which had been four feet high, was flattened and mud covered. Daniel and the others worked in pairs, carefully straightening where they could, one holding the stalk upright while the other pressed the sodden soil around the roots as best they could, mounding it in an effort to keep the damaged plant stable. Jane and Maddy joined them, working until the sky was dark and their fingers were cut and muddy, their efforts yielding little success. The raucous call of a laughing jackass mocked them from a nearby tree.

Ten

Wednesday, 8 February 1832—*very pleasant, cool morning*

'The cow calved overnight,' Daniel told Maddy by way of greeting. Steam wafted from his cup and she held her own half-full cup in both hands. Noticing her hands as she drank the remains of her tea, she frowned. Her skin, once milky white and soft, was now brown and a little calloused; her palms and fingers were still scratched and sore from the sharp edges of the maize stalks. Working outside with Jane, and at times the men, had exposed Maddy to a tanning she would once have considered unbecoming, and yet now it was her norm.

'Good morning, Mr Coulter. That's good news.' Although she'd grown quite used to taking her tea black, the butter she'd purchased from Tillington was getting low, and to have their own fresh cream would be a luxury.

'It's a heifer, which is good,' he said.

'Yes.' Maddy's thoughts were not on the cow and calf but on the man who stood quietly beside her. In England he wouldn't have been considered a gentleman as such, and yet he was more one than anyone she'd ever met. Certainly more than a few she'd encountered recently.

'Have you heard a word I've said?' Daniel asked, sounding amused and a little miffed.

'Sorry, I was wool-gathering.' She turned her face away and hoped he didn't think she had permanently flaming cheeks. She could hardly admit she'd been comparing him to the likes of Mr Francis Platt, no matter how favourably he fared.

'I said I'll leave the twins suckering the maize.' He glanced at Maddy for approval of this decision. She nodded. Suckering the maize was a tedious chore, requiring one to be bent over in order to remove secondary shoots from the main stalk.

'And,' he continued after a moment's hesitation—Maddy turned away from the view to face him, not wishing him to think she wasn't listening—'Phil, Lester, Charlie and young Joey are preparing the top field for sowing the swedes.'

'Mr Garrick has already sown most of his swedes,' she commented.

'Yes, but he has a greater acreage under cultivation than we do, and more convicts.' While his tone was level, Maddy sensed a hint of reproof.

'I'm sorry, Mr Coulter, I did not intend to criticise. It was merely an observation.'

He nodded. 'Joseph and I will continue cutting timber for the barn.'

'Mrs Garrick is coming to pick me up in her buggy after midday, as we are paying a call at Cragside.' While she was looking forward to seeing Mrs Everette the Younger, and to a lesser degree Belle and Amelia, it was a pity she'd also have to suffer Mrs Everette the Elder. 'Jane is baking, and I may send her down to Tillington to take instruction on cheese- and butter-making now that we shall have fresh milk. I know we have the facility, but not much knowledge to go with it.'

'Good. I'll dig out the butter churn from the store,' he said, grinning.

'It's a shame neither Jane nor I have much by way of agricultural experience.'

He laughed at this, his eyes sparkling with amusement. 'What Jane lacks in knowledge and experience, she makes up for with enthusiasm.'

They stood smiling at each other for a moment, and then Daniel sobered and stared across the valley. His change in demeanour perplexed her. It was as if there were a line, and somehow she'd crossed it.

'I think I'll inspect our new addition,' she said, waving the now empty cup at the kitchen, 'as soon as I drop this off.'

'I'll bid you good morning then.'

'Aren't you going to come with me?'

He hesitated, and his withdrawal was like a cloud crossing the sun, leaving her feeling as if everything were a little less bright.

'If you like.'

'No, it's fine. I won't keep you from your work.'

He nodded, gave her a quick glance and turned on his heel. Perplexed, she watched him go.

Her mood was not lightened when she came across Lester by the cow shed.

'Good morning, Mr Lester.' Maddy tried to inject a note of warmth into the greeting.

'Miss.' Lester nodded politely but offered nothing more as he checked the latch on the gate and turned away. Maddy opened her mouth to speak, intent on engaging him in conversation, to perhaps iron out the odd wrinkle between them.

But realising she wasn't up to forcing the issue, she closed her mouth and watched him walk away. That he wanted as little to do with her as she did with him was obvious and more than a little irksome. She had no idea what she had done to set him against her.

The calf was sweet, its toffee-coloured hair still damp and combed into swirls by the cow's rough-tongued cleaning. Tail swishing and head bunting, the tiny heifer drank from a contented-looking mother.

'Well done,' Maddy told the cow when it stared in her direction, then she smiled and after a moment turned away. Mrs Garrick would arrive soon enough, and she didn't want to keep her waiting.

Maddy was ready when Mrs Garrick arrived with young George asleep in a basket on the floor of the buggy. Bowman the groom rode behind on a heavy-set bay.

'Good day, Maddy,' she called as Joseph crossed the yard to take hold of the horse's bridle. Maddy smiled her thanks to the man as she climbed in to sit beside Mrs Garrick.

'Mrs Garrick, it is good of you to call for me.'

'It's no trouble,' she said.

Maddy smoothed the skirts of her gown and smiled, recalling Jane's good-natured complaints about the tiny buttons as she adjusted her bonnet. They set off, the wheels creaking a melody in time with the rhythm of hoof beats and jangle of harness, the groom keeping a respectable distance behind. All this was accompanied by the undulating buzz of the cicadas. The smell of the forest, which Maddy had come to enjoy, encompassed them as they travelled along the narrow trail until it met the new road from Maitland to Patrick's Plains.

'How are you settling in?'

'Well enough, though the mosquitoes make sleep hard work,' Maddy said, stifling a yawn. 'The farm is coming along—the tobacco is shoulder high, and we had a new calf born overnight. We even managed to revive most of the maize after last week's storm.'

'Yes, Alex said it wreaked havoc on the crops.'

Young George snuffled sleepily in his basket and Maddy bent down to adjust his coverings. 'Where are Tida and Edwin?'

'Edwin has been a little unwell, and I'm not sure if Tida is coming down with the same malady, so they are staying with Beth and Ann. Though neither were happy to be left behind.'

Maddy smiled, imagining the outrage at such harsh punishment. 'I believe they shall both survive.'

The steady clip-clop of the horse lulled them into a companionable silence, but as they were conveyed along the road, a sense of trepidation crept over Maddy. Mrs Garrick had promised there would be several other women of the area present— Mrs Wyndham, Mrs Harpur—and she thought perhaps Eliza Ogilvie, who was closer to Maddy's age and was visiting with the Harpurs from a property further inland. Her stomach squirmed at the thought of meeting new people. While she mostly looked forward to getting to know her neighbours, the ensuing speculation and possibly indiscreet questionings were less attractive.

The house at Cragside was lovely: two storeys with large verandas wrapped around both levels; and surrounded by established trees more suited to an English manor than the banks of the Hunter. Mrs Garrick slapped the reins on the horse's rump, and they rolled along the tree-lined drive, easily the smoothest piece of road Maddy had travelled on since arriving in New South

Wales. Viewing the house produced a pang of hopelessness when she compared the beautiful home ahead to her own humble circumstance. Maddy lifted her chin and straightened her spine; she would see her house built and it would be every bit as lovely. They left the horse and buggy to be dealt with by Bowman and headed for the front door.

They entered through a large panelled hall, where they were greeted by a servant who whisked young George in his basket away to the nursery. They removed their bonnets and handed them to another waiting maid. Maddy and Mrs Garrick were conveyed to a crowded sitting room, where conversation hushed as they came through the door. Maddy was relieved to have worn one of her better gowns: though not black, it was a dark grey, and she felt frivolous after so long in mourning black.

Maddy perused the faces of the seven women seated in a semi-circle, all occupied with knitting or sewing. She hadn't brought any busy work and looked around, a little confused.

'Susannah, Madeleine,' Mrs Everette said, placing her embroidery in the small basket at her feet. 'Do come in.' Indicating a small and unoccupied settee, she added, 'Please, sit down.' Her words were accompanied by a chorus of welcome from the other ladies in the room.

'Thank you, Catherine,' Mrs Garrick said, smiling acknowledgement of those who greeted her warmly.

Maddy smiled and murmured a greeting before following Mrs Garrick to the settee. She was relieved to notice Mrs Garrick didn't appear to have any sewing either.

'Miss Barker-Trent, Maddy, allow me to introduce you to the fine ladies of the valley. Mrs Wyndham of Dalwood.' She nodded to a smiling woman with very dark hair and eyes so dark they appeared black. 'Mrs Everette, my mother-in-law, you have already met.'

Maddy nodded and managed to smile despite her lips being so dry they stuck to her teeth. The elder Mrs Everette's mouth twisted slightly and Maddy wondered if the strange movement was supposed to be her smile. 'And this is Mrs Harpur of Oswald, our neighbour on the Maitland side.' Again, nods and smiles were exchanged. Amelia, Belle and a girl Maddy didn't know but presumed to be Eliza Ogilvie sat closest to the windows, and all looked at her expectantly. What did they want? Before she could pursue this line of thought Mrs Everette the Younger continued, 'Of course you know Amelia and Isabelle, and this is Miss Eliza Ogilvie of Merton; she is visiting on her way to Sydney with her papa, who is out with Mr Everette inspecting the river.'

'Good afternoon. It's lovely to meet you all,' Maddy said, baring her dry teeth at them. She had never been so pleased to see the arrival of the tea tray as she was that afternoon. Outside the temperature had steadily risen, and in the crowded room the heat was stifling. Mrs Everette poured tea and the maid handed out the cups, starting with the elder Mrs Everette, then Mrs Wyndham, Mrs Harpur, Mrs Garrick, Maddy and Miss Ogilvie next, and finally Amelia and Belle. Maddy had to force herself to sip it slowly though she longed to gulp it down.

'How are you faring, my dear?' asked Mrs Wyndham.

'Quite well,' Maddy said, replacing the three-quarter-empty cup on the saucer and trying to concentrate on the conversation rather than the liquid. 'It's certainly different from England, but I find it greatly to my liking.'

'It was a dreadful thing to happen, your father's sudden death.'

Maddy nodded and blinked away the ever-waiting tears. She smiled, grateful that someone had mentioned Papa, for sometimes it felt as if he had never existed. 'Yes.'

'Did Mr Platt visit you?' Amelia asked Maddy from across the room before Maddy could respond further.

'Ah, yes he did, a few days ago.' It took her a moment to catch up with the sudden change of topic.

'There have been a plethora of young bucks happening upon the area,' Mrs Everette the Elder said, her eyes narrowed as she gave Maddy a shrewd look.

'Hardly that,' Mrs Harpur murmured, barely loud enough to be heard, though her smile and tone were both kind and gentle. 'Most are inclined to visit my husband,'—she turned to Maddy—'as he was an assistant surveyor, but alas, his sight failed him utterly, and he now enjoys the tales and company of all who visit. Our son William has stepped into rather large shoes and is determined to be his father's eyes.' Her face clouded a little as she spoke. Maddy remembered Mr Garrick had mentioned Mrs Harpur as one of the women who ran their husband's properties, and Maddy marvelled at this soft-spoken woman's air of quiet strength.

The afternoon tea and conversation were pleasant, if some-what centred on children, servants, and goods not readily available in the Hunter Valley. While it was nice to meet her neighbours, Maddy felt no connection with these women. Her life was now filled with crop yields, ledgers and expenses, and feeding those who relied upon her. She'd rather have talked with Mrs Harpur about how she managed the farm. Losing the thread of chatter again, Maddy looked from face to face and noticed Amelia gazing out the window with a bored expression. Belle and Eliza Ogilvie were deep in conversation, and as she sat listening, or trying to, Maddy found it difficult to join in with any of the different topics. She stifled a yawn and blinked several times. She had been awake since before dawn and sitting in the warm room half listening to conversations she didn't relate to was making her drowsy.

'I wish we could have a party,' Amelia said, her tone wistful.

'I agree,' Mrs Wyndham said. 'We have seen some very hard times recently, and I think a party would be just the thing to brighten us up.'

Maddy's ears pricked at this.

Amelia leaned forwards, her face shining with excitement.

'An Autumn Ball,' Mrs Everette the Younger suggested.

'But Miss Barker-Trent is in mourning,' said Mrs Everette the Elder.

'Yes, but it was her father who died, not her husband,' said Mrs Everette.

'I think it's a wonderful idea, and it wouldn't be for a few months yet, when the weather is a little cooler,' Mrs Garrick said, and then to Maddy, 'It's entirely up to you if you would like to participate.'

Maddy nodded, grateful to her neighbour for giving her the choice. She loved and missed both her parents, of course, but so much had happened and changed, it felt much longer than a few months since Papa had died, and it was more than a year since Mama's death.

'I think it would be nice to have something to look forward to,' Maddy told them, and it was true.

Her agreement seemed to seal the matter, and a flurry of chatter and plans filled the room with an excited buzz. They all, with the exception of Mrs Everette the Elder, were brimming with ideas, and it made Maddy's head spin as they all chattered at once.

'Shall we hold it at Oswald or here?' Mrs Harpur asked.

'Will there be sufficient space?' Mrs Wyndham frowned.

'How many do you expect to come?' Mrs Everette the Elder asked somewhat caustically.

'At least one hundred,' said Amelia.

'Surely more than that,' said Belle, sounding more enthused than Maddy had heard previously.

'Do you intend to include the smaller landholders?' Mrs Wyndham asked.

An odd silence filled the room.

'Oh, yes, of course.' Mrs Everette the Younger was the first to break ranks.

'Indeed, the entire community should be invited,' Mrs Harpur said, she then turned her attention to Maddy. 'Maddy, before your arrival we had some very tough times: fires, hail storms and the relentless heat. It all has taken a toll on many of those on smaller properties with fewer resources.'

'I agree: everyone should be invited,' Mrs Wyndham said.

'How can you invite everyone?' Mrs Everette the Elder snapped. 'They won't fit in any of the houses around here—not even yours, Mrs Harpur.' Maddy took that to mean Oswald was bigger again than Cragside.

'That's true,' Mrs Harpur agreed. 'But we could have an evening picnic, and some music. There is a lovely flat by the river.'

'Not exactly a ball,' Mrs Everette the Elder sniffed.

'Perhaps not, Mother Everette, but it will still be fun, and that after all is the aim.'

'When shall you hold it?' asked Eliza. 'I do hope I can attend.'

'You must,' Belle implored, her eyes wide.

'We need a date,' said Mrs Wyndham.

'We must settle on the venue,' said Mrs Everette.

'We must have a theme,' said Mrs Garrick.

'We must create a guest list,' Mrs Harpur said with a laugh.

'We must, we must,' Mrs Everette the Elder grumbled.

Eleven

**Monday, 27 February 1832—hot and dry, with a
thundery afternoon**

The rooms adjoining the kitchen were almost complete, and
Maddy looked forward to a little more privacy once the final
layer of plaster was applied to the walls. However, it would have
to wait as the men were needed to complete the fences in preparation for a small herd of cattle Mr Garrick and Daniel had
purchased at Wollombi. Jane had taken tea down to the field
to save the men traipsing back to the yard, wasting time and
energy. Work on the land was arduous at best, but the dry hot
winds that tore through the valley in recent days made it tor-
ture. Everyone was thankful for the refreshing southerly breeze
that blew up most evenings, bringing a modicum of relief and
enabling sleep.

When Maddy was finished her meal and tidied the mess away,
she took up the pail of kitchen scraps and headed for the chicken
yard. As usual her gaze went to the foundation trenches for the
house. The only thing changed since she'd arrived was the dimin-
ishing depth as the surrounding mounds of earth trickled back

into the holes. There was so much else to do on the farm that must take precedence she despaired of ever seeing the house built. A melodic yodel filled the air, and she scanned the treetops for the family of magpies who shared the ridge. She couldn't see the birds anywhere.

Maddy was halfway across the yard when the sound of an approaching horse caused her stomach to flutter. For a moment she thought it would be Daniel, but of course his horse was still in the field. She frowned: both Daniel's mare and her own horse stood at the rail, ears pricked, staring along the drive. It sounded as if the approaching horse was galloping. Standing in the middle of the farmyard with the bucket of vegetable scraps, she waited for the horse and rider to appear.

A cloud of dust rose in wake of the thundering hooves and Maddy saw too late that the rider had his face covered and wore his hat low over his eyes. She dropped the bucket and ran for Daniel's hut. Maddy hoped his gun had been left behind, though she didn't know how to use it, and it was more likely he had it with him. There were a lot of snakes about in the fields by the river. Papa's gun, which she'd threatened to learn to use, lay uselessly under her bed.

'Stop,' the man bellowed as the horse skidded to a halt only feet from where Maddy fumbled with the latch on the door. She scanned the tree line, hoping Jane was out there somewhere and would go for help. Changing her mind, she prayed Daniel had taken his weapon.

The man's face was obscured by a sweat-stained kerchief and the low brim of his hat. She wouldn't be able to identify him should she manage to survive his visit. She prayed someone would come.

'What do you want?' Maddy asked. A rush of cold anger filled her and she forgot to be afraid.

'Hand over your money.' He waved the long musket barrel towards the door of the hut.

'I have no money,' Maddy said, and it was true: the best she could do would be to write him a note. She had a few shillings in her room, but Mama's jewels and her other valuables were buried in a cache beneath the hen house, and only she and Daniel knew about it.

'Get in there,' he barked as he dismounted, the gun barrel pointed unwaveringly at Maddy. Her hand was on the latch and she turned away from him to open the door. The cold steel barrel pressed into her spine, forcing her to step over the door plate and inside. She was momentarily blinded in the dimness after the bright sunshine and blinked as her eyes adjusted to the gloom.

'Move.' He jabbed the gun at her.

'I have nothing, unless you want soap.' Her nose wrinkled at the stench of him. He ignored her as he scanned the contents of Daniel's neat living space. She'd not been inside since moving to the kitchen and had no idea where to find anything valuable. The best she could do was keep him occupied until someone came and realised there was something wrong.

'I tell you, there is nothing of any value,' Maddy said, striving to remain calm.

'I'll be the judge of that,' he spat, thrusting his face so close to hers that his rancid breath reached her through the kerchief. She recoiled but saw in an instant the desperation and fear in his face. He stepped back, his eyes once more darting as he searched the contents of the room. His returned his attention to her before he spied a small shelf above the bed.

'What's that then?' He pointed the musket at the small chest on the shelf. Before Maddy could answer, he swung the weapon at her, herding her towards the bed. Blood thundered in her ears, but her feet refused to move.

'Get it!' He shoved the barrel hard into her middle and she stumbled, twisting and bashing her shins on the metal bedstead as she retrieved the tea caddy with shaking hands. She was almost as reluctant to hand it over as she would have been if the chest was full of gold, for tea was nearly as valuable. Still, she was dealing with a desperate man, and if he wanted the tea, Maddy knew she would be best served to give it to him.

'Open it,' he said.

'I don't have the key.' She didn't know if it was locked, but knowing Daniel, it probably wasn't.

'Give it here,' he said, holding out one hand while pinning the gun stock between his elbow and ribs. He placed the caddy on a trunk and tried to open the barrel-shaped lid. It stayed closed. 'Where's the key?'

'I told you, I don't have it.' Aiming to stall him, she continued, 'It might be in the drawer,' and nodded at the desk; she could only hope it didn't contain anything valuable to Daniel. She glanced at the still open door and wondered if she could get past him while he searched for the key. He waved the barrel a few times, dissuading her of the notion, and so Maddy did as he wished. With the small chance of escape gone she thought she had to distract him and keep him occupied until someone, anyone, came. She began to talk.

'It's only tea—surely you can see this is a tea caddy.'

'Shut yer gob and give me the key.' He lifted a shaking hand and pushed the brim of his hat up a little, revealing a wide scar above thick dark brows and hooded dark eyes; he looked gaunt. Maddy pulled open the shallow drawer, all the while keeping her attention trained on him. He tossed a furtive glance outside but quickly returned his attention to her. Not that she could have done anything, for he was between her and the open door. The room was dim, and he stepped closer to peer into the drawer himself.

'What's that? That one, the key there, give it to me.'

She picked up the largish key, obviously far too big for the tiny caddy lock, and reluctantly handed it over. It was the key to the store. He took the key in his grimy hand and retreated to the trunk where he'd left the tea caddy. Stupidly he tried to shove the key into the minuscule lock and swore his frustration when it didn't fit.

'It's quite evident it is not the key for that lock. I tell you, it's a tea caddy, not a treasure chest.'

'What's this for then?' he said brandishing they key.

'I don't know, but the men will soon return from the field, and you will be captured.' She straightened, lifting her chin. 'There are ten men due to return for their tea at any moment.'

He sniffed the air, as if he might catch their scent on the breeze. 'I can't smell no cooking.'

Maddy almost laughed: he'd not been trying to smell their approach.

'I baked yesterday, so there's salt beef and bread in the barracks,' she told him; at least she hoped there was at least a heel of bread left from yesterday evening's meal.

He swallowed and Maddy wondered how long it was since he'd eaten. Deep shadowed hollows beneath his eyes told their own story.

'Why don't you let me get you some food? I'll tell them that's all you wanted.'

He hesitated and glanced out the door, then moved slightly closer. The gun was still pointed in Maddy's direction, but it wavered a little as he leaned out and looked across to the other buildings.

She heard him swallow again.

'It's good and fresh, and the bread was baked only yesterday. And there might be eggs.' Maddy hoped the mention of food might be enough to send him in search of it in the barracks.

He stepped closer to the door; the barrel of the musket dropped. Before she realised what she was doing, Maddy grabbed a pot of blotting sand and flung it at his head in the same instant as he turned his face back towards her. He stumbled backwards, tripping over the door plate. He grasped the gun, pulling the cock to full. It fired, blowing a hole through the thick layers of bark roof. The sound of the report resonated within the confines of the hut, deafening her, and the billow of smoke obliterated her vision for a moment. She saw his legs working as he rolled to his feet. Maddy rushed to the door, shoving it closed and jamming the gun barrel against the door frame. She leaned her body against the door, trying to the keep the weapon trapped in the gap. The smell of gunpowder was suffocating in the small room. He levered the few inches of metal tube still visible inside back and forth and Maddy wasn't sure what to do. She shoved hard against the timber of the door, using all her weight and praying he wouldn't pull the gun clear. If she could keep him from reloading, Daniel and the others might come in time.

Instead she was flung back and wedged between the partially open door and the wall, her face smashed by the unfinished timber, the back of her head and shoulder taking most of the impact as she was whacked into the wall.

'Hey!'

Though her ears were still ringing from the gunfire and her senses were addled from the impact, Maddy recognised Phil's outraged cry.

The pressure on the door eased and she pushed it away, sucking air into her tortured lungs. She heard the sound of running and peered around the door. The man had lost his kerchief in the scuffle and as he raced across the yard to his wandering horse, she was certain he seemed familiar. Maddy noticed in that moment the condition of the skinny brown horse and realised it too must have had a hard time of it as it stood observing the goings-on, a tuft of grass drooping from its lips. Sensing the man's fear it lifted its head and backed away from him. He lunged at the dangling reins, but the horse bounded sideways. Maddy saw Phil at the top of the path, and then another movement drew her attention. It was George Lester. The fugitive turned, his gun at his shoulder, on full cock and ready to shoot. Had he reloaded? Maddy didn't think he'd had time, but she couldn't risk it. She pushed the door closed and leaned against it.

Through the door she heard the man yelling almost incomprehensibly and, unable to help herself, she opened it a crack and peered out.

'Here, take the horse and go,' Lester told him. Lester dropped a saddle on the ground near the horse yard and vaulted the timber-framed gate. Baby fled, galloping to the furthest corner of the field. Lester grabbed Red by the mane, and though the horse tried to swing away, it was too slow. Lester flung the reins around the horse's neck, preventing any escape. Within moments Red was bridled and led from the yard. While Lester saddled her horse, the outlaw kept his gun trained on Phil, who stood frozen at the edge of the yard. He seemed to have forgotten her presence in the hut.

Lester led Red from the yard as the outlaw backed across the farmyard, grabbing a coil of rope that had been left hanging on a fence post as he passed it. He continued, bypassing his own horse still busily snatching at any grass it could, and grabbed the reins from Lester. The bushranger sprang onto her horse. Red snorted and pranced beneath the unfamiliar rider, eyes rolling as he shook his head. Before Phil or Maddy could do anything, the bushranger drove his heels into Red's flanks and galloped away, leaving Lester standing by the yard.

The last Maddy saw of her horse was his tail lifted flag-like, streaming behind him as he was ridden away. The outlaw's riderless horse galloped after them. Maddy sagged against the door jamb for a moment before straightening and going outside to find Phil rushing towards her across the farmyard. A loud crack of thunder hurt her ears and she yelped.

'Miss Maddy, are you unharmed?'

'I'm fine,' she said through gritted teeth, ignoring her racing heartbeat. Beyond Phil, Maddy saw Daniel, Charlie, with Betty the dog on his heels, and then the twins, all running towards her, and dark storm clouds billowed low over the hills beyond them. Lester stood where he was, his gaze meeting hers across the yard and for a moment she saw something, but before she could grasp its meaning he looked away, shoulders slumped, his chin dipped. A wave of angry frustration welled in her gullet.

'That rogue took my horse,' she said, glaring at Lester, 'and you helped him do it.'

Twelve

Tuesday, 6 March 1832—fine day, warm

The hair rose on Maddy's arms when she heard the sound of a horse approaching. *Not again?* Of course the men were all out in the fields. Again. She spun around and raced towards the kitchen, where Papa's gun was propped behind the door. She had no intention of losing anything more to the louse-ridden bolters of the bush.

'Hello, the house,' came a guttural and yet feminine voice. Maddy skidded to a halt and retraced her steps until she could see the visitor through the trees. There were two horses, one ridden by a slouched figure, the other her own Red. The saddle had slipped half off, and he was covered in mud and scrapes along his flank, but Maddy was relieved to see he appeared sound enough.

Forgetting the gun, Maddy hurried to greet the visitor. As she drew closer three faces, horses and rider, all turned in her direction. Red nickered reproachfully and Maddy reached out a hand to rub beneath his forelock. She took his reins from the rider's hand before peering up into a wrinkly sunken face. Black button eyes gleamed in the woman's withered features, her smile friendly and toothless. She rode astride, ancient and hunched, but seated as if she were glued to the saddle.

'Good day, lass, been meaning to drop by.' Her voice was as rusty as a gate hinge in need of oil. She levered her leg over her mount's rump and slid down to thud on the ground.

'Ah, hello,' Maddy said, reaching out to steady the creaky woman. She'd thought her plump when she first saw her, but Maddy realised the woman had a large leather satchel strapped over her shoulder and was severely stooped.

'That your horse?' she asked.

'Yes. Yes it is—where did you find him?'

'He was by the road between here and Anville Creek.' She shuffled to the timber bench beneath the awning on the front of Daniel's hut.

'How can I ever thank you? He was stolen by a bushranger who'd come here to rob us. I feared I'd never see my horse again.'

'Yes, I heard of it. Not much around here that old Molly doesn't hear.'

Maddy realised this was the Molly Hunt she'd heard mentioned several times. 'Mrs Hunt, may I offer you refreshments? We can go to the kitchen and have tea and freshly baked bread.'

'That would be grand,' she said, rising slowly and painfully to her feet.

'Stay there for a moment: let me tie your horse and unsaddle poor Red, and give him a handful of grain.'

She settled back down onto the bench. 'No need to tie my horse, he'll just pick around for a bit of feed.'

'Very well,' Maddy said. She led her horse to the hitching post and pulled the saddle straight in order to undo the girth straps. 'I wish you could tell me where you've been, old boy, and what happened.'

By the time Maddy had her horse settled and had given a handful of cracked corn to Mrs Hunt's horse as well, Jane had appeared and was chatting happily with the old woman.

Maddy joined them in time to hear Mrs Hunt sharing some of her story with Jane, though from all that Maddy had heard of the legendary woman, this version was severely edited. Or the gossip had been elaborately embellished.

'I've outlived two husbands, maybe more, the memory's not so grand these days. But I made sure the last one would not die afore me, got a young 'un this time.'

'Time for tea,' Maddy said and held out her arm to Mrs Hunt, who heaved herself to her feet so they could make their way to the kitchen.

Mrs Hunt drank down her tea without milk and scalding hot, then held out her cup to be refilled before Maddy had taken her first sip. Maddy grinned and poured.

They spent the next hour entertained by Mrs Hunt's lively tales of her times in the valley. A full pot of tea had been consumed.

'I'd best take the men some food,' Jane said, rising from the table and picking up the basket she'd prepared before Mrs Hunt's arrival.

'Good day, lass,' Mrs Hunt said, beaming up at her, head waggling.

'Good day, Mrs Hunt,' Jane said, then turned to Maddy. 'I shouldn't be long.'

Maddy nodded. Jane had been reluctant to leave her on her own since the bushranger's visit, so she waved her off with a reassuring smile. She and Mrs Hunt watched Jane leave through the open door.

'Shall I make another pot?'

'Why not? I've a thing or two I want to say to you,' she said, her face suddenly serious.

What could the woman possibly have to say that caused her expression to change so dramatically? She pushed the kettle back onto the hob and pulled open the firebox to check the flame. It didn't need it, but Maddy placed a log inside anyway. *Sit down and hear her out*, Maddy told herself, and she sat back down opposite and waited for the water to heat and the woman to speak.

'Lester,' she began.

Maddy froze.

'He's a bad'un.'

She'd knew she'd not taken to the man—but what could Mrs Hunt have against him? 'I know he's not the most genial of men, but he has given me no trouble.'

'I told yer pa to send him back to Sydney,' Mrs Hunt said, not letting the subject go.

'Oh,' Maddy said, 'I didn't know Papa had trouble with him.' Why had no one mentioned it?

'Aye. Well I've met men like him a time or two, and they ain't to be trusted.' She pinned Maddy with a penetrating stare. 'And not long after he came to Shelby a girl ran off.'

Maddy bit her lip as she considered Mrs Hunt's words.

'What do you mean?'

'Yer pa had Phil and Charlie assigned to Shelby, and a girl to help out around the place. Everything was fine until Lester arrived, then she took off,' she said, pinning Maddy with her beetle-eyed stare.

'It doesn't mean he —'

'Bit of a coincidence, I reckon. There's gotta be a reason she run off.'

'I see,' Maddy said, considering. Why hadn't anyone told her? Surely Mrs Garrick would have said something? Lester had rarely spoken to her, to anyone, but he hadn't done anything untoward that she knew of.

The kettle began to steam, and Maddy took advantage of the distraction, her mind racing. 'And the girl, what became of her?'

'She turned up at Tillington and was sent back to Parramatta.' Molly wrinkled her nose and shrugged.

'Why?'

'I think yer pa decided having women at Shelby was more bother than it was worth until yer ma came to manage them.'

'I see,' Maddy said.

'Think on it.' Mrs Hunt's small dark eyes narrowed, and she nodded sharply as if to emphasise the directive.

'At least I have the horse back, mostly unharmed, and for that I can't thank you enough.'

Molly deemed it time she was away, and Maddy walked with her to the farmyard. She watched as the hunched figure caught her horse and led it over to a tree stump; before Maddy could speak, the old woman had dragged herself into the saddle.

'There ain't mounting blocks all over the place in the scrub: best you learn to ride astride,' she said by way of a parting comment, and with a wave of her gnarled hand, she cantered away.

Maddy shook her head, Mrs Molly Hunt both intimidated and inspired her in equal measure.

Jane was still in the fields, probably talking poor Charlie's ears off, and so Maddy made her way back to the kitchen. Laying a hand against the side of the teapot she found the contents still warm so refilled her cup, added a splash of milk and went outside, replaying Molly Hunt's words over and over. Could what she said about Lester be true? Walking past the trenches Maddy leaned against the rough surface of a huge ironbark gum tree, clutching her cup to her chest as she stared at the view of the valley.

There seemed to be no answers, only more questions.

She had to speak to Mrs Garrick. And Daniel: perhaps he would know something and he was the more accessible. But what to ask?

She could hardly march down to where they were working and demand he tell her why no one had seen fit to mention there might be something sinister about Lester. Surely if there'd been even a hint of impropriety Papa would have sent him away. Maddy had to know. She flung the untouched tea onto the ground and went back to the kitchen. She would go down to see where the men were working. And if an opportunity arose, she would ask Daniel.

The framework for the barn was complete, and the sound of axes could be heard in the distance as she headed towards where the men were cutting shingle for the new structure's roof. The rasp of a saw and the thunk of axes disguised her approach as Maddy drew closer. She paused for a moment to watch the work, grateful Papa had at least furnished the property with suitable tools for the job.

The strong wiry twins, Michael and Patrick, were using a two-man saw about six feet in length to cut the trunk into shingle lengths. Phil, Lester and Joseph were splitting and trimming the hard red timber blocks into neat shingles, ready to be nailed into place on the roof batons. The air was sweet with the smell of fresh-cut timber.

On the far side of the work, Maddy saw Charlie and Jane talking by the draught horses. At least Jane was talking—Charlie was listening. Daniel and Joey were chopping away at a massive tree and when it began to sway, they ran clear, axes held aloft, faces exhilarated.

'Timber down,' yelled Joey with delight as a loud crack rent the air. Everyone stopped what they were doing and turned to watch the tree slowly list and then with a great whoosh of air smash through the branches of the surrounding trees and crash down with a ground-shuddering thud. They all cheered. There was a level of gaiety despite their hard work that Maddy wished she could enjoy.

'Miss Barker-Trent,' Daniel said, having spotted her through the trees, 'are you well?'

'I'm fine, Mr Coulter,' Maddy said, and on impulse continued, 'but if you have a moment?'

He looked baffled but nodded, and giving Charlie instructions, he leaned his axe against the unhitched dray and joined her. Daniel knew Lester as well as anyone seemed to, and he'd never hinted at his being dangerous in any way.

'Is something wrong?'

'Let's walk down to the river.' She didn't know where to start, or what to ask.

'Jane said Molly Hunt brought your horse back.'

'Yes, it's fortunate she found him. I imagine others may not have been so honest.'

'He's a fine animal, and recognisable. I wonder how he got away.'

Maddy squinted up at him: did he mean to imply Mrs Hunt wouldn't have returned her horse if he hadn't been recognisable?

'The saddle was hanging off one side, so I assume Mr Lester, in his haste to help the bushranger, didn't tighten the girths sufficiently,' she said.

'Seems likely,' he agreed. Why wasn't he bothered by Lester helping the bushranger?

'Mrs Hunt told me that Lester had been suspected of'—she hesitated, feeling heat rise in her cheeks; she examined the uneven ground and hoped he didn't notice her discomfiture—'having something to do with a convict girl running away from Shelby.'

'Ah,' he said.

'Ah? What is that supposed to mean?' Maddy rounded on him; anger brought heat rushing up her chest and neck.

'It means that she's told you her theory.'

'Theory?'

'Yes, Molly Hunt has a theory that the girl was'—it was his turn to hesitate—'assaulted by Lester, but only Mrs Hunt has ever suggested his involvement, and the girl herself didn't accuse him.'

At his words, the temperature of her outrage lowered to a simmer.

'Even so, why would Papa keep a man here who was suspected of a, er, the like? Mama and I were due to join him, so surely he'd not wish to have even the hint of such threat?'

'Because there was never any suspicion of Lester having anything to do with it. Other than Mrs Hunt's accusations, there was absolutely no hint he'd had anything to do with the girl. I do not think, and as you can be assured your father did not believe, that you are in any danger from that quarter. I would never keep him here if there were even a sliver of doubt.'

'I see,' Maddy said, and as Daniel's eyes remained locked on hers, she knew he spoke the truth. If Mr Garrick and Daniel trusted Lester, perhaps she should trust their judgement. As to her father's judgement, she thought of the house and his letters and knew she couldn't be as certain on that count.

'If there'd been any real proof, or even a small window of opportunity, he wouldn't be here,' Daniel continued, misinterpreting her ongoing silence as disbelief. 'The men are locked in at night, and there was no evidence he'd been away from the men's barracks. I believe the girl should have been safe in her bed, but she ran away.'

'Wait, you *believe*?'

'I wasn't here,' he confirmed. 'I came to Shelby only a few months before your own arrival.'

'Oh, of course.'

'Your pa was at a low ebb when you and your mother didn't arrive when expected, so Mr Garrick asked me to help out here for a time, until Mr Barker-Trent was able to cope once more.'

He'd only come to Shelby temporarily. And yet he'd stayed on? Did he feel obligated by her own circumstances to stay? Should she offer him the opportunity to leave? But she couldn't manage without an overseer, and she doubted it would be easy to find anyone equal to Daniel.

He sighed and Maddy glanced up to see he inspected the same patch of dirt she'd been examining. 'While Mrs Hunt is a stalwart for the convicts around the settlement of Newcastle, Maitland and even Patrick's Plains, if she takes against someone, there is no redemption.'

'And she took against Lester?'

'It seems so; she insisted he was responsible for the girl.'

'I see.' Maddy looked up the hill. Daniel and Mr Garrick had both proven themselves to have her best interests at heart in the short time she'd been in the colony; while she knew almost nothing about Mrs Hunt. 'Well, I think a close eye should be kept on him, and if there's any trouble, we will send him back to Sydney and find a replacement.'

'I don't know why Molly Hunt took against Lester, but he is a quiet chap, does his work and keeps his opinions to himself,' Daniel said, starting down the hill towards the river once more. He paused to meet her eyes and Maddy saw only sincerity there. 'His actions possibly saved your life. What if the bushranger had shot you through the door? He was a desperate man and life in the bush is difficult at best. Why do you think so many convicts stay on the properties they're assigned to? There's little food to be had in the bush, and though the bushranger had a gun he may not have had much ammunition, which is probably why he came here.'

'No ammunition? But he'd fired the musket.'

'Only once, then he ran. Even so, he could still have hurt you—could have assaulted you with the stock.'

They continued to walk in silence until they came to a small stretch of pebbly beach beside the slow-moving water.

'Do you believe Papa drowned?'

'He must have.' He looked at her. 'What else could have happened? The river has submerged logs and cold undercurrents in places.'

Maddy didn't want to voice her fears aloud: to do so would make it a real possibility. She shook her head. She didn't want to believe Papa might have taken his own life, but she couldn't shake off the suspicion he'd done so.

Thirteen

Saturday, 17 March 1832—rain all night

The relentless mosquitoes surrounded Maddy in a cloud as thick as the storm brewing on the horizon, their assault cruel and without mercy. She flapped her arms in a vain effort to keep them from her face as it already appeared as if she were suffering from the pox. The air was a wet blanket, heavy and stiflingly hot as she pulled the almost dry washing from the line strung between the trees.

Jane was putting the chickens in the pen and moving the cow and her calf into the newly finished barn. The weather had been oppressive for days, and though Maddy feared for the severely parched crops after the last storm had flattened the maize, she longed for the relief a downpour would bring. Another five acres had been cleared, ploughed and was ready for sowing. If it rained and soaked the newly turned soil, all the better. It wasn't a given, no matter how promising the sky: more than once she'd seen the clouds head directly towards Shelby, only to be swept north and away until distant mountains disappeared beneath a deluge while Shelby received not a splash.

This time they were fortunate. The first drops were plump and sent up tiny clouds of dust as they bounced on the parched ground. Maddy rushed inside, her arms full of fresh clean sheets. She pushed her face into the soft cotton and breathed the smell of the lavender Jane had put in the rinse water.

She looked forward to sleeping in her newly completed room between the crisp clean sheets.

The door banged open behind her and Jane fell in through the door.

'Made it by the skin of me teeth.' She grinned, showing off her slightly crooked teeth.

'There's tea in the pot,' Maddy told her, putting the sheets on the scrubbed table.

'And there's a wedge of fig tart left—we could share it,' Jane suggested.

Maddy grinned; Jane had a sweet tooth, and the gift of early figs from Mrs Wyndham had been delighted over. 'Very well, add a bit of cream, and we'll celebrate the rain.'

'The good Lord knows we need it right enough.'

Maddy nodded and Jane pulled the jar of cream from the crock where it was stored before it would be churned into butter.

Maddy peered out the window at the veil of water obscuring even the closest trees from sight. The rain she'd experienced thus far in New South Wales came by way of storms that blew in, wreaked havoc, and blew away to the coast, but this was heavy and vertical. She noticed a movement through the window and saw Daniel running through the downpour to skid to a halt beneath the wide veranda. Her heart did the usual flutter. The sound of rain on shingles muffled his knock, and if she'd not seen him, she might not have known he was there. Maddy pulled open the door as he removed his coat and hung it on one of the pegs attached to the wall.

'Come in,' she said and stepped back to allow him entrance.

'Thanks.' He swiped his hat from his head and entered.

'Tea?' Jane offered.

'Yes, please.' He smiled at her and placed the hat on the floor by the door.

Jane poured three cups, picked up the sheets and took them from the room. Daniel and Maddy sat down at the table. She was momentarily struck speechless as she considered the difference of her circumstances from last year. A year ago she'd been in England with Mama, living in rented accommodation in Wiltshire, waiting for Papa to make Shelby ready for them. But with Mama often taking to her bed Maddy spent more time with the servants than with her mother. Her parents had never discouraged her from being friendly with the servants, far from it, though she'd been aware such friendships had been deemed unsuitable by many; now Maddy was seated in a kitchen with a convict and a hired overseer, about to share a pot of tea. Her life was reduced to two thousand acres in a colony on the far side of the world and she'd never been happier.

'It's good we finished the barn roof,' he said as he took a seat at the table.

'Yes, Jane has moved the cow and new calf inside.'

'I saw.' He grinned.

'Here, have this.' Maddy pushed across the slice of tart to him, leaving the other for Jane.

'No, that's yours,' he said, pushing it back.

'Really, you have it, I don't want it.'

'Let's share,' he suggested.

'Very well.' Maddy smiled and retrieved another fork from the caddy. They simultaneously cut a forkful from each end of the slice. Jane returned in time to watch this and snorted.

'Miss Maddy, you should have mine,' Jane said.

'I am content without, Jane, only that Mr Coulter refused to have any unless we shared.'

Jane shot Maddy a curious look before collecting her own cup of tea from the sideboard and joining them at the table.

'I saw Mr Garrick and Mr Wyndham earlier. Mr Wyndham had the mail from the *Sophia Jane* and there was a letter for you,' Daniel told her.

Maddy blinked. Who would be sending her a letter? She hadn't stayed in contact with anyone in England; and she knew none of her living relatives. Maddy supposed Mama's family were still alive, but as she'd not met any of them, she doubted they would write to her.

Daniel retrieved the damp epistle from inside his waistcoat and handed it to her. Maddy's fingertips tingled as they brushed against his. She took in the unfamiliar handwriting, embellished with such pretty flourishes Maddy was certain a feminine hand had written it. But who?

'Aren't you going to open it?' asked Jane, peering over at the square. '*Miss Barker-Trent, Shelby Estate, Hunter River,*' she read aloud. Her reading was coming along exceedingly well.

'I'll look at it later,' Maddy said and pushed it into the pocket of her apron. She knew Jane was disappointed, but she and Daniel had other things to discuss.

'Mr Wyndham mentioned a dairy herd that is coming up for sale: a small landholder near Maitland has sold up, and the buyer doesn't wish to take the animals. Mr Garrick agreed it would be worth consideration as the herd would be a good addition to Shelby. I thought I could ride out this afternoon and take a look at them.'

'How many?' Butter and cheese were both in high demand, having a good market in both Sydney and Newcastle.

'Ten, I think,' he said, 'and a bull.'

'If Mr Wyndham and Mr Garrick, and yourself, believe this to be a suitable purchase, then I shall write a note. And leave the negotiation to you.'

'I'll set off shortly then and be back before nightfall.'

Maddy nodded and then glanced out the window. 'This rain won't make for a pleasant ride.'

'I'm counting on it.' He grinned.

Maddy lifted a brow at this.

'If it's raining, perhaps no one else shall venture out today and I can secure a sale.'

'Ah, good idea.'

Jane and Maddy settled to an afternoon of mending by lamp-light, for the day had grown dark beneath the lowering sky. They were comfortable enough in the cosy kitchen, but Maddy's vision blurred as she grew weary peering at the fine stitching of her gown. She let the dress fall into her lap and stared out the window at the rain flowing over the veranda roof; sewing was her least favourite chore and she'd never do it if it could be avoided. With a sigh, Maddy rethreaded the needle.

The rain continued to lash the roof, and the ground surrounding the kitchen disappeared; the foundation trenches were lost altogether as sheets of water flowed across the clearing towards the precipice and down to join the river.

The darkness drew in by degrees and Maddy was stoking the fire in the stove when a loud knock was heard over the rain hammering the roof. Jane looked at her and she nodded. Jane rose, leaving the sock she'd been darning on the table, and crossed to open the door. It was Phil, drenched and shivering.

'Come in by the stove,' Maddy told him.

'No, miss, I'm not stopping, just letting you know I'm going to move the sheep up onto the hill beyond the quarry. The river is rising fast, so I thought it best to be safe than sorry.'

'Yes, and will you need any help?'

'No, miss, you stay here; the boys and I will move them. But if you don't mind, we might put the horses in with the cattle—it's grown cold, and we have the space enough.'

'Yes, of course.' The air leaking in around him was indeed chilly.

'Right you are then,' he said, stepping back from the open door.

'Is Mr Coulter back from Maitland?'

'No, and he probably won't get back tonight either, as if the river is up, then the creeks and streams will be too.'

'Yes, of course,' Maddy said, and her heart plummeted to rest unhappily in the pit of her stomach. She took comfort from Daniel's presence always only a few hundred yards away. Even one night without him being in residence was dispiriting.

'I hope this rain lets up soon, or our new field will be washed down the hillside.'

'True. Well I'm away to get those sheep shifted.'

He quickly disappeared beyond the curtain of water.

'I think we've had enough rain for today,' Jane said, as if they had control of the situation and could turn it off.

'Yes, I agree.'

'That's the problem with this place, it either don't rain at all, or it rains so much we're in danger of being smothered in it.'

Maddy couldn't disagree.

Sunday, 18 March 1832—rained all day, eased somewhat in afternoon.

Maddy flopped her head down on the pillow. No matter that she couldn't hear anything at all over the downpour battering the roof, she'd spent the night straining to hear Daniel's horse. The sky was lightening when she finally drifted off, only to jerk awake at a sound. She heard Jane rise and run along the flagged veranda to the kitchen door. Maddy opened gritty eyes and pushed back the covers to slip out of bed. She picked up the small polished stone Daniel had given her and rubbed a thumb over the smooth cold surface. She held it for a moment before replacing it on the dresser. She'd never get back to sleep until she knew Daniel was safe, so she dressed and pulled on an oilskin coat, boots and Papa's battered hat before hurrying down to the farmyard.

There was no sign of Baby in the small field, but then she remembered Phil had moved the horses out of the weather and into the barn. The timber chimney attached to the end of the barracks leaked a thin wisp of smoke, and Maddy realised the men hadn't yet emerged. Indeed, why should they? There was little they could do outside in such miserable weather. She sloshed along the strip of dimpled water covering the footpath past the milking bail and chicken pen to the new barn. Pulling open one side of the wide double doors, she was greeted by the loud lowing of the milking cow; the calf had been penned in a corner so as to reserve the milk. After milking, Jane would let the little heifer back in with her mother for the day. Maddy walked over to the barricaded area designed to keep the horses away from the small haystack and bags of feed. Red and the draught horses whinnied a chorus of welcome. Baby wasn't with them.

'He didn't get home then?' Phil said from the open doorway.

Maddy spun around. 'It doesn't look like it,' she said, her voice flat.

'He will have stayed in Maitland.'

'I'm sure you're right.'

'I've been down at the river,' he said and took off his hat and gave it a vigorous shake to remove the water.

'And?' Maddy said when he didn't elaborate.

'I drove a stick in at the water's edge last evening, and it's risen a good eighteen inches overnight.'

'Surely we've not had so much rain?'

'There's a number of tributary streams feeding in up the river, and if it's been raining all up the valley like it has here …'

'I suppose.'

There was nothing to be done but wait and hope. Wait for the rain to stop and wait for the river to go down. Wait for Daniel to return. And hope he would be safe.

'And the fields?' Maddy asked, dreading his answer.

'A good bit of the north corner of the newly ploughed patch has been washed away,' he said, 'but the maize is closest to the river, and so far, it's not holding up too badly.' He looked out the door. 'If it lets up soon we should be right.'

Maddy followed the line of his gaze. The rain continued to fall but didn't seem as heavy as it had been the previous night.

'I'll go down and take a look after breakfast,' she said.

'Let me know and I'll come with you.'

The field of maize was a foot under water, with the stalks swaying in the current, which was thankfully flowing much slower than the central channel where the river bed was hidden beneath the expanse. Logs, dead beasts and even an entire tree swept past as they stood watching the fast-moving water carry off anything and everything within reach. Maddy prayed no one had been caught in the torrent, for nothing could survive the onslaught. For once she was glad Papa had chosen to build the homestead far from the river's reach.

'Come on, let's walk around and check the tobacco,' she said, and together they sloshed along the muddy track to the next field. The tobacco was planted higher up the hill, and she was pleased to see there was no damage, though the ground was sodden, and she didn't know if it would adversely affect the crop.

The walk back up to the farmyard was hard going and her boots collected a layer of sticky mud with each step until several inches clung to the soles. They reached the yard to find Charlie and Patrick approaching from the far side, dressed in oilskin coats and looking as mud-splashed and bedraggled as Maddy felt.

'We walked down to check the little creek near the road,' Patrick said. 'It's overflowing and has formed a sort of dam against a fallen tree.'

Maddy turned at Charlie for clarification.

'Yep, seems a tree went down when the water undercut the roots and it's blocking the flow, so everything coming behind it has made a bank and the water is damming up, and the far side is clean washed away,' said Charlie in one of the longest sentences Maddy had ever heard from him.

Without a word Maddy and Phil kept walking, the boys turning to follow them.

'The rain in Ireland ain't nothing like this,' said Patrick.

'Nor in Yorkshire,' agreed Phil.

Charlie, reverting to type, said nothing and merely nodded in agreement.

'I think it's easing a bit.' Maddy looked up at the grey mass of clouds, as raindrops spattered against her upturned face. 'I'm sure the clouds are starting to break up.'

The others also peered from beneath hats at the lowering sky.

Phil nodded. 'Could be.'

The creek was as the boys had described, swollen to double the usual width, with filthy water engulfing the scrub ten yards each side of the creek bed. The usually dry gully and shallow ford had disappeared, and there was a deep chasm beyond the mass of jammed trees and branches. Maddy realised with dismay they were cut off entirely. Shelby ridge was essentially an island.

'That's going to take a bit of clearing,' Phil said, examining the jammed debris blocking the water flow.

She realised Daniel wouldn't be able to get home until the water receded. As if the thought had conjured him, Maddy saw movement in the trees and peered through the rain to see him astride Baby, trotting up the ridge of ground between the water-filled wheel ruts.

Silently they stood and watched Daniel take in the state of things. Beneath him his horse stood, ears drooping and head held low; and looking utterly miserable as the rain ran down its face in rivulets.

'Good morning,' Daniel called across the expanse.

'Morning, Dan,' Phil said.

Charlie and Patrick grinned; and Maddy gave him a dismal wave. Though she was relieved to see he'd survived the night unscathed, an irrational part of her was annoyed that he'd not been there when she needed him. Had she needed him.

'I don't suppose there's anywhere else I can cross?'

'I don't think so,' Phil called back. 'There's a mess of tangled branches all the way, too dangerous to bring the horse through. Probably break a leg.'

Daniel nodded and slipped down from his horse and tied it to a sapling before walking to the edge of the water.

'This is a bit of a mess.' His eyes met Maddy's across the expanse.

'Indeed,' she said and smiled; her resentment was ridiculous. It was hardly his fault the way was blocked. He had, after all, been away on estate business. Investigating a potential investment. For her.

He made his way upstream along the water's edge, head down as he examined the swirling mess of branches, grass and brown foam.

'It's not safe to try and cross,' she called out to him, suddenly fearful he might try. He looked up, nodded and returned to his horse.

'I'll go back to Cragside,' he said, 'and I'll ride out again this afternoon and see if it's gone down at all.'

Cragside—was that where he'd stayed overnight? Surely he could have stayed at Tillington?

'Back to Cragside?' Maddy said, obviously louder than she'd intended, for he sent her a sharp look and nodded.

'Yes, I stayed there last night. I stopped in to see Mr Everette and was persuaded to stay as the rain hadn't let up.'

Maddy bristled: she'd been fretting all night long and he'd been enjoying a cosy evening with Belle and Amelia.

Fourteen

Monday, 19 March 1832—sunshine, fair with a cool breeze

The sky was clear when Maddy rose the next day and took her customary cup of tea outside to watch the sunrise. Were it not for the sogginess of the ground beneath her boots she could almost have forgotten the rain of the past few days, until she saw the river was swollen to overrun the flats on the north bank, submerging much of Mr McLeod's crops.

She knew Daniel was not at Shelby, yet she hoped to hear his approach, her heart leaping at any foreign sound. She longed for him to stroll up with a cup of tea to join her for their morning planning. *Stop it*, she told herself, *he will return as soon as he is able*! Stumbling over a small ridge of debris pushed up by the previous days of rain, Maddy spilled tea down her front. Teeth gritted, she muttered a curse. Swearing was one of the less admirable attainments she'd gained since working alongside the men.

Pulling the damp pinafore away from her dress, she felt something in her pocket. It was the letter Daniel had given her. Maddy frowned; how could she have forgotten it?

Thankfully only one corner was a little damp. She tossed the remaining inch of tea onto the ground and hurried back to the kitchen. Using a knife, she broke the seal and unfolded the letter.

My Dearest Maddy,
I hope this missive finds you well.

Scanning the page, Maddy frowned, none the wiser as to who it was from. As she read, the author revealed herself by tone and topic. Henrietta Atkinson wrote of her newfound interest in biology, and how they'd all expected George Macleay to propose to Rosa, but he had returned to Brownlow without doing so.

The letter continued along the same vein, until Maddy reached the last paragraph.

I thought it prudent to advise you of Chase Hobson's intention to return to the Hunter River in the coming weeks and his plans to call on you at Shelby Estate. Forgive me for saying so, but you and your estate are a much-discussed topic among the young men of the colony. For not a few like their chances to snaffle a prize such as yourself.

Maddy sat staring at the sheet of paper, unsure how she felt or what she thought.

'Miss Maddy.' Jane stood in the open doorway, her eyes as large as saucers. 'We, er, we have visitors.'

What? Surely not. If Daniel couldn't cross the swollen creek, how could Chase Hobson have managed it? She glanced down at the letter on the table and checked the date, tenth of March. No, it couldn't be him. But who?

Maddy watched, bemused, as Jane stepped back a little to reveal Mrs Rose McMahon and her son standing beneath the edge of the veranda roof. The woman was looking down at the flagstone paving, the boy gazing up at the underside of the shingled roof above him, his expression unreadable. Maddy examined the boy; she'd not seen him since the day she arrived, and she thought he'd grown taller. He was a wiry child, but his cheeks were plump and round, framed by a mop of yellow and gold curls. While he appeared well nourished, his mother did not. There were dark circles beneath her eyes, and her pale cheeks were hollow. Maddy hadn't given Mrs McMahon and her son much thought since she'd returned to Shelby. But here they were, wet and bedraggled. The boy sported a coat far too small for him and his trousers were ragged and filthy about the hem. Mrs McMahon wore a man's coat, and they both had muddy bare feet. What had happened to them? Where had they been in the months since Papa had died?

'Mrs McMahon, please, come in,' Maddy said. The woman's gaze flickered over Maddy's face and she shook her head. Maddy shot a glance at Jane, who was unusually silent, to see her gaping.

Maddy gave Jane a reassuring smile and stepped outside. 'Jane, perhaps you can find something for Mrs McMahon and her son to eat.' And to their visitors she said, 'Mrs McMahon, do come in, is there anything I can help you with?'

The woman shook her head again. 'I need to speak to Mr Coulter.'

Maddy blinked. She hadn't been expecting that. 'He's at Cragside; he's not been able to make it home over the flood waters.'

'I have to see him.'

'He's not here, but can I help?'

'No, I'd best speak to him.'

She gazed around; an air of desperation emanated from her.

Maddy tried again to explain. 'He stayed with the Everettes at Cragside last night. He can't get back as the creek is flooded.'

Jane came out with two tin cups, one of tea, the other half full of milk. She offered the milk to the boy, who stepped behind his mother and didn't take it until given permission. Then his hand snaked out to take the cup before he retreated behind her coat again.

'Did you get food?' Maddy asked Jane.

'Yes, miss, I just thought I'd bring them a warm drink first.'

'Here, give me the tea, you get the food.' Maddy took the cup from Jane and led the visitors to the bench seat beneath the kitchen window. 'Please, at least sit for a moment while you drink this.' She gave the tea to her guest.

Mrs McMahon inhaled the fragrant aroma before taking a cautious sip. Jane came with a tray laden with thick slices of buttered bread and offered it. The woman looked at Maddy, and, with a half-smile, picked up a slice with elegant long fingers and handed it to her son. He put the empty cup on the ground at his feet and snatched the bread, gobbling it down before gazing longingly at the remaining slices. His mother gave him a second portion and finally took one for herself, eating it more delicately than had her son.

'Mr Coulter is not here—please tell me I may help you?' Maddy offered again, she could not imagine why the woman needed to see Daniel so desperately.

She shook her head. 'No, I'd best speak to Mr Coulter.'

She quickly ate the remaining slices of bread, handed Maddy her empty cup, took hold of her young son's arm, whispering something to him in a serious tone, and straightened.

'I'll go to Cragside. Luke will have to stay here.' Her eyes met Maddy's; there was a steely glint of determination.

'You'll never make it: the creek is flooded, there's no way across.'

'I'll be fine.'

Luke stood silent beside Maddy as his mother walked away, her bare feet slapping through the puddles, the hem of her skirt, already wet and muddy, twining around her ankles as she crossed the clearing and disappeared into the trees. Maddy realised her mouth hung open when a fly buzzed into it. She gagged and coughed, expelling the insect.

Looking down at the silent boy she wondered how long his mother would be. The rest of him was exactly as filthy as his feet. What on earth was she going to do with him?

'Jane, can you put on a cauldron of water? Luke will need a bath if he's going to be staying with us.'

It was Jane's turn to gape, and then she turned to Luke, her mouth closing to form a kind of grimace. Maddy frowned at her and Jane coloured, muttered something indecipherable and hurried to do as she was bid.

It took them several attempts to persuade the boy to undress and get into the large tub of warmed water. He uttered not a word, and yet he left them in no doubt that he wasn't going in without a fight. By the time they'd soaped and scrubbed him there was very little water left in the tub, while Maddy and Jane were saturated, as were most of the surfaces in the room. Luke sat on a chair by the fire, scowling, swathed in a blanket and holding a conciliatory cup of hot chocolate in his hands. With his face shiny clean, the colour of his eyes was noticeable as he watched her and Jane tidy up. His grey eyes met Maddy's. Grey eyes with a darker ring around the pupil. Eyes very similar to those she saw in the mirror every morning. A seed of suspicion germinated in Maddy's mind and refused to be weeded out.

'I have this: it might fit him,' Jane said, returning from her room. She held up a plain blouse, which was worn and looked as if it was too small for her. Maddy nodded, but her attention was elsewhere as she watched Luke's gaze move to Jane.

'Least it will do until we wash and dry his britches.' Handing Maddy the garment, she scooped up the rags they'd stripped from the lad and carried them outside, her nose wrinkled with distaste.

A strained silence filled the kitchen as Luke watched Maddy, who studiously tried to avoid looking at the boy. Maddy released a pent-up breath when Jane returned; her brisk clattering as she removed the tub and chattered to Luke, who didn't answer, did much to dispel the tension.

Maddy left them to check on how the men had fared overnight. She found Lester on the roof of the barracks, straightening layers of bark that had shifted beneath the onslaught, with Joseph hand-ing up the lengths of pole used to secure the bark in place; Phil and the twins were attending to the listing hen house; and the released hens scratched and pecked as was their wont. As always with Lester, she was conscious of his silent appraisal. She really didn't like the man at all and was certain the feeling was mutual. She said good morning as she passed Joseph, and nodded politely if somewhat coldly to Lester, and continued on her way to Phil.

'Morning, miss,' he said, smiling at her as he paused from hammering in a stout peg.

'Phil, could I speak to you for a moment?' She couldn't bring herself to engage in polite niceties.

He frowned, nodded and handed over the hammer to Michael. 'You boys, carry on.' He turned and indicated Maddy lead the way.

'What's on your mind, Miss Maddy?'

They walked until they reached the top of the path to the fields and she turned to face him. 'Where is Mrs McMahon's husband?

'Bill McMahon?' Phil's glance slid away. 'He died a few years back, he was a soldier.'

'How many years?' She was made suspicious by Phil's odd reaction, as if he didn't want to discuss Rose McMahon.

'About ten.'

Maddy went cold. She swallowed hard before she spoke. 'Who is the father of the boy?'

Phil blinked, reddened a little, and coughed. He didn't answer.

'Mr Hardy?'

'No, not me, I'm not,' he gulped, 'I've never—'

'I'm not accusing you. I just want to know who his father is.' Maddy believed him, but she wanted to know if it was … it didn't bear thinking about.

'Well,'—he did not meet her eyes—'I don't rightly know.'

'Is it someone from Shelby?' She couldn't bring herself to ask him directly.

He didn't respond for some time, but when he spoke Maddy knew he spoke the truth. 'I truly don't know, miss,' he said, his voice solemn. She sensed there was *something* he wasn't telling her, but short of threatening him, she knew she'd hear no more on the matter. Did she really need Phil's confirmation? She gave herself a mental shake: she would not entertain such dreadful suspicions. She dared not even think it.

'Very well, I'll leave you to your work.'

Maddy had turned to go when he spoke. 'What's brought this on, missy?'

'Mrs McMahon wanted to speak to Mr Coulter—she left the boy at my quarters and has gone to Cragside. The lad …' She hesitated, her voice wobbling.

'He's here?' Phil looked past her as if he might see Luke lurking somewhere nearby.

'Yes, he's in the kitchen with Jane.'

'What did Rose want with Daniel?'

'She wouldn't say, just said she must speak to him. She left the boy and went.'

Something alerted her to a presence behind her and Maddy turned to see Lester standing within earshot, obviously listening.

'What do you want, George?' Phil snapped, seeming to have come to the same conclusion.

'Just wanted to see what you want us to do next. The roof is as good as it's ever gunna be. It needs proper shingling.' His tone was even, but the words held an accusation.

'Yes, well, so long as it's waterproof for now,' Phil said.

'For now,' Lester agreed grudgingly.

'Right, help the twins finish the hen house, then take them and Joseph down to check the fences of the bottom field.'

Lester gave Maddy another of those looks she couldn't decipher before letting his glance slide back to Phil, nodding as he walked away. Maddy frowned, remembering Molly Hunt's suspicions—could he be as bad as the woman implied?

Fifteen

Tuesday, 20 March 1832—cloudy and showers, cool

Daniel walked into the yard the next day as Jane and Maddy, with young Luke tagging behind, carried milk and eggs respectively.

'Good morning,' he called out cheerfully, his dimple flashing. He was as handsome as always, but he seemed different from the day before. Maddy's heart did the customary leap.

'Mr Daniel,' Jane greeted him enthusiastically, 'how did you get here?'

'I found a way over the debris with the water somewhat receded. I left Baby at Tillington.'

'Did Mrs McMahon find you?' Maddy asked.

'Who?' He frowned.

'Mrs McMahon, the woman who found Papa ...' she hesitated, 'drowned.'

'Oh, Rose, no, I've not seen her since, er, since your father, er, the day your father ...' he said, his smile sliding away.

Dread bubbled within Maddy's breast. Could Daniel be the boy's father? If he were, didn't he feel any obligation to see Luke was well cared for? Raised decently? No, she couldn't believe that of him.

When she didn't respond, he looked at her with eyebrows raised, and then at Jane. Luke stood holding his egg and watching the conversation unfold.

'Why?' Daniel's brows dipped into a frown as he took in the tableau. 'What is Luke doing here?'

'Mrs McMahon,' Maddy began, then a lump of dismay blocked her throat. She coughed a little to clear it, before continuing, 'She came here yesterday wishing to speak to you. She was insistent that she speak to you. I told her you were at Cragside, and so she left the boy and went off to find you.'

'I stayed at Tillington,' he said. This information would have pleased her yesterday, but now it annoyed her.

'You said you were going to return to Cragside.'

'I'll take the milk and eggs,' Jane said, reaching for the basket Maddy carried, 'to the kitchen.'

Maddy let the handle slip from her fingers.

'Come along, Luke,' Jane said and together they continued across the yard and away from the tension.

'Miss Barker-Trent, what's happened?' Daniel seemed confused.

'Why would she want to see you?' Maddy said. Surely she was mistaken.

'I don't know,' he said and stepped closer. Maddy backed away. 'Maddy?'

'Who is the boy's father?'

Daniel grew still. His gaze flicked away from hers.

'Do you know who his father is?' she persisted. Please, she silently begged him, let there be some other answer.

'Are you implying I am?' Daniel's tone and face were incredulous.

'Of course not. I'm simply asking if you know who his father is.'

'It isn't me,' he said, and a muscle twitched in his jaw.

Maddy lifted her chin and swallowed. Tears threatened as relief rushed through her. Of course he couldn't be; he'd not been there long enough. She knew that, but was the alternative any more palatable? Maddy made her way to the bench on the veranda, her legs shaking. 'I'm sorry, of course you aren't. Do you know who it is?'

'I couldn't be certain,' he said, and then more firmly, 'No, I'm sorry, I don't.'

'Do you have a suspicion?'

'I'd be wary of accusing anyone.'

'That tells me nothing,' Maddy snapped, annoyed at his side-stepping her question. Her mind whirled. She longed to share her fears with him, but deep inside she could barely acknowledge them.

'I don't know, Maddy.'

Their eyes met and held. Maddy broke the contact and tried to relax her clenched jaw.

'Why did you not return to Cragside?' An image of Luke's grey eyes flashed through her mind and her insides went cold.

'I saw Alex along the way, and he invited me to stay at Tillington.'

Maddy registered the confusion in his face. He wasn't the only one confused. She had been jealous when he'd stayed at Cragside, now she was annoyed that he hadn't. Was she losing her mind? But the boy? The need to know who his father was clawed at her insides.

'Maddy, what is troubling you?'

'Nothing, I'm fine.' She turned away. 'Is there anything else?'

She could feel his gaze on her back, but she didn't turn around.

'Ah, yes, I purchased the dairy herd.'

Which was why he'd been away, Maddy reminded herself. She turned back to face him. The breeze ruffled the leaves and the fresh scent of eucalyptus enveloped her.

'Very good, and did you get them for a fair price?' she asked, forcing herself to think of something other than Luke. After all, plenty of people had grey eyes.

'Aye, very fair.'

'Good,' she said again, for want of something better. Her well of words had dried up. 'I'd better get on,' she said after a tense silence.

'Yes, so had I. Where are the men?'

'Repairing the new field, the bottom corner suffered somewhat in the rain.'

'Right,' he said.

'Well, good day.'

❧

Saturday, 24 March 1832—*fine and cool*

'No, Luke, you must use your fork,' Jane said, her voice patient as the boy held a fork in one hand, only to pick up his food with the fingers of the other, 'like this.' She guided him, holding his hand and skewering a piece of meat.

Maddy sipped her tea and tried to ignore the pair of them. The boy had been with them for five days, and though he was no trouble, he'd not said a word the entire time; he only stared at them in silent reproach and did as he was asked. It was imperative they discover what had become of his mother. No one had even mentioned the poor woman nor seemed interested when Maddy broached the subject. That Rose was an outcast was clear, but no one would discuss the matter and so she let it go and hoped the woman would come back soon.

Maddy had spoken to Daniel little since the flood, only exchanging necessary information regarding the running of the farm. The twins had begun digging over a small patch of earth behind the kitchen, as the haphazard garden behind Daniel's hut was positioned in the worst soil on the ridge, and everything planted there struggled to survive let alone produce anything edible. Maddy wondered, not for the first time, whether Papa had sought advice and ignored it, or had he simply not asked. He'd done so many things that seemed contrary to good sense, and then there were his letters. Surely he'd have known the deception was ludicrous—would be uncovered when she arrived?

A knock sounded at the door. Maddy started, slopping her tea; she muttered a curse that drew a frown from Jane, stood up and opened the door to find Daniel standing outside.

'Mr Coulter,' she said. For some reason Maddy didn't understand, something had changed between them. 'Please come in.'

'Thank you, no. I've only come to let you know the fences for the dairy fields are finished, and the work on the expansion of the milking shed should be done in the next day or so. I thought I'd send Phil and the twins to Maitland to walk the herd back tomorrow. If you agree?'

'Of course, if that's what you recommend.'

'Daniel.'

Maddy spun around and stared at Luke. It was the first word she'd heard the boy say. They were all looking at him, and Luke ducked his head; and with barely any discernible movement, he slid from the chair and disappeared beneath the table.

'Well,' said Jane, 'at least we know he can speak.'

'Yes,' Maddy agreed, as she'd been beginning to wonder.

Daniel squatted down in the open doorway and peered at the boy under the curtain of the oiled tablecloth.

'Hello, Luke,' he said, his voice soft.

But Luke didn't respond. After a few minutes it was obvious nothing more was forthcoming, and they all straightened. Daniel turned to Maddy. 'Can we have a word in private?'

Her stomach clenched; why were they suddenly so formal with each other?

'Of course.' What else could she say?

They walked past the foundation trenches to the gum tree where they had met each morning. In the days since the floods Maddy had deliberately stayed inside, telling herself it was too cold. But in reality she felt shamed by her own fears and suspicions.

'Has there been any sign of his mother?' he asked.

'No.' Maddy was worried. 'Do you think we should send someone to Cragside and see if she's been there?'

'I thought Phil could stop in on the way to Maitland.'

'Yes.' She stared out at the large pools of dirty water lying on the flats below that were left behind as the flood receded. The breeze lifted and the stale smell of mud and rotting debris reached them even though they were high above it. 'Has she ever left the lad here before?'

'Not to my knowledge.'

Maddy nodded. A tense silence filled the air between them.

'Have I done something to upset you?' Daniel surveyed the valley, tension visible in the tautness of his jaw.

Had he? 'Of course not,' she said.

'Then why are you behaving as if I had?'

'I don't know what you mean.' Maddy turned to look at him. Could it be she who had changed?

'You have been distant since the flood.'

'I am merely concerned for Rose,' she hesitated, diverting her gaze, 'and the boy.'

'If having Luke with you is difficult, he can bunk in with the men, or even with me.'

For some reason this irritated her, though Maddy knew his offer was kindly meant. With great effort she kept her tone even. 'He is fine, and Jane seems to be quite taken with the lad. I think she misses her own brothers and sisters.' Maddy sighed and met his eyes. 'Though we must find his mother.'

Daniel stared at her for a long moment, then nodded and turned to face the valley. 'We're going to take the dray down the hill now the track is dry enough. When the water receded, we found much of the ploughed soil from the corner of the field banked up near the water's edge. I thought we can haul it up here to improve the soil in the vegetable garden.'

Maddy nodded.

'Maddy, I'm not Luke's father.'

She blinked. 'I know.' Is that why he seemed so distant? Had her mad questions driven a wedge between them?

He stepped into her line of vision and his gaze met hers. Maddy could see the sincerity in his face. She nodded again and looked away, hoping he wouldn't notice the tears suddenly filling her eyes. The obvious answer to the boy's parentage wasn't to be considered; she couldn't countenance it. There must be another answer and she would find it. She hoped Mrs McMahon would return for the boy soon.

'I know you are not,' she said again and met his stare, and she felt for one moment the connection between them as solidly as if they were touching. 'Well, we're making soap today, so I'd better get on.'

She turned and hurried away before he could respond.

Along with a pail of lard, Mrs Garrick had given Maddy instruction on soap-making, and thankfully Jane knew how, having helped her mother with the task. It was Maddy's first attempt at the chore and she welcomed the labour; anything to take her mind off the disappearance of Rose McMahon and the parentage of Luke.

Jane was melting the lard on an outside fire while they prepared to make their first batch of soap. Maddy wrinkled her nose at Jane; the process was smelly, and she was grateful they were working outdoors. Feeling useless, she watched as Jane put the ashes collected from the stove and fires in a wooden trough built specifically for the process.

'Now we just pour this water through the ashes,' Jane told her, nodding at the buckets she had ready, 'and we catch the lye water in the bucket under here.' Jane had assured her they would make enough soap to last half a year. Maddy donned her apron to help, and with Luke nearby drawing odd shapes in the dust, he was far enough away from the fire to be out of harm's way but close enough for them to keep an eye on him.

'You might want to put this on.' Jane folded a square of cloth and handed it to Maddy.

'What do I do with it?'

'Tie it around your head, to cover your nose and mouth.'

Maddy shrugged and did as instructed.

'It stinks a bit, and this might help to keep the stink outta your hair,' Jane said and handed Maddy a mobcap, the same as she and most female servants wore. Maddy pulled it on and tucked the stray tendrils of hair beneath it before pulling the drawstrings tight to keep it in place.

Jane poured the lye water into a large cast-iron cauldron suspended on a tripod over a well-tended fire and handed Maddy a wooden paddle. 'Now stir, and keep stirring.'

Doing as she was bidden, Maddy watched as Jane melted the lard in another cauldron in the coals. Keeping an eye on the simmering lye she was careful not to inhale the fumes as she stirred and stirred. As the liquid heated, Maddy averted her face from the caustic steam, while watching the milky liquid slowly began to grow clear.

'I reckon the lye should be just about perfect,' Jane told Maddy as she carefully placed a raw potato into the liquid. They watched as it began to sink, but before it was fully submerged it settled, floating with only a small circle of the potato left dry. Jane grinned at Maddy, seemingly unaffected by the smell of the lard and lye, while Maddy's eyes watered.

'Doesn't it bother you?' Maddy asked, wiping away tears with her sleeve.

'Not as much as it does you,' Jane said, laughing as she poured the now liquid lard into the lye. 'You stir it again and keep on stirring until it thickens.'

Maddy did as she was instructed and, though her arms ached, she continued to stir. Jane dragged the coals from directly beneath the cauldron with a metal poker, checked on Maddy's progress and instructed her to keep stirring.

'I'll ready the moulds,' Jane said.

Maddy glanced around to see Luke had climbed a nearby tree and still seemed happy playing by himself. She returned her attention to Jane, who had dampened some old cloth and lined the long wooden soap box. Meanwhile Maddy continued to stir. There was a decent breeze for which she was grateful, as it cooled her and swept away the worst of the smoke and the strong smell of the soap. She considered how little she knew of Jane's past. She may have been transported, but she would never be treated like a criminal at Shelby.

So intent was Maddy on her thoughts that she didn't hear the approach of the Everettes' buggy. The first she knew of the visitors was when Amelia spoke.

'Hello, there.'

Maddy looked up to see Amelia and Belle standing a hundred yards from the fire where she continued to stir and their horse being led to the farmyard by the Cragside groom. Jane grew still and Maddy ceased stirring for a moment, but at Jane's frown, she resumed, her arms aching.

'Good morning,' Maddy said, her voice muffled by the cloth covering her mouth.

'Is your mistress at home?' Amelia was looking directly at Maddy. Maddy blinked. Amelia didn't recognise her. Of course, with the cap, apron and kerchief, she would hardly be distinguishable from a convict maid.

'Amelia, it's me,' Maddy said, pulling the kerchief away to reveal her smile.

Both Amelia and Belle frowned uncomprehendingly.

Without a word Jane crossed and took the large wooden stirring paddle from her.

'Maddy, what are you doing?' Belle stared, dumbfounded.

'We're making soap,' Maddy told them. She understood their confusion—she hadn't known anything about it either. And it really did smell awful.

'Why are *you* making it?' Amelia backed away.

'We need it, and the Garricks had slaughtered a pig and gave us the lard.'

'Slaughtered a pig?' Amelia's mouth twisted, revealing her distaste.

'Lard?'

Maddy grinned. 'Yes, the lard is made from pig fat.'

'But why are you making soap? Isn't that what you have the girl for?' Belle said.

Maddy's smile slid away. She knew neither of the Everette girls had ever been required to do anything more industrious than embroidery, but Maddy's life had never been one of idleness.

'I don't wish to be rude,' Belle continued, oblivious to Maddy's reaction, 'but surely you don't have to do such rough work yourself?'

Maddy opened her mouth to respond, then closed it. Belle was right, she didn't need to do any of this herself, but she couldn't countenance expecting Jane to do it alone. Besides, she really didn't mind the hard work; if she tired herself sufficiently with work during the day, she could sleep at night rather than endure the endless tossing that had been occurring since Luke had been left with them. She gritted her teeth against the hasty words that sprang to mind and forced a smile before responding. She did not need to explain anything to the Everette girls.

'I'm afraid it's all hands on deck at Shelby. And if Jesus thought himself not above washing the disciples feet, I'm not above making the soap.' Maddy smiled brightly at them, and smoothed her apron before returning her attention to Jane. 'Can you manage without me for a little while?'

Jane nodded, cast a narrow-eyed glance at the visitors and continued stirring.

'Don't try to pour it into the moulds without me,' Maddy told her. 'Call me when you're ready.'

'But, miss—' she began.

'I mean it, Jane, it's dangerous. Call me when the soap is ready to be transferred.'

'Yes, Miss Barker-Trent,' she said demurely.

Maddy held her gaze for a moment; she had her doubts as to whether Jane would call her, but she wouldn't pursue the topic with an audience.

Maddy turned back to Amelia and Belle. 'Come inside and we can have a cup of water, or tea if you'd prefer.'

'Tea would be nice,' Amelia said.

'We won't take too much of your time: water will suffice,' said Belle, her words clipped.

'I can easily make tea,' Maddy said once they were in the kitchen, pushing the kettle onto the heat. She poured a cup of water and drank it thirstily. Soap-making was hot work; she could see why Mrs Garrick recommended it be done in the cooler weather.

Maddy remembered Rose. 'Actually, it's good that you popped by: did you by any chance see Mrs Rose McMahon at Cragside?'

'I don't know anyone by that name. Who is she?' Belle said.

'She lives on a small holding nearby,' Maddy said and cringed inwardly. She didn't actually know where the woman lived but had the merest idea of the direction of the woman's home. 'She's the widow of'—Maddy groped for the name Phil had told her— 'Bill McMahon, who was a soldier.'

'A soldier's widow. She would hardly have come to the house.'

Maddy turned away and busied herself with the tea, inwardly fuming at Belle's attitude, but she made no comment; after all, it was true—Mrs McMahon would probably have approached one of the women servants or even one of the men in the fields.

When Maddy turned from the range she found the Everettes gazing around the interior as if they'd never seen a kitchen before. She frowned. They probably hadn't. At least not one like this.

'To what do I owe the pleasure of your visit?'

'We came to discuss the ball,' Amelia said.

'We need to change the venue—the field has been flooded and won't be dry in time for the full moon,' Belle said, standing rigid; her hands were clamped closely to her sides, as if she didn't want to inadvertently touch anything.

'Where would you move it to? Wasn't the river bank chosen to accommodate everyone from the area?' Maddy was certain she knew where this was going and gritted her teeth.

'We thought with the weather having made the field unusable, we should pare down the numbers and hold it at Cragside.'

'But what of those who will have to miss out?' She was unable to look at Belle's self-satisfied expression. If Belle didn't want to invite anyone below her own social position, then Maddy herself should not be included, for she was quite sure she no longer measured up.

'It's unfortunate,' Belle said.

'Perhaps alternative arrangements could be made.' Amelia smiled brightly. 'They could have their own dance.'

'Or,' Maddy said with her own forced brightness, 'we could change the date to allow the field to dry and carry on with the original plans.'

'It would take too long; after all, it is to be an Autumnal Ball,' Belle said stubbornly.

'Then we shall make it a Winter Ball, and everyone can have something to look forward to, not just those who will fit in at Cragside.'

'But—' Amelia began.

'What do Mrs Garrick and Mrs Harpur say?' Maddy interrupted her.

'I don't know, for we came here first,' Amelia admitted. Belle's expression was rigid.

'Then I would recommend until the matter is discussed with all the ladies no firm decisions be made.'

Maddy put the teapot on the table. 'Do you take sugar?' she asked, glancing from one to the other. The door opened and Luke stood in the entrance, staring wide-eyed first at Belle and then at Amelia. Without a word, he backed away and let the door close once more.

Sixteen

Tuesday, 27 March 1832—fine day with light showers in the evening

They found Rose McMahon's body wedged in a jumble of flotsam. Maddy was on her horse and about to ride over to Tillington when George Lester and Joseph came along the track from clearing the debris blocking the creek. They carried a make-shift litter between them on which lay a pitiful shape. At first, Maddy didn't comprehend the significance, but Daniel and Phil, who were on their way back from checking the newly acquired dairy herd, realised what it was the men carried and ran across the farmyard to assist.

Beneath her the horse grew tense, head high and ears erect. He snorted loudly, unsettled by the scent of the burden borne by the men. Maddy slid to the ground and hurriedly tied him to the rail before turning back to the four men who stood around the litter on the ground. Her breath caught in her throat.

'Rose?' Maddy gasped, taking in the distorted features of the once handsome woman. Not again, not another drowning. Rose's long thin arms were bare and strangely mottled from being in the water. Maddy shivered. Wasn't water supposed to be life-giving? Her experience so far convinced her life on the river bank extracted an expensive price.

'Come away, miss, you don't need to see this,' Phil said, taking Maddy's arm and urging her back from the body. 'We'll take care of things.'

She nodded; the men would do what was necessary, and she didn't wish to burden Jane with the unhappy assignment.

'What happened?' Maddy looked up at Joseph. 'Where was she?'

'Up stream from where the creek was blocked; she must have got caught in the roots of a tree,' he said.

Maddy stared at him for a long moment. Phil's hand dropped away from her arm.

'She didn't make it to Cragside?'

'It doesn't look like it.'

'No one there saw her,' Phil said.

'What do we do now?' Maddy asked no one in particular.

'Bury her,' said Lester, his tone matter-of-fact.

Maddy looked at Daniel. 'What about her family? Shouldn't we inform them?'

'Who knows who they are,' Lester said. 'She lived over on a place on the western boundary and never talked about her people back home.' His tone was dismissive, as if the poor woman had been worth less than nothing.

'That makes no difference,' Maddy snapped, 'her family still need to be told.' Then she remembered Luke. 'And the boy: shouldn't he return to them?'

'I don't think ...' began Phil, but his words trailed off.

'Perhaps Mr Garrick will know more about her, or Mr Ever-ette: they've been in the region the longest, so I imagine they would know if anyone does,' said Daniel.

Maddy stared at the slack features of the woman and winced. 'Can someone please cover her?'

Joey nodded and hurried to the store. He returned with a length of canvas and laid it gently over the body.

While the men dug a grave a little further down the slope from where Papa was buried Maddy knew she had to tell Luke of his mother's fate. He must at the very least have an opportunity to say goodbye to his mother. And so she left the men and made her way to the kitchen to find him.

'Miss Maddy.' Jane's face was full of anguish and Maddy knew at once that she'd been told of poor Rose's fate.

'Yes, I know.' Maddy looked around, but there was no sign of the boy. 'Where is he?'

'He's looking at the pictures in the book you loaned me, in my room.'

'Very good. Have you told him about his mother?'

'No, I wasn't sure—'

'Come along, let's get it over with. The grave has been dug.' While Maddy's voice was level, her heart was thundering, and she felt sick. Jane looked as miserable as Maddy felt.

Luke sat cross-legged on the pallet at the foot of Jane's bed, peering up at her, his grey eyes dark and fathomless. His expression was impossible to read, and she glanced away for some heartbeats.

'Luke.' Maddy forced herself to meet his gaze and was beset by a deep pain in her chest. He was so young to lose his mama. Afraid she might buckle altogether should she soften towards him, Maddy squared her shoulders and pushed aside the empathetic ache in her heart.

'Luke, I've some news. We've found your mama.' He straightened, his expression expectant, and Maddy suddenly found herself by his side, her hand on his shoulder. 'I'm sorry to say she was caught in the flood.' He dropped his chin to his chest.

Maddy bit her lip. 'She has died, Luke. I'm—' She stopped. The child's lip was trembling. 'Would you like to come and say goodbye?'

Maddy felt Jane staring at her, but she couldn't meet her eye, and with a lump clogging her throat, she turned and left the room, leaving Jane to bring the boy to the graveside. A part of her wanted to clutch him tight against her, to comfort him in his grief. But she couldn't forget the question hanging over his paternity. Not yet. Maybe never.

They silently followed, and Maddy held herself rigid, her chin high, unable to watch, but she sensed the movement as the boy approached his mother's wrapped body. There were no tears, no wails of sorrow, only his customary silence, before Jane urged him back. After barely a moment Daniel tucked the shroud around Rose's face before he and Phil lowered the wrapped body into the grave. Maddy couldn't look at Luke, desperately ashamed of her callous behaviour towards the boy. Instead she observed Lester as he watched the proceedings, then she saw his expression alter as he turned his attention to Jane and Luke. His mouth twisted slightly as his eyes narrowed. What was it with the man that made him so disdainful of everyone?

As she'd intended to ride to Tillington, Maddy continued with her mission. Seizing the excuse to flee the situation, she told herself she needed to inquire about Rose McMahon's family and what was to be done with the boy. Curse it, why had the woman been so insistent that she see Daniel? What had been so urgent? This question niggled at Maddy as she rode along the track alone, having refused Charlie's offer to accompany her. She needed the solitude and time to think. The certainty that everyone was keeping the truth from her ate at Maddy. They all knew who the child's father was—of that Maddy was convinced.

When she saw a rider approaching, she had cause to regret declining Charlie's company. She relaxed only when she registered who it was.

'Morning, Miss Maddy,' she greeted Maddy with a frown, 'you look like you're bearing the worries of the world.'

'Oh, Mrs Hunt.' Maddy tried to smile, knowing it was but a poor facsimile. 'Good day.'

'Call me Molly, everyone does.'

'Oh, of course,' Maddy said. 'Molly.'

As usual, Molly sat astride, deep in the saddle, her skirts caught up around her knees, revealing long knitted stockings over twig-like legs; her feet in men's work boots were jammed hard into the stirrups. Molly was slouched and easy, while Maddy was corseted and perched stiffly upright on her respectable side saddle. Not for the first time Maddy wished opinions bothered her as little as they did Molly Hunt in this regard.

'Where are you off to?' Her button eyes peered at Maddy from beneath the brim of her hat.

'I'm on my way to Tillington. Unfortunately Mrs McMahon was found drowned in the flood.'

'Another drowning?' Her expression disbelieving.

'I'm afraid so. She was on her way to Cragside.'

'Cragside? Why would she want to go there?'

Red fidgeted beneath Maddy while Molly's horse stood calm, head low and ears flat.

'Mr Coulter was forced to stay there when the creek became blocked by debris damned by a fallen tree. She insisted she must see him and ...' Maddy couldn't finish, imagining the poor woman attempting to cross the swollen creek and being swept along until caught in the branches, struggling until her strength was exhausted and she succumbed to the onslaught. Tears filled

Maddy's eyes. Molly became still and tense enough that her horse jerked his head up, ears pricking as he sensed her agitation.

'What about the boy?'

'Oh, he's at Shelby, she left him with us.'

Molly relaxed visibly, and in turn, her horse lost its alertness, settling back into the former sleepy stance.

'I'm on my way to Tillington to see if Mr Garrick knows of her people's whereabouts. I think they should be informed.'

'Ah, yes, she and her husband came out after Waterloo.'

'You knew them?' Relief filled Maddy. 'I need to let them know of the woman's death, and that we have buried her. To make arrangements for the boy.'

'Don't know as they left anyone close behind in the old country.'

'Where does she—er—where *did* she live?'

'She had a little place north of yours.' She frowned. 'Don't think she owned it though.'

'Well Luke can't go back there on his own.'

'You're right about that. Well, I'm off.'

'But what about the boy? There must be some family? We have to find somewhere for him to go.'

'Nah, there's likely no one,' she said, again peering at Maddy, her expression curiously intense. 'And if there is, they probably won't want him, even if you could find them.'

Maddy sagged a little in the saddle.

'Good day to ye.' With a click, she urged her horse on, heading towards the small settlement of Black Creek.

'Wait, Mrs Hunt, what about the boy?'

She wheeled her mount around to look at Maddy once more. 'What about him?'

'What will I do with him?'

'Take care of him.'

Molly turned her horse once more and drove her heels into its flanks until they were cantering away. With little else to do, Maddy steered her own horse's nose in the direction of Tillington.

She found only Beth and Cookie at the homestead, as Mrs Garrick and the children were visiting Mrs Wyndham. Maddy declined Cookie's offer of tea and a quick catch up. Unusually, there was no sign of Bowman the groom, who must also have been working on the mill. Leading her horse towards where the men were working, Maddy was interested to see the progress of the construction of a water mill. The millpond had been dug, with only the few intervening yards to be cleared so the diverted water from the creek could flow and turn the giant wheel and the industry of flour milling could begin. Her approach went unnoticed and she stood and watched as the wheel was manhandled into place with the aid of four large horses straining to bear the weight while it was fitted to the shaft.

A cheer rang out as the wheel slid into place and, despite her misgivings about the boy, Maddy smiled. One of the men noticed her presence and spoke to Mr Garrick, who, with his shirtsleeves rolled up, laboured alongside the men.

'Ah, Maddy.' He grinned up at her as he climbed the stone-lined water race. 'What do you think of our watermill?'

'It looks wonderful—when will it be operational?' The mill, in addition to servicing smaller farms along the river, was a canny business investment for Mr Garrick as the price of flour was considerably better than that of un-milled grain.

'Not too long now, for the mill stones are to be fitted in the coming weeks, and then it's just a matter of letting the water in.' His boyish enthusiasm was infectious, and Maddy almost forgot why she'd come to see him.

'To what do we owe the pleasure?' he asked, wiping his hands on a kerchief he'd pulled from his pocket. 'I'm sure you know Mrs Garrick is away to Dalwood.'

'Yes, I called at the house and saw Beth and Cookie.'

'You came to see me then?'

'Yes. I'm afraid Rose McMahon's body has been found in the debris after the flood waters receded. She left her son at Shelby and I'm not sure what to do with the boy.'

'I see,' he said, his expression growing serious.

'Yes, I ran into Molly Hunt on my way here, and she seems to think there is no family, and that, should I find any, they wouldn't want him.'

'Mm, she may be right. I believe the woman … er, she lived on the edges of society. Spent more time with the Wonnarua than with other white settlers, unusually enough. Susannah thinks perhaps they were kinder to her.'

'I see,' Maddy said, but she didn't. She didn't understand at all.

'Where is the boy?' He lifted his hat and wiped the sweat from his brow with his forearm.

'At Shelby.'

'What do you intend to do with him?'

'Well, I'd thought to return him to his family, but I don't know who his father is.' Maddy frowned. 'No one seems to know.' Or be willing to say, she thought.

He nodded slowly but said nothing for a long while. 'You could send him to Hawkins—there's probably a family willing to take him on, as a stable boy or the like.'

Maddy blinked. She couldn't send him away to be little more than a slave. 'No, I don't think so.'

'It's up to you, my dear, but do think about it. You don't need to encumber yourself with a stray.'

Maddy didn't like his inference—Luke wasn't a stray—but she saw Mr Garrick's point. She didn't want to raise a child. She didn't know how to.

'Yes, I'll give it some thought.' She rubbed Red's forehead. 'Do you know who his father is? Surely the man should be the one to take responsibility?' She wished she had the courage to ask him outright if it was Papa.

The silence stretched between them, and when he finally spoke, Maddy felt as if he'd punched her in the stomach. 'I think you'd best forget about that.'

Maddy lifted her chin, though her knees wobbled. 'I have asked Daniel, and he says he is not the boy's father.'

'No, he couldn't be, as he wasn't yet in the colony when the child, er …' His neck reddened and he cleared his throat. 'No, Daniel hasn't been at Shelby long enough. Perhaps you should send the lad to Hawkins; he'll be well taken care of. You have enough to contend in running an estate such as Shelby.'

Although Maddy knew Daniel was not the boy's father, could not have been, she was relieved to hear it again from Mr Garrick. Still, she refused to give credence to her nagging suspicion of who else the boy's father could be. There had to be someone else, and she would find out who he was. Though he managed to dodge the issue, something Mr Garrick said pointed towards Luke's father being from Shelby. No, she blinked, no, she'd not countenance it.

'Come and have a look at the mill,' Mr Garrick said, jerking her back to the moment. Maddy nodded and followed him to where the men were busy putting the mill wheel together.

After Maddy was shown the grist mill's workings and had discussed the condition of her newly acquired dairy herd, she left for home. As she rode she continued to contemplate Luke's parentage. With Daniel and Phil eliminated, it left only Lester and young Charlie, and Maddy was certain the latter was not Luke's father. Lester? Maybe, yet something in the way the woman had skirted him on the day of Papa's death struck a chord and Maddy considered whether perhaps Mrs McMahon had been an unwilling recipient of his attentions. If one could describe it thus. Had she been assaulted? Surely if it had been so the woman would have accused him outright—a widowed woman must be required to explain the appearance of a child, must she not? And Lester in that case would be long gone. Maddy couldn't imagine her father would sanction his presence on Shelby if he had done such a thing. It made no sense. Deep down she knew there was only one solution that did. She shook her head to rid herself of the disquieting thought. Instead she ran over her options as to what she must do with the boy. He could stay at Shelby and bunk in with the men, or Daniel for that matter. It would surely be better than sending him away to be little more than some colonial's slave. She would discuss it with Daniel, seek his advice.

Seventeen

Friday, 30 March 1832—showery

For the third night since Rose McMahon had been found, Maddy's sleep was fitful. After hours of restless tossing, she climbed out of bed, pulled a shawl around her shoulders and went barefoot into the kitchen. Lighting a taper and placing a block of wood in the firebox, Maddy thought if she couldn't sleep, she could attend to the ledgers. Her grandpapa's pendulum clock, one of the few things Papa had kept when he'd sold the mill, stood in the corner near the door and read just past midnight. Its chime had probably been what had woken her.

Though she'd discussed what to do about Luke with both Daniel and Phil, Maddy couldn't settle on what to do next. She couldn't bring herself to send him away nor to have him sleep in either the barracks or in with Daniel, so he remained on the pallet on the floor of Jane's room.

Soon another female servant would be coming and would have to be housed in with Jane. As Jane was in the smaller room, and there wasn't room for another bed, Maddy decided the best course of action would be to have the smaller room herself and move Jane and the new woman into the larger one.

'Miss Maddy,' Jane said quietly.

Maddy looked up to see her standing in the open door. Maddy blinked; she hadn't heard it open.

'Come in, Jane,' Maddy said, 'and close the door—it's quite cool tonight.'

Jane did as she was bidden, and when she saw Maddy had stoked the fire, she pushed the kettle onto the heat.

'Would you like me to make you a chocolate?' Jane asked.

Maddy nodded, grateful she'd followed her instinct that day at Parramatta. Jane was a wonderful companion, a hard worker, and Maddy had come to consider her more family than servant.

'Only if you'll join me.'

'I never say no to chocolate.' Jane grinned.

'What are you doing awake at this time of night?'

'I heard you and wondered if you were unwell.'

'I am quite well, only suffering a little from insomnia. So I thought I'd check the accounts.'

Jane frowned.

'I couldn't sleep,' Maddy explained.

'Are you worried?' Jane asked as she gathered the makings of the chocolate.

'It's nothing in particular, just a lot of small things swimming around in my mind.' Maddy remembered the rooms. 'Though there is something I'd like to discuss with you. As we have a new girl from the Female Factory coming to help with the dairy herd, I was considering changing rooms with you so there will be more space for two beds, and I shall have the smaller room.'

'If you wish, but what about Luke?' A small frown creased her usually smooth brow, and Maddy felt bad—Jane had so loved having her own room. But there was nothing else to be done until the house was built.

'I'm not sure: both Mr Coulter and Mr Hardy have said they'd be happy for him to bunk with them, but I don't know if it's the right thing to do.'

'He don't seem to like the men much,' Jane said as she prepared the drinks.

She was right, now that Maddy thought of it—Luke hadn't made any attempt to connect with any of the men at Shelby. Unlike young Edwin Garrick, who spent every moment he could with either his father or Bowman—and sometimes even the field hands—Luke seemed content to stay close to either Jane or herself, even though Maddy hardly encouraged him to do so.

'Well, I suppose he could share with me,' she said, feeling a little queasy even as she suggested it; she didn't want to examine her feelings too closely when it came to the boy, but she had to admit it was the best solution.

'There'll be room enough for the pallet in the bigger room,' Jane said.

'We'll see.'

'Tell me about your life in England, Miss Maddy?' Jane said, placing a steaming cup of chocolate on the table before her, and sitting down opposite, her shawl pulled snugly around her shoulders. The fire kept the chill at bay, and Maddy relished the warmth on her back. Tucking her feet beneath her, she took a sip. Jane did the same as Maddy considered her request.

'My mama was often sick, so Papa would take me to the mill with him. Grandpapa owned a cotton mill in Wiltshire, and I used to spend a lot of time with him. He taught me to keep the accounts. Papa was not terribly good with figures. Grandpapa used to say his head was in the clouds. Mama said he dreamed big dreams and would one day fulfil them all.' Papa hadn't fulfilled any dreams, though he'd been full of them. Angry tears filled her eyes. She blinked hard: perhaps if Mama had lived it would have been different.

'Why did he come to New South Wales if he had a business in England?'

Maddy considered how to explain. To tell her the entire truth felt like a betrayal, but she found herself unable to resist the desire to talk of her past.

'I think Papa was restless. Certainly he was never interested in his father's business, so when Grandpapa died and Papa inherited, he sold the mill to fund a move to New South Wales, to build his own life. Mama said he always wanted to have land. Mama's family owned a great estate, and I think Papa had always felt somewhat lesser because of his industrial roots.'

'Was your ma a lady?'

'No, but she was born into a prominent family. She forfeited her position when she married Papa.'

'Oh, how romantic,' Jane breathed, eyes wide and sparkling in the flickering candlelight.

'Romantic?' Had it been romantic? 'Yes, I suppose it was. They met when Mama's horse bolted. Papa was a great horseman, and he galloped after her and caught the reins, pulling up the runaway horse and saving Mama from certain death.'

'And it was love at first sight?' Jane asked, sighing as she sipped her chocolate.

'Indeed, they always claimed it was.' Maddy smiled; their love had been palpable. Her first clear memory was of feeling left out of their insular love for one another.

'Did you live in a fine house?'

'I suppose it was, though not as fine as the one Papa had promised to build here for Mama.' Promised and lied about, Maddy remembered. And then there was Luke. She was no longer certain she wanted the matter answered, as the likely truth became clearer in her reluctant mind.

'One day you will build the fine house,' Jane said, not a hint of doubt in her words.

'I hope so, Jane, for it's my one desire to see Shelby as my parents had planned.'

'You said your ma was sick?'

Maddy examined Jane, sensing a lot of questions she'd probably wondered about since coming to Shelby. 'Yes, Mama had been frail since I was born. She'd been close to death after my birth and Grandpapa said she'd never fully recovered.' Maddy had always felt it was her fault that her mother suffered so, though it had never been said aloud. Maddy knew Papa had blamed her—she'd sensed it in his attitude at times. It was why she feared he'd killed himself rather than continue without Mama, rather than be saddled with the cause of his heartache. She lifted her chin: that was as it may be, Maddy would build Shelby and fulfil their dream.

'Why did you and your ma stay in England instead of coming with your pa?'

Good question. At the time they'd told her it was so Papa could reserve all his attention for preparing the property, but now Maddy was in the colony she knew that the women came with their husbands and children; infants were even born at sea. She'd recently begun to wonder if there'd been more to it than had been shared with her.

'Your life must have been different from out here in the bush,' Jane said, eyeing Maddy from behind her cup.

Maddy sipped her own fast-cooling beverage. 'Yes, it was different, but not better.'

'Aye, I feel the same. I miss my ma and kin, but here there's food aplenty, and it's not so cold.'

'But the heat is awful,' Maddy reminded her.

'Not as awful as being freezing and hungry,' Jane said, her expression full of sorrow.

Maddy had never in her life been hungry nor cold beyond a point of slight discomfort. But she had been lonely and, were it not for Grandpapa, that might have been its own kind of unbearable.

'Tell me about your family,' Maddy invited, not wishing to peruse her own story any further.

'There's seven of us, and I'm the eldest. It worries me how Ma will be getting on without me, but she's a careful woman, and Tom is handy—he'll get a job with Pa and hopefully help keep him sober.' This was the first time Jane had mentioned her father. Maddy wondered what Jane's life had been like without the certainty of an income.

'Where does your pa work?'

'Harrington Hall is nearby, and all the village men work there, but Pa is …' She paused and Maddy sensed she didn't wish to be disloyal, which was something Maddy could appreciate. She hurried to ask an alternative question and alleviate the need for Jane to expound the topic of her father.

'And your other brothers and sisters?'

'Well, as I said, there's Tom, he's fifteen and strong as an ox: he was attending the parish school, and he can read, but with me gone, I imagine he'd have to work on the estate now. After Tom comes May. She's almost thirteen—no, it's past her birthday, so she would be thirteen already.' Jane paused, obviously saddened, but she continued. 'Ann, she's a year younger than May, and she is already a fine seamstress. We all helped Ma with her piece-work, but Ann is the only one of us who had Ma's gift for it. I'm that bad, Ma didn't even ask me to help, so I took on most of the household chores, leaving Ma and Ann to do the sewing.'

'I'm sure you were a great help to your family,' Maddy said.

'I'm not much help to them now though, am I?' Jane didn't sound bitter; she was merely stating a fact. 'After Ann is Katie—she's a sweet girl though a right tomboy—and then there's John, he's nine, and little Billy, who is four.' She grinned at a memory. 'His middle name should be mischief—always into something.'

'Do you miss them terribly?' Maddy wondered what her own life would have been like if she'd had a brother or a sister.

'I do, but at least there's one less mouth to feed.'

'Do you write to them?' Maddy didn't recall ever seeing a letter for Jane from anyone.

'When I learn to write properly, I'll send a letter and tell them how good it is here. Tom will be able to read it. Maybe he will write back.'

'Then I will help you write to them tomorrow,' Maddy told her, ashamed of her own selfishness at not noticing that Jane had never been able to let her family know she was safe and well.

Jane smiled and yawned. 'Aye, that would be nice.'

'Then we shall, but first I think we should head back to bed, for the dawn will come soon enough. And tomorrow we'd best make a start on swapping rooms as well.'

Jane rose and took the cups to the bench. 'Yes, Miss Maddy, I'll be away to my bed, and you too.'

'Yes, I will. I doubt I could concentrate on the accounts now.'

'Good night,' she said and made her way back to her bed, leaving Maddy to do the same.

Maddy fell asleep almost immediately when her head touched the pillow, but it was not a restful slumber. She was plagued with frantic dreams, torturous anxiety and feelings of imminent doom. Dreams where she wished for assistance from familiar faces. Daniel, Phil and Mr Garrick all featured prominently, and none did anything to rescue her from the faceless terror that pursued. She was sweating and frightened. Rose's features swam before her in the darkness and there seemed to radiate from her a wave of expectation.

'What do you want?' Maddy tried to ask, but she couldn't move no matter how she struggled against the strangling covers. She called out for help, for Rose to help her, but no sound would come.

'Miss Maddy, are you unwell?'

Maddy jerked awake to see Jane standing in the open doorway of her room.

'I don't know, just a bad dream.'

'You've been dreaming a lot.'

Maddy blinked: had she? She confessed, 'I'm worried about what will become of Luke—no one seems to know who his family is.'

'Do you think they'll take him away?' Jane asked, concern creasing her brow.

'It would be best if they did.'

'Oh no, Miss Maddy, we can't let that happen.'

'Jane, we must try to find them: he should be with his family.'

'But we're his kin now,' she said, quietly but stubbornly. 'That Rose, she left him here with you. You're his kin.'

A sudden angry storm burst within Maddy. 'Jane, you will not speak such nonsense,' she snapped. 'He has a family somewhere and as such he should be returned to his own. I will place an advertisement in the newspaper.'

Maddy ignored Jane's shocked face, refusing to be moved on the matter. It was for the best. Far better for Luke to be with his real family.

Tuesday, 10 April 1832—fine, beautiful weather

It was after lunch by the time Maddy caught up with Daniel, who was with Phil near the kitchen garden. The men had been ploughing a newly cleared field, preparing to plant wheat. Her own morning had been long and arduous after so little sleep; the little she'd had having been disturbed and hardly restful.

'Good morning, Miss Maddy,' Phil greeted her, a wide grin encompassing his ruddy features.

'Good afternoon, Phil,' Maddy said, emphasising the hour.

'Is it that already?' He frowned. 'Well the day don't half get away on one.'

Daniel smiled at Phil, but the look he sent in Maddy's direction was impossible to read.

'I was wondering if I might have a moment?' she asked, not meeting his eyes.

'Right enough,' Phil said, turning to leave.

Maddy watched him go.

'What is it you wish to speak about?'

Maddy turned back to look at him; she opened her mouth to speak, but nothing came out.

'Maddy, what is it?' Daniel's eyes clouded and he stepped closer to her, one hand outstretched.

'It's Luke,' she gasped around the sob caught in her throat.

'Luke? Not this again—'

'No, no.' She shook her head. 'I know you aren't his father,' she hurried to say.

'That's good,' he said, sounding still uncertain.

'I'm worried about him—he hasn't spoken at all since his mother left him here. He just watches us silently. He didn't even speak when his mother was found.'

Daniel didn't respond, just watched her, his scrutiny penetrating the carefully constructed facade she'd barricaded herself behind.

'I am afraid Papa must be Luke's father.' Maddy blinked rapidly to keep the tears at bay. Her throat ached; she'd said the words and there was no retreating from it now. When Daniel took her arm and led her to the seat on the veranda of his hut, she didn't resist.

He spoke, calm now and kind as ever. 'It's possible, of course, but does it really matter? No matter who his father is, it's up to you whether you keep him here or send him away.'

Maddy looked up at him through tear-drenched lashes, her heart a rock in her chest. She longed to ask if it mattered to him but didn't dare.

'You could acknowledge him, or you can just let him stay on at Shelby and say no more about it if you don't want to send him to Hawkins,' Daniel continued.

'I can't,' she said, swallowing hard around the lump in her throat, 'I can't send him away.'

∼✦∽

Tuesday, 1 May 1832—heavy shower at night

'I ain't sleeping with that ill-gotten whelp in the room. I heard all about him.'

Mary Brown arrived on the first of May and immediately the newcomer galled Maddy when she was shown her accommodation. Jane and Luke had already been moved into the room Maddy formerly inhabited.

With lank brown hair and a sallow complexion, Mary had flounced down from the back of the Garricks' wagon with the airs of a lady. Maddy noticed the sly smile she sent Bowman who drove the wagon, before her green eyes gleamed with interest when they turned on Daniel, but his businesslike tone had soon set her straight, and so Mary had turned her attentions to the other men at Shelby.

Jane had been commissioned to show her around and had been doing so when Maddy overheard Mary's statement. She paused, unsure how to deal with the situation. Luke was still at Shelby, sleeping on a pallet in with Jane. He'd drawn Mary's attention as he lurked in the doorway of the room the women would share with the boy.

'He's not a brat,' Jane said, her tone indignant.

'I won't be sharing a room with that scrap—look at him, can hardly tell it's a boy with all that curly hair.'

Maddy stepped up behind her. 'Mary, Luke is staying with us for a time, and I will not have anyone treat him with disrespect.'

Mary spun around, her expression mutinous. Maddy gave her a hard look and after a moment, the woman backed down and nodded. It was obvious she had taken against the boy even before she'd laid eyes on him. Maddy knew gossip was rife between convicts, and there was nothing she could do about it.

'I'm a respectable woman.' Mary paused to cast a disparaging glance over Maddy, her opinion that she didn't consider Maddy to be at all respectable obvious. 'I don't want my name sullied by associating with the likes of him.' Mary continued to mutter about what she'd heard of the boy. Her demeanour was affected, but her speech was rough, and Maddy wondered if she wasn't attempting to portray a loftier position than she was due. The way she simpered around Daniel revealed Mary's intention to pursue a route taken by many female convicts, that of marrying out of her assignment as soon as she could. That it irked Maddy was ridiculous and she knew her jealousy was unfounded, but she couldn't seem to help it when it came to Daniel.

'Jane, move Luke's pallet into my room,' Maddy said, reassuring herself it would only be for a short while: just until she could arrange suitable accommodation for him. 'Mary, I will not permit you to treat Luke badly—if you do, you will be on the first steamer back to Parramatta.'

Mary nodded, but Maddy couldn't help noticing a satisfied smirk cross her face as she turned back to the business of settling herself in.

'Jane, when Mary is finished here, you can take her out to the field and show her how to bring in the herd and separate the calves.' Earlier she'd instructed Jane to show Mary around and give her the rest of the afternoon off, but now Maddy thought they'd be better served by keeping the newcomer busy.

Up until Mary's arrival, Jane and young Joey had been milking the cows with calves. The practice was to lock the calves away from their mothers in the barn overnight, then after milking return them to the fields with the herd to feed as they liked during the day. So far only a third of the herd had calves at foot, and the rest were all in various stages of pregnancy. For the time being the milking and cheese-making were still man-ageable, but once the rest of the cows delivered their calves, they would need at least one more dairy maid. Maddy intended that Jane would remain her companion, and so she would need to send to the Factory for another woman, which meant having more accommodation built to house them.

'I don't know how to milk a cow,' Mary said. 'I am a lady's maid.'

'Well, here you're a milk maid,' said Jane, and her tone brooked no argument.

Eighteen

Wednesday, 2 May 1832—day clear and warm, night and morning cool

'I'm sure the girl is no better than she ought to be.' The voice came from the other side of the drawing room door. The Cragside maid shot her a furtive glance as she began to open the door. Maddy placed a gentle hand on hers to stall her. They stood together, silent in the dimly lit hall of the grand house, waiting to hear any response to the old woman's statement; for there was no doubt Mrs Everette the Elder spoke of her.

'Mother Everette, how can you say that? She's a lovely girl.'

'We came upon her making soap with her convict,' Belle interjected, her tone disapproving.

'I made my own soap when I first came here,' said Mrs Wyndham.

'Hardly a disreputable occupation,' said a voice Maddy thought she recognised.

Were it not for the maid standing beside her, Maddy might have taken flight. She wanted to run away from the room full of

genteel busybodies who waited on the other side of the door. She
didn't belong there. They knew it, and she knew it.

'She'll never find a decent husband if she continues to live like
a convict. The latest is she's taken in a nullius filius.' ·

Bile rose in Maddy's throat: Luke wasn't *nobody's child*, but there
was little to be gained by reacting. Swallowing hard, Maddy nodded to the girl, her face carefully devoid of expression as the maid
pushed open the door and stepped into the room.

'Miss Barker-Trent,' the girl announced and Maddy followed
her in. With her features schooled into a semblance of pleasant
friendliness, Maddy found the room filled with smiling-faced
women. Well, most of them: Belle did not appear to be pleased
to see her, and Mrs Everette the Elder turned to glower over her
shoulder. It made sense that she'd not be happy to see Maddy—
she could hardly continue to gossip about her when she was
present.

'Oh Maddy, do come in. Let me pour you a cup of tea,' Mrs
Everette said with an apologetic smile.

'Thank you, Mrs Everette. Tea would be lovely.'

Mrs Everette the Elder, Mrs Garrick, the younger Mrs Everette and Mrs Wyndham were seated at a round table set with
plates of sandwiches and cakes. Mrs Harpur sat beside Belle on a
chaise situated between French doors leading to the wide veranda;
and Amelia was alone on the opposite side of the room. Maddy
took the cup of tea the young Mrs Everette offered and crossed
to sit beside Amelia, who smiled warmly at her. Amelia might be
flighty but she wasn't a prig.

An awkward silence filled the room until Mrs Wyndham
broke it, shifting slightly in her seat to address Maddy. 'How are
you, Miss Barker-Trent? I've heard you've achieved great things at
Shelby. Your papa would be proud.'

Maddy smiled gratefully at her. 'I am quite well, Mrs Wyndham, and thank you for your kind words.'

'I believe you had a bit of an adventure with a bushranger?' Mrs Harpur said, and Maddy realised she had been the other speaker who'd defended her against Mrs Everette the Elder. Maddy smiled at her gratefully.

'Yes, it was a storm in a teacup,' she said, having no desire to hold the focus in this distinguished little group.

'Oh my,' said Amelia, staring at Maddy, 'how awful. Were you terrified?'

'I was, but he got away with little. And no one was harmed.'

'I heard your horse was stolen.' Belle stared malevolently at Maddy across the room. What had she done to the girl to incite such dislike?

'Indeed. However, the girths weren't tightened properly and so my horse managed to rid himself of the bandit and was returned to me, unharmed.'

'Very fortunate.' Mrs Garrick smiled and continued, 'As you know, Maddy, we're gathering today to discuss the ball. The river bank where we'd intended to hold the event has been flooded and it is likely that it won't be suitable for some time, so we are discussing options for a change of venue.'

'I thought it had been decided to pare it back and hold it here,' Mrs Everette the Elder said tartly.

'We mustn't be hasty, as there's been a great many looking forward to such an event in the district. I've heard even the Mudies and Lanarchs of Castle Forbes intend to come,' said the younger Mrs Everette. She turned to Mrs Wyndham and said, 'George says John and Emily Lanarch's new house is coming along well.'

'All the more reason to maintain a certain level of society,' Mrs Everette the Elder interjected before Mrs Wyndham could respond.

'But what of the free settlers in the region? Aren't they to be invited?' Maddy blurted impulsively. She'd met so few people from the valley and had anticipated getting to know more of her neighbours. Biting down on the words that rushed to her lips, Maddy knew it wasn't her place to have an opinion.

'I agree,' Mrs Wyndham said, her expression serious. 'Many of the smaller holdings have suffered greatly with the drought and then floods. I think the event must be open to all, for they have suffered far more than we.'

'Surely they should hold their own dance?' said Belle, lifting her chin defiantly.

'Oh, Belle, don't be so stuffy. There are so many decent folk in the area, and I think they should all be welcomed,' said Mrs Everette the Younger.

Maddy was relieved to see Mrs Wyndham and Mrs Everette were in favour of including all the people in the valley. She looked at Mrs Garrick, wondering on which side of the battle she would sit.

'There's a good flat piece of ground at Oswald that is on higher ground than the site originally chosen at Cragside,' Mrs Harpur chimed in.

'Wonderful: it's much better if we can include the entire community. As Mrs Wyndham said, there are many who have had a difficult few years, and a party for everyone would no doubt bolster their spirits,' Mrs Garrick said, declaring her allegiance. Maddy could have hugged her. Suddenly she was pleased she hadn't run away.

With the matter settled, and only Mrs Everette the Elder and Belle displeased, the plans for the ball continued. A new date for mid-May was chosen, and Maddy found herself swept up in the excitement of the coming social event. Mrs Wyndham, Mrs Garrick and Mrs Harpur all promised to discuss the building of a dance platform on the river flat at Oswald with their husbands, and they were certain labour would be supplied by all the nearby properties willingly.

'I'm certain Mr Coulter and our workers would be happy to contribute,' Maddy said.

'Very good. I shall tell Alex to speak to Daniel about a date.' Mrs Garrick glowed with excitement.

'How are you, Maddy?' Amelia asked quietly.

Maddy smiled genuinely at her. 'I am well, truly.'

'I had a letter from Mr Hobson,' Amelia said, her voice low so as not to be overheard.

'How is Mr Coulter?' Belle asked before Maddy could respond to Amelia.

Maddy turned to Belle. Schooling her features, she refused to respond to her goading. 'He is well enough.'

'He is very handsome. I do envy you. Though I've no doubt you shall have your pick of men as soon as your time of mourning is finished.'

Maddy's body jerked involuntarily at her words; why would she say such a thing? 'I am not interested in my pick of anything beyond good seed and livestock,' Maddy said a little more loudly than she'd intended.

A hush fell over the previously chatting group as everyone's attention turned to her. She stared down at her clenched hands as heat rushed to her cheeks. 'I have no intention of marrying any-one. I am committed to building Shelby into the farm and home my mama and papa planned.'

'Well, I never!' Mrs Everette the Elder spat the words into the intervening silence.

Maddy looked up at the woman's usually benign features, now twisted with maliciousness.

'A decent gentleman would not wish to sully his reputation with the likes of you—an upstart who lives and works alongside criminals. I've heard you have a stray whelp living with you—in your own bedroom no less.'

A series of gasps and Mrs Catherine Everette's reproachful 'Mother-in-law!' affected the old woman not at all.

Maddy gaped at her for a moment. How the old woman knew so much about the goings-on at Shelby she had no idea, but indignation swept through her. She slowly rose to her feet and stared down the horrid termagant. She'd had enough of her bullying.

'I beg your pardon, Mrs Everette.' Maddy turned her gaze to the younger Mrs Everette, whom she considered to be the host of the party, if it could be called that. 'I think I should leave now, but I thank you for the tea.' Maddy nodded to the other women, not sparing a glance for either Belle or Mrs Everette the Elder. 'Good day.'

'Wait, Maddy, please don't leave, I'm sure Mother Everette meant no censure,' Mrs Everette the Younger said, her expression imploring.

'With respect, Mrs Everette, I'm quite certain she did. And so I shall remove my upstart self from her company.' Maddy straightened her skirts with shaking hands and looked once more at her host. 'I apologise for any discomfort I've caused you. Please send word when the work is to be done for the dance floor and I'll send the promised labour. And if there's anything else I can contribute, do let me know. But I shall not inflict my company on those who find it distasteful.' Maddy glared at the back of Mrs Everette the Elder's head. And with that, she exited the room.

She'd barely made it out the door when she came across the maid, who blinked owlishly at her. Maddy knew she'd been listening at the door again. She sent the girl to find her bonnet and cloak and was still waiting when Mrs Garrick and Mrs Everette joined her in the hall.

'Please, Maddy, don't feel you have to leave.' Mrs Everette looked and sounded abashed.

'Maddy, please, we do not consider you to be anything but a lovely young lady with a very kind heart,' Mrs Garrick said.

'My mother-in-law is a nasty woman with little else to do but criticise anyone and everyone.'

Her obvious displeasure with her relation's behaviour softened Maddy's heart, and her spine, held ramrod straight, relaxed.

'Thank you, dear Mrs Everette,'—Maddy turned from one face to the other—'both of you. But I have no wish to be where I am not welcome.' It was hardly a new thing to be an outcast. Hadn't it been so her entire life? She'd never felt as if she fit in anywhere, not even with her own family; for most of her life it had been only Grandpapa who'd made her feel special. She'd been a fool to think it would be any different in the colony.

'But you are welcome—it is Mrs Everette the Elder who is not,' Mrs Garrick said, then gasped and looked at Mrs Everette. 'Oh, Catherine, I do apologise.'

'Please, Susannah, there is no apology required, forgive me, but the woman is a heartless old termagant, and I fear I don't know how my dear Douglass could possibly be related to her.'

A gasp of laughter bubbled within Maddy, and she saw Mrs Garrick's eyes also sparkle with humour.

'I beg you, please don't allow her to drive you away,' Mrs Everette said, her tone and expression sincere.

'Thank you, but truly, I must be on my way. There's much to be done at Shelby, and as yet I find myself unable to leave the running of the place to Mr Coulter entirely. He does a magnificent job, but he can't be everywhere at once.' And she preferred the company of convicts to some of those women, though she restrained herself from saying so.

'Maddy, you must believe us when we tell you that you are doing a tremendous thing. Alex tells me Shelby is coming along nicely. There are a great many of us who admire you. Don't let the opinion of a few spoil the ball for you.'

'Yes,' Mrs Everette said, her eyes shining, 'and with the postponement, you shall be out of mourning and will be able to wear a pretty gown.'

'You shall accompany me to Sydney, where we can have new gowns made,' Mrs Garrick announced. Maddy hesitated; she couldn't leave Shelby for so long.

'You are so terribly kind, but I have a suitable gown brought with me from England.' Mama was certain there would be some form of society to be found in the colony and had spared no expense on the walking, tea and evening gowns she had commissioned to wear when not in work gowns. Maddy's mind clouded with the memory of Mama's planning. How could she have forgotten how happy they'd been when all her mother's attention had been focused on Maddy?

'Very good, and Maddy?' Mrs Garrick paused, and Maddy saw her face was full of compassion. She bit her lip against a rush of threatening tears. 'Please don't take any notice of what some folk say. Those of us who've lived here a little longer realise what great advances you have achieved in the short time you have been here.'

'Thank you, Mrs Garrick, it means a great deal to hear you say that. And Mrs Everette, please don't concern yourself.' Maddy smiled reassuringly at both women. 'You both have only made me feel welcome. Now, I will find my horse and be away.'

Nineteen

Friday, 4 May 1832—sunny and mild

'Miss Maddy, Mary still won't milk the cows!' Jane's tone brimmed with frustration.

'Well, it's the only thing she freely admitted being unable to do,' Maddy said, for Mary had promised all manner of skills, and so far no effective work had been forthcoming. Her sewing was dreadful; her cooking, if possible, was worse; and when asked to clean anything, she did so with such petulance and bad grace that Maddy was more and more inclined to send her back to Parramatta.

'Where is she?' She placed her cup of tea in the saucer and rose. The accounts would have to wait a little longer.

'I left her at the bails—she's still trying to pull the milk from poor Petal.'

Jane had named each of the herd, and one particularly calm beast sported a small patch of white on her forehead which vaguely resembled a flower.

'I don't know what to do with her,' Maddy said as she crossed the yard, 'but she will have to learn how to milk or go back to Sydney.'

'Aye, miss, but I don't think she can do much of anything. Beyond lying: she's mighty good at that.'

Maddy felt sorry for Jane, as she was almost invariably the one to complete Mary's leftover chores. Mary was supposed to alleviate Jane's workload, not increase it.

'I'll deal with her, and you go back and get on with your own chores,' Maddy said, though she was not entirely confident of her own ability to keep Mary at one task.

'Yes, miss,' Jane said, and she left Maddy with the milk maid who wouldn't milk.

The cow was still in the newly built timber milking bail, a small rectangular pen constructed to closely surround the cow, with a feed trough at one end and a chain across the back to stop it backing out until the milking was done. Maddy saw the bucket was kicked over, which made no difference, as Mary had barely squeezed a drop of milk from the ill-treated beast. She looked around for the problematic maid, who was nowhere to be seen.

Maddy had a reasonably good idea as to Mary's whereabouts and, ignoring the bellowing of the calf that was waiting to rejoin its mother, headed for the barracks. As she approached, Maddy could hear the woman's voice and knew Mary would be chatting with one or other of the men. This time it was Joseph O'Brien who had drawn Mary's eye, and she was leaning against the door jamb of the barracks, laughing coquettishly at something the large broad-faced man had said. Joseph was a gentle giant with a soft Irish accent and an unassuming manner, but Maddy didn't believe he was so smitten as to do Mary's chores for her.

'Mary!'

Mary jumped and spun about to face her mistress. Joseph grinned and quickly withdrew into the barracks.

'What are you doing here?' Maddy asked, making no effort to hide her annoyance.

'I was just asking Joe to help me milk the cow, miss,' she said sulkily.

'Get yourself back to the poor creature you've left standing in the bails and milk it,' Maddy said, fuming at Mary's indolence. Maddy knew she'd been spoiled by the exceptional behaviour of the other convicts assigned to Shelby, but she was not going to have this woman take advantage.

'I tried, miss, but I couldn't get any milk from her. I told you I don't know how.'

'Then you shall just have to learn.' Maddy followed the reluctant milk maid back to the bails, where Petal, having finished the measure of grain and responding to the plaintive bellowing of her calf, was pushing and shoving in an effort to escape her confines, causing the entire structure to wobble alarmingly. Mary halted a few yards from the cow and with an insolent glower at Maddy retrieved the upturned bucket, snatched up the milking stool and positioned it beside the cow; she sat down ready to milk. With jerky movements, Mary began tugging and pulling at the teats. Her rough treatment produced a kick but not a drop of milk. It hardly bumped the woman's shin, but it sent her scuttling backwards away from the flashing hoof.

'Give her some more grain and start again,' Maddy told her, having more sympathy for the cow than the woman. It had only been a glancing blow and had barely connected.

'I ain't touching that savage animal!'

'Unless you wish to return to the Parramatta Factory, that is exactly what you will be doing.'

'What's going on here?' Phil's voice came from behind her. Relieved to have someone to show the useless woman how to milk, Maddy was about to ask him when Mary launched into a woeful lament.

'Oh, Mr Phil, it's this darn cow. I do not know what to do with it, it's too bad, sir. I've tried and tried, but it won't let me milk it at all. It kicked me and all, even kicked over the milk.' The last said with a definite tremble. Maddy gaped at her, dumbfounded by the maid's dramatic performance.

'Why, old Petal here is no trouble at all to milk. Are you, me darlin'?' Phil approached the cow and gave her an affection-ate scratch. He straightened the stool and bucket, sat down and, resting the top of his head against the cow's flank, began to strip milk quickly and easily; the bucket was soon half full of steaming white milk.

'Excuse me, Phil, but Mary needs to learn to milk the cows: you have more than enough to do, and that is why she's here.'

'Oh aye, miss, I don't mind.' He continued with the chore, the milk foaming with bubbles due to the speed with which he milked. 'There's plenty more cows to milk, so Mary can do the next one.'

'I will never be able to do it—I'm afeared of the beasts. And they don't like me.'

'It's Mary's job to milk the cows, and if she is not up to the task, then she will have to go back to Parramatta, and someone more suitable found.'

He rose from the stool, swiftly shifting the pail of milk out of striking range of Petal's hooves, and turned to Mary, who was leaning against a nearby tree. 'Well then, Mary, there's nothing else for it, you will have to learn to milk. You won't get a better place to work than here at Shelby: believe me, I know.'

'But I can't, they hate me,' she whined.

'Nonsense,' Maddy snapped, 'you will learn to milk. Every chore you're given you have managed to worm out of, and enough is enough. Milk or leave.'

Phil unchained the cow and allowed it to back out; without a word, he ushered in the next, tipped some grain into the trough and stepped back.

'Oh, very well then.'

Mary took her place on the stool and began to milk in earnest. Maddy stared in amazement, and Phil gaped at her. While not as fast as he, Mary managed the task with remarkable success and Maddy wondered if all her other failures had been similarly intended to get her out of working at all. The woman put more effort into avoiding work than was required to actually do it. Well, no more. Maddy had her measure, and any further attempt from Mary to get out of her chores would see her sent packing.

'Excellent, Mary. Now when you finish the milking, you can help Jane with the washing.'

'Actually, I had—' she began, looking up at Maddy.

'That was not a suggestion.'

She sighed heavily and with a reluctant 'Yes, miss,' returned to the job of milking but muttered something unrepeatable about hating cows.

Leaving Mary with her newly discovered ability, Phil and Maddy walked across the yard to the hitching rail. Charlie had tied the big grey draught horse there, still harnessed to the dray, after unloading the newly cut shingles. Maddy ran a hand along Pepper's shoulder, and the enormous beast turned his head and nickered a gentle acknowledgement of her caress.

Daniel and Lester stood outside Daniel's hut, and both turned towards them at the yards. Lester was his usual silent self and managed to avoid meeting her eye. She reminded herself his only fault was being surly, and, when weighed against his skill as a stonemason, it was no valid reason to accuse him of any wrongdoing, nor to send him away.

Both men stepped away from the small porch and headed towards Phil and Maddy. Lester loosed the horse, mumbling something incomprehensible that she took to be a greeting. Maddy nodded and murmured a response, watching him as he led Pepper across the yard to unharness the dray.

'Miss Barker-Trent,' Daniel greeted her, his expression serious.

'Mr Coulter.' Maddy's tone matched his for formality, and she wondered what the matter could be.

'If I could have a word,' he said, his eyes were dark, and a shiver of apprehension ran up her spine.

'Of course.' She glanced at Phil.

'Right, well I'll head down to the fields and check on the progress of the boys then, shall I?' Phil said, his glance shifting first to Daniel and then to Maddy. His deference to Daniel momentarily annoyed her, then she drew in a calming breath. She'd been on edge since the flood. She could trust these men.

'Yes, thanks, Phil.'

Phil nodded and with what looked to Maddy like a relieved glance at Daniel made good his escape.

'What is it?'

'Shall we sit for a moment?' He indicated the bench seat on the porch. What could he wish to discuss that required her to be seated?

'Certainly.'

They crossed and sat down, with each of them at the furthest reaches of the long bench—easily enough space in between for a third person to sit.

'Well,' he began, and uncertainty hung on the word. Maddy turned her head to look at him. He stared across the yard, and she took advantage of their proximity to examine his profile: the fringe of sweat-soaked hair stuck to his forehead, and lashes long enough for any girl to covet; his nose was straight, but his usually full lips were pressed into a thin line, and his strong jaw was tense. Whatever could it be?

'Mr Coulter, tell me what the matter is?'

'It's Lester,' he began, still not looking at her.

What had Lester done? 'I saw you speaking to him—is there a problem?'

'Not a problem, exactly,' he said, finally his focus fixed on her.

'Then what, *exactly*?' she murmured, feeling very warm. Suddenly the conversation didn't feel like it was about Lester at all. She twisted the fabric of her gown between her fingers.

Daniel frowned. 'He has served four years of his seven-year sentence and, if you grant it, he could have his ticket of leave.'

Maddy breathed a sigh of relief; she'd been afraid he was going to tell her he wanted to leave Shelby.

Daniel continued. 'He would have to stay in the colony, but he would essentially be a free man.'

'But what about the house?' Panic rose in Maddy like a wave: she knew it was selfish, but the house at Shelby was everything. Building the house was imperative. 'Do I have to grant this ticket of leave?'

Daniel frowned and she knew immediately that she'd made a faux pas; she cringed inwardly at her selfishness but was unable to withstand the panic that gripped her.

'It's common to grant a ticket of leave to convicts who've been well behaved.' His tone was level, but she knew she'd disappointed him.

'I see,' Maddy said, her stomach sinking; Shelby would never be built.

'You could pay Lester to stay on and build the house,' he said, identifying her reluctance. 'Perhaps he'd be a more willing worker knowing you respected him enough to grant him his freedom.'

When Maddy remained silent, Daniel continued, 'It's obvious you don't like the man, but I don't understand what he's done.'

'He helped the bushranger,' Maddy reminded him, her voice pitched a little too high, 'and he doesn't try to hide his dislike of me.'

'He doesn't like anyone,' Daniel said with a sigh. 'Try to understand his situation. He was a master mason in England, while here he is less than nothing.'

'He's a criminal,' Maddy snapped. 'Why do you persist on defending him?'

'He was transported for fishing in an estate river,' Daniel spoke quietly. 'He was an artisan sought for his skill and expertise and was sent to the far side of the globe for something he and his family had done for centuries. He caught a fish to fill his pot. He's hardly a hardened criminal. He resents being in the colony, that is all. He is a hard worker, and I think you will get more from him if you grant the ticket of leave—certainly more than if you keep him here by force. I don't know why you've taken such a dislike to him.'

She didn't know how to explain how she felt about Lester. In light of Daniel's words, she was beginning to wonder if she'd misjudged him? Had she allowed Molly Hunt's suspicions to colour her opinion? Probably, she conceded. Daniel was right: other than Lester having helped the bushranger, he hadn't done anything untoward.

'Many convicts granted their ticket of leave are happy to stay on as paid workers,' he said when she didn't respond.

'I will give it some thought.' Was he right? Would Lester be willing to stay on at Shelby if she did as Daniel suggested?

'If he's being paid to build the house, you will have someone dedicated to that task alone. We can send for a replacement for the farm work, and the house will become his priority,' Daniel said, and Maddy rose; it was her turn to scan the far horizon.

She exhaled. 'As I said, I will think about it.'

Twenty

Monday, 7 May 1832—warm and sunny

Daniel didn't bring up the topic of Lester's freedom again for a few days, though Maddy thought of little else. Once she'd have talked through her fears and the ramifications of granting the ticket of leave with Daniel, but ever since he'd mentioned the matter, she felt awkward around him. She knew it was selfish, but fear made her indecisive and reluctant to reveal it to Daniel.

Instead she decided to ride to Tillington and discuss it with Mr Garrick. After all, she reminded herself, Mr Garrick had far more experience with convicts than either she or Daniel did, and she could visit with Mrs Garrick and find out what was happening around the valley. Her life on Shelby was busy, and they rarely had visitors as they were a little out of the way for passers-by, and without suitable accommodations available, most travellers stopped instead at Oswald, Cragside, Tillington, and even Dalwood.

Maddy was in no hurry and so allowed her horse to walk along the track while she took the opportunity to examine the progress of the fields the men were clearing. The paddock, previously left untouched, with its proximity to the river was to be sown with tobacco, and the fields on higher land would be good for grazing and had access for watering from the boundary creek.

The running and development of Shelby was a constant juggle in which Maddy had to decide between progress and facilities. If she were to employ free men she would have to pay them, but were she to request more convicts, she would need to build more accommodation, which would take men away from the fields when either planting or tending of crops and livestock took precedence. Not for the first time Maddy wondered if she'd been mad when she'd decided to take on such a mammoth task. Attempting to build a successful estate in a land she knew nothing about, not to mention having absolutely no experience or knowledge of farming at all, was ludicrous. Such an endeavour would have been doomed were it not for the advice and efforts of Daniel, Phil, Mr Garrick and Mr Wyndham. Without their help, and that of Mrs Garrick in regards to running the domestic side of things, she'd have been forced to sell Shelby and return to England defeated.

As she rode towards the boundary, Maddy looked over the escarpment at the two long fields bordering the river: a long stretch of flat ground perfect for cultivation. Her heart swelled with a bittersweet satisfaction as she examined all they'd accomplished. One of the fields directly below was sown with tobacco, and the other wheat. Even from a distance she identified Joey, Charlie, Patrick and Michael chipping weeds from between the tobacco plants. Maddy smiled: Shelby was a hive of activity, and if progress at times seemed slow, today it was visible. The arrival of an additional four men had gone a long way to increasing the speed at which the farm was beginning to take shape. Having produced several crops that would be sent to Sydney, and with the dairy herd for cheese-making, and a growing flock of sheep, there was no doubt that in the coming year they might see a small profit rather than just an endless outpouring of funds spent on the estate's establishment.

Maddy pulled Red to a halt and turned him so she could take it all in. She was proud of their accomplishments. They'd all worked so hard—even Lester, she had to admit.

A movement caught her eye as a figure approached the gate where the dray stood; the draught horses were still harnessed with nosebags attached, and they chewed contentedly whilst waiting for the next trip up the hill to the yard. Maddy frowned, certain it was Mary. The maid must have dropped her chores and set off almost as soon as Maddy left the farmyard, taking the foot-path down the steep hillside rather than the easier track along the river bank. What was she doing? For a moment Maddy considered going back to the yard to ask Jane what had happened. She exhaled and shook her head. What was the point? Mary would no doubt be back at the house by the time Maddy reached the fields, but she determined she would investigate the matter on her return.

She watched the men labouring and, as far as she could see, none of them had noticed Mary's arrival. The maid seemed to hesitate by the side of the dray, peering over towards the men and ducking down to avoid being seen. She stayed there for a few moments before hurrying away; she quickly disappeared back into the line of trees. Maddy breathed a sigh of relief. Mary had prob-ably been looking for Joseph, in whom it seemed she had taken a special interest. She could only hope Mary was going back to her chores and would not continue searching for the big Irishman to do it for her; perhaps it would be best to just let the matter go. The constant need to be on the woman's back was exhausting. She would speak to Jane, find out what Mary had been up to. With a little too much force Maddy turned Red's head, dug her heels into his flanks and cantered towards Tillington.

Tida and her mother were in the courtyard when she arrived. Tida only allowed Maddy to go and see Mr Garrick when she'd promised to visit with her as soon as their business was done. She found Mr Garrick in his office, accepted a small measure of sherry and sat down opposite him.

'To what do I owe the pleasure, my dear?' Mr Garrick said.

'Mr Coulter has mentioned that George Lester is eligible for a ticket of leave.'

'Indeed.' Mr Garrick nodded, but when he added nothing further, she began to feel uneasy.

'I fear that if I grant him his leave, I should be left without a stonemason, and I am afraid the house will never be built,' Maddy blurted, shamed by her own selfishness but determined to be honest.

'I understand why you would feel like that. Perhaps you could ask Mr Lester what he intends to do should you grant the ticket of leave.'

Of course, that was what she should have done immediately. But again Maddy hesitated. 'Isn't it better that I should give the matter due consideration, even make a decision before I speak to him?'

'Why do you think that?' His gaze bored into her, and Maddy felt uncomfortable beneath the scrutiny.

'Because if I do grant it, then I have no way to make him stay and build the house.' The words rushed from her and heat flooded her cheeks.

'The house will be built, Maddy,' he said, his expression sympathetic.

She offered him an embarrassed smile; how she wished she could believe it.

When Maddy said nothing, he continued, 'You could assign one of the men to work with him, as his apprentice, so to speak.'

An idea sparked. 'Perhaps if I promised to give one of the boys to him as an apprentice, if they build the house, he could then take him on as assigned labour, having trained him without the expense of paying him while he is learning.' Maddy began to feel excited as the plan took shape.

'Maddy, you can't just pass assigned labour to another; it has to be done through the governor.'

'I'm certain something could be arranged. Lester would have an assistant and could train him while building Shelby.'

'You would need to replace two convicts for the farm,' he reminded her.

'Yes, and to do so, I'd need to extend the barracks. And we're only just managing to feed ourselves.'

'It's up to you, Maddy. While you need to keep the farm going, you also do need to build yourself suitable accommodation. You can't continue to live with the convicts long term.'

Though Maddy knew he was right she bristled at his words, certain it was due to Belle and the old Everette woman's comments that anyone else even gave her living arrangements a thought.

With Mr Garrick's words running loops around in her head Maddy thanked him and made her way across the courtyard to the main house.

'Oh, Miss Maddy,' Tida said when she saw her enter the hall, 'whatever has taken you so long?' The child stood in the open doorway of the parlour, hands on hips, feet planted wide, appearing more like a miniature Cookie than the young lady she was supposed to be.

'Good day, Miss Garrick,' Maddy responded. 'Please accept my humblest apologies—I was caught up discussing business.'

'Oh Maddy, don't be silly.' Tida grinned and relaxed her stance. 'But do hurry: Mama said we have to wait for you before we can have tea, and I'm starving.' She turned back into the room. 'Mama, Maddy is here, so can we have the cake?'

'Tida, please, calm yourself. Let poor Maddy inside.' As usual, Mrs Susannah Garrick's voice was tinged with amusement at her daughter's forthright manner despite the reprimand.

'Good day, Mrs Garrick,' Maddy greeted her and was surprised to see Mrs Wyndham seated at the table opposite her. 'Oh, Mrs Wyndham, I'd not realised you were here.'

'It's lovely to see you,' Mrs Wyndham said, her dark eyes were warm and as welcoming as Mrs Garrick's.

'Please come and sit,' Mrs Garrick said, indicating the vacant seat to her right. Tida walked around the table and climbed up onto the other empty chair.

'I hope you didn't wait for me.' Maddy took the seat suggested and watched Mrs Garrick pour tea into the remaining cup. On a crystal stand was a layered cream and strawberry sponge cake and Maddy could see why poor Tida had been practically salivating.

'Not at all,' Mrs Wyndham reassured her, 'I have only now arrived myself.'

'Forgive my intrusion.' Maddy was conscious of her visit being unplanned and wondered if she should make her excuses and leave.

'Not a bit of it,' Mrs Garrick said. 'We were just having a chat and Tida wanted to be included. She's quite grown up now you see.' She turned an indulgent smile in her daughter's direction;

the minx was grinning happily, but not taking her attention from the cake.

'Then I appreciate the invitation and am honoured to be able to join you.'

The conversation was easy and suitable to a small girl's company as they sipped tea and each indulged in a large wedge of sponge cake. Mrs Garrick instructed Tida on the niceties of afternoon tea and, before Maddy knew it, an hour had passed. The large mantel clock struck three and she reluctantly acknowledged it was past time to head back to Shelby.

'Thank you for the tea, but I'd best be on my way.'

Mrs Wyndham placed her cup in the matching saucer and nodded. 'Yes, I too must be going. Perhaps we could travel part of the way together?' she said, looking at Maddy.

Maddy glanced at Mrs Garrick and then nodded. 'Of course, that would be delightful.'

Maddy had a feeling this wasn't as spontaneous an offer as the women hoped it would appear. She wondered what Mrs Wyndham wished to speak to her about and why she chose not to mention it in front of Mrs Garrick.

'Yes, do,' Mrs Garrick said, and Maddy saw a glance pass between them.

'Lovely,' she agreed, forcing a smile. They said their goodbyes and headed outside.

Within a few minutes, Mrs Wyndham's buggy and her horse were brought around by a stable boy.

'Could you tie Miss Barker-Trent's horse to the tailboard, please?' Mrs Wyndham asked the lad. Right, Maddy thought, I am to ride with Mrs Wyndham in the buggy.

Maddy offered no protest but climbed up beside her. When she was settled, Mrs Wyndham slapped the reins on the horse's rump and with a 'gee up' they set off for the road.

'Thank you for the ride,' Maddy said when they'd ridden beyond the Tillington boundary onto the North Road and Mrs Wyndham hadn't yet spoken.

'You are most welcome. I thought it might be a good opportunity to speak to you in private.'

Maddy pushed down the wariness that the words caused and waited for her to continue.

'Maddy, I hope you understand that what I have to say has no bearing on my own opinion of the situation.'

Maddy eased away from her a little but said nothing.

'There's been much discussion of your living arrangements.'

Maddy could imagine.

'I understand why you are keeping the boy at Shelby, but it's probably not in your best interests long term.'

Maddy watched the rolling rump of the horse in the shafts, praying Mrs Wyndham didn't know anything at all.

'Perhaps the boy would be best served if you sent him to Reverend Hawkins,' Mrs Wyndham said. Though her voice was gentle and her tone soft, it took all Maddy's strength of will to stop from blurting out that Luke was, in all likelihood, her brother; and in that moment, she knew she could never send Luke away.

'Of course I don't want to offend you,' Mrs Wyndham said hurriedly.

The horse took several strides before Maddy was able to respond. 'I know you don't, and while I see your point, I feel it would be best for the child if he stayed at Shelby.' Her words were stiff and awkward.

'I've no doubt of that, but what of your own reputation?'

'Mrs Wyndham, I am convinced you have my best interests at heart, but I was not raised to follow the accepted conventions. My mama forfeited a life in society to marry beneath her, and Papa sold a lucrative business to pursue his dream of a new life in the colony. I travelled alone to join him here and, against advice, have stayed and am well on the way to fulfilling their dream. I am no stranger to criticism and censure, and I don't intend to start worrying about what anyone else thinks now.'

'Of course, my dear, but surely you have dreams of your own?'

Maddy's chin wobbled and the horizon grew blurry.

'I meant only to offer a little advice. I respect your decision to keep him. I, and many others, admire what you have done in such a short time. I didn't know your mother, but I know your papa would be incredibly proud of all you have achieved. And'—she cleared her throat—'your kindness to a poor motherless boy.'

Maddy nodded: if only she could truly be assured of that. She bit down on her trembling lip until she was confident she could speak without weeping. 'Thank you.'

'You must follow your own instincts, for they have served you well so far.' After a long moment of silence, she continued, 'Perhaps if you could attend a Sunday service occasionally?'

'Perhaps,' Maddy said, reluctant to agree. She happily sent the staff of Shelby to whichever property was holding the services, and if the weather was inclement, Daniel did the reading and she attended. But Maddy was not a church goer and didn't think it likely she would change in the foreseeable future.

As they turned onto Shelby land, Maddy glanced down towards the fields on the river flats and saw the small figures of Wonnarua children, and with them was Luke, running and laughing as they played in the shallows. Even from a distance she could see his smile. Could he ever be so happy with her?

'And you could try to wear a bonnet, for I fear your complexion is growing almost as dark as the faces of the men who work out in the sun all day,' Mrs Wyndham said, dragging Maddy's attention away from the children playing below.

Maddy lifted a hand to her bare head and groaned: she'd left her bonnet behind again.

Mrs Wyndham dropped Maddy off at the yard, and with a kindly goodbye, she drove her buggy back out along the road. When she was out of sight, Maddy led her horse to the rail to be unsaddled and saw Lester approaching from the barn. Maddy sighed: why did it have to be Lester?

'You want I should sort the horse, miss?' he asked.

'Yes, thank you.' Maddy wondered fleetingly if she should speak to him about the ticket of leave. Before she could address the matter the sound of Mary's lilting laughter came from the direction of the barracks. Maddy glanced at Lester, who lifted an ironic brow, and she couldn't help smiling. Lester's lips twitched, and not for the first time Maddy wondered if she'd had the man wrong all along.

'Before you let him go, could you ride down and get Luke: he's playing with the Wonnarua children, and it's getting late.'

'Yes, miss,' Lester said, but his expression had lightened somewhat at the unexpected privilege.

Twenty-One

Thursday, 10 May 1832—fresh and clear skies

The days preceding the ball were dry with warm breezes that cleared the air and freshened the mind. Preparations for the coming event were in full swing. The Oswald field where the ball was to be held was well trodden by busy feet as folk from all over the valley worked together to construct the temporary dance floor, set up a large marquee, lay out trestle tables, and pull logs into a large semi-circle to provide seating for the entire community.

'Oh, Miss Maddy, it's going to be so grand,' Jane said, watching as lanterns were strung from branches and tall torches were placed around the perimeter of the tent.

Maddy returned her grin; it was indeed going to be beautiful when the riverside field was full of light and revellers. She did a slow pirouette to take in the activity happening around them. Daniel and Mr Garrick were busy with the tables, laughing at something young Edwin said. Daniel clapped the lad on the shoulder, and she realised she'd not seen Luke for a while. He'd travelled down on the back of the dray with Phil, Jane and her, the three of them perched atop Shelby's contribution of materials; the lengths of sawn planks were intended for the extension of the barracks and would be used thus when the dance floor was dismantled. Maddy scanned the area but Luke was nowhere to be seen. Jane saw her frown and, realising who Maddy was looking for, without uttering a word began to search.

'Luke?' Jane called, drawing the attention of men who were scything the grass near the river.

'Is something wrong, lass?' one of the burly men asked her, as he and another abandoned the chore and crossed to inquire.

'Yes, I'm looking for a small boy—his name is Luke?' Maddy told them, as she picked up her skirts and hurried to the dray to peer into the back.

'What does the lad look like?' the second man asked. A murmur ran through those working nearby and several more folk stopped what they were doing to join the search.

'He has dark gold curly hair,' Jane said.

'He is Mrs McMahon's son,' Maddy said.

The men who'd come to assist froze in place. The larger man's mouth twisted.

'Oh,' he said and turned away. 'It's the McMahon whelp,' he said to the men gathered, who all looked suddenly uncomfortable.

Maddy stilled and rotating slowly to look him in the eyes replied, 'He is a little boy.'

Beth, the maid from Tillington, hurried down the slope, 'Miss Barker-Trent, is Miss Tilda and young Edwin down here? We're about to go back to Tillington and I can't find them anywhere.' The men who'd been reluctant to help search for Luke were suddenly all action. Maddy pushed aside her outrage and walked towards the thick rushes along the water's edge, calling all the children's names as she went.

'Here they are, Miss Maddy,' Jane said, dragging first Tida and then Luke from the reeds. Tida stood wide-eyed and woebegone

beside Jane. Relief surged through her, but before Maddy reached
the muddy pair, Beth the Tillington maid raced past her, grabbed
Tida by the arm and demanded to know where Edwin was. Wide-
eyed, Tida told her he wasn't with them. Beth looked around as if
to verify the little girl's information and before Maddy could inform
her she'd seen Edwin with Daniel earlier, she had marched her
away, accompanied by a blistering barrage for playing so close to the
river and with *that* child. It took every bit of Maddy's self-control
not to demand an apology of Beth; she'd always liked the girl, but
resentment and hurt rose in her now like bile. Forcing down her
ire, she turned her attention back to Luke: his feet were bare and
his legs muddy to the knees. What had he done with his boots?
Keeping Luke shod was proving harder than getting him to speak.

'Ah, you've found him,' Daniel said, appearing beside Maddy.
He smiled at the men. 'Thank you for your help. As you've
probably heard, the lad's mother died in the flood and Miss
Barker-Trent has kindly taken him in.'

'I see,' one of the men said, and with a polite nod he turned
away.

She noticed the meaningful glance he sent to his companion,
who said, 'Well, glad they're unharmed.'

The men returned to their work and Maddy hurried across the
mown field to where Jane was scrubbing at Luke's feet and chastis-
ing him for losing his boots.

'Luke, you must not wander off or play so close to the river,'
she told him, her voice far harsher than she'd intended. A cold
shiver ran along Maddy's spine at the thought of what could
have happened to the two small children. Luke stared impassively
at her.

'Miss Barker-Trent, can I have a moment?' Daniel asked.

Still feeling shaky, Maddy turned distractedly in his direction. Daniel walked a few yards away from everyone else and she
followed.

'Yes?' she said as he halted near a small scrubby bush that looked like it should be best served if someone tugged it up by the roots.

'I think you should consider leaving Luke at home tonight; his presence won't be welcome, and it will only serve to upset some of the people you'd be better off having on your side.'

Maddy frowned at him. 'What are you talking about?'

He sighed and she could see he thought she was simply being difficult.

'Maddy,'—he looked into her eyes, his own dark with concern— 'surely you must realise what people will say?'

'I don't care what people say.' Maddy lifted her chin.

'Maybe you don't care for yourself, but what about the others, what about Luke?'

'How can what people think, or even say, about him make the slightest difference to him?'

He opened his mouth, then as if he thought better of what he'd been going to say closed it again.

'Mr Coulter, please tell me straight. What are you trying to say?'

'Oh, Mr Coulter, Maddy, I'm so glad you're here.'

They turned to see Amelia Everette hurrying towards them, a small parasol held aloft, presumably to keep the sun from her milky white skin. Maddy realised she'd left her bonnet on the seat of the dray once again. Oh well, if she was tanned, so be it. She hated wearing hats anyway.

She saw Phil, Jane and Luke were all on the dray and about to head back to Shelby.

'I must go,' Maddy said to Daniel as Amelia reached them.

'Good day, Miss Everette,' he said to Amelia, ignoring Maddy.

Maddy saw that Phil was looking around and waved to indicate to him she was coming, but when he saw her, he seemed to mis-interpret the gesture and with a nod he slapped the reins against

Pepper's and Minty's rumps and the big horses moved off. Maddy exhaled: she could call out and run across the busy field, but to do so would draw more attention than she felt she could endure.

'Well, there goes my means of escape,' Maddy muttered.

'I'll take you back,' Daniel said.

'Maddy,' Amelia said, with a warm smile. 'Mr Coulter,'—she peeked up at him from beneath dark lashes—'the ball is going to be wonderful, don't you think?'

Maddy's stomach squirmed and she saw Daniel's lips twitch with amusement.

'Yes, wonderful,' he agreed.

'Lord, give me strength.'

Daniel jerked and looked down at Maddy, and she realised she must have said her thought aloud. Heat rushed to her cheeks.

'Well, I must be off. I seem to have been left behind and it's quite a walk.' Thankfully, the day was sunny and cool, and the walk along the river should be pleasant enough, and though she liked Amelia Everette, she did not much enjoy the sight of her batting her eyelashes at Daniel Coulter.

'Oh, I was hoping you could help me with the tables. Aunt Catherine has provided some lovely greenery for decorations.' Amelia bit her lip in consternation.

Maddy knew it would be she who did the work, with Amelia giving the orders.

'I'm sorry, but I have to get back to Shelby if I want to be ready in time,' Maddy said. She nodded at Daniel, and to Amelia said, 'I'll see you tonight,' and started walking down the slope.

She had reached the path by the river when Daniel caught up with her. Maddy looked around, a little startled to find him so close.

'I'll walk you back,' he said.

'You have your horse,' she reminded him.

He looked dumbfounded. 'Oh, of course,' he said and he turned around as if the mare should be behind him. Maddy couldn't help but smile at his expression.

'Thank you for the offer, but I'll be fine. I can walk back along the river, and then up the track from the bottom fields,' she said, her tone more kindly than it might have been moments before.

'Yes, but I don't think it's a good idea for you to be wandering around alone.'

'What do you mean wandering around? I'm walking back to Shelby, and I've no intention of getting lost. The way is quite clear and easy to navigate.'

'I know, but ...' His voice trailed off and then, as if stumbling across an idea, his eyes widened. 'But I have to return to Shelby now anyway, and if you come with me, we will both be home safe and sound far more quickly than if you walk.'

'That is true, but whatever will people think if I ride on a horse astride rather than side saddle?'

He ignored her sarcasm. 'I've not noticed you bowing to convention before, so why start today?' he said, one brow lifted in question.

'That too is true.' Maddy smiled. 'Very well then, fetch your horse and I'll meet you at the gate.'

He nodded and jogged off to where he'd left his horse tethered.

When Daniel arrived with Baby in tow, Maddy suggested they both walk until they were at least out of sight of the good folk of the valley.

'It's enough for them that I allow convict women and a pitiful orphan to live under the same roof as myself.'

'Indeed,' he said, his lips twitching again.

'What?'

'Nothing.'

'I can see your struggling to contain your mirth—why are you laughing at me?'

'I'm not laughing at you. I'm laughing at the thought of Mrs Everette the Elder seeing you sitting astride a horse and behind a mere overseer to boot.'

'It's almost worth it, other than knowing Mrs Everette the Younger would be forced to listen to the old woman's tirade about me again.'

'Again?'

Maddy told him of the overheard conversation at Cragside.

'It hardly matters,' he said, but there was something in his expression that made her wary.

'What?' She stopped and turned to look directly at him.

'Miss Barker-Trent, you must realise having the boy share a room with you is, well, unconventional to say the least.'

'Of course I do, but what would you have me do?'

'He could stay in the barracks. He likes Phil well enough. Or with me for that matter,' he suggested. As he spoke, he turned Baby so that he could assist her to mount.

'What about you?' Maddy asked, indicating the horse.

'I'll walk; you can ride.'

'I can easily walk as far as you.' She was indignant.

'I don't doubt it, but you don't have to,' he said patiently.

'I thought we were both to ride,' she reminded him. He looked as if he was about to protest, but he nodded and placed his own foot in the stirrup; he swung up into the saddle before reaching down a hand to her. Maddy placed her hand in his and her foot on top of his boot, and with one smooth action he hauled her up to land behind him, her skirts over the mare's rump and her arms around his waist. Maddy's heart thundered and her stomach fluttered at his closeness. Reluctantly she let her arms fall to rest on her thighs as the horse began to walk steadily towards Shelby.

'Have you given any more thought to Lester?'

Maddy stiffened. She had but still wasn't sure what to do. She'd half hoped it would just be forgotten. Which was ridiculous: the man would want to have his future secured. And there had been that moment when he'd seemed, well, almost friendly.

'Yes,' she said.

'And have you made a decision?'

'I'm not sure,' she said, but perhaps she should talk it over with Daniel; he would be able to point out the merits and the perils of her idea. 'I'd thought to perhaps ask him to apprentice one of the lads, and, if I grant him his ticket of leave, I will pay him to build the house. When he's finished, he'll have a trained assistant.'

He twisted around in the saddle to face her. The movement caused his shoulder to brush her breasts and she shivered.

'That's an excellent idea,' he said, then turned back to face the road ahead. She felt more than heard his sigh. 'It would leave us short in the fields, though.'

'Could we apply for more convicts to replace them?'

'Yes, we could, though we've been extremely fortunate with the men we've been sent: according to Alex, it's not often that convicts are so amenable.'

Maddy admired the back of his head, noticing the brown skin of his neck and how it grew pale as it disappeared beneath the protection of his shirt collar. It took her a moment to comprehend what he'd said. 'Are you saying we shouldn't grant Lester his freedom?'

'It's up to you, as I've said all along. It's not my place to do otherwise.'

'I'm asking for your opinion.'

He didn't answer for a long time, and the roll of the horse beneath her did little to soothe the rising tide of frustration.

Dealing with Daniel was becoming more and more complicated as she scrambled to untangle the knot of feelings he evoked.

'I think you should do as you see fit.'

'No, Daniel, you can't do that: you cannot refuse to answer me.'

'I can, and I do. It's not for me to decide. You are the mistress of Shelby.'

What was wrong with him? Maddy wanted his opinion, had asked for it—that he now refused to give one when he'd raised the topic was maddening.

'I insist you say what you would do if you were given the same circumstances.'

The silence stretched on so long that Maddy thought he was not going to answer.

'I would give him his freedom and offer him the opportunity to build the house,' he said eventually.

Well, what had been so difficult about that? 'Isn't that what I've just said I'd like to do?'

'Yes, it is.'

'But?'

'But … I don't know if he will accept your offer,' he said finally.

Maddy didn't like the sound of that, and then, as if from nowhere, the question popped from her. 'And what of you, Mr Coulter? Surely you wish to be master of your own establishment? I take it that was your intention when you first came to the colony?'

'I am in no hurry to make any changes.'

'You are not?'

'For now.'

And she could tell by the tension in the set of his head and neck this was all he would say on the matter.

Twenty-Two

Tuesday, 15 May 1832—full moon, cool morning and evening but clear warm day

The sun had dipped beyond the horizon and the moon was a giant globe of orange lighting the fields as the dray bumped along the track to the Harpurs' field. The air smelled of freshly cut grass, eucalypts and burning whale oil.

The grounds being already full of people, carts, buggies, horses and more people, the air fizzed with excitement. Maddy sat beside Phil, while Jane, Mary, Luke and the boys and men from Shelby were squashed in the wagon. Daniel rode alongside on his horse. Only George Lester had declined the invitation to accompany them. She knew she needed to speak to him, and soon, but the idea of discussing his freedom made her cold with dread: what if he refused to continue at Shelby? But could she in good conscience keep him a convict? She shook off the questions—she would speak to Lester after the ball. She was determined that for this one night she would just enjoy herself, and she'd leave worrying about Shelby until tomorrow. The wagon creaked down the slope to the field, and her heart skipped with anticipation as she took in the scene by the river.

The lanterns glowed and flickered, adding to the romance of the evening. Maddy saw the refreshments tent teemed with industry as the ladies of the valley delivered their contribution for the supper. Everyone was dressed in their best: the men in clean shirts and shined boots, and the ladies in their finery. Maddy glanced down at her own gown, the first colourful item of clothing she'd worn for over a year, and felt as light and frivolous as was possible while balancing a basket of cakes.

The field faded away and for a moment melancholy filled her as she recalled visiting the seamstress with Mama as they excitedly planned their new life with Papa in New South Wales. She wore the gown Mama had chosen for her: a soft green silk with embroidered roses and puffed sleeves, and the matching fringed mantlet was draped over her knees.

The dray lurched over the uneven ground, jolting her from her reminiscences. Squeals rose from the wagon as they all clutched at anything and anyone in order to steady themselves. One of Maddy's hands left the basket and grabbed for the low rail beside her. There was much laughter and giggling from the back of the dray, and as she turned, her eyes met Daniel's and with that look the distance between them fell away.

'Oh, get away with ye,' Jane said, but she sounded delighted, and Maddy saw young Charlie grinning like a fool. Well, well? Maddy mused, smiling. She noticed Mary was nestled beneath Joe O'Brien's arm at the back corner of the dray. Mary wore a neat dress with a pretty embroidered shawl draped around her shoulders. Maddy wondered where it had come from. She'd never seen her wearing it before and had no doubt that Mary would wear something so pretty given any opportunity. Big Joe O'Brien seemed content to be snuggled up with the maid. Maddy wondered if she should be careful to put a bit of distance between the two—no, not tonight. Tonight Maddy intended to enjoy the music, company and moonlight. Her heart swelled as she took in the river shining silver beneath the enormous full moon.

Daniel tied his horse and was soon standing beside the wheel, reaching up to relieve Maddy of the basket. A string of random musical notes drifted across the field from the small tent beside the dance floor as the musicians tuned their instruments. Maddy looked down at Daniel; how handsome he was, with his cravat neatly tied, the breadth of his shoulders emphasised by a fine coat and pristine linen shirt. She was glad the awkwardness of the afternoon wasn't to be carried into the evening. When he'd placed the basket on the ground beside the wheel, out of the way, he turned and reached up a hand to help her down.

'Thank you,' Maddy said, taking his hand as she stepped down, careful to keep her skirts clear of the dirty wheel.

'My pleasure.' He searched her face and for the space of several breaths, Maddy could not look away. Blood thundered through her body and somewhat reluctantly she let her fingers loosen. After a heartbeat, Daniel released her hand and stepped back. He picked up the basket and handed it to her.

'Thank you,' Maddy said again.

'Promise to save a dance for me.'

Their eyes met and Maddy nodded. 'I will.'

He grinned and turned back to help Phil with the horses.

Maddy fairly skipped as she took her contribution to the supper tables, but as she drew closer she saw only the women of the smaller holdings working in the tent. Maddy paused as she registered those around her, and she realised no other convicts were present, save those who'd come from Shelby. Her heart was thudding hard in her chest and she wasn't certain if she was going to collapse in dismay or explode with rage. She'd been under the impression that the ball was to be for the entire community.

Maddy saw Mrs Garrick crossing the mown clearing and leaving her basket by a tent pole, so she hurried over to speak to her neighbour.

'Mrs Garrick,' Maddy said a little breathless.

'Oh, Madeleine, I'm so pleased you're here. Now, do tell me Daniel is with you?' She peered over Maddy's shoulder looking for him.

'Ah yes, he's helping the men.'

Before she could wonder overly much why Mrs Garrick wanted to know if Daniel was there, Mrs Garrick continued, 'Good, that's good. Now, I need someone to organise refreshments for the band: could you help?' Her expression was a little harried, making Maddy wonder what was the matter.

'Of course,' Maddy said, 'but where are the other ladies?'

Mrs Garrick looked at Maddy. 'They will be along soon.'

'But—'

'Maddy,'—Mrs Garrick met her eyes, her expression serious— 'the women of our small society aren't inclined to do the preparations themselves: they send in the servants.'

Nodding slowly, Maddy let the reality sink in—of course they wouldn't help, it was enough they'd sanctioned the event.

'I understand. Who do I see regarding the refreshments for the band?' There was no point in berating the one woman who didn't consider it beneath her to work beside the servants. Maddy decided to ignore the hypocrisy and follow Mrs Garrick's lead.

The moonlight cast curious shadows all around by the time the so-called respectable of the valley's inhabitants arrived. Chase Hobson stood with the Everette girls by the punch table, and Maddy searched for someone, anyone, else to talk to. Mrs Wyndham and Mrs Harpur were with Mrs Garrick. She cast a wary glance around for Mrs Everette the Elder, intent on avoiding her company at all costs. Thankfully the old woman was nowhere in sight so Maddy crossed to join them.

She heard Mrs Wyndham say, 'He is going to be so surprised,' as she drew closer and the band finished tuning up.

Before Maddy reached the ladies, Mr Francis Platt stepped in front of her. She took in his square handsome face. His eyes gleamed in the lamplight. 'Miss Barker-Trent, I hoped I might see you tonight.'

Maddy smiled. 'It was very probable that you should.'

His smile faltered and she repented of the retort. 'I apologise,' he said, frowning, 'I had not meant to offend you.'

Contrite, Maddy put a hand on his arm. 'No, Mr Platt, it is I who should apologise, and I do.'

Still looking a little crestfallen, he nodded, and a tight smile crossed his lips briefly.

'I fear my sense of humour can be somewhat caustic,' Maddy continued. 'Please. Forgive me.'

'Of course,' he said, but his expression remained peevish.

'Have you been back in the valley long?' she asked, hoping to distract him from indulging in fragile sensibilities. Maddy cast a glance around for a means of escape, but everyone was moving towards the dance floor as a lively tune filled the crisp night air.

'Only a day or two. Mr Hobson, Chase, arrived in Sydney and told us of the dance to be held here, so we came.'

'We?' Maddy glanced around once again.

'Alex Middleton and I,' he explained. As he said the words she saw Mr Middleton speaking with Mr Wyndham. His brooding eyes met hers across the clearing and for a moment Maddy felt skewered by his gaze. She felt as if he were assessing her. She looked away.

'Would you do me the honour of ...' Francis Platt held out his hand in invitation and Maddy nodded. Relieved to have something to do beside stumble around awkwardly from conversation to conversation, she allowed herself to be led across the twenty or so yards to the dance platform and up the steps. They joined three other couples to make a set, and her heart sank when she saw one of the couples was Daniel and Belle; and Amelia seemed very happy to be on the arm of Mr Chase Hobson.

The music started and they began to dance. Her feet kept up of their own accord, but Maddy's mind was awash with misgivings. She wished she'd said no to Mr Platt. Maddy didn't want to dance with another man while watching Daniel dance with Belle, though she had no right to feel so. All too soon she found herself face to face with Amelia, who dragged her besotted gaze from Chase to smile brightly at Maddy. Maddy's hand rested lightly on hers as they met in the centre and, star-like, spun until they moved onto the next partner and then Maddy was in Daniel's arms and her heart began to thunder in earnest. He looked down at her and she was ensnared as surely as a butterfly in a spider web. They spun and stepped, and too soon Maddy was swept into Mr Platt's arms once more.

Maddy struggled to concentrate on the intricate steps of the dance and couldn't keep her eyes from returning, between turns and spins, to Daniel. More than once their gazes locked before he'd disappear behind another to turn and twirl with Belle, who didn't look one bit as if she was enjoying the dance. The next time the dance delivered her to Daniel his hand had barely touched hers when she felt his attention shift. His feet stilled and Maddy stared up at him in alarm. She saw his expression go slack with shock. Maddy turned her head to see what had affected him so strongly. Before she could identify the source of his disquiet he continued with the dance, though his movements had become stiff and mechanical. The remaining minutes of the dance were completed automatically on Maddy's part too. She tried peering at Daniel and searching the faces around the dance floor, seeking out what or who had upset him so much.

Maddy watched as he curtly thanked Belle and hurried from the floor. Maddy made to follow him, but Francis Platt kept hold of her hands as the music started for the next dance, and, having missed the opportunity to refuse, she could do nothing but let him lead her through steps of a second dance. Each twirl and slide that faced outwards was an opportunity to scan the faces for Daniel. The dance went on interminably and Maddy was forced to concentrate after several missed cues. The minute it finished, she thanked Mr Platt and excused herself.

Hesitating at the top of the steps, Maddy saw Daniel with a small group: Mr and Mrs Garrick, a man of similar age to Mr Garrick, and two women who Maddy hadn't seen before, one with pale blonde hair arranged in an intricate style, and a golden gown that made the rest of the women seem dowdy. Maddy drew in a sharp breath when she saw her lay a proprietary hand on Daniel's arm. He did not remove it.

Maddy's heart began to beat erratically. Her feet moved of their own accord and she found herself standing on the edge of the group. Daniel noticed her and their eyes met. His expression was unreadable, but his lips were pressed into a thin line. Maddy's heartbeat faltered.

'Ah, Maddy, come my dear.' Mrs Garrick's smile was wide and welcoming. 'You must meet Mrs Clinton, Daniel's sister and my dearest friend.'

Maddy blinked. Daniel's sister? He'd rarely mentioned his family, let alone that they were due to visit.

'Mrs Clinton, I'm honoured to meet you.' Maddy's words were stiff and awkward.

'Oh, Miss Barker-Trent, I'm so pleased to meet you at last. My brother hardly ever writes.' Daniel's sister smiled at Maddy before turning a playful frown on Daniel. 'Thankfully Mrs Garrick has told us much of what he's been engaged with here in the colony.'

Maddy returned her smile; the woman's eyes were so similar to Daniel's, and yet she felt herself sized up in an instant and found somewhat wanting.

'And you must allow me to introduce Daniel's betrothed, Ella Whitfield.'

Maddy met the frosty blue stare of the blonde woman she'd seen from the dance floor. Maddy swallowed a gasp of shock, coughed, apologised and smiled mechanically.

'Oh, Charlotte, we are not yet affianced,' said the golden Ella Whitfield.

Maddy's gaze flew to Daniel. He didn't meet her gaze; his expression remained stony. 'Miss Whitfield, a pleasure,' she said, her voice surprisingly even.

'Miss Barker-Trent—may I call you Maddy?' she said, her voice was low pitched and sultry.

Seeing her standing beside Daniel, Maddy thought they would make a handsome couple. A perfect couple. 'Of course,' Maddy said.

'We've surprised Daniel, and you appear as shocked as he.' She gave Daniel a long look before diverting her attention to glance at Maddy, who noted she hadn't been invited to call Miss Whitfield by her Christian name.

'Ah yes, I must admit your arrival is a great surprise. You must be delighted, Mr Coulter.'

Daniel nodded slowly, but a muscle in his jaw ticked.

'And Maddy,' said Mrs Garrick, 'this is Charlotte's husband, Mr Matthew Clinton; Matthew, this is our lovely neighbour and Daniel's employer, Miss Madeleine Barker-Trent.'

Matthew Clinton nodded politely. He was a bull of a man, and Maddy thought he seemed as if he'd rather be anywhere other than where he found himself to be.

Mrs Garrick laughed. 'I see you really are just as surprised as the rest of us.' She gave Daniel a fond smile.

With the exception of herself, Daniel and Miss Ella Whitfield, the small group laughed. Maddy smiled and said she was pleased to meet them all, and then quickly excused herself, refusing to give Daniel another glance. She turned and hurried to the supper tent.

Maddy's mind reeled. How could Daniel have failed to mention a fiancée? He'd hardly referred to his sister, which was strange enough, but to omit that he was betrothed?

'Maddy.' She heard her name called and jerked around to see Amelia beckoning.

'Oh, Amelia,' Maddy said and hurried to where the Everette sisters stood with three men: Messrs Hobson, Platt and Middleton.

'Maddy, who is that with the Garricks?' Amelia asked, not trying to hide her curiosity.

'Amelia, don't be such a busybody.'

'How cruel you are, Belle. I'm not a busybody. Surely being curious is not something unexpected when our friend Mr Coulter seems to have visitors?'

'It's Mr and Mrs Clinton, Mr Coulter's sister and her husband,' Maddy told them.

'And the girl? She seems quite familiar with Daniel.' They all turned to see the girl leaning close as she spoke to Daniel; his attention was trained on the ground before him, his expression unreadable.

'A Miss Ella Whitfield.'

'Are she and Mr Coulter acquainted?' asked Belle.

'Yes,' Maddy said.

'Who is she?' asked Alex Middleton, his expression intense as he observed the newcomers.

'I, er ...' Maddy couldn't bring herself to say it. 'Ah, there's Mr Hardy trying to catch my attention. Please excuse me.'

Without waiting for a response she hurried away.

Maddy found Jane and Charlie, Mary and Joe, and the twins partnered by two women she didn't know, dancing on the grass fifty yards from the main dance floor. While the dance they performed wasn't strictly in keeping with the formal version being stepped out above, it seemed to Maddy a great deal more enjoyable, if the enthusiasm and laughter were anything to go by.

Phil, Luke and young Joey stood by watching and grinning as Michael swung his partner off her feet to reveal her petticoats, causing her to squeal with delight. Even Luke was smiling and clapping along in time with the music. Phil's expression sobered as he saw Maddy's approach. He came around the dancers and crossed to meet her.

'Miss Maddy, whatever is the matter?'

Was she so transparent? Maddy attempted a reassuring smile, but it did nothing to alleviate his concern.

'I'm feeling a little unwell,' she said, touching her brow, 'only a slight daze, but I thought I might feel better down here away from the noise and music.'

'Shall I fetch you a drink?' He leaned down to peer at her.

A drink? 'Yes, please.'

'Here, sit down and I'll be back in a jiffy.'

Maddy sat down on the nearest log and resolutely kept her attention on the wilder dancing of the workers and did not allow herself to look at those on, or near, the dance floor. She had to get away, but if she insisted on returning home so early, the others would have to miss out as well. And they were all having such fun. She couldn't do it. But she could stay well away from the Garricks and company.

Maddy managed to keep a respectable distance from Daniel Coulter and his family and friend for the remainder of the evening, but for her the enjoyment was gone. She'd not had her dance with him, and now she was grateful. Better not to grow used to his arms around her. Much better.

For the remainder of the evening Maddy accepted every dance when asked, but she was merely going through the motions. No one commented on her lack of enthusiasm, but she knew it hadn't gone unnoticed. Her only relief was in that she didn't see Daniel and Ella on the dance floor.

The servants from different properties who'd helped with the preparations for the night danced on the grass or stood tapping their toes as they watched the festivities. Maddy realised she'd rather have stayed with Jane, Phil and the others than spend the evening dancing with land-seeking men, some of whom were older than her father had been.

It was almost midnight and the moon had crested the zenith: the night was still bright beyond the lanterns and torches, and Maddy took a few moments away from the crowd. She blinked away tears and tipped her head back; the stars were dim in comparison with the bright lunar light and she wondered whether perhaps she suffered with a sort of lunacy. She snorted a bitter laugh and stood staring at the gleaming water flowing past. She'd never travelled north of Shelby or seen where the lifeblood of the Hunter Valley sprang from, but she knew where it finished, and she recalled the first time she'd entered the heads at Newcastle. Although she'd arrived with sad tidings, she hadn't expected to be stranded and alone in the valley within two days.

Suddenly the immensity of her circumstances hit Maddy, and her legs wobbled.

'There you are,' Daniel said.

She brushed the tears away and lifted her chin. 'Yes, here I am.'

'I believe the last dance is about to begin—would you do me the honour?'

Maddy stilled. How could he ask this of her? 'Wouldn't your betrothed have something to say about you dancing with someone else?' Her tone was much colder than she'd intended, and Daniel's lips thinned.

'Miss Whitfield is a dear friend of my sister's. I have never asked her to marry me.'

'Has anyone told your sister?'

'Maddy, please, I didn't even know they were making the journey here.' His eyes were dark and unreadable. Maddy stared at him. Daniel had never done anything to deceive her before, so surely he wouldn't lie now. He couldn't lie about something like this. 'I would have told you if I had known. Surely you know that?'

Maddy nodded slowly, as relief flooded through her.

'Miss Maddy, the wagon is ready to go.' She found Jane standing mere yards away, and Maddy glanced back at Daniel. The music began, and she knew the opportunity to dance with Daniel had been missed.

'You should take the day tomorrow, Dan—Mr Coulter, to visit with your family.' Again her words were frosty and she immediately wished she could withdraw them when she saw his hurt expression.

'Very well, Miss Barker-Trent.' For a moment she thought he was about to say more, but instead he merely said. 'Thank you.'

He turned and walked back to the Garricks and his family … and Miss Ella Whitfield.

On the drive home the moonlight seemed harsh and probing. It sent the bush into eerie shadow and gave their faces a cold blue cast.

The cheerful chatter behind her in the wagon ebbed until everyone, tired and sated, was lulled by the rocking motion of the dray into a drowsy silence, leaving Maddy with no distraction at all from her whirling thoughts.

Twenty-Three

Friday, 18 May 1832—partly cloudy, cool night

'Maddy, you cannot continue to avoid me,' Daniel said, his frustration evident.

It had been three days since the ball and the appearance of his family and Miss Whitfield. Three days of little contact, and then only when Maddy couldn't evade him. There was always plenty to be done, and she found it easy enough to keep out of his way. In the evenings Daniel visited the Garricks, and in the mornings, when she would once have met with him to discuss the coming day, Maddy stayed away and didn't allow herself even the small luxury of looking to see if he'd wandered up from the yard to speak to her.

'I don't know what you mean,' she said stiffly. She stared at him, watching the colour creep up his neck.

'Of course you do: since the ball you've not given me a chance to explain. You've rarely left your rooms.'

Maddy bristled. 'I fail to see what business it is of yours how I spend my days.'

'As the overseer of Shelby, I need to discuss certain matters with you.'

'And here I am, so what do you need to discuss?' Even as she spoke, her heart longed for their former easy communication. Why was she behaving so?

'Maddy, I didn't invite Ella to New South Wales. We have not corresponded,' he said quietly.

'Nevertheless, she is here,' she said, but deep inside the tiny flicker of hope was reignited.

'Yes, and so are my sister and her husband. And I'm delighted to see Charlotte, but I was never engaged to Ella, nor had I ever intended to be.'

'I hadn't taken you for a cad.' Her mouth seemed to have a mind of its own.

'I didn't trifle with her either, Maddy, I promise you.'

'It's none of my business.'

'No, I suppose it isn't.' He sounded as if he was exhausted.

'Why did she come then? If you were not betrothed, or if she had not been given to believe you would be?' Maddy swiped away a stray tear, suddenly desperate to be reassured, unwilling to let it go now the conversation had begun.

'My sister and Ella have been best friends since childhood. Our families were close. I think it was expected that one day a union between us would join the families. When I expressed my desire to emigrate to the colonies, Ella was adamant she could never live in such a place. It didn't concern me, because I'd not considered it an option.'

'Do you love her?'

'I care for her, but I do not love her.'

'Did you ever?' She had to be certain his affections were not so fickle that he had let Ella believe there would be more.

'Not in a romantic fashion, and I didn't allow her to think it would ever be anything more than friendship. But Charlotte hoped I would fall in love with her, and nothing I could say to the contrary seemed to penetrate. I came to the colony to make my own way, my own future, and not merely fall in with the wishes of my sister and her friend. Charlotte is a wonderful sister—it's only in this matter that she seems unable to concede defeat.'

Maddy stared out over the valley for a long while, unsure how to respond. Part of her was thrilled at his words, but a small practical part hesitated. What could any of this mean to her? Hadn't she promised herself never to marry? At least not until Shelby was complete.

'Daniel, why do you stay on here at Shelby?' Maddy forced herself to look at him.

'Do you really have to ask?' His eyes were dark and unreadable.

Maddy's heart stilled. Was there some hope for them after all?

'Maddy, I have loved you since the moment I first saw you, when you strode out across the field in search of your father.'

Maddy's heart began to beat again, the rhythm erratic and thunderous. She didn't know what to say.

'Maddy, please, say something?' Tension filled his words.

She shook her head. Then opened her mouth to speak, but nothing came out. Tears filled her eyes and she tried once more to tell him how much she loved him. Again, no words came and she shook her head.

'I'm sorry, I should never have spoken.' His shoulders, usually so square and straight, drooped as he turned away.

'No, no.'

He stopped.

'Please, Daniel, you must know—'

'I do. I know, and I am sorry. I beg your forgiveness.'

He started back along the track to the yard, the back of his neck flushed deeply.

'Daniel, *wait*.'

He stopped but didn't turn around.

'Please, Daniel, please, look at me.'

He pivoted slowly on his heel, his face set.

'You must know I love you.' The words came in a rush.

He didn't react at first, then a smile widened his mouth as comprehension dawned. With two long strides he crossed the space between them and grasped her arms. 'Do you? Do you really love me?' His eyes dark and intense held hers captive.

'Of course I do—how could you not know it?'

He took her face in his work-roughened yet gentle hands and lowered his head. Maddy's eyes drifted closed as she felt the first touch of his lips. Soft and gentle, he kissed her. Maddy's heart ached with the sweetness of his mouth on hers.

He drew back and gazed into her eyes, his face tender and brimming with the love she'd craved her entire life. Daniel loved her.

'Oh, Maddy, you have made me the happiest man in the colony. The world.'

Maddy smiled. He smiled. They both stood beside the foundations of Shelby homestead and grinned at each other like fools. Maddy tingled with happiness as she stood staring openly at the man she'd loved since first he'd smiled at her across the rough-ploughed soil of a field.

'Miss Maddy?' She turned to see young Luke standing on the far side of the building. Daniel's hands dropped, but he didn't step away.

Maddy glanced at Daniel. He smiled at Luke and then at her and she knew it was true. She wasn't dreaming this wonderful moment.

'Yes, Luke?' Maddy said, facing the boy, but leaving her hand on Daniel's arm.

'There's a buggy coming up the road.' As was his habit, Luke roamed silent and all-seeing through the bush, popping up unexpectedly and as if from nowhere. He was often off playing with the Wonnarua children; they liked to scratch around the creek bank for the small crayfish and sometimes he brought them home to be boiled and shared with the men. Maddy had tasted them only the once and found them muddy and unpalatable. He'd obviously been down near the creek and seen the visitors approaching along the road. He was barefoot again, and Maddy hoped he'd not lost his boots.

'Who is it? Do you know?' she asked him.

'It's Mrs Garrick's buggy,' Luke said, his face as usual darkly expressionless, 'and there's riders too.'

Maddy swallowed.

'It's probably my sister.'

She looked into Daniel's face, and a sudden fear filled her. 'Will you tell her?'

'Yes,' he said, his expression clouded.

She remembered Luke and turned back to the boy. 'Luke, can you find Jane and tell her we're expecting visitors, please?'

'Yes, miss.' He turned and ran off around the side of the kitchen.

'Daniel, I'm afraid.'

'Why? Maddy, everything will be fine.'

'But she thinks she is here to resume your relationship, and ...' Maddy's heart was thudding once again, but this time it wasn't with joy but with trepidation.

'There is nothing to resume. I will speak to her,' he said, his expression determined, 'and once it is settled, we shall declare our love to the world.' He paused, sudden concern flitting over his face. 'You will marry me, won't you?'

'Oh, Daniel,' she gasped, tears pricking her eyes, 'of course I will.'

'But first I must talk to Ella, clear the situation between us.'

'Daniel,' Maddy said, loving the feel of his name on her tongue, 'you must be kind.'

'I doubt it shall break her heart.'

'I hope not.'

'Come, I can hear the horses.' He held out his hand and Maddy placed hers in his grasp, thrilling at the sensations that buzzed through her. Realising they could not be seen holding each other, at least not before he'd spoken to Ella, Maddy reluctantly slid her fingers from his. Their eyes met and he gave an understanding nod.

'Soon,' he said firmly.

Maddy gave him a wobbly smile and hoped he was right.

They had reached the farmyard by the time the buggy appeared between the trees, with Mrs Garrick and Charlotte Clinton seated beneath the black canopy. Maddy frowned. Where was Ella? Then the sound of cantering horses reached her, and she saw a flash of colour through the trees. Three horses came to a dusty halt behind the buggy. Mr Garrick on his big bay; Mr Clinton, grinning with delight on a grey mare Maddy knew Mr Garrick had purchased from Mr Wyndham recently; and on the black stallion, formerly dear Papa's horse, was Miss Ella Whitfield. Maddy drew in a sharp breath. Why was she riding Papa's horse?

'Oh, he is an absolute joy,' Ella announced loudly, her thin lips stretched into a genuine smile and her milky complexion enhanced by a pretty blush. Ella's peacock-blue riding habit was a blaze of brightness against the muted colours of the bush and Maddy brushed her too-brown hands over the front of her own serviceable grey gown.

'I declare, how she is not afraid to ride such a beast is beyond me,' Charlotte Clinton said with a laugh.

'Indeed, you sit a horse well,' said Mr Garrick, smiling at Ella. 'If I'd not seen it with my own eyes, I would not have believed you capable.'

Ella laughed. 'I feared you would not allow me to ride him.' She ran a matching blue-gloved hand down the horse's shining black neck.

A surge of jealous anger reared up inside Maddy. Who did she think she was? Thinking she was to marry Daniel, and riding Papa's horse? In that moment, it mattered little that Maddy had sold the stallion to Mr Garrick.

'Daniel, I must have this horse,' Ella called imperiously as Daniel and Maddy approached the small group.

He didn't respond, but after shooting Maddy an apologetic glance, he approached the buggy and helped first his sister and then Mrs Garrick down. The stallion danced and fidgeted beneath Ella, and Maddy noticed she held a tight rein, so his mouth dripped with foam; his sides were heaving. It was obvious the horse had been ridden hard. Annoyance flashed across Ella's features as she watched Daniel help Mrs Garrick down.

Phil, Lester and young Charlie all appeared in the clearing, and as Ella nudged the horse towards the mounting block. She kicked her foot from the stirrup and unhooked her knee as Charlie hurried across to hold the stallion's head while she slid gracefully from its back. Her polished boots were briefly visible from beneath the skirts of her colourful outfit, and once again Maddy was painfully aware of her own plain garb. How could Daniel truly love her when this vision of elegance and refinement was his for the taking? Instead of the owner of Shelby, Maddy felt as if she were one of the convicts she worked alongside when compared to Ella Whitfield. She longed to run to her room and change into something more suitable for receiving visitors. Instead she lifted her chin and crossed to Mrs Clinton, offered her hand to her future sister. 'Mrs Clinton, welcome to Shelby Estate, humble as it may be.'

'Miss Barker-Trent, thank you,' Charlotte said, hesitating only a moment before she took Maddy's hand.

'Please, you must call me Maddy.'

'Maddy, it is,' she agreed and then she shot Daniel a questioning look that Maddy could not interpret. She had little time to consider it any further when Ella crossed to Daniel's side and placed a proprietorial hand on his arm: the same place Maddy's hand had been only minutes before. Daniel politely stepped away from her touch, but he listened as she spoke to him. Trying not to appear ignorant to Mrs Garrick and Mrs Clinton, Maddy watched them walk across the farmyard.

'Maddy, I do hope you don't mind our thrusting ourselves upon you without warning. It's a lovely day and we decided to take a ride, and as we were close, Miss Whitfield and Charlotte wished to see where Daniel lived, and so we came.' Mrs Garrick's smile was apologetic. Maddy returned her smile. She imagined Miss Whitfield was well used to having her way.

'I've arranged for tea, if you'd like to come this way.'

Mr Garrick and Mr Clinton were talking to Phil and dealing with the horses, and Maddy reluctantly left them behind and led the way along the path to the kitchen. She was conscious of each billow of dust as they walked; although Maddy knew Mrs Garrick understood the hardships of life in the colony, her neighbour now lived in a proper house. Maddy could imagine Mrs Clinton's life in England. Her own life in Wiltshire felt as if it belonged to someone else.

They came into the clearing to find Jane and Mary had set up a trestle table and carried out the bench seat and several chairs. It seemed they were to have a picnic tea. Maddy could have wept with relief. She would thank Jane at the first opportunity.

The best china was set out, and Maddy saw her mother's lovely embroidered cloth laid over something she imagined was a plate of scones fresh from the oven or the pound cake Jane had made earlier that morning. Jane carried the last chair from inside, and Maddy saw Mary behind her in the doorway, hurriedly chewing, her mouth stuffed full of some stolen morsel. Maddy frowned and hoped their visitors hadn't seen her.

She glared at Mary, who quickly drew back inside, mouth puckered as she tried in vain to disguise her chewing. Maddy wished she didn't find it necessary to steal food when it was readily available. There was nothing she could do about it for the moment or possibly ever. She sighed.

'This is delightful,' Mrs Garrick exclaimed when she saw the tea laid out.

'Yes,' Maddy agreed. She turned to Jane. 'Thank you, Jane, it's a lovely idea.'

Pleasure flooded Jane's face as she nodded and hurried back to the kitchen.

'Where do you live, Miss Barker-Trent?' Mrs Clinton asked. She started to remind her to call her Maddy but closed her mouth on the words.

'As is common in the colony,' Mrs Garrick began to say, but Maddy interrupted her.

'Jane, Mary and I share the accommodations here in the small rooms off the kitchen.'

'Really?' Mrs Clinton's brows rose to disappear beneath the sweep of her carefully arranged hair. Maddy was suddenly conscious once again of her own plain toilette. She wore her hair pulled back into a serviceable knot when working. There was hardly time to bother with curling tongs and pins every morning when there was a farm to be run.

'Yes; work on the house has begun, but I'm afraid it's a very long way from habitable.'

Charlotte Clinton looked around, her face a mask of dismay. 'It's all terribly primitive.'

'Oh, this is quite luxurious,' Mrs Garrick told her. 'Maddy has made enormous progress here in only a few months. Her papa lived in a slab hut for several years.' Then, as if recalling that Daniel now inhabited the same hut, she snapped her lips closed.

Daniel and Miss Whitfield came into the clearing, followed by Mr Garrick and Mr Clinton. Maddy knew immediately when she saw Daniel that he hadn't spoken to Ella. Ella's expression was no different from when she and Daniel had walked across the farmyard. Daniel gave her an almost imperceptible shake of his head. It was understandable, she supposed; it was hardly the time. He would have to approach the subject carefully. It was the honourable thing to do. Yes, Maddy realised, the idea of speaking to her today, with an audience, had not been a good idea. She sent Daniel an understanding look and turned back to Mrs Garrick, who'd said her name.

'Oh, I'm sorry, I was daydreaming.' Though, she thought, watching Ella with Daniel was more a nightmare than a dream.

Mrs Garrick's brow furrowed a little, 'I asked if you would like to show us the progress on your house?'

'Of course, not that there is much to see yet. But with the first course of stone laid, you can at least see the shape of things to come.'

'Garrick here tells me you are most fortunate to have secured a stonemason,' Mr Clinton said.

'Yes, it was fortuitous. I'm given to understand that it's quite unusual to find skilled workers in the colony.'

The men stood at the end of the table, and Miss Whitfield, beside Daniel, studied the display, making no effort to hide her opinion of what she saw; her lip curled disdainfully.

'Ella dear, sit down and have tea first,' Mrs Clinton said, her expression not having changed since she'd taken in Maddy's living quarters.

'Tea would be nice,' Ella said, suddenly giving in to her friend's urging.

'Alex, you will love this cake, it reminds me of the one we would have for tea with your mama in England,' Mrs Garrick said to her husband. He sent his wife a loving glance that quickly transformed into a boyish grin.

'Very well, I shall indeed.' He pulled out one of the vacant chairs and sat down. 'Has it currants?'

Maddy smiled and nodded. 'Yes, Jane has become quite the accomplished baker.'

Mr Clinton took the seat beside his wife, which left the chair beside Maddy for Ella, or the one between Mrs Garrick and Mrs Clinton. Without hesitation, she started towards her friend, and Daniel followed, holding the seat for her. He then moved around and sat down beside Maddy. In order to hide her delighted smile she reached for the pot and poured the tea. Jane slid into the space at the corner of the table and cut several slices of cake before withdrawing once more. Maddy tried to concentrate on the tea, and not on how good it felt to have Daniel seated beside her.

The conversation followed the usual ebb and flow of farmers and neighbours talking, with the men discussing new agricultural techniques and the women discussing the ball. Ella didn't contribute, but instead seemed to have eyes only for Daniel, who was engaged in the debate about the import of Merino sheep. Maddy too found herself inclined to listen to the men's discussion on the merits of one breed of sheep over another.

When the tea was finished and the guests began to murmur about being on their way, Mrs Garrick reminded Maddy she'd been going to show them the foundations of the house. Maddy agreed and led the way but noticed as they walked to the far side to admire the view that Daniel and Ella had lingered near the table. They were speaking, or at least Ella was. Daniel stared at the ground while he listened, his expression carefully guarded, and Maddy wondered what Ella could be saying.

'They make a handsome couple, don't you think?' Mrs Clinton said, her eyes, so much like Daniel's, assessing Maddy.

Thankfully Maddy was saved from having to reply when Mr Garrick, who stood on one of the large flat foundation stones, asked whether Maddy planned to import the marble for the dining room fireplace. Mr Clinton asked who the architect was and when she glanced back at Daniel and Ella, she saw they'd turned away and were headed back towards the farmyard. Maddy forced her attention back to Mr Garrick, who was discussing the dimensions of the various rooms with Mr Clinton. She looked at the large stone blocks soon to be buried beneath the next course. Buried and never to be seen again, and yet the entire house depended on their careful placement. She saw Daniel and Ella briefly before they rounded the bend in the track and were out of sight. A cold shiver ran along her spine.

Twenty-Four

Friday, 18 May 1832

Daniel and Maddy stood staring at the plume of dust billowing in the wake of the buggy as the visitors finally left.

'I'm going to check the sheep—would you like to come with me?' he asked, not looking at her.

Maddy nodded and they turned in unison and walked to the fields.

'I wasn't able to broach the subject with Ella.'

'It was folly to think you could with everyone here.'

He turned his face towards her, not breaking stride.

Maddy shrugged and said. 'It wasn't an appropriate time.'

'No, I need to speak to her privately, give her an opportunity to rage at me without an audience.'

'Why ever should she rage at you? You didn't encourage her on this quest to retrieve you.'

'How did you know?' He stopped and faced her; they were far enough from the yard to be free with their words.

'Know what?'

'She insists I return to England and work for her father.'

Maddy gaped at him. She hadn't meant that at all. Her heart thudded with a wild panic.

'I told her I had no intention of returning to England, at least not permanently.' He paused and frowned. 'But that wasn't what you meant, was it?'

'No, I merely thought she intended to bring you to her side.'

'To heel is more likely what she expects.' His tone was that of someone who didn't know whether to be amused or annoyed. They began to walk once more.

'Maddy, can you be patient?'

His eyes gleamed dark beneath the shade of his hat. She nodded. Not that she had a great deal of choice. A laughing jackdaw broke the silence. Maddy looked up into Daniel's face, at his lips, soft and full, and heat ran through her as she recalled the feel of his mouth on hers. She had no right to withhold her understanding. She could be patient—after all, they had the rest of their lives to be together.

'Of course.' She stepped towards him and reached up to place a hand on his warm cheek. 'You must do what's right. I can wait.'

He watched her, his eyes darkening until they appeared to be black.

'Oh Daniel, please, don't look at me like that.'

He stepped closer until he was touching her skirt. 'Like what, my love?'

Maddy felt the muscles of his face move beneath her hand as he smiled.

'It isn't fair, Daniel. You look at me like that and my bones turn molten. I don't understand what's happening. I've never felt like this before.'

His face lowered until she felt his breath on her cheek. He kissed her and, if possible, it was even more thrilling than the first time. The warmth of his body pressed against her branded her. She never wanted the kiss to end.

A crack of a branch snapping had them yards apart in an instant and scanning the bush around them. Daniel laughed and Maddy giggled.

'Come on, we'd better inspect the sheep,' she said, still laughing as she continued along the track. Daniel didn't follow straight away, and Maddy paused to glance back at him. He peered into the scrub once again, and then with an almost imperceptible shrug, he caught up with her in a few long strides.

'Tonight, I shall go to Tillington and see Ella.'

'Very well.'

He took Maddy's hand in his, and they walked along the track and into the future. Together.

Just before dark Maddy ventured out, leaving Jane and Luke happily reading and Mary mending a tear in her gown with bad grace. Mary didn't think it necessary, and had said so, several times, but Maddy had insisted she repair it before she went to bed.

'I shan't be long. I'm just going to take a bit of air,' Maddy told them.

Everyone in the room looked up at her, their expressions varied. Jane was puzzled but accepting, Luke's expression was as unreadable as usual, and a smirk lingered at the corner of Mary's mouth.

Maddy opened her lips to explain further but realised it would only make it worse, so closed them again. Pulling her shawl around her shoulders she stepped out into the crisp night air. The chill that ran along Maddy's spine wasn't completely due to the temperature, though the feel of winter whispered on the breeze as it lifted the loose tendrils of her hair, wrapping them around her face. Maddy was aggrieved for Daniel; he shouldn't have to do this. As he hadn't proposed to Ella in the first place, he shouldn't have to extract himself. But, her conscience reminded her, what of Ella? She'd hung her hopes on a future as Mrs Daniel Coulter, and it was not to be. Maddy hurried along the path, wanting, no, needing to see Daniel before he went. To be reassured that it wasn't a dream.

The bush was silent as the night crept in and the day creatures settled to sleep. Soon enough the nocturnal set would begin to move, and different sounds would be heard.

As Maddy drew closer to the yard, the soft murmur of someone speaking and the jingle of harness reached her. Beneath the darkening sky and the half-moon high above the horizon, the clearing had a magical feel. Daniel was saddling Baby, his head bent low as he tightened the girth. The usually steady mare was more jittery than Maddy had ever seen her, and she realised Daniel must be nervous and his anxiety was transferring to the horse.

He ran a soothing hand along Baby's neck as he turned to look at Maddy. He didn't seem surprised to see her.

'Did you hear me coming?'

'No, but I thought you might be along.'

'Do you think she will be terribly upset?'

'I don't believe so,' he said, sounding a little distracted as he glanced over at the barracks, where a light glowed warmly from the small window, and smoke drifted from the chimney. For a moment Maddy thought he was going to take her in his arms, but instead he turned back to the horse and thrust his foot into the stirrup. He swung up into the saddle and said, 'I may as well get this over with.'

'Yes,' Maddy agreed, all the while longing to pull him back down and tell him to stay with her—to send Ella a letter. For reasons she couldn't fathom, Maddy didn't want him to go. With his hat shadowing his face, he seemed as cold and remote as a statue staring down at her in the twilight. Maddy placed a hand on his boot, wishing she could stop him. He nodded and she knew he understood.

'Well,' she said, making her voice as cheerful as she could manage, 'you'd best be off.'

'Yes.' He lifted his chin and Maddy had a glimpse of the taut line of his jaw before he looked down once more. 'Don't wait up; we can talk in the morning.'

Maddy nodded but couldn't speak for the lump that had formed in her throat.

'Good night,' he said, and the horse moved off.

Maddy stood watching him go, only becoming aware of her surroundings once more when he had disappeared from view. She sighed and started back to the house.

A branch cracked behind her and she turned to see Lester standing at the corner of Daniel's hut. Where was he going? He stood as if frozen; it was obvious by his expression he hadn't been expecting to see anyone, particularly not his mistress, standing in the clearing.

'Good evening, Mr Lester,' Maddy said. For a moment she considered tackling the subject of his ticket of leave, but she was far too churned up to discuss anything rationally, particularly with someone who made her uncomfortable.

'Miss.' His nod of acknowledgement was almost imperceptible.

'Did you want Mr Coulter?' He had been heading for Daniel's door, of that she was certain.

'Um, yes,' he said hesitantly, then more firmly: 'Yeah, I wanted a word.'

Maddy wasn't certain she believed him.

'Well, it will have to wait, I'm afraid—he has ridden over to Tillington. To see his sister,' Maddy explained, silently cursing herself. There was no need to justify Daniel's movements.

'I see,' he nodded, 'well, good night then, miss; I'll head off to bed.'

Maddy muttered a cursory good night and, without waiting to see what he did, she hurried back to the kitchen. Her body might be at Shelby, but her heart rode to Tillington with Daniel. As she hastened through the darkening night, Maddy realised she'd not heard the door to the barracks open before Lester had appeared. Where had he come from? Had he been lurking, listening to their conversation?

The sound of Mary laughing reached her before she stepped into the pool of light from the window. Maddy paused, for though it was cool, she was reluctant to go inside. Feeling raw and unready for conversation with the prating maid and her chimerical notions, Maddy skirted the veranda and continued to the precipice, where she viewed the moon-washed valley. Drawing the shawl closer around her shoulders, she leaned against the wide trunk of a towering gum and gave way to her racing thoughts.

Would Daniel have arrived yet? How would he broach the subject with Ella? Despite his assurances, Maddy couldn't help but feel for the woman. She must love him. How could she not love Daniel? He is handsome, and kind and clever, and, Maddy realised, full of integrity. Which was what caused her some misgiving. What if Miss Ella Whitfield were to refuse to release him? Could she do that? When they had never been formally betrothed?

Maddy's heart began to thud and she forced herself to stop. There was nothing to be gained by worrying. Daniel would do as he'd promised. He'd explain to Ella that he didn't love her and had never meant to mislead her, but he didn't wish to marry her. Surely she wouldn't try to hold him when he didn't love her? No, of course she wouldn't. Her pride was at stake. Maddy trusted Daniel to be kind. He would do as he promised Maddy, but with as much care and gentleness as was possible. Ella may not like it, may even be hurt, but she would have to accept it. With that small reassurance, Maddy straightened and cast one more glance at the valley as a cloud drifted in front of the moon and threw the land into shadow. She retreated to the warmth and lively chatter of the kitchen.

On more than one occasion during a night of fitful sleep, Maddy imagined she heard the jingle of bridle, but though she held her breath and strained to hear there was no way to be certain from inside the room. The soft puff of Luke's breathing calmed her jangling nerves as he slept on, oblivious to her anxiety. At one point she considered leaving her bed to see if Daniel had returned, even going so far as to sit up and swing her bare feet to the floor. She realised if she opened the door it would doubtless wake the boy and so slumped back onto her pillow.

Never had she so longed for a night to be over. Maddy eventually dozed, but the hours in her bed were far from restful. She imagined all manner of scenarios that may have taken place— some that eased her harried thoughts, and some that only served to increase the discomfort.

'Are you sad, miss?' Luke's quiet voice came from the darkness.

'I'm sorry, Luke, I hadn't meant to wake you.'

'Is it for Mr Daniel?'

Maddy was glad of the darkness that hid her embarrassed surprise. Was she so obvious in her desire for Daniel that even a boy could see it?

'Whatever do you mean?' Maddy said, hoping her voice didn't betray her chagrin.

'Mr Daniel rode away and he's not back.'

Maddy blinked and sat up once more. 'He isn't?'

'No, miss, he's not come home.'

He couldn't know that. But something in the assured way he spoke convinced Maddy he was right. What could have happened? She flung back the quilt and felt around on the cold stone floor for her slippers. Perhaps he'd been overcome by bushrangers, or his horse had spooked and thrown him? She imagined him lying on the ground hurt and helpless. Scrambling into her robe she pulled wide the door and let in a gust of icy air: the dawn was almost upon them. With no care for her inadequate footwear or state of undress, Maddy raced along the path to the yard and saw in an instant that the mare wasn't in the yards and there was no plume of smoke to tell of Daniel's presence in the hut.

As she stood shivering in her nightwear, Maddy saw young Charlie hobbling barefoot, wearing only his nightshirt, and presumably returning from the privy. She froze and hoped he wouldn't look over and see her standing like a spectre in the trees in the early morning half-light. When he hurried into the barracks without giving any indication that he'd seen her, Maddy returned to her room to find Luke's bed empty. She crawled back beneath the covers and let the silent tears fall.

She eventually rose, despite having slept little. She couldn't lie in bed any longer, no matter how tempting the thought. Snatches of conversation and warped scenes from the previous days had haunted her dreams, leaving Maddy feeling both restless and exhausted. Pulling on a coat over her nightgown against the still chill air, she hurried to the kitchen, lit a lamp and stirred the coals to life before adding wood to the stove.

The cold of the flagstones seeped through her slippers as she carried the lantern back to her room and hurriedly dressed in a sombre grey gown, suitable for work but drab in comparison to the pretty colours Ella wore. In the lamplight Maddy examined her features in Papa's small shaving mirror as she twisted her hair into a neat knot at the base of her neck. She couldn't help comparing her own plain features to Ella's pretty countenance. She stared at her reflected image: her eyes were the colour of storm clouds, and, compared to the brilliance of Ella's blue, were as plain and common as dish water; her hair was so riotous as to resist the civilising effect of any tongs or pomade, while Ella's face was framed with perfect ringlets; Maddy thought her lips too thin and Ella's a perfect rosebud; Maddy's cheekbones were high and angular, and Ella's round and soft; and Maddy's skin was tanned and freckled where Ella's was pale as milk.

Maddy grinned at her reflection. *At least my teeth are straight,* she thought. She'd chosen this life, and she loved it. To be discontented simply because she didn't look like a delicate English rose was ludicrous, as she never had. She was too tall, too thin, and too plain. And, Maddy reminded herself as she pulled on the heavy leather boots, she'd never suited pink. But she had to admit she was glad to have a little colour in her wardrobe again, for she'd worn mourning black for long enough. Before leaving the room, she ran a caressing finger over Daniel's gift: the small polished stone.

Twenty-Five

Saturday, 19 May 1832—clear and cold

The morning stretched endlessly and Maddy's ears ached as she strained to hear any hint of an approaching horse; her heart thudded painfully at every noise. It was almost midday when Daniel finally rode into the yard, and his lateness only underlined her fear that things had not gone well with Ella. Maddy was torn between wanting to go to the yard to see him and an almost irresistible desire to hide.

Dry mouthed, she made her way to where Daniel was dismounting, his entire countenance downcast. What had happened?

'Daniel,' she said, coming up behind him. He turned slowly and their eyes met. 'What happened?'

'Maddy, might we talk later? I'm sorry, but I need to check on the men, and I don't want to— We have much to discuss and I don't want to be interrupted.'

'But what happened? You were gone all night.' Maddy searched his face for reassurance and found none. A hard lump filled her throat as she took in the shadows beneath his sorrowful eyes.

'So many things, and I've hardly slept. But first I need to check on the men.'

'But …'

'I'll come and see you later.' His tone was weary.

'Yes, yes of course,' Maddy said, taking a step back, her breath catching as she met his eyes. His desolate expression escalated the fear coursing through her. Without saying anything more he resumed unsaddling the horse, and, unwilling to stand waiting like a fool, Maddy hurried back to the house, her heart a cold stone in her chest.

All day her emotions swung between dread of what he would say and wanting to beg him to explain. By the time the day's chores were done and the evening meal preparations were underway, she had settled somewhat and was prepared to give Daniel the benefit of the doubt.

She was in the kitchen garden picking herbs when she saw Daniel come in from the fields. Without hesitation, Maddy shoved the rosemary she'd gathered into the pocket of her pinafore and hurried towards the yard. Before she was halfway her step faltered. Why was she running to him when he had been unwilling to speak that morning? He'd left her in misery all day. Pride redirected her steps back towards the garden; she would continue with the task she'd come outside to do.

Before she'd retreated a dozen steps he called her name. She froze. Now that it came to it, she wasn't sure she wanted to know. In her heart of hearts, Maddy knew something was terribly wrong. If it wasn't so, he would have come straight home the night before or spoken to her first thing. She took another step, continuing towards the garden. Annoyance flared deep in her: why had he kept her waiting all day?

'Maddy. We need to speak.'

Are those the same words he said to Ella? she wondered. His tone filled her with trepidation. He was much closer than she realised and she turned to look at him. Daniel's eyes were shadowed and his lips were pressed into a thin line. Maddy nodded and knew she couldn't speak even if her life depended on it.

'I'm sorry,' he said, his gaze finally meeting hers.

She opened her mouth, but no sound came; she grew cold and clammy; her entire body shaking as she willed herself to remain upright.

'Ella wasn't there,' he said, stepping closer.

Maddy retreated a pace on wobbly legs.

'Maddy, please,' he begged.

She turned her face away. For a moment she'd imagined happiness stretching into the future. Maddy shook her head. The surroundings blurred as tears filled her eyes.

'I must explain.'

Still she stood with her face averted and her blood thrumming painfully.

'The women had gone to visit Mrs Close at Green Hills. I took the opportunity to speak to my brother-in-law. I told Matthew of my predicament. He wasn't sympathetic.' His tone was flat. 'I don't know what I expected of him, perhaps a degree of under-standing, but I was mistaken.'

Maddy looked at him then and went cold. 'What do you mean?'

He stepped closer. 'Can we walk? This isn't a conversation I particularly wish to be overheard.'

Maddy nodded stiffly and fell in step with him. He headed towards the field track, and they walked side by side in silence. He was only inches from her, and yet it felt like an ocean separated them. When he steered her onto the track down to the glade, she hesitated. It was a beautiful place, her favourite hideaway in sum-mer, with the cool water of the spring and the mossy trees. Now it was bound to be damp and cold on a late autumn evening. She visited the glade each Sunday when everyone else went to church, taking a few moments of peaceful solitude. Maddy didn't stop until she reached the large boulder that shielded the small pond from view of anyone coming down the trail.

'Ella is convinced we were to be betrothed, and would have been married, had I not come to the colony. I explained to Matthew it wasn't true. I'd never spoken for her.'

'What did he say?' Maddy croaked, then cleared her throat and licked her dry lips.

'I shan't tell you his exact words: suffice to say he told me the expectation was that I must return to England and marry Ella.'

'Return to England?' she whispered. A band tightened around her chest.

'Yes, apparently, they feel that I should go back; I've had my adventure. You see I'm to inherit a small estate from an elderly aunt one day, and my sister's husband has … well shall we just say he's made some bad investments.' His bitter tone revealed Daniel's opinion of his brother-in-law.

'I see, but what has this to do with you?' She choked a little on the last.

'It pains me to say, but I suspect he has borrowed heavily from Ella's father, and if I read between the lines, I believe he hopes it will relieve him financially. Ella isn't without means, and I would have control of her money if I marry her. He didn't say that precisely. He would never admit to such chicanery.'

'I see,' Maddy said, but she didn't. She shook her head. 'But you came to the colony to settle and make a new life for yourself.'

'I did, and I've no desire to return to England, not even for a short while.'

'So, what …?'

'If I were to send Ella home, she would be embarrassed, but more importantly to me, it would put my brother-in-law, and therefore Charlotte, in a social and financial predicament. It seems my sister isn't privy to Matthew's financial indiscretions.'

'Is that why they came?'

'It seems so, though I don't know how he convinced Charlotte. I don't imagine he shared his true motivations. In Charlotte's letter at Christmas she said Ella had been talking about my imminent return. I can only surmise the journey stemmed from that until I speak to her myself.'

'I see.' What else was there to say? Daniel was trapped in a situation not of his own making every bit as much as his sister was, even though she was oblivious.

'Maddy, I don't know what else I can do.' His voice trembled a little and she found herself unable to look at him. She couldn't stand to see the pain in his eyes. 'I know you might not have seen it, but Charlotte is kind. She and I were close before she married Matthew. I couldn't do anything to hurt her.'

'It's very simple,' Maddy said, and her voice sounded flat, foreign to her own ears. 'You mustn't.'

'I've no desire to marry Ella nor to return to England, but I owe my sister so much, and I can't see her humiliated and destitute,' he continued as if she'd not spoken.

'Then don't, don't do it,' Maddy shot back. 'I have money, I could—'

'I could never countenance it.' Daniel's expression was intractable. 'Nor will I be party to Matthew's machinations. But I cannot see my sister humiliated.'

'What will you do?' With a sinking feeling, she knew he would never be hers. She'd been a fool to have believed anything different. No one would ever choose her: she knew it.

'I must protect Charlotte.' He dropped to sit on the boulder, swept his hat from his head and slapped it against his knee. 'I am not returning to England. If Ella was to insist we marry, she would have to remain in the colony. Matthew and Charlotte can have my inheritance, and if it isn't enough to clear his debts, it should be enough to alleviate them somewhat. In that regard it matters little which country I reside in.'

Maddy stood staring at him for a moment and then sat down beside him. For a long time she stared at the damp ground and the lichen-covered tree trunks and wondered what she was doing there.

'But if you offer to help Matthew, why must you marry Ella? Surely repaying the debt is enough—'

'I fear the debt is far greater than my small inheritance. If I were to marry Ella, her father would likely settle the rest. He wouldn't permit Ella to be tainted by public embarrassment. Even if it is only by association.'

Maddy couldn't make sense of any of it. How could her emotions swing so violently? One day her future was to be viewed with joyful anticipation, and now with dread.

'Do you intend to buy a property in the colony?' she asked after a long moment.

'I had, but then I came to Shelby, and ...'

'And you stayed. Far longer than you'd meant to?'

'Well yes, but I was very happy here.'

Was? Maddy realised in that moment that she had truly lost him. She swallowed hard. Should she be pleased? After all, she'd been saved from giving away her independence. Yes, she must see it thus. Fate had saved her from her own covetous heart.

'All we truly have is our honour, and you must do what is honourable,' Maddy said, rising and straightening her skirts. For a moment Maddy considered asking where was his honour when it came to her? Had he not said he wanted to marry *her*? Her mind roiled with words she wanted to throw at him, but she sucked in a breath and blinked away angry tears. She would not beg for his love.

'But Maddy,'—he too got to his feet—'I love you.'

'Don't,' she said, unable to keep the frostiness from her words, 'don't say it ever again. You must do what you feel is right for your family.' She gritted her teeth in a determined grimace. It was over before it ever began, and Maddy wished it had never been. She couldn't look at him.

'Yes,' he said, his voice sadder than anything she'd ever heard.

Though the loss of him was more painful than losing both Mama and Papa together, it was a pain that must go unacknowledged, she realised. As was the case with their affection for each other.

'When will you leave?' Maddy was surprised at how unemotional she sounded when she asked the question. Her heart was a block of ice, numbing her entire self—body and mind.

He blinked, swallowed and eventually said, 'I won't leave you until we find a suitable replacement.'

'That's not your responsibility.'

'It's my duty.'

'Duty.' She nodded; tears she'd managed to hold in began to spill over and she averted her face, not wanting him to see. 'Yes, we must all do our duty.'

Twenty-Six

Friday, 1 June 1832—cool with clearing skies

Daniel's words of duty echoed endlessly in the following weeks. Maddy understood duty. She too had a duty: a duty to Mama and Papa; and one to Phil, Charlie, Jane and the others. A duty to fulfil a promise. As did Daniel. She could not resent him for it, no matter the pain it caused.

She slept little and ate less, working each day until she dropped, only to lie on her bed staring into the darkness. She and Daniel were polite, but the sadness and longing that stretched between them was tangible. As there was always plenty to do, it was relatively simple to keep him at a distance. Far easier than her contrary heart would wish for.

The weather grew cold and miserable with occasional icy showers; the grey skies matched her melancholy mood. Taking advantage of a break in the drizzle one morning, over a week after Daniel's terrible decision, Maddy pulled on boots and coat and headed down to the fields where the men were harvesting the last of the potatoes. She should be elated, as with the colder weather there was less to do on the farm, and on the quieter days the men quarried stone for the house; but it seemed a hollow effort with Daniel's departure looming. She watched as the large horses pulled the potato plough through the damp soil. Michael, Patrick and young Joey worked ahead of the horses, clearing away the dried stalks and allowing the plough to turn the soil and expose the tubers. Young Charlie drove the team and controlled the plough, while Daniel, Phil, Lester and Joseph followed, collecting the yield into sacks that were then sewn up and stacked on the waiting wagon. The damaged tubers were left to be gleaned for stockfeed when the harvest was done. The scene brought back the memory of the day she'd arrived and Maddy swallowed around a lump of emotion.

As had occurred that fateful day, Lester was the first to notice her standing by the side of the field, and once again, he merely watched, his face expressionless—and yet somehow she felt as if he could see right through her. After more than half a year, he was as remote as he had been when she first met him. A few paces from where Maddy stood was the wagon, stacked high with sacks stamped SHELBY ESTATE, HUNTER RIVER, and she felt a momentary flash of pride. It was a good harvest, with plenty for their own consumption and surplus to be sent to market. The elation was soon eclipsed as she watched Daniel carrying a bulging sack across his shoulders, navigating the uneven ground with ease as he came towards her. Maddy braced for a painful conversation. Every word they spoke to each other was fraught with regret and caused them both discomfort. Regardless of her understanding his reasons, it still hurt.

'Miss Barker-Trent.' He nodded politely, avoiding looking directly at her.

Tears pricked Maddy's eyes.

'Mr Coulter,' she said, having to clear the croakiness from her throat. She nodded at the laden dray. 'It is a decent crop.'

'Yes, I wasn't sure how it would go, as the weather wasn't favourable, and with the flood we were fortunate they didn't rot in the ground.'

'Yes.' Maddy nodded. An awkward silence stretched, and she wished she hadn't come down.

'Actually, I'm glad—' he began.

'I was wondering—' Maddy said at the same instant.

'You first.'

'No, you.'

His lips twisted in a momentary flash of humour, then levelled once more and he nodded. 'I'd like to take a day or two off, if you don't mind.'

Maddy nodded. She desperately wanted to ask him why, but she was afraid of the answer; instead she nodded again and kept her questions to herself.

'There's a piece of land on the Allyn River going to auction next month, and I'd like to ride up and take a look.'

'I see,' Maddy said, sounding more composed than she felt. She knew he must leave Shelby eventually, but the reality pierced her heart. 'Yes, yes of course. When were you planning to go?'

'When we take this load to the steamer I'll continue up the Paterson River from there.'

'I see.'

A tense silence swelled between them as she searched for something to say.

'What were you wondering?'

'What?' Maddy met his stare—she had no idea what he meant.

'You said you were wondering …'

'Oh, yes.' She hardly wanted to know the answer any more, for each word felt as if it were a nail in the lid of the coffin holding her dreams. 'I wondered if you'd mentioned to anyone else that I'm looking for a new overseer here.'

'Ah, yes. I told Mr Garrick and Mr Everette when I was last at Tillington.'

Maddy nodded. There was little point in hiding it, she supposed.

'They said they would keep an eye open for someone suitable.'

She nodded again. Her chin trembled a little. He saw it.

'Maddy, I won't leave until we find ...'

His replacement, she silently finished the sentence. She nodded; unable to look at him, she turned away. She couldn't do this. Perhaps it would be better if he went all the sooner. She would advertise for someone.

'May I have a word?'

Lester glanced up from the block of stone he was preparing and scowled at Maddy. He put down the tool he used to chip the facing of the stone and joined her. With the men cutting stone in the quarry, and Lester busy on the house, progress was at last being made, so Maddy felt even more hesitant to broach the subject but knew she could put it off no longer; she'd waited too long as it was. However, she didn't intend to have such a discussion where anyone could wander by. She owed George Lester her full attention, and with Mary and Jane scrubbing sheets nearby in the house yard, it was hardly conducive to a private conversation.

'Come into the kitchen and we can have a cup of tea and talk.'

His eyes narrowed but his face remained impassive as he laid down his tools and followed her without comment.

Maddy pushed the kettle onto the heat and invited him to sit down. He pulled the kerchief from his neck and mopped his face before doing so.

'Mr Coulter has told me of your eligibility to be granted a ticket of leave,' she said, sounding as stiff and awkward as she felt.

She groaned silently: she needed to improve relations with the man, not make the divide wider.

He stared at her, his eyes as always merely watched her. She cleared her throat, feeling suddenly nervous and inept in his brooding presence.

'Do you have any firm plans for the future?'

'I've an idea or two.' His voice was gravelly with disuse when he finally spoke; his expression gave nothing away.

'Very good.' The water began to boil and Maddy turned her attention to making the tea. She could feel his stare on her back as she placed the leaves in the pot; it brought to mind her first morning at Shelby when she'd shared tea with the men, before she knew of Papa's death.

'I have a proposal for you,' Maddy said, pouring the tea into her mama's delicate porcelain cups. Lester's eyes met hers across the scrubbed pine table. He said nothing, only sat waiting. His silent perusal made Maddy squirm in her seat. She forced herself to be still. She was about to make the man an offer he couldn't refuse, so why was she the one who was nervous? After all, his future freedom was in her hands.

'I would like to grant you your ticket of leave and employ you to complete the house.' Maddy examined his features, still unchanged. She hurried on. 'I will apply for another assigned servant, and he shall be under your charge; in the meantime, I will pay the other men to work on the stone if they wish to earn extra. As I still have to run the farm, I can't offer you extra help on any permanent basis, but perhaps the inducement of being paid for their labour will be sufficient.'

'Why would you do that?' he asked, his tone disbelieving. 'They're convicts; they have to do what you say. We all do.'

'Because I want the house built and I want everyone on Shelby to be happy. They work hard as it is—if more is required of them, they should see some benefit.'

'You're certainly a strange one.' He picked up his tea and took a sip. 'But so was yer pa.'

Maddy ignored the reference to Papa though it rankled. 'When the house is done, I will make arrangements to have the man you've trained signed over to you, and I doubt you will have any trouble finding plenty more work in the colony.'

He drained his cup and placed it back into the saucer. His gaze drilled into her and Maddy was hard pressed to meet it. Why did he make her so nervous? Though he was somewhat belligerent, other than keeping a silent watchfulness he'd done nothing to warrant her distrust. A muscle in his broad temple pulsed as he examined her for a long while. Far longer than was comfortable.

'Do you mean it?' he asked when she thought he would never say anything at all—not even acknowledge the offer.

'Yes, of course,' she said, 'I'd not have spoken to you had I not meant it.'

His lips twitched and his dark eyes crinkled and almost disappeared as a wide smile transformed his face for the first time ever in her presence.

'Then, Miss Maddy, I'd be honoured to build your house.'

Relief flooded through her and she felt suddenly limp. Maddy grinned and reached a trembling hand to him across the table. His smile didn't falter, but he hesitated a moment before grasping it in his large calloused fingers and shaking it vigorously.

'I didn't think I'd ever want to work for a woman,' he said, looking at her with his dark assessing eyes.

'And you do now?'

'The way I see it, miss, you ain't just any woman.'

'I'll take that as a compliment,' Maddy said, smiling.

He nodded. 'You won't regret this, miss,' he promised.

'I know I won't, George.'

Twenty-Seven

Monday, 4 June 1832—foggy and cold

With Daniel riding his horse, and Phil and Lester atop the dray packed high with Shelby Estate potatoes, the men were about to leave for Green Hills with the produce to be shipped to Sydney markets the next morning.

Jane and Mary were busy working through a list of chores while Luke practised writing on the slate Maddy had purchased for Jane. She took advantage of the small window of freedom to change into her riding habit. Though she knew her penchant for riding alone was frowned upon, she wished to clear her mind and a morning ride was exactly what she needed. It was so long since she'd ridden purely for enjoyment that she'd almost forgotten how much she loved it.

'Morning, Miss Maddy,' Charlie greeted her as she approached. He smiled, taking in her attire. Maddy marvelled at how he had come out of himself since she'd first met him. Not long ago, he'd barely have dared even to look in her direction, let alone smile and speak directly to her. Being in charge of the horses suited him.

'Good morning, Charlie.'

'I'll saddle Red.' He nodded towards the yard, where the gelding stood leaning over the rails, ears pricked, nickering expectantly. Charlie's dog Betty was busy rolling in a fresh pile of dung. Maddy shook her head and turned her attention back to Charlie.

'Yes please, Charlie.'

He headed for the store to retrieve the tack, calling for Betty to come away, and Maddy crossed to her horse, revealing two carrots to Red, who stamped his foot and whinnied his approval.

She held out the first treat, and he delicately snapped off one end, chewing delightedly, eyes half closed and ears drooping with pleasure. The sight brought a smile to her lips and she thought she'd not smiled since Daniel had left for Tillington to see Ella.

Charlie returned with saddle and bridle, placed the tack on the fence rail and entered the yard.

'Where are you off to, miss?'

Maddy blinked. An initiated conversation, and now a question: Jane obviously was good for him. She'd seen the pair talking quietly and knew they frequently went for walks together.

'I'm not sure. I was thinking I would go towards Dalwood, and perhaps call on Mrs Wyndham.'

'Would you like me to come with you? I could throw a saddle on old Pepper.'

The very reason she wished to ride was to get away and have some time alone. She needed to think. 'Thank you, Charlie, but no. I'll be fine.'

'Well, be careful, miss, you know there's been talk of bushrangers about the place.'

There had been talk—there was always talk—but she took little notice. Runaway convicts were hardly out of the norm. Maddy wondered where they'd run from. Some of her peers insisted a heavy hand was required to keep the convicts under control, however the men Maddy considered her mentors managed assigned labour with decency and compassion, and she saw no reason to stray from their example.

'What have you heard, and where did you hear it?'

'George told me.' By this time Charlie had the bridle on and was lifting the saddle from the rail.

'Where did he hear it?'

He grunted as he tightened the girth and turned to look at her. 'I'm not rightly sure, miss.' He checked the saddle was firm. She imagined Lester had probably spoken to someone from Tillington when attending Sunday services.

'I shall only be an hour or so,' Maddy said as she led Red to the mounting block. Perhaps she should learn to ride astride. It would certainly be convenient. And what was a little more scandal?

Maddy pulled her bonnet off as she rode, looping the ribbon over her wrist. The winter sun shone through the trees and warmed her bare head as she let her horse wander along the track. She could have taken the road, but instead she'd ridden out past the quarry and taken a little-used footpath that cut through the bush to rejoin the road closer to Mr Wyndham's property.

The sound of birds, rustling leaves and the steady clop of her horse's hooves soothed her frantic mind, and she found herself immersed in the moment. Maddy's hips rolled with the gait of the horse beneath her, and she concentrated at first only on her surroundings. She inhaled deeply, enjoying the smell of eucalypts and something undefinable but particular to the bush. It seemed such a long time since she'd done anything purely for the pleasure of it.

As Maddy rode her attention drifted to the question of her future at Shelby. Deep down she feared her life would stretch out in a long and miserable existence without Daniel. Maddy had to choose between continuing alone or marrying someone else, though she found it impossible to entertain the latter idea. The Lord knew there were plenty to choose from, some who might even be tolerable companions, but she'd never go down that avenue. The thought that had been lurking at the back of her consciousness suddenly swarmed to the forefront of her mind. She could sell Shelby to Daniel and return to England. Daniel was already familiar with the property. He'd developed the majority of the improvements. To force him to start again when he'd done so much seemed unjust. And, Maddy forced herself to admit, she doubted her own ability to stay and see him marry Ella and begin a family. To witness him with another woman, living the life of Mr and Mrs Coulter that she'd dreamed of, was more than she could endure. Not even for Mama or Papa.

Maddy was almost at the juncture where the path met the road to Dalwood when she heard the sound of approaching hooves. Down the hill a cloud of dust billowed behind two riders galloping towards her. Her horse stopped in response to the pressure on the reins but pricked its ears as it watched the approaching horses. One horse was black and ridden by a woman in brilliant blue and both were immediately recognisable. Maddy was surprised Ella hadn't accompanied Daniel to see the property. Red stayed completely still and quiet, as if he too hoped Ella would gallop by unaware of their presence. She had no desire to speak to the woman at all. In fact, if it were possible to accomplish without being seen, she'd have turned Red and ridden in the opposite direction. Thankfully she was far enough away from the road that Ella didn't notice her.

They went by so fast she didn't have an opportunity to identify the groom riding several yards behind Ella and the stallion. Maddy muttered an unladylike curse beneath her breath and fumed. Ella not only had Daniel, but for her to have claimed Papa's horse and to gallop such a fine animal all over the countryside ignited a fury in Maddy she could not have hidden in that moment. No, it was best to avoid a meeting. Maddy exhaled only once they'd passed and after a few moments urged Red forwards once more. She assumed Ella had been to Dalwood, and Maddy was no longer inclined to go there. It was silly, but she felt as if she disappeared from view when Ella was around, and she couldn't bear the thought of hearing about Ella's visit and the excitement over her betrothal to Daniel. Maddy wasn't ready to face the furore the upcoming marriage would incite. Or worse, sympathy and understanding—for she was certain that the more discerning women of the district would know where Maddy's affections lay. No, she would save herself the humiliation.

On impulse she turned her horse in the same direction Ella and the groom had gone and urged it into a steady ground-covering trot. She didn't know why she followed, but Maddy wanted to see where Ella went. To observe Daniel's betrothed without her knowledge was an impulse Maddy didn't even try to resist. Did she dislike Ella on her own account, or was it because of her relationship with Daniel and his family? Maddy had to admit being irked by the ease with which she rode Papa's horse. Even Mr Garrick, a strong man, had struggled with the difficult stallion.

The air tasted of dust for about a mile, and as she rounded a slight bend it suddenly cleared and there was no sign of the two horses. It was as if they'd not ridden this way at all. Maddy slowed Red to a walk and peered around. The scrub was sparse, but she saw no obvious place where they might have left the track. She held her breath to listen. The only sounds heard over the clopping hooves of her her horse were the usual song of the breeze in the trees and twitter of birds. Where had they gone? The road stretched empty ahead, with not even a residue of dust floating to mark their passage. Perhaps there was a trail off to the side she'd missed while caught up in her own bitter thoughts. Maddy turned Red back the way she'd come, and, walking him slowly, scoured each side of the track. She found nothing obvious and after a few minutes she decided to ride home by the road.

It had been a silly impulse to follow them and even more to believe they'd simply vanished. They must have just ridden harder along the straight and were gone from sight before she'd rounded the bend. But what of the dust? There was always a trail of dust lingering when a rider passed. The breeze was quite fresh, so it had most likely blown the dust away, she reasoned. Satisfied with her conclusions, Maddy laughed aloud at her silliness. Steering her horse homewards, she dug her heels in and thrilled at the instant response as he lunged into an exhilarating gallop, leaving their own trail of dust behind.

As she rode into the easterly breeze her eyes began streaming, and she reconsidered her conclusion: if the breeze was coming from the east, it would have blown the dust towards her, not dissipated it. Maddy shook her head. What did it matter where they'd gone? It was nothing to do with her. She'd come out to clear her thoughts of the woman, not to chase Ella all over the countryside.

Twenty-Eight

Monday, 4 June 1832—cold winds in evening

'I think I'll go to bed now,' Mary said, folding away the mending she'd been playing about with. Jane sat in a chair by the stove with Luke on her lap, reading a Bible story by turn: the soft murmuring of their voices was a comforting backdrop as Maddy inspected the monthly accounts. Mary liked neither reading nor listening to someone else read, and Maddy wondered if she intended to sneak out to meet Joe.

'Yes,' Maddy said, 'it's been a long day. I think we should all make our ablutions and head to bed.'

Mary frowned. Maddy saw Jane duck her chin to hide a mischievous smile. Maddy was wising up to Mary's tricks and was glad she'd forestalled any night-time antics. For now.

Jane agreed and, shoving a grinning Luke from her lap, she stood and placed the Bible on a shelf, out of harm's way, before following Mary out of the door. 'Wait, Mary, I'll walk to the privy with you.'

Maddy heard Mary say something in response but couldn't make out the words. She looked at Luke, who stood silent beside the range. Though he was completely relaxed with Jane, the boy remained wary and silent around Maddy, and she wasn't sure what she could do about it. There was something in her that wanted to keep him at arm's length, despite the fact that he lived under her roof and even shared her room.

'Your reading improves daily, Luke,' Maddy said, meaning to sound encouraging, but the words came out stilted. She tried a smile, but when he averted his gaze, she sighed.

She heard the dog begin to bark, and thoughts of her relationship with Luke flew from Maddy's mind as the sound of horses quickly followed the warning. She hurried to the door and pulled it open to see Daniel, Mr Garrick and Mr Clinton on horses that had obviously been ridden hard.

'Daniel, what's happened?'

He looked into her face, and though it was dark, Maddy could see the tension in his jaw.

'Is Ella here?'

Maddy shook her head. 'No, why would she be here?'

'She rode out and did not come home,' Mr Garrick said.

It took Maddy a moment to comprehend what he meant. When she'd seen Ella it had been late morning. How could she not have returned to Tillington?

Maddy turned to Daniel; she'd expected him to be away for several days. What had brought him home so early?

'When did she go?' Maddy asked. For reasons she didn't examine she didn't admit to having seen Ella earlier.

'She rode out after morning tea,' Mr Garrick said.

'She had a groom with her, but neither has returned,' added Mr Clinton.

'Where did they go?' Maddy asked.

'Charlotte said she'd intended to go to Dalwood,' Daniel said.

'Have you been there?'

'Yes,' he said, 'apparently she didn't arrive.'

'Perhaps she changed her mind and went to Cragside, or Oswald?'

'We thought it best to check here first as it's closer,' Mr Garrick said.

'Of course. Do you want me to come with you?' Maddy's mind was racing. Still she didn't say she'd seen her, and now it was too late. She opened her mouth. But nothing was forthcoming. Why did she hesitate?

'No, we'll ride to Oswald and hope she's there and then, if we don't find her, to Cragside,' said Daniel.

'Surely she'd have sent word by the man if she'd intended to stay away overnight.' This came from Mr Clinton.

'Perhaps she didn't realise how late it had grown?' Maddy suggested, immediately realising the idiocy of the statement. I must tell him, she thought, but then Daniel frowned at her, and she found again she didn't have the words.

'Sorry to have disturbed you, Maddy, we'd best continue,' Mr Garrick said, and he turned his horse to retrace their way.

'Perhaps the men may have seen her,' Maddy suggested, starting to walk towards the yard.

'Yes, you go inside out of the cold,' Daniel said. 'We will check, and then be on our way if they know nothing.'

Maddy nodded. The men turned their horses and were gone before she could confess to having seen both Ella and the groom. Turning to go inside she paused, she knew she must tell them. Jane and Mary stood in the open doorway, and Luke, who'd joined her outside, followed Maddy into the light and warmth of the kitchen.

'What's happened, miss?' Jane asked, her brown eyes wide and worried.

'Miss Whitfield and a groom went out riding and haven't returned.'

'Good riddance,' Mary muttered. Maddy spun to glare at her, but Mary held her stare with an insolent gleam in her eye for a moment before finally lowering her chin. 'I'm for me bed,' she announced and left the room.

Maddy no longer cared if Mary snuck down to see Joe. Wracked with remorse, she didn't know why she'd lied. By omission, admittedly, but still Maddy hadn't been truthful, and she was ashamed.

'Was she riding the black horse?' Luke asked, startling her.

'Yes,' Maddy said, looking down into his upturned face. 'Why? Did you see her?'

His gaze held hers and a guilty flush rose to Maddy's cheeks; he must have seen her too.

'I saw the tracks. Where she rode the horse,' Luke said.

'Then we'd better catch the men and tell them,' Maddy said and headed for the door. She hesitated and beckoned to him, 'Come along.'

He followed her out into the cold night air. She had to admit she'd seen Ella, and she needed to do it immediately. Maddy was only too pleased for the darkness to hide her flaming cheeks.

'Daniel!' Maddy called out when she saw they were leaving the farmyard. Her voice was loud and easily heard in the still night air. Maddy knew it was Daniel who drew up and turned towards the path to the house, and he who steered his horse to meet her. Mr Garrick and Mr Clinton reined in their horses but waited on the road.

'Daniel, I saw Miss Whitfield earlier today.' Maddy didn't bother with any explanation; he had to know, and she had no excuse for not having spoken up earlier.

Even in the dark she sensed his disbelief. 'You saw her?'

Maddy nodded but couldn't speak.

'Where?' He didn't ask why she'd not mentioned it earlier. Maddy wished he had, for his simple acceptance of her behaviour was far more damning than if he'd grown angry.

'She was coming from Dalwood. They were headed back towards the North Road.'

'Did you speak to her?' His tone gave nothing away.

'No, I wasn't close enough to speak; I only saw her through the bush.' Maddy glanced at the waiting men, knowing full well they could hear every word in the quiet night.

'I see,' Daniel said.

'She was going fast, at a gallop. I didn't have a chance to speak to her. She didn't even see me.'

'And the groom?'

'He was with her.'

'Did you speak to him? Did he see you?'

Maddy was aware of Mr Garrick and Mr Clinton urging their horses closer. 'No, and I don't think so. As I said, I was in the bush, on the small path from the quarry. I wanted solitude, so I didn't try to draw their attention.'

'But they didn't go to Dalwood,' Mr Clinton said.

'I thought they'd come from there.'

'What time was this?' Mr Garrick moved his mount even closer.

Maddy looked up at Daniel. 'I'm not sure of the exact time. I'd been dawdling along the path, but I'd left Shelby around eleven, and it couldn't have taken me much more than half an hour.'

'That wouldn't have been long after she left Tillington,' Mr Clinton said.

Maddy and Luke stood watching the three mounted men. Luke moved closer to Maddy's side, as if for comfort. Automatically she placed a hand on his shoulder and drew him against her.

'Luke said he saw the stallion's hoofprints,' Maddy said, her gaze fixed on Daniel. Shame kept her talking, but pride kept her chin up. She'd been stupid to try to keep her surveillance of Ella a secret: it served no purpose, except to reveal her selfishness.

'Where did you see them, Luke?' Daniel asked.

'This is nonsense: we must find her. She must be at the Everettes' or Harpurs',' Mr Clinton snapped.

'Don't be hasty, Matthew,' Daniel said, not looking around at his brother-in-law. 'If Luke saw something that may help, we must listen to what he has to say.'

But Luke's small bony shoulder grew tense beneath her hand, and Maddy felt him shrink away, though he didn't move. When Luke didn't say anything, Daniel stepped down from the saddle and crossed to crouch down in front of the boy. Daniel's entire attention was on Luke; his movements were jerky and his face pinched with worry as he peered at him. The child stepped behind Maddy, as if repelled by the intensity radiating from Daniel.

'Luke,'—Maddy leaned down and took both his hands in hers— 'you must tell Mr Daniel where you saw the tracks of the black horse.'

With his chin on his narrow chest, Luke refused to look at her. Maddy glanced up at Daniel.

'Come, this is wasting time—let's go to the nearby properties and see if they have any news of Ella,' Mr Clinton said, harshly pulling his horse around and digging his heels into its flanks. His horse exploded forwards under the harsh treatment and he soon steered it towards the road once more.

'Luke, no one is upset with you,' Daniel told him, his voice quiet, but still tight with anxiety. When Luke didn't respond, or even look at him, Daniel glanced at Maddy and said, 'I'm sorry I frightened him. Can you try to get it out of him?'

Maddy continued to hold Luke's hands, certain that if she let them go, he would melt away into the bush. If he withdrew any further they'd never find out what he knew.

Luke allowed her to lead him back to the kitchen after the men had ridden away. He said nothing further and Maddy wasn't sure what she could do to entice him to speak. For a moment she'd had his trust, but it seemed she'd lost it again. And she felt that loss keenly. Instead Maddy made him hot chocolate, which he drank silently, his dark eyes huge and watching while she relayed everything to Jane.

With the hot chocolate consumed they retired soon afterwards. Maddy lay on her bed, wide awake, her cheeks burning with shame at her disgraceful behaviour. Where could they have gone? It then occurred to her that the groom's name had not been mentioned. He was missing too. Was he not worthy of consideration when compared to Ella Whitfield? Or was a convict worth nothing at all? The thought angered her more than she could have ever believed possible.

It took a little while for Maddy to identify the intermittent sound coming from the pallet on the floor. 'Luke?'

There was no answer, just an abrupt silence, as if he'd clamped his chattering teeth together. It was not especially cold in the tiny room, so Maddy concluded his shivering was more a reaction to the night's goings-on than the temperature.

'Come up here,' she said and held up the quilt for him to slide in beside her. At first there was no further sound, then the shush of his quilt being moved aside and the soft pad of his bare feet on the flags. His slender body slid in beside her, and Maddy dropped the covers over him. Freezing flesh touched her legs, and she squeaked and pulled away from him. Maddy was delighted to hear a soft snigger.

'You did that on purpose,' she accused.

His amusement developed into a giggle. Maddy gave him a good-natured poke in the ribs and lay back down.

He squeaked and wriggled and Maddy smiled into the darkness. After a few moments he settled and she could hear his breathing in the almost total darkness.

'Luke?'

He didn't respond, but Maddy sensed he was listening.

'Was it near the road that you saw the horse prints?'

She waited so long for his answer she didn't think he was going to respond. Then she felt him move as he nodded. She let go the breath she'd not realised she held.

'Do you think you could show me where you saw the tracks?'

'Yes.' He spoke so softly, at first Maddy was unsure she heard anything. She pressed a light kiss to his curls before letting her head fall back onto the pillow.

Maddy sighed and nodded. 'Good boy.'

Twenty-Nine

Tuesday, 5 June 1832—heavy mist, cold

Luke and Maddy were out of bed and ready to go before dawn. Jane stood in the door of the kitchen and watched them leave, a concerned frown still lingering on her brow. Maddy carried a small bag holding a heel of bread and a slab of cheese, as well as a canteen of water. She had no idea where Luke would lead her, but she didn't want to be forced to return home due to thirst or hunger. She was dressed in her most worn gown and sturdy boots as they were to walk. Luke insisted they needed to be on the ground to see the tracks, and not wanting him to withdraw again, she did as instructed. With Papa's hat clamped down on her head, and her warm coat, Maddy felt vastly overdressed when she saw Luke wearing the ragged clothes he'd worn when his mother had left him at Shelby. She realised how much he'd grown when she saw the length of exposed leg and bare feet, and she wondered why he didn't want to wear his new clothes. Maddy sighed and realised it was not the time to take him to task on his dress. She wondered if they would ever get him to wear shoes for more than a few hours.

Daniel's horse wasn't in the yard, and with a sinking sensation in her chest, she knew they'd not found Ella. Or the groom, she reminded herself.

By the time the first blush of dawn crept over the range and revealed that the valley floor was draped in a blanket of mist, they'd walked through the bush to where she'd seen Ella and the groom the day before. Luke crossed to the far side of the road and continued south east without hesitation; it was the same way Maddy had seen them go the previous day. He followed the road as it dropped down into a gully; he hesitated only when they reached a point a little beyond where Maddy lost sight of the pair. She wondered how much he could see in the dense fog. When he reached a place that seemed no different to her from any other, he stopped and crouched down to examine the ground, straightened, and headed off into the bush.

'Have you seen something? Is this where you saw them?' She peered at the ground but could see nothing unusual.

He glanced around at her and nodded before continuing without further explanation. Maddy followed at a small distance, not wishing to blunder through any signs he might be able to see but which she could not. She hoped he knew what he was doing. Luke often played with the Wonnarua children, and sometimes the police used tribesmen to track bolters, and Maddy guessed some knowledge had been passed on, though Luke was a white boy.

They walked for miles, with Luke pausing occasionally to peer at the ground. The sun crested the hills, bathing the countryside in a cold light which only served to emphasise the morning chill. Maddy shivered and hoped they would find Ella safe and well. As the sun inched higher she could discern the prints of horseshoes in the dust, but Luke seemed to see so much more than she could.

It was as if he followed a map. Sometimes he circled away from the narrow track and found some sign indiscernible to her, before continuing. When he located the place the pair had run into trouble, even Maddy could see the ground had been disturbed by more than two sets of horse tracks. The soft sandy soil of the ridge was churned up considerably.

'Why did they come this way?' Maddy asked the question aloud, not expecting any answer, but Luke surprised her.

'Chasing a wallaby,' he said.

Maddy lifted a brow: she supposed it made some sense, but she didn't know why Ella would want to. Maddy knew some folk liked the meat, but the one time she'd sampled it, she'd thought it wouldn't ever be her first choice. But, she acknowledged, that might be down to Jane's cooking rather than the meat.

'And they've obviously come across at least one other rider,' Maddy said, noticing the prints of an unshod horse as she examined the disturbed ground.

Luke nodded in solemn agreement. 'Yes, miss.'

'Only one?'

He shrugged. 'Think so.'

'Do you know where they went?'

He looked up at her. 'Me and Ma saw the bad man talking to a man from the big house.' His grey eyes narrowed. 'We saw the men and Ma came to Shelby to see Mr Daniel.'

Without giving her time to process what he'd said, Luke cautiously made his way around the disturbed ground, careful not to add his own footprints to the melee, and all the while his head was bent as he searched for the next clue.

'Wait, Luke, what bad man? Which big house?' But he didn't seem to hear her, only continued following the horse's tracks. Maddy hung back and wondered what he was talking about. Had Rose wished to speak with Daniel because she'd seen the bushranger? The bushranger who, she was starting to glean, had kidnapped Ella and the Tillington groom?

After a few moments of circling, Luke headed off once more, and she followed. This time she could see the trail quite clearly. They twisted through thick scrub, following the tracks left by the horses. Maddy watched Luke as he moved through the country, confident and easy, and marvelled at his skill of following the trail even when she could discern nothing. As they wended their way further from Shelby, her misgivings grew. Perhaps they shouldn't have gone out alone. If a groom and Ella could be captured, and they had been on horses, what chance did she and Luke have should something similar occur?

Luke froze, one hand held out to stop and possibly silence her. For though he moved through the country like a ghost, disturbing nothing, and absolutely silent, no matter how hard she tried, Maddy could only stumble, crunch and puff her way along behind him. She stood now stock-still, her ears straining to hear whatever it was Luke heard. He held out his unwavering hand: an instruction for Maddy to remain where she was as he crept forwards, his bare feet placed slowly and deliberately, each step taken with excruciating care. He lifted his head and sniffed the air.

Maddy peered around, her ears aching with effort as she tried to discern any sound that didn't fit. And then she too heard it. The tell-tale jingle of harness worn by a restless horse, or horses. She squinted, peering through the tree trunks, trying to determine where the sound came from, all the while struggling to remain silent. The squeal of a horse sounded close by. Could it be Papa's stallion? She gasped and was shot a stern glance from Luke. A laughing jackdaw began its mocking call, and as it did, Luke beckoned her forwards and they moved under the cover of the raucous bird call.

They continued to creep through the scrub, and Maddy could only hope Luke wouldn't lead them into trouble. Trying to make as little noise as he did, Maddy followed his step forwards, pause to listen, and then another advance of half a dozen paces. Each time she made a noise he turned; his face was ever impassive, but still he managed to make her cringe at her own clumsiness.

When a strange mound finally came into view, Maddy marvelled that they were so close before she saw it. It was at least twenty feet high and looked as if several large boulders had been dumped by a giant's hand amongst the trees and shrubs. It was similar in size to the remains of an ancient hill fort Papa had once taken her to see, but Maddy didn't think the original inhabitants of New South Wales built such ramparts, and there was no corresponding ditch, so she concluded it was most likely natural. She caught the scent of wood smoke before she saw it waft through the trees. She stared wide-eyed at Luke. He nodded, though what he meant she wasn't entirely sure. Perhaps that this was where Ella Whitfield and the hapless groom were being held.

From the mound Maddy heard a woman's voice. It was high-pitched and frightened, and Maddy was certain it must be Ella's. The words were unclear, but her fear was not. Next came a man's harsh response and Ella screamed.

Maddy's breath caught and she turned to Luke, who crouched beside her. He watched her, his grey eyes dark and afraid. His fear flowed to Maddy and she peered around, searching and desperate to run away but knowing she couldn't leave Ella behind.

'What can we do?' Maddy whispered.

'This is the place the bad man lives.' He backed away a few steps.

Maddy glanced over her shoulder and felt a shiver of apprehension. They couldn't barge in.

'Go and find Mr Daniel,' Maddy whispered.

He looked in the direction of the mound once more, and then back at her, a concerned frown marring his smooth brow.

'Can you find him and bring him and the others back here?'

Luke nodded but didn't move. Maddy realised he was reluctant to leave her alone. 'I'll be fine; I'll stay here and keep an eye on them.'

He nodded, then slowly and silently, he stepped away from where she crouched. She flicked a quick glance towards the mound once more and when she turned back to watch him go, he had already disappeared from sight. Maddy's heart began to thud. Though he was a small boy, his presence had imbued her with a confidence that had left with him. She could only hope she hadn't made a mistake.

The muscles in her legs began to cramp as she crouched behind a medium-sized tree. The cold had been kept at bay by the long walk through the bush, but now it penetrated her clothing and seeped into her bones. She straightened slowly, stopping when her shifting weight snapped a twig, the sound as loud as a pistol shot in the silent bush. Maddy froze, staying as still as her shaking legs and thundering blood would allow; halfway between crouched and standing she waited to see if she'd alerted the bushrangers to her presence. When no outraged outlaw appeared, she straightened from the excruciating crouch and breathed once more.

She scanned the surrounding bush for the horses. Having heard Papa's stallion but not seen any sign of the mounts, Maddy decided to make her way to the far side of the mound and see if they were there. With a vague plan to capture the horses and foil any escape the bushrangers might attempt, she tucked the canteen and bag behind the tree and set off, trying to keep her attention on both the mound and the ground before her, wary of making too much noise or tripping on a branch or tree root. Edging her way around the perimeter of the odd little hillock, she'd gone no more than a hundred yards when she heard movement. Standing as still as a statue of a running man, with one foot lifted to step forwards and the other not terribly well placed, Maddy forced herself to remain immobile and wished she'd thought to bring Papa's gun. Frantically she scanned the top of the mound for any sign of movement, and after several long moments she placed her foot carefully between the branches of a scatter of twigs. Considering her position, she wondered if she could get closer to the base of the mound: she might be less likely to be seen there by anyone looking down at the surrounding bushland.

She set off, heading directly for the largest boulder, hoping it would provide her a level of protection. As much as it pained her, she resisted the urge to hurry, and instead placed her feet carefully, avoiding stepping on anything that would alert anyone to her presence. She'd barely reached the cover of the boulder when she heard a male voice; she was close enough to distinguish the words.

'I'll be back shortly. You keep an eye on her.' Maddy realised there was more than one bushranger, and she wished she'd stayed back where she started. Now what?

'No, I'll do it: this place gives me the shivers.'

'Don't be ridiculous.'

'It's all right for you—you've only been here one night.'

'Go then. But be quick about it.'

Next she heard a thud, a curse and the sound of someone moving towards her. Maddy swallowed; whoever it was, they were much too close for comfort and so she crept slowly backwards, taking refuge behind the large rock. Glancing around she realised she needed to be wary of stumbling into the coming man's path. She had no idea where he would appear and so she hunkered beneath the slight curve of the rock and prayed not to be seen.

From where she crouched, she heard the rustle and snap of bushes as the man walked through the low shrubs. He'd emerged from behind a bush carrying a water canteen. He was close but thankfully he turned away from her and disappeared into the scrub. She wished she knew how far away the source of water was so she could gauge how long he would be gone. She thought he was probably the man who'd raided Shelby and taken Red, but who was the other brigand? And what had become of the groom who'd been out riding with Ella? Maddy's heart stilled. Had they killed the poor man? She'd seen no sign of any violence—nothing like she imagined murdering someone would leave. Surely Luke would have discovered blood, or a body, if there'd been any lying about. No, the groom must have been captured as well.

She could stay where she was, or she could continue with her quest to liberate the horses, and hope to find a suitable hiding place should the man return before she made it back to where Luke had left her. She glanced around and frowned; unable to tell where she'd come from anyway, Maddy continued with her original course of action. She would free the horses. Bent low, she moved across the forest floor in a stealthy creep, staying as close as possible to the base of the mound and praying that the water source and the man sent to collect it were far, far away.

'You won't get away with this,' Ella said, her voice shaky but clear.

'Shut up or I'll gag you.'

'You will hang,' she continued, a level of defiance creeping in. Maddy frowned: Ella wasn't speaking loudly, so she knew she must be directly beneath the place where the woman was being held.

The accomplice snorted with disdainful humour.

'You think you won't be caught?'

'You think anyone will bother trying to find you?' he taunted.

'My fiancé will come, and all the men of the valley.'

'Your fiancé'—his tone was mocking—'has his eye on the Shelby bitch.'

Maddy paused, frowning.

'Anyone with eyes can see it. It's the talk of the valley. She's rebuffed every eligible buck in the colony, but lowly Mr Coulter is going to make good with the heiress of the Shelby Estate,' the man continued tauntingly.

Maddy bristled with indignation, knowing she must continue to move, but something welded her to the spot as she listened. Her heart thrilled on one point—she knew Daniel loved her—and sank with another—Ella would never let him go.

'Nonsense: she might have land, but Mr Coulter has money enough to buy his own. In fact he is away inspecting a property on the Allyn River.' Annoyance lent strength to Ella's words.

She shouldn't have told him that, Maddy thought. Though Daniel was back, and he would come soon and rescue Ella.

'Away, is he? Then we are bound to keep you a little longer.'

'What do you mean?'

Yes, what did he mean?

'If he can afford to buy land, he can afford to pay a good ransom.'

Maddy frowned: who was he? Could it be Chase Hobson? Luke had said he and Rose had seen the bushranger with a man from the big house. For Amelia's sake she hoped not. But she was certain the voice had the ring of education, and unlike the majority of convicts he sounded more like a gentleman than did many of the settlers. Between that, and the news they hoped for a ransom, she began to hope that at least Ella would not have been assaulted.

'You will never get away with it.'

'We'll see.' He sounded dismissive, as if he'd had enough of the conversation.

'Mr Garrick will not rest until he has tracked you down.'

'Mr Garrick will never see me again.'

'He treated you well.' Concern crept into Ella's voice, and Maddy realised she knew who it was.

'Yes, he did. More fool him.'

Thirty

Tuesday, 5 June 1832

It was Bowman. Ella and the groom hadn't been close enough for Maddy to recognise him, but she was certain the man speaking was Bowman, Mr Garrick's trusted convict head groom. A wave of relief swept over her momentarily. Not Mr Hobson then. But what on earth had happened? Maddy stood frozen for several long moments, then, with a start, recalled her purpose and knew she must continue. By freeing the horses, she'd remove the kidnappers' ability to leave the area. With this in mind she moved off once more, carefully placing each step; she mustn't draw their attention.

They'd tied the horses in a small lee at the base of the mound, so, set behind a thick barrier of scrubby bushes, they were quite well hidden. The closest horse was the skinny brown gelding the bushranger had ridden into Shelby; beyond it the bay Bowman had been riding, both tethered and standing quietly. She shook her head. If she'd not heard him herself, she would have found it hard to believe Bowman was in league with a bushranger. Tied a little away from the other horses was Papa's stallion. Maddy saw the beast had managed to tangle the reins around a shrub, with one front leg trapped in the mess.

It would be best if she could free the stallion first—less dangerous to have him away before she dealt with the other two horses, and she needed the flighty beast to lead the others away. Fear churned in her gut and she hesitated. Should she do this? What if the horses were never recovered? No, far better to remove all means of escape for the bushrangers. Dozing in the dappled sunlight, the first two horses barely gave her a glance, unlike the stallion. It stirred restlessly, tangling itself more as it jumped sideways at her appearance. Maddy wished for a sharp knife and the strength to cut through the reins. She had neither.

The stallion snorted as she approached, ears pricked and eyes rolling wildly as it scrambled and tugged at the bush, back bowed and rear legs straining as it tried to free itself. How was she going to untangle it? Maddy moved forwards as slowly and as silently as she was able. The horse thrashed once again and managed to twist free its tangled hoof. Well, that was a start, Maddy thought and steadied her breathing as she listened for the bushranger's return. When she heard nothing but the normal sounds of the bush, she started forwards once again. Murmuring reassuringly to the animal, and hoping she couldn't be heard from the mound, she managed to place one hand on the stallion's quivering shoulder while she examined the twisted leather straps and spiky shrub it was caught around.

'Hush,' she soothed, slowly stroking up its neck. The stallion continued to twitch but stood still for the moment. If she could undo the throat-lash and perhaps slip the bridle off, it would be free. The horse allowed her to get the strap through the first part of the buckle before he lunged away. Maddy swore softly and started again on the bridle.

'Hush now, we'll have you out of this mess in a jiffy if you just stay still.'

She eased the prong free of the strap and pulled it loose. Gently, so as not to spook it again, Maddy softly stroked her way to the head-piece and began to lift it over its ears.

'Oy! What do you think you're doing?'

Maddy looked around, unable to see the man, at the same time as the stallion pulled back; her fingers still held the bridle, and with a tug and twist the beast managed to free itself, wrenching her arm in the process. In a trice, it was galloping away, head high and tail aloft like a flag of triumph. Ignoring her aching shoulder, Maddy dropped the bridle and raced for the next horse. She might be caught, but she could make the outlaws' escape as difficult as possible.

'Help, help me,' Ella screamed, 'Help m—' Her cry was cut short.

Maddy hesitated. She had enough time to free both the other horses before the bushranger reached her. The bushranger's horse danced away, so she raced to remove the bridle from Bowman's mount. She returned to the last horse and managed to undo the throat-lash before rough hands grabbed her shoulders and pulled her away. Maddy twisted, trying to wrench herself free of his grasp. The horse shied, pulling back hard, but the bridle held. The bushranger's fingers tightened, and Maddy bent her head and bit down hard on his hand, kicking backwards at him simultaneously.

'Ouch, you bit me!'

Maddy kicked and twisted again.

'What's going on there?' called Bowman. Maddy looked up to see him standing near a large tree trunk at the top of the mound and staring down at them. She kicked backwards again, glad of the heavy-soled yard boots she wore as she felt her heel connect with the bushranger's shin. He swore, but his grip didn't slacken. He shoved her forwards and Maddy fell to her knees in the dust.

'What the hell is going on?' Bowman was closer now, and Maddy realised there was more than one way down from the top.

'The bitch bit me,' the bushranger complained, rubbing the side of his hand where she saw the imprint of her teeth. She had left a decent mark.

Good.

'I caught her releasing the horses,' he explained, still rubbing at the bite mark.

William Bowman joined them and the face she'd known previously as polite and solicitous was cold and expressionless. He stared at Maddy for a long moment, then turned to scan the surrounding scrub for the horses he and Ella had been riding. He swore.

'Your habit of snatching gentrified women is going to get us hanged,' he told his accomplice, sending the other man a withering look.

'I forgot your taste runs more to convict wenches,' the bushranger muttered with a sideways glance at Bowman, who didn't seem to have heard. He continued more audibly, 'I didn't snatch this one, she just turned up, and she let the horses loose. What're we gunna do now?'

'Shut up! Just take her up with the other one. I need to think about this.'

Maddy watched this interchange with interest: still on her knees in the dust, she knew then that Bowman was the leader and brains of the duo. She scanned the bush, searching for some means of escape. How long until Daniel came? She wasn't sure how long it was since she'd sent Luke for help. The bushranger reached down and she saw the wide scar above his brow, confirming he was the same man who'd held her at gunpoint and stolen her horse. He pulled Maddy roughly to her feet, his grip on her wrist savage as he twisted it up behind her and shoved her towards the base of the mound and an apparently impenetrable clump of scrubby bushes.

Before they reached the base Bowman strode past without a glance and disappeared from sight beyond the thicket. Maddy wondered what conclusion he'd come to. They rounded the same clump of shrubs and she saw a narrow trail winding up the side of the bank between the rocks and trees. She was amazed; it had been completely invisible until she was shoved past the bushes. She saw why the horses had been tethered at the base of the mound rather than at the top: it would be impossible to lead them through the undergrowth without making the entrance visible to anyone who ventured nearby. When they reached the top Maddy saw it really was a perfect camp for concealment. It was a mostly flat space, with a scattering of boulders large and small; tall willowy trees reached skywards with little foliage beyond a clump of sun-seeking leaves at the very top.

A rough lean-to of bark and branches had been constructed near one of the larger boulders, and slumped beneath it on the ground, with her back against the rock, was Ella Whitfield.

Ella looked up at Maddy, her face blanched with the exception of a large red mark on her cheekbone; she radiated fear. Maddy noted Ella's tied ankles poking from beneath the hem of her riding habit, and she saw her wrists were bound behind her. Maddy was certain she'd last seen the same rough rope at Shelby—the only thing the bushranger managed to keep hold of when he'd attempted to rob them. There was no time to dwell on that as she was certain the men intended to secure her in the same fashion, and it would be a good idea to distract them and, if possible, keep from being tied too. She had to give Luke time to find and bring help. Ella still hadn't moved at all.

'Ella,' Maddy exclaimed, and Ella turned to Maddy, her blue eyes wide in her pale face. She tried to give her an encouraging smile, though Ella's dazed expression wasn't reassuring. How hard had he hit her?

Maddy knew she had to keep the men's attention on herself as long as possible. 'You can't think to get away with this,' she said when the bushranger shoved her roughly towards Ella. She stumbled, and, in a moment of inspiration, cried out and clutched her ankle.

'What's wrong with you? Get over there,' the bushranger said, but Maddy heard a note of concern in his voice.

'My ankle—I twisted it.' She held the joint in both hands and kept her head down. 'I can't walk,' she wailed.

'Then crawl,' Bowman said, his voice cold, then, to his accomplice, 'Tie her up.'

'It's broken,' Maddy whimpered.

'Good: you won't be able to run away,' Bowman told her.

'There ain't no more rope.'

'Any more rope—Good God, man, can't you speak like an Englishman?' Bowman sounded more concerned over the bushranger's abuse of the language than the health of his prisoners.

'What happened to the rope?' Bowman asked when the bushranger didn't respond.

Maddy chanced a glance at Bowman; he lifted a billy can from the smouldering embers of a small fire, seemingly unconcerned by his partner's difficulties.

'I used it to make a shelter: it's been cold living out here for months.'

'Then tie them together and use the same rope, or pull down the hut. I don't care, just tie her up. And stop your snivelling.'

Maddy took a moment to examine the shelter and saw he had indeed used a great deal of rope to tie a sapling between two trees to form his roughly triangular structure in the lee of one of the larger boulders.

The bushranger glared resentfully at Bowman for a moment before turning to contemplate his hut, and then Ella. For a moment Maddy thought he would deconstruct his shelter rather than untie Ella. Had she put up a fight? If so it had certainly gone out of her now. What had happened? She didn't look as if she'd been harmed. She could worry about Ella later. First they had to get free, or at least stay safe until help arrived.

'Mr Bowman,' Maddy said, still keeping hold of her ankle and hoping her deliberately pained expression was convincing. He continued to stare into the tin cup of tea he held. 'Please, you must quit this folly—you know it will go much better for you if you give yourself up.'

He laughed as he looked down at her, his face full of a genuine amusement that quite softened his features into the handsomeness she'd seen before.

'You can't hope to get away: there's help coming for us right now. They're on their way.'

'So you say, but how do they know where we are?' He examined her as one might an insect he would like to crush beneath his heel.

'Young Luke guided me here, and he's gone to get Mr Garrick and Mr Coulter.'

'Where did you leave your horse?' he asked, as if he'd not heard.

'At Shelby in the field. We walked.'

'Walked? All this way?' His expression barely changed, but there was a tension in every movement that told Maddy she needed to be careful. His handsome face somehow made his lack of compassion all the more disquieting.

'Yes, Luke followed the tracks,' she told him. She had to say something, and although Maddy knew she needed to be wary of him, she thought the truth was probably her best option. She clutched her ankle once again, wincing. She only hoped it was credible: if they thought she was injured, they may not bother to bind her.

'Ah, Rose McMahon's kid. I've seen him lurking about.'

Maddy lifted her gaze to meet his once more but said nothing.

'I heard you'd taken him in. As it should be I suppose. Your papa was pretty fond of his mother.'

Maddy's breath caught in her throat and she glanced down. Calculating eyes searched hers out again and this time Maddy refused to look away. No matter what, she would not be ashamed of Papa.

'It was good of you to take in your brother,' he drawled, watching for her reaction. 'Not many women would want to admit they had a bastard brother.'

The usual sounds of the bush suddenly went silent and Maddy was aware of Ella and the bushranger listening, of them judging Papa, and in due course, Maddy herself. A raging heat prickled her brain and she longed to hit the arrogant smile from his face. How dare he sneer at Papa? At least Papa was not a convicted criminal sent to the other side of the world. And poor Luke, an innocent victim of birth.

'I care nothing for his parentage. He is a child in need, and I'd turn no one away in such circumstances.'

Bowman merely snorted and turned away.

The bushranger made no move to either dismantle his abode or untie Ella. Maddy could appreciate his reluctance in both instances. She glanced at Ella, but the girl had not moved.

'I thought you went for water!' Bowman snapped at his hapless companion.

'I did, but ...' The bushranger's eyes flew to Maddy, as if that was explanation enough.

'Where is it?' Bowman tossed the empty cup onto the ground and started towards the trail.

'I dropped it when I saw her freeing the horses,' the bushranger said, his tone peevish.

Bowman didn't respond but continued down the path, and he was soon out of sight. The bushranger gave Maddy an assessing glance, then crossed to the fire and pulled the billy from the coals, checking the contents and retrieving the cup Bowman had dropped. He wiped away the dust clinging to the side, then pulled the corner of his shirt from his trousers and used it to clean the rim before pouring himself the remaining tea. As if he were entirely alone in his eyrie, he squatted beside the fire, picked up a small branch which he added to the glowing embers, and sipped the tea.

Maddy looked at Ella, who stared at their captor; her chin dimpled, and her lips trembled. She was trussed up like a chicken, sitting in the dust, and she was frightened. Tears spilled down Ella's cheeks and Maddy wished she could offer her some comfort. Soon Daniel would come and they would be safe. At least she hoped it would be soon.

The three of them sat in silence and Maddy wondered if Bowman had returned to the creek for more water, or more likely if he was searching for the horses. After what must have been a good half-hour, he still had not returned. The bushranger got to his feet with a grunt, picked up a rifle from the ground and strode across to the top of the path.

'The mongrel,' he said and with a few long strides he too was gone from sight.

Thirty-One

Tuesday, 5 June 1832

Maddy was on her feet in an instant. Ella still didn't look up as she approached. She was certain Bowman had taken the remaining horse and made good his own escape, leaving his accomplice to deal with the men who would surely arrive soon to rescue them. Maddy had no plan other than to untie Ella so they could at least move. Or run, should they get a chance.

'Ella, lean forwards so I can untie you.' Ella didn't respond to Maddy's whispered instruction. She sighed and pushed at her shoulder. Ella shifted enough to give Maddy access to her rope-wrapped wrists. Maddy made short work of the loose ties, the rope being so stiff it hadn't tightened on itself. (Which was why Phil had deemed it useless and left it looped on the fence post.) Ella's wrists were chafed by the abrasive coils and Maddy hoped the marks would not mar her skin permanently. The rope was soon dispensed with, and Maddy rubbed Ella's hands gently, hoping to stimulate the circulation. When she stopped rubbing, Ella's hands flopped to her sides, and she made no move to untie her own ankles. Maddy cast a quick glance over her shoulder; neither the bushranger nor Bowman had returned.

'Ella, untie your feet and I'll go and make sure no one is coming.'

Ella stared up at her blankly.

Maddy saw that a blue-purple bruise had developed. 'How dare he hit you,' she gasped.

Ella still made no move to free herself, so with a muttered curse Maddy bent to dispatch the ropes herself. Straightening, she waited for Ella to get to her feet. She didn't move.

'Ella, come along, get up.'

Still the woman remained unresponsive. Maddy bent down and took hold of her by the arm and lifted it encouragingly. Perhaps she was stiff and sore after sitting on the cold ground, tied up and immobile overnight. Suddenly Maddy realised the terror poor Ella had endured. With more compassion than she'd previously felt for the girl, Maddy gently tried to urge Ella to her feet.

'Come, you must stand up and get your blood flowing.'

Ella made no effort to stand; nor did she react to Maddy's encouragement. Maddy fought down her frustration and bent low to look her in the face. Ella's eyes remained downcast and Maddy reached out to lift her chin and force Ella to listen. Ella pulled away with a whimper and Maddy saw Ella's jaw was also swollen and discoloured.

'Ella, I know you've been hurt, but we've an opportunity to escape, and I need you to stand up and be ready to run. I cannot carry you.'

Ella's gaze was unfocused and her expression uncomprehending. *Curse it!* Should they just wait for help to come?

'Ella,' Maddy hissed, deciding they had to move, 'get up now!' Ella blinked at the intensity of Maddy's command and shifted a little. Well, it wasn't much, but at least she'd reacted.

'I'll help you. I know your legs are painful, but it will get better as you move about a bit.' Maddy hoped she was right. Taking both Ella's hands in hers, Maddy pulled her up. She finally moved, tucking up her legs and straightening slowly. Maddy puffed out a relieved gasp as Ella stumbled forwards and she managed to steady her before they both ended up on the ground. Ella squeaked with pain at the jolted movement and Maddy cringed sympathetically.

When Ella was able to stand unassisted Maddy left her to hurry across the uneven ground to the top of the trail. She peered down and saw no one. Where was the bushranger? The horse she'd been unable to free was gone and neither man was in sight. She couldn't blame them; if they'd stayed they'd have been trapped atop this hill in a medieval-style siege, Ella and Maddy with them.

In the distance Maddy heard the muted cry of a male voice and thought it might be one of their rescuers, but she didn't call back, in case it was the bushranger calling out for Bowman.

She wasn't going to wait there for him to return: he still had a gun. Maddy spun around to find Ella still standing where she'd left her. This was going to be difficult. Ella must be in terrific pain, but they had to get off this mound and away as soon as possible. The more desperate the outlaws were, the more likely they were to be brutal. Better that they should run now and get away. If they could get clear of the immediate area, they were sure to come across Daniel and Mr Garrick. Maddy hurried back to Ella.

'Ella, both the men are gone, so let's walk down the hill and start for home. I'm certain Daniel will be along shortly, but we should leave here. Come with me; we'll start out.' Ella didn't respond, but she didn't resist. Maddy led her towards the far side of the mound and hoped they might find another track. Trying to choose a path as smooth as she could through the trees, she cast a glance back at Ella, who winced with every step. Had they broken her jaw? There was no blood, but the bruising was spreading.

Frantic, she searched for a way down—they didn't dare go the way the bushranger had in case they ran right into him and were recaptured.

Maddy led a stumbling Ella through the trees and around the boulders until at last she saw a small, barely discernible trail, probably made by an animal of some kind, and with only the slightest hesitation she started down. Ella followed without protest and, when the way became crowded with bushes and trees, Maddy let go of her hand and hoped she would follow. She did.

They had gone about halfway down the side of the mound when the animal track dwindled to nothing. Maddy continued, pushing a route through the thick scrub and spindly tree trunks, ignoring the scratches and tears the branches inflicted on her and her clothes. The sharp report of gunfire ripped the still cool air. Maddy froze, holding out a hand to halt Ella's dogged steps behind her. She listened in vain for the next shot, swinging her head from side to side. Where had the shot come from? Who had fired the gun? She heard nothing but her own frantic breathing, and the sudden silence of the bush. All the creatures had gone to ground or were waiting, as was Maddy, to see if danger was imminent.

She turned to find Ella crouched down, utterly motionless and looking like a startled rabbit, with tears streaming down her face. They couldn't stay there, halfway down a steep incline, with someone shooting. Maddy knew they needed to get down and keep moving.

'Come on,' she whispered, beckoning Ella to follow. She didn't wait, just started down the trackless slope. Not hearing Ella following, Maddy turned to see she hadn't moved. She scrambled back up to her.

'Ella.' She crouched down and took hold of her trembling hands. Ella sat on the ground, utterly silent with her eyes tightly shut and tears dripping from her chin. Maddy saw the dark bruising again.

Anger mingled with her fear, but she didn't have time to worry about it—they had to make good their escape. She pulled Ella to her feet and, holding her unresisting hand, led her. Sliding from tree to tree, they made their way down. At the base of the mound, Maddy realised this side was far higher than the place the bushranger and Bowman used to access the top. She was relieved to have reached level ground and hoped the dense scrub would give them better cover should the gunman be searching for them. So far there'd been no repeat gunfire, and the birds had resumed flitting through the branches, chirping unconcernedly. Maddy was sweating beneath her warm cloak and wished they had time to stop and regain their breath, but with Ella following placidly now, she didn't want to risk her baulking again, so they kept going.

Still holding Ella's hand Maddy pressed on, with no idea which direction they were headed; it was away from the mound and the bushranger's camp and that was the best she could do.

How long they trudged through the bush she wasn't certain, but she wondered if by now they should have come across Daniel. She paused, trying to get her bearings. Instead of thinning to clearer ground, the trees had become even thicker; a mass of tall spindly gums was reaching up for a share of light between the thick canopy of leaves. The giant cedars blocked out the sky almost entirely, and Maddy had no idea what time it was, nor which direction they were headed. She looked back and saw only a few yards before the dense bushland became a wall of moss-covered trunks.

'Moss,' she said, 'grows on the north side of trees in England, but is it the same here?' Ella merely stared at her, her face a mask. Maddy frowned at her. 'Ella, what happened? Why won't you speak? We are free now, there's no need to be afraid.' Ella remained mute, her blue eyes swollen and red rimmed from crying. Maddy examined the moss once more. If England was in the Northern Hemisphere, she reasoned, and the moss grew on the north side, perhaps in the Southern Hemisphere it grew on the south. Which meant they were heading south. There was no settlement to be found in that direction until Wollombi, a distance of at least twenty miles. Maddy peered at the thick scrub and knew they'd never find the place should they try to walk there through the bush.

'If we turn left, we should be heading east, and back towards Shelby and the river,' Maddy told Ella.

There was no reply.

'This way,' Maddy said, and with Ella's hand still grasped in hers, she changed direction and headed for home. At least she hoped that was where they were headed.

They walked for what seemed to be hours, and Maddy grew thirstier than she'd ever been in her life. The going was slow as the bush was thick and difficult to traverse. Ella remained silent and Maddy was forced to pull her onwards when she began to lag. She ignored the suspicion they were hopelessly lost and tried to jolly Ella along.

'We're almost home,' she told her. They stood in the relentless sameness of the trees and Maddy hoped she didn't sound as unconvinced as she felt. Ella stared at her blankly.

'Come on, Ella.' Maddy knew she sounded frustrated. 'I know you're frightened, but we have to keep our wits.' The girl flinched away from her and she experienced a flood of compassion, pushing aside her annoyance.

'I'm sorry,' Maddy said, crouching down to take both Ella's listless hands in her own, 'I'm sorry, it's just that I'm a little bit tired. And you must be too, but we must keep on.'

Ella nodded and relief flooded through Maddy; she certainly didn't want to spend a night out in the bush. Although not as cold as England on a winter night, it was cold enough, and Ella had already endured one night. Maddy knew when they stopped moving they would likely stiffen up with soreness as well as the cold. She checked the canopy and saw that the leafy covering was sparser than it had been and took comfort that the sky was still blue, and that dappled sunlight patterned the forest floor.

'I wonder what time it is?' Maddy glanced at Ella. 'I don't suppose you have a time-piece?'

Ella shook her head, so Maddy straightened and left her resting on the log. At least she was responding, she thought, and swallowed dryly. Thirst made Maddy feel a little mad, and she thought perhaps they should try to find water. If they changed course, Maddy wondered if they would stumble across a creek or rivulet. But what if they became more lost? She looked around. They couldn't be any more lost.

In order to distract herself from thirst, Maddy tried to calculate the approximate time. She and Luke had headed off before dawn, reaching the place where Ella and Bowman had left the road to Dalwood as the sun rose at around seven. They'd walked for around another couple of hours before finding the bushranger's hideout. Perhaps it had been ten before the men had discovered her freeing the horses, and at the latest eleven before she and Ella had made their escape. It felt like they'd been walking for days, but the sun was still quite high and, though they were thirsty and tired, Maddy thought it not much later than mid-afternoon. They had around an hour before the cold would begin to draw in, and maybe two and a half hours before the sun would set. How far south had they travelled before Maddy realised they'd been going in the wrong direction? A half an hour? Perhaps more. A wave of panic filled her chest and she forced herself to remain calm. No good could come of them both being insensible.

'Ella,' Maddy croaked, swallowed dryly and continued, 'I think we're heading east, but perhaps we should divert and head north east. Are you a little rested?' She spoke mostly to keep herself from being overwhelmed by the fear that they would never be found, that they would die out here. Probably of thirst. She'd not had a drink since the water on the trail before she and Luke had come across the bushranger's lair. She recalled the canteen of water she'd left hidden and blinked back tears. She couldn't afford to waste moisture crying.

'Come on, we must keep moving.'

Ella stood up. Well, Maddy thought, that is one thing at least, she is responding to me. 'Ella, we're safe now.' At least they were safe from the bushranger and Bowman.

Ella nodded. The eyes that met Maddy's were still frightened, but at least she was aware of what was happening. Maddy wasn't certain she had been earlier. She checked the trees and adjusted their course as well as she could and started off again, trying not to think about water. She swallowed what little moisture her mouth contained and kept walking.

Thirty-Two

Tuesday, 5 June 1832

They'd walked for perhaps another half an hour when Ella tugged her hand from Maddy's to stumble over and flop down onto the trunk of a fallen tree. Exhausted and more than a little scared, Maddy followed her. They were hopelessly lost. Maddy's legs ached, and exhaustion that went beyond the physical enveloped her. A stinging pain on her leg made her cry out and she jumped to her feet. Her first thought was she'd been bitten by a snake and so she sprang away from the log, lifting her skirts high. There was no snake: only several large red ants crawling over her boots and one further up on her stocking. Maddy flicked them off and laughed shakily. Ants, only ants. She rubbed at the burning bite and stomped her feet several times. On the ground beside the log Maddy spotted a swarm of the same ants and realised she'd been sitting near a nest.

'Come on, Ella, there are ants here, and they've a horrible sting; we'd better move.'

Maddy took Ella's hand and once again hauled her to her feet. Ella stood, but still she made no sound. Had Bowman broken her jaw? Maddy examined the other girl's bruised face. She didn't think it was broken—it was swollen, but not misshapen. Certainly it must be painful. 'Come along now, not far to go,' she said, but she no longer believed it was true.

As they walked Maddy began to feel dizzy. She blinked away a strange blurriness that gave everything around her a halo. She continued trying to encourage Ella, but it was becoming more difficult to think with each step she took.

'We're nearly there,' she croaked, not daring to stop talking for fear she might pass out if she did. 'I'm sure we're almost home.' It was difficult to breathe. Everything was growing dark when she realised she'd heard something. She heard it several times before she realised what it was. Someone was calling her name.

'Daniel,' Maddy croaked, and the black receded a little and she licked her dry lips and tried again. 'Daniel, we're here!'

Ella suddenly came to life, let go of Maddy's hand and, arching like she was possessed, let out a terrifying scream. She screamed again and again and Maddy realised she too was calling for Daniel.

'Daniel, I'm here.' Tears flooded down Maddy's cheeks as she gasped for breath. A detached part of her was surprised she had enough moisture left in her body to shed a single tear. The rescue party thundered through the bush towards them and Maddy clutched a tree trunk in order to stay upright. Relief overwhelmed her and her knees buckled. Daniel. He had come. He'd found them. Maddy was barely aware of the others with him; desperate, she watched as his horse came through the bush. He flung himself from the saddle before the horse came to a complete stop and swept Maddy into his arms. In an instant, relief flooded through her.

'Daniel,' Maddy gasped, gazing up into his beautiful eyes.

'Daniel,' Ella screamed and Maddy felt him stiffen. And then he was gone. Someone else took his place as she watched him go to Ella. Maddy began to cry, dry, wracking sobs of pain and relief.

A canteen of water was offered to Maddy, and she looked up to see she was held by Chase Hudson. Where had he come from? She took the unstoppered flask and guzzled the water. She drank until her stomach hurt.

'Slow down,' he said, gently pulling the container from her lips.

Maddy relinquished the precious water reluctantly. She saw Ella resting in Daniel's arms. Maddy longed to push Ella away and climb into Daniel's lap, to feel his strong arms around her. Instead she tried to focus on Chase Hudson.

'What—'

'Helping in the search for you,' he said before she could stammer out a question.

Maddy met his eyes. 'Really?'

'My God, what happened to you? Did the brute beat you?'

'What? No.' Maddy was confused.

'Your face, it's swollen—what happened?'

'Nothing.' She lifted a hand and felt her lips, the skin felt oddly tight. It was Ella who had been hit by Bowman. Maddy looked at him. 'I'm all right,' she slurred, glancing over at Ella and Daniel before forcing herself to refocus on Chase. She tried to say, 'How did you come to be here?' but she sounded odd, her speech thick and slow. Maddy repeated herself, carefully enunciating each word.

He frowned at her but answered, 'I was at Dalwood when a boy came and told us about Miss Whitfield, and so I joined the search party.'

Maddy nodded, too exhausted to speak. They must have pulled together a search party in the night. Had it only been one day? She looked around at the half-dozen men and saw Molly Hunt and Phil standing a small distance away.

'Phil,' Maddy croaked, 'what are you doing here?'

Phil had hung back, but at her question he hurried forwards, sweeping his battered hat from his stringy red hair. His bright blue eyes swam with tears.

'What has happened?' Maddy's heart thudded with fear: surely nothing else could have occurred.

'Nothin', missy—it's just that I was afeared we'd never find you.' He sniffed, wiped his nose on the sleeve of his coat, and gave Maddy a wobbly smile.

'How did you find us?' She peered around at the sameness of the bush, and still had no idea where she was.

'We heard you.'

Heard her? 'What?' She looked over at the others. Along with Mr Garrick were Mr Wyndham, Molly Hunt and Mr Everette. Where had they all come from?

'When Daniel and Mr Garrick came back this morning to get more people to search, we saw yerself and young Luke were gone.' He shuddered. 'It was Daniel who knew you musta gone looking yerselves.'

Maddy nodded, struggling to stay focused; she was having trouble seeing. 'What happened? Did Luke find you?'

'He found Mrs Hunt, who was out visiting, and he told her he was looking for Mr Daniel. She tossed him up behind her on that old horse of hers and galloped to Shelby to find out what was going on. Mr Garrick and Mr Clinton had ridden back to Tillington to wait for everyone to gather, and she, reckoning she knew where this place was, left Luke at Shelby and rode to Tillington. 'Twas her led us there.'

'Did you capture them?'

'Yes and no.' He hesitated a moment before continuing in a lowered voice. 'Mr Clinton shot one bloke, and when we got to the hideout, no one was there. We found Miss Whitfield's saddle and another old battered one, but no sign of any of the horses, nor Bowman. We don't know if the bushranger fellow killed him or if he too escaped.'

'Oh, he escaped all right,' Maddy muttered.

'Missy, you don't look at all well, you just rest now, and we'll get you home.'

Maddy nodded, the effort to speak had become increasingly difficult, and her breath was coming in short gasps. 'I might lie down for a bit,' she murmured.

Maddy woke to find she was being carried on a horse. It took a moment to identify Mr Garrick riding behind her. She twisted to see Phil riding old Pepper. Though she still felt a little odd, the dizziness had receded somewhat. Where was she? Maddy tried to straighten.

'Steady there,' Phil said, and Mr Garrick reined in the horse and helped Phil lower her to the ground.

'How are you feeling, missy?' Phil asked.

'Much better,' she told him. When she turned to Mr Garrick, she saw he was staring at her with a concerned expression.

'Would you like to rest for a bit?'

'Please,' she said, nodding, 'and can I have more water?'

'Of course.'

Maddy drank deeply and lowered the canteen to find most of the search party gathered around her, only Daniel, with Ella in front of him on his horse, and Mr Clinton staying a little apart.

'Can you tell us what happened?' Chase Hudson asked.

'There's time enough for that later,' Mr Garrick said firmly.

'No, it's fine. I am fine. You said the bushranger was shot?'

'Not by me. But yes, he's dead.'

Maddy nodded. She felt a little sorry for the hapless outlaw. It had been obvious that he had played second fiddle to the handsome Bowman.

'What happened?' Phil asked, curiosity getting the better of him.

'I set the two Tillington horses free, but I was unable to untie the bushranger's horse before I was discovered.' She paused and took another mouthful of water before continuing. 'Mr Bowman, when he realised you were looking for us, that I'd sent Luke for help, he took the last horse and ran away. He is a wicked man,' Maddy finished. She didn't know what he'd done to Ella, but she'd never forget the fear in her face when she'd first seen her. Maddy looked past Phil to see Mr Clinton and Daniel helping Ella drink from a water flask.

Mr Garrick and the others were watching her, waiting for her to continue.

'Maddy, however did you escape?'

'They had Ella tied and were going to do the same to me, but I feigned an injured ankle and they didn't get around to doing so. When the bushranger followed Bowman I managed to untie Ella and we ran.' Maddy looked over at her again. 'Is she all right? She didn't speak at all until we saw Daniel.'

'Yes: in shock I think,' Mr Garrick said.

'I still don't understand how you found us. And where are we?'

'You had walked almost to Oswald, only you're a bit further inland,' Mr Garrick told her, smiling.

'Really?' She wondered how they'd managed to miss Tillington.

'Yes, we were heading back to get more searchers, and some torches, and we heard you.'

'Heard us?' Maddy gazed from one face to the next.

'Aye, we all heard you,' Molly Hunt chimed in, chortling a little as she nodded. 'We could hear someone yelling, and we followed the sound until we found you two.'

'Yelling? Me?'

'Yes,' Mr Everette said with a smile. 'You were yelling at Ella to keep moving. That you were almost there.' He grinned. 'And you were.'

Maddy shook her head. She didn't recall yelling at Ella. 'I was trying to encourage her, but surely I wasn't yelling.' She frowned, trying to recall the last few hours before they were found. Perhaps she had been encouraging Ella a little more vigorously than she'd intended. Ella had been getting slower and slower, and Maddy knew they mustn't stop. They'd needed to find water.

'Yes, well, she wasn't very well, and we had to keep going.' Maddy paused, thinking. 'When we stopped to rest one of those large red ants bit me, and things were a little hazy after that. But surely we should have come across Black Creek?'

'You were in a kind of funnel between two creeks,' Mr Garrick told her, shaking his head with wonder. 'You managed to miss both of them.' He nodded in the direction Maddy assumed they'd been travelling. 'If you'd kept going, you'd have eventually come to Black Creek where it turns south. Essentially, you've been travelling parallel to it.'

Maddy wasn't sure if she wanted to laugh or cry. Instead she shook her head and reached for the flask of water. All the talk about creeks reminded her of the relentless thirst. 'I can't believe we travelled so far.'

'Let's get you home and we can worry about the rest later,' Mr Wyndham said, his kindly eyes crinkled with his smile.

Maddy nodded. 'Yes, I long for a bath and to get my boots off. I'm certain my feet are two large blisters.' Maddy looked at Ella. 'And poor Ella must be worse—she is wearing riding boots.'

When they'd reached Shelby, Jane took Maddy in hand: washed and dried her and put her to bed. She held Maddy prisoner in her room, feeding her broth and insisting everything on the farm was fine. Maddy was to rest, no arguments. Mrs Garrick visited and reinforced Jane's regimen. But eventually her swollen face resumed a normal shape and she had nothing to do but lie in bed and think. After much discussion and a visit from the doctor, with snake bite ruled out, the consensus was that the ant bite had caused a strange reaction, and as no other explanation was obvious, Maddy didn't argue. But she remembered Papa's swollen face and the ants on him, and, coupled with the bite she'd suffered the day he died, Maddy wondered whether her—and his—swelling had been caused by the ant bite. She was certain she'd not swollen up that day like she had this time, but if Papa had been bitten, and become disoriented as she had, perhaps he'd fallen into the river, and not deliberately drowned himself as she'd feared. Maddy clung to the explanation with relief. Papa hadn't killed himself.

Thirty-Three

Friday, 15 June 1832—strong winds

It was several days after her adventures before Maddy began to
feel her normal self. The place where the ant had bitten her was
still swollen and red, and though it itched like the devil, the bouts
of lethargy had become few and far between. She hadn't seen anyone besides Jane and Luke, and having escaped her bed, she was
permitted to sit on a bench in the sunshine and rest.

When she heard a horse whinny a welcome and an answering call of an approaching horse, Maddy rose and made her
way slowly along the track to the farmyard where she found
both Mr Garrick and Daniel's brother-in-law, Mr Clinton,
dismounting.

'Maddy, how are you?' Mr Garrick said, his expression full of
concern as he tied his mount and crossed to meet her.

'Good morning, Mr Garrick, Mr Clinton. I am much recovered, thank you.'

Daniel and Phil appeared from the far side of the yard and
joined them.

'Daniel, Phil.' Mr Garrick nodded a greeting before turning his attention back to her. 'If you're well enough, Maddy, we thought to enquire about the circumstances of yours and Ella's— misadventure?'

'Of course, how is Miss Whitfield?' During her convalescence, she'd often run over the strange time she and Ella had spent together, but shame at her own behaviour had not permitted her to call for Daniel and enquire; she castigated herself for failing to admit she'd seen Ella and Bowman riding together. For if she had told him immediately, the men might have found the hideout and saved Ella, and herself, from such a harrowing experience.

'She is recovering,' Mr Garrick said. 'Come, you mustn't stand here, you need your rest.' His face a picture of concern.

'Come along, missy,' Phil said, 'sit ye here.' He led her to the long bench on the porch of Daniel's hut. Daniel watched on, saying nothing, and Maddy could not bring herself to meet his eyes.

'Thank you,' Maddy agreed and did as she was bidden.

'How were they captured?' Mr Clinton asked from where he stood beside Daniel. Maddy met his eyes for a moment and tried to scare up a little pity for the man.

'I'm not sure,' she said after a moment. 'Luke said they chased a wallaby into the bush, then we found the ground quite churned and so we assume that was where they'd come across the bush-ranger or been ambushed. What's his name? I've not heard anyone mention it?'

'His name was Samuel Bowman, a distant cousin of William Bowman.' Mr Garrick said the last with disgust in every syllable, his face full of sorrow. 'My dear, how can I ever apologise for everything inflicted upon you, at the hand of someone in my charge? I'd no idea he was so ruthless.'

Maddy reassured him, 'Mr Garrick, you could not have known. He had been all charm and propriety itself whenever I saw him at Tillington.'

'Yes, you're right. He's been with me for three years and I've never seen the bad in him. He was convicted for a highwayman—I'd put it down to youthful hijinks—he was of minor gentry stock you know. He could have gone far in the colony, had he kept his head. That he raised a hand to my guest is unforgivable.'

Maddy recalled the bruise on Ella's face. 'Will she be all right?'

'I think so.' He looked at Maddy. 'Do you know what happened to her? She will not speak of it at all.'

'No, but when I first found their hideout, I heard her speaking to Bowman,' Maddy hesitated, 'and she was telling him how much trouble he'd brought on himself with what he'd done.'

'I see,' he said, the planes of his face stiffening.

'Then when they captured me, she seemed dazed and didn't speak at all until we saw Daniel; it was then she began to scream.' Maddy found herself unable to look at Daniel.

'What had he done to her?' Daniel interjected.

'I don't know, she is bruised and has a swollen jaw, which I thought might have been from … blows, but perhaps she merely stumbled, as the ground up on the top is quite rough with boulders and fallen branches.'

'We must catch the—' Mr Clinton began.

'I don't think it was William Bowman's intention to kidnap Ella. When Samuel Bowman caught me trying to release the horses, William told him he would get them hanged if he continued to snatch women of the gentry.' Maddy paused. 'Perhaps when Ella is recovered, she will be able to tell us exactly what happened.'

'Yes, it's all terribly confusing. But you are both recovering, that is the main thing.'

Maddy's conscience still niggled at her involvement, much of it possibly unnecessary. 'Mr Garrick, I'm very sorry that I set the stallion and your other horse free.'

'I'm sure they'll turn up somewhere. Everyone knows who owns the stallion, and if I offer a reward of a free service.' He reddened.

'That's an excellent idea,' Maddy said, ignoring his embarrassment. A sudden wave of tiredness enveloped her. 'If you will excuse me.'

In the days that followed, Maddy went about as before but felt all the more listless. She had grown tired of being the strong pillar everyone at Shelby leaned against. Milk production was down as the cows grew heavy with calf; future crops needed to be planned and fields chosen to prepare for planting when the weather began to warm. She gave the men their instructions when Daniel was away, which was often and yet not quite frequent enough to be able to cut ties with him. No word came of a possible replacement, either. Mary and Jane seemed to be squabbling over every chore, and Luke silently floated around the edges of their lives. During the day, he would disappear, sometimes to follow the men to the fields, or else wander off playing with the Wonnarua children near the bank of the river; and sometimes he silently hung about the house, not exactly beneath Maddy's feet but around enough to remind her of the question of his paternity. Who else could she ask? Maddy began to think she'd never know for certain. Would finding out make any difference? Luke was here to stay.

Of Ella she'd seen nothing, and though Maddy would have liked to have left it that way, she knew she needed to see her. The time they'd been together in the bush had forced Maddy to help Ella, but it had not endeared her to Maddy. For all Ella looked down her nose at the colonials, she had been utterly useless in a crisis. Deep down Maddy knew she was being unfair, but she despaired for poor Daniel should he decide to stay in New South Wales when he married Ella. Sometimes Maddy couldn't help thinking he'd be better off allowing Ella and Charlotte to persuade him to return to England. Lying in her bed each night, listening to the bush and watching the moon shadows creep across the walls and floor, Maddy hoped Ella would triumph and take him away.

She'd not seen Daniel's sister or brother-in-law at all but both Mrs Garrick and Mrs Wyndham had been to see her, embarrassing her with praise Maddy felt was undeserved. She imagined Charlotte Clinton would have been frantic with worry for her friend; Mr Clinton was likely dreading what would become of his finances should Daniel be robbed of the opportunity to marry the rich heiress and relieve himself of some debts. Anger flared momentarily on Daniel's behalf: how selfish they were to foist their difficulties into his lap. Maddy sighed. He could refuse to take them on, but he would never do such a thing, especially not with Charlotte his only living relative. Maddy knew he would do anything to protect her.

The men were cutting posts in preparation to fence another section of land, and as Daniel was with them, Maddy decided to ride over to Tillington and see Ella. Charlie would be working around the yard. Maddy paused and heard the ring of a hammer in the forge, where he was likely shoeing one of the horses. She returned to her room and, with Jane's disapproving help, changed into her riding habit.

A young man met Maddy at the yard gate of Tillington homestead and assisted her down before leading her horse off to the stables while she visited. Not sure of how she would be received by Ella, she wished she'd been able to warn the house of her call. Removing her gloves and straightening her skirts, Maddy took an extra minute to adjust her bonnet before entering the courtyard.

'Oh, Miss Maddy, how lovely to see you again—it's been too long, it has indeed. Too long.' Cookie's dark raisin eyes shone with delight from her flushed round face as she wiped her flour-dusted hands on her pinafore. Her plump figure exuded welcome as she stood on the flagged veranda outside the kitchen door.

'Cookie, how lovely to see you.' Maddy crossed and spontaneously bent to give her flushed cheek a peck. She had always been so kind.

'Oh missy, you're making an old woman blush,' Cookie said, dimpling happily. 'Are you well? That man—'

'Is Mrs Garrick at home?' Maddy interrupted, smiling at her, as she had no desire to discuss Bowman. Her stomach felt as if a swarm of bees had invaded.

'Indeed she is, and you'll find them all in the sitting room.' Cookie glanced over Maddie's shoulder. 'Bridget, go and tell the mistress that Miss Barker-Trent is come to visit.'

Maddy heard a scurry of feet and turned to see a young red-haired girl hurrying along the opposite wing of the veranda. 'Is she new?'

'Oh aye, and she's a good lass, poor thing: her family in Ireland all died, and she was only trying to keep body and soul together. Poor lassie cried every night for a week, but she's settling in now.'

Cookie was a hard task mistress, but if an assigned servant was a willing and hard worker, she was kindness itself. It was an entirely different story if she came across one who was slovenly or lazy. If Cookie was the girl's champion, she was in good hands and likely had a bright future ahead of her.

Bridget held the parlour door open and Maddy entered the room to find Mrs Garrick coming towards her, arms held out in welcome.

'Oh Maddy,'—she pulled Maddy to her and held tight for a moment—'how can we ever thank you?' Beyond her shoulder Maddy saw Mrs Clinton staring down at the table, her expression set.

'Come in,' Mrs Garrick said, then added to a hovering Bridget, 'Bridget, please bring in a fresh pot and another cup and saucer for Miss Barker-Trent.'

Maddy glanced around to smile her thanks to the girl, who bobbed an awkward curtsy and pulled the door closed as she went.

'Oh Maddy,' Mrs Garrick repeated, shaking her head in wonder, 'what an ordeal.' She peered into Maddy's eyes. 'You seem quite recovered?'

Maddy nodded, then glanced past her to Mrs Clinton once again. 'Good day, Mrs Clinton,' she said, and it was only when addressed directly that she looked at Maddy.

'Good day, Miss Barker-Trent.' She turned her attention once more to the cup on the table before her.

Maddy had no time to contemplate the woman's coldness before she was invited to sit. Mrs Garrick shot her a sympathetic look. She found herself seated opposite Daniel's sister, examining the top of Charlotte Clinton's carefully arranged hair. The smooth shine and delicate curls that swung around her ears reminded Maddy that she'd not dressed her own hair before leaving home but had placed her hat on the usual tidy knot she wore around Shelby.

'Is Miss Whitfield recovering well?' Maddy asked Mrs Garrick when Mrs Clinton continued to keep her face averted.

'Oh, Maddy.' Mrs Garrick's face clouded.

Alarmed, Maddy looked from Mrs Garrick to Mrs Clinton and back again. 'What is it?' Maddy knew Ella hadn't been well, but surely she was relatively unharmed.

Mrs Clinton focused on Maddy, her blue eyes so like Daniel's, and yet cold where his were warm.

'She is quite fine physically, but she hardly speaks,' Mrs Garrick said, tossing a concerned glance at her friend.

'Could I see her?'

'Haven't you done enough?' Mrs Clinton said, her tone frosty.

'I—' Maddy began: what did she mean? Maddy sent Mrs Garrick a questioning glance.

'Charlotte, you can't blame Maddy for what happened.' Mrs Garrick reached over and rubbed her friend's hand.

Mrs Clinton snatched it away, her eyes never leaving Maddy's face. 'I can, and I do.' She continued to glare across the table.

'I beg your pardon?' Wide-eyed, Maddy glanced at Mrs Garrick as if for clarification.

'All this is your fault,' Mrs Clinton spat and stood up so abruptly the chair fell to the ground. She left the room without righting the furniture or looking at either woman again.

Maddy watched her go, bewildered. She turned back to Mrs Garrick.

'Oh dear,' Mrs Garrick said, a deep frown marring her brow.

'I'm afraid I don't understand.'

'No dear, and why should you?'

Bridget entered through the still open door carrying a tray with a fresh pot of tea, crockery, and piping hot scones. The young maid glanced at the chair, placed the tray on the sideboard carefully, then removed the used crockery and replaced it with the new supplies. Maddy and Mrs Garrick watched her in silence, and, when she'd been thanked and asked to convey her appreciation to Cookie, Mrs Garrick stood and righted the chair.

'I'm afraid Charlotte blames you for the rift between herself and Daniel.'

'Rift?' Maddy didn't know there was a rift.

'Yes, you see Charlotte wants Daniel to marry Ella and for them to return to England. It's why they came.'

'I know.'

'It's …' She hesitated and gave Maddy a look that could only be described as penetrating. 'Well, you see, it's quite obvious Daniel has feelings for you, and although he seems to be going along with this ludicrous plan to marry Ella, he has stated that he has no intention of returning to England. So if Ella wishes to marry him, she will have to stay here.'

Maddy nodded, bit her lip, and poured the tea with a trembling hand, placing the pot back on the table with a bit of a clatter. Normally she'd have loved to indulge, knowing how wonderful Cookie's baking was, but the aroma caused Maddy's stomach to churn. After a moment of silence she said, 'Why does she blame me for Ella's state of mind? I take it that is what she meant?'

'Please, Maddy, don't take it to heart. Charlotte is quite highly strung, and she must have someone to blame. Matthew is, ah, quite intent on seeing Ella and Daniel married, and so ...'

'But Daniel intends to marry her.'

'So he says, but anyone with eyes can see it will be under duress.'

'I see,' Maddy said and plonked three spoons of sugar into her tea. She stirred it slowly.

'Time will tell,' Mrs Garrick said, and she rested a hand on Maddy's, halting the relentless stirring.

'I fail to see how I am responsible for any of this.'

'Of course you aren't. How could you be? But they are all terribly distraught and ... well, Charlotte, as I said, needs someone to blame.'

Maddy shook her head. She was at a loss. 'And Ella hasn't recovered from the ordeal?'

'She has, but she's ...' Again Mrs Garrick frowned and then after a moment of seeming to search for the right words said, 'Well, I don't exactly know what to make of it. She barely speaks to anyone. And she only wants to be with Daniel, and then it's only to weep all over him. The poor man doesn't know what to do.'

A weeping insipid Ella didn't match the haughty young woman
Maddy knew her to be. Then she recalled the mute and distressed
creature she'd led through the forest.

'I think she might be trying to force Daniel to return to
England.'

'I hope she succeeds,' Maddy said with more force than she
intended.

Mrs Garrick's eyes widened at Maddy's outburst.

'If Daniel was to force her to stay here, it would no doubt prove
a miserable existence for them both,' Maddy continued.

'I agree, but Daniel loves it here,' Mrs Garrick said. 'You must
understand, Charlotte is not heartless: she adores Daniel, and he is
her only close living relative.'

'So Mr Coulter has told me,' Maddy said, but she'd seen no
evidence of the woman both Mrs Garrick and Daniel claimed
Charlotte Clinton to be.

'Yes, well,' Mrs Garrick hesitated, and then as if compelled to
defend her friend's behaviour, 'She ... Well, perhaps if she'd been
able to have children. Suffice it to say her life has not met her
expectations. I believe she has pinned her hopes on Daniel and
Ella giving her an opportunity to be an aunt, to be part of their
children's lives.'

'I see.'

'Maddy, I'm terribly sorry, you—'

'I must be going. Thank you for the tea,' Maddy said, cutting
her off. She rose from the table as the door opened to admit Ella.
She was somewhat pale but dressed and primped. Maddy saw the
bruising on her cheek and jaw had faded to a murky yellow, and
the edge of a white bandage was visible beneath the cuff of her
sleeve.

'Ella, do sit down,' Mrs Garrick invited quickly.

'If you don't mind, I wish to speak with Miss Barker-Trent alone,' Ella said, addressing Mrs Garrick tonelessly.

'Of course, my dear.' Mrs Garrick sent a curious glance in Maddy's direction, and then, after a moment, rose and muttered something about another cup and saucer and left the room.

'I'm pleased to see you recovered,' Maddy said.

'Thank you; please do sit down.'

'I was just about to leave.'

'I shan't delay you much more than a moment, but let's sit.'

Maddy lowered herself back into the chair.

'I wanted to thank you for what you did.'

'I, er, you're welcome.' Maddy wasn't sure how to respond, for Ella's words were what one would expect, but there was something in her manner that wasn't right. She seemed flat, as if the episode had dulled her shine.

'And I feel I owe you an apology for getting you into such a situation.'

Maddy stared at her wide-eyed. Before she could respond Ella continued after a short pause.

'I was careless and chased after a kangaroo, the groom followed me, and we came upon the bushranger. That is what they're called, isn't it?' she asked.

Maddy nodded.

Ella continued in the same monotone. 'It was obvious they knew one another, and so then I think the groom, Bowman's his name, panicked. So you see, it was my own fault. All of it.'

Maddy stood and crossed to take Ella's hands in her own. 'No, Ella, it wasn't your fault. They didn't have to do what they did. William Bowman could have taken care of you and got you away from the bushranger, but instead he decided to take advantage of the situation and take you hostage.'

Ella glanced at her, then at the table, and sighed. Maddy found herself staring down at the perfection of her neatly parted hair, the glossy ringlets, and wondered how she would survive in a bark hut. Perhaps if they kept a house in Sydney, and Daniel could buy land closer to the town?

'How did you find us?'

Maddy met her eyes, brilliant and blue, and containing something of an accusation. 'I didn't. At least not on my own. Young Luke followed the trail. I sent him for help when we realised we'd found their lair.' She returned to her own seat.

'The boy?' Her disbelief was obvious.

'Yes.' Maddy said, trying to keep the anger from her voice.

'Is it true?'

Maddy knew what she meant but didn't wish to delve into the subject. 'Is what true?'

'That the boy is your half-brother?'

Maddy averted her gaze, unsure how to answer. It may be the truth, but there was no way to prove or disprove it. 'I do not know who his father is.'

'Bowman seemed to think he was—'

'I'm sure there's much speculation, but I have no idea; nor does it matter.' Maddy cut her off and then drew in a deep breath. She wanted to leave, and good manners or not, she would go. She rose, leaving the tea unfinished. 'The lad has no family, and whether he is,'—she had been going to say 'my brother' but the words lodged in her throat—'whoever his father is, I intend to care for him, and he is welcome at Shelby as long as he wishes to stay.'

Thirty-Four

**Monday, 23 July 1832—cold, came into rain
mid-afternoon**

With winter drawing to an end and George Lester working full
time cutting stone for the house, along with anyone who could
be spared, progress was made. The sounds of industry—the ring
of hammers on chisels, and George Lester's instructions—should
have been music to Maddy's ears, but somehow she couldn't
dredge up any enthusiasm. According to Lester, the Shelby
quarry produced a good quality fine-grained stone, which was
easy to cut. The draught horses were kept busy hauling blocks
of stone from the quarry on a specially designed sled. The stone
was then stacked ready for shaping and manoeuvring into place.
Shaped and finished blocks were mortared to the large foundation
stones, and soon Papa's house sprang out of the ground, much like
spring-planted seedlings jumped after a shower of rain. The progress was constant, and yet Maddy still felt deflated.

Since Papa's death she'd been determined to see the house he'd
described become a reality, and though that had never been closer
to happening, uselessness and disappointment seemed to have

taken her over. Without the hope of life with Daniel, everything had palled. Much as she tried, Maddy struggled to elicit even a little of the determination she'd had when she'd first decided to fulfil her parent's dreams.

In need of a break from the decision-making and constant questions, Maddy retrieved her shawl and headed for the glade, pausing only to let Jane know where she was going. Since the episode with the bushrangers, Jane watched over her like a mother hen.

She walked along the clifftop track, intending to avoid the busy farmyard, and Daniel. The track skirted the bottom of the horse fields and she was at the corner when she heard the sound of a horse approaching. Maddy sighed and paused to see it was Mr Garrick. Maddy could hardly slink off into the bush now she'd seen him, so she changed direction and followed the fence line up the slope to the farmyard.

Mr Garrick had dismounted and was speaking to Daniel and Phil by the time she reached the yard.

'Ah, Maddy,' Mr Garrick said when he saw her.

'Mr Garrick,' Maddy said, including Daniel and Phil in her somewhat forced smile.

'I came to deliver these.'

'Thank you,' she said, frowning a little as he handed her two dirty squares of paper: letters, both addressed to Papa. Maddy blinked back sudden tears when she saw her own handwriting on one. It was the letter she'd sent from England. The letter he'd never received. Tears filled her eyes. If only he'd received it, he might be alive today. There had been so much left undone. Maddy tried to hide the flood of emotion by examining the other letter. The familiar curling flourishes were immediately recognisable as Mama's.

Maddy gasped. Conscious of the three men watching her, she looked up and met Mr Garrick's gaze. 'Thank you so much, but where did they come from?'

'Reverend Hawkins saw my stallion and the gelding in the bush near Black Creek; he tried to capture them, but the stallion spooked and took off.' He grinned. 'Clinton and I and a couple of grooms went out this morning. As it seemed to me that they weren't far from where Bowman had holed up, we went back there to see if we could find them.' He frowned. 'Frightfully difficult to locate the place again—we hardly knew we were upon it until it rose up amid the trees. A dashed good hideout.'

'Did you find the horses?' Maddy asked, though the squares of paper she held were really what she wanted to ask about.

'Oh, yes, yes we did. Delivered them safely home before I rode back here with the letters. I knew you'd want them.' He gestured at his horse and she saw a filthy sack hung behind the saddle. 'While we were there, we had a look around the plateau and found a mail bag—no one had ever even missed it, or its carrier. There wasn't much inside but those.' He nodded at the letters she held. 'I've a few more to deliver, but I thought you'd want to see them sooner rather than later.' He suddenly seemed awkward, and a quick glance at Daniel and Phil revealed they also seemed uncomfortable.

'Thank you, thank you so much, Mr Garrick.' Maddy glanced down at the letters once more, conscious of both Daniel and Phil watching. The letters in her hand scalded both her curiosity and her skin. 'It's good to have them.' She flapped them a little, longing for privacy to read them.

When had the mail bag been stolen? Had they been hidden in the bush ranger's hideout all these long months? She shook her head in wonder. Maddy dragged her attention back to the men. 'I hope the horses were not any the worse for their time running in the bush.'

'Both were in remarkable condition—nary a scratch nor a bump on either of them. Of course they'd thrown all but one shoe between them. But nothing a good trim and currying won't put to rights,' Mr Garrick assured her.

'Good news, that is,' said Phil, 'very good news indeed. Well, I'd best be about my chores.' He brushed a finger along the front of his disreputable hat in salute and departed.

'And I'd best be on my way,' Mr Garrick said, 'it's been quite a day, and I wish to deliver those'—he nodded to the mail bag— 'and get myself home. Mrs Garrick will be bursting to know what has transpired.'

'Yes and thank you so much for finding these.' Again Maddy wafted the letters a little. Hurry up and go!

Mr Garrick mounted his horse and within a few moments had cantered away. She stared awkwardly at Daniel's boots.

'The work on the house is coming along well.'

Maddy nodded. There seemed nothing to say, but she searched and snatched at the first thing she could think of. 'How is your search going?'

His eyes were blue in the sunshine, and she watched as they clouded over into a stormy grey. 'Search?'

'For land.'

'Oh, yes. Ah, not terribly well. I'm—' He paused, then continued in what Maddy was certain was a different direction from the one he'd started to take. 'I'll find something soon enough, I imagine.'

'Yes, I'm sure you will,' she said and longed for their old easy companionship. 'Well, I'd better get on.' She flapped the letters once more.

'Yes,' he agreed. She looked up to see he was examining her. Unsurprisingly, their glances barely brushed before they both turned from one another and walked away.

Thirty-Five

My Darling Robert,

Dearest, let us move on from recriminations and apologies. You have been gone a long time, and it's longer since we have been able to be together as man and wife. These things are important to a man and I do not condemn you for it. As for Madeleine, I shall speak to her and I'm sure she will, in time, come to understand.

I like the sound of this Daniel—he does indeed sound like a suitable match for Madeleine. However, you must not interfere, as neither man nor woman appreciate a contrived match, no matter how well intended.

My darling it is with a heavy heart I write this last. I fear I shall never be in health suitable for the journey to New South Wales. The autumn has been particularly miserable, and I have suffered greatly. I know that you believed the warmer weather would bring about an improvement for me, but I am simply too ill to survive six months aboard a ship. I lament my own cowardice on this, but as willing as my heart is, my body has betrayed me, and I do wish to be buried on English soil, and not tossed into the sea to be devoured by the fishes. I love you,

*and I know you understand me as no one else ever has and you
will understand my decision to remain.*

*As for the house, please be assured, I understand, I truly do.
The house was never important to me. I only wish that you
give your small deception not another thought. As I shall never
join you, I think your suggestion for Maddy to reside with the
Garricks is a sound one, at least until the house is built.*

*I will send Madeleine to you, and together you will make
Shelby all that we dreamed. I hope you and Madeleine, and
your son of course, can find a way to create a future together.
Enjoy your life, and take care of our girl. I treasure this time
I've had with her. I suspect we have neglected her, but I trust
you shall make up for it.*

*Please be happy, my darling, and know that you have given
me more love than I could ever have wished for.*

Love always,

Your wife,

Sophia

Tears streamed down Maddy's face. A sob ached in her chest as
she sat staring at the sheet of paper and tried to reconcile the letter
with her memories of Mama. She'd not mentioned any of this.
She had been so brave during the final months of her illness. The
letter must have been written when Maddy'd gone to Trowbridge
to see Papa's solicitor, only to return to find her mother's condition much worsened. Had Mama been too unwell to speak of
it? Maddy's mind raced. And Papa? Rose? Her heart ached with
sorrow for all the things that might have been. Maddy recalled
sitting with her mother's arms around her, looking out the window of the parlour, Mama telling stories of her own childhood, of
growing up in a grand house. A family and home she'd forfeited
for her love of Papa. Was that why he'd written of the house?

Had Mama written other letters of her illness? Had he known she would never join him? Why had Mama not told her? What else was there?

She stared at the letter; Papa had liked Daniel for her. And it was all too late. Mama, Papa and even Rose were all dead. Which left only Luke. What next? Unsure how she felt, Maddy rose from her bed and refolded the letter. Her mind raced with questions that could never be answered. Questions she could never ask. Mama had always been so indulgent with Papa. She could see it now. But surely not this? How could he do that to Mama? How could her mother be so accepting of his infidelity? Her head ached as unanswered questions flooded her.

How could Maddy face the polite society of the valley now? It was one thing to associate and work alongside convicted criminals, but was it worse to have an illegitimate brother? When she'd only suspected it, she had thought it wasn't, but now it was confirmed, she was no longer certain.

She would go. If she returned to England no one would have to know. Her fingers clenched around the letter. She could easily burn it, and all evidence would be gone. No one ever need know.

Luke's face swam before her: his dark grey eyes; his wary expression. She couldn't leave him to fend for himself. She glanced at her own letter, resting innocently on the bed. Her remembered innocence mocked her. Papa's reaction to the news of Mama's death. His rejection. Had he killed himself? Had his grief overtaken him? Or had it been a reaction to the ant bites? The questions buzzed around in her brain like angry wasps, and yet there were no answers to be had. Maddy considered the letter once more. She wanted to destroy it, but this was Mama's final letter to Papa, and she found she could not. Instead she pressed the creases flat, pulled the portmanteau from beneath her bed and placed the letter inside a satchel of documents she kept there. On impulse she snatched up the stone Daniel had given her and placed it on top of the letters. Relegating it all to the past.

Tuesday, 14 August 1832—warm and sunny

Spring bounced into the valley and with it came a drastic change in the temperature. The black and white magpies swooped the men if they ventured too close to their nests; the pretty wood ducks by the river could be seen waddling along in pairs; and a sweet duo of wagtails sang merrily as they worked industriously, building a nest on a branch of a gum tree near the gate to the kitchen garden. A clump of wild orchid growing on a boulder beside the path down to the glen budded to life.

Phil had sown spring and summer vegetables and was forced to hover over his patch with a maternal ferocity to keep the pink and white galahs and flocks of dark olive birds she'd yet to identify away from the tiny shoots. Newly born lambs were bouncing, lively tails jiggling, as they played in the fields.

Regardless of the progress, weather and new life around her, Maddy remained listless and miserable. She tried to hide it, but more than once she noticed Jane cast a concerned glance in her direction. Maddy avoided any conversation that might include questions as to what was wrong. She couldn't have borne the sympathy.

'Miss Maddy.' Jane found her leaning against the wall, watching the wagtails coat their nest with what looked like spider webs.

Maddy smiled at her. 'Jane, have you seen the nest today? They are putting on the finishing touches, and I imagine they will lay their eggs soon.'

Jane glanced at the nest with little interest and then returned her attention to her mistress. 'Miss, you don't seem to be yourself.'

Maddy couldn't help the wan smile. It seemed she was not going to be diverted, and it was typical of Jane to get straight to the point.

'I'm fine,' Maddy assured her.

'No, miss, you ain't.' She stepped closer and rested the back of her hand against Maddy's forehead.

'I don't have a fever.'

Jane frowned, bent a little and peered into Maddy's eyes. 'Then, miss, whatever is the matter with you?'

Maddy looked away, biting a suddenly trembling lip. She would not cry. She was determined to keep herself together, but Jane's brusque concern cut right through her fragile carapace.

'Oh miss, don't cry,' Jane said. 'I didn't mean to make you cry—I'm just that worried.'

Maddy drew in a breath and managed a shaky smile. 'I'm fine, Jane,' she said and continued when Jane's features twisted into a disbelieving cast, 'Perhaps I'm just a little tired.'

'Well, miss, you get yourself inside—I'll bring you a cup of tea, and you have a lie down. There's nothing needs doing so bad that we can't manage without you for an hour or so.'

Maddy began to protest, but then nodded. An hour away from the demands of Shelby would be welcome. She hadn't lied: she was tired.

'Thank you,' she said and turned away, tears filled her eyes once more.

Sleep however was elusive, and Maddy lay staring up at the rafters and considering her future at Shelby. With Daniel absent much of the last weeks of winter, it became all the more apparent the direction her life would take when he finally found a home of his own, to share with Ella. The moment drew closer each day, while Maddy firmly ignored the need to find his replacement and had so far avoided placing an advertisement. Maddy

considered asking Phil to take on the role of overseer, for he had
been at Shelby longer than even Daniel, but she didn't think he
would suit the position. He was far too obliging, and should she
ask him, he would accept so as not to let her down, but Maddy
knew he wouldn't want to do it. She sighed: to be able to sleep
would be wonderful. She pushed away the matter—she would
think about it later.

Maddy had seen little of Ella, and while there'd been few
social situations to avoid, she knew she couldn't stay on in
the colony when Daniel and Ella were married. To see them,
to socialise with them, to watch Ella have the life she longed
for … She shook her head; no, it would be far better to remove
herself.

She could sell Shelby to Daniel. From what she had gathered,
even before Papa died there'd been little done of any consequence
before Mr Garrick had insisted Daniel work on the property. Why
should Daniel have to purchase other land and start again? Her
chin began to tremble. Maddy knew to leave Shelby would be a
terrible wrench, and to leave Daniel behind would be paramount
to having a limb removed. No—to leave him was to have her
heart excised. But the incision had already been made. It would
be better to get the worst over. Tears stung her eyes. She scrubbed
them away.

Even as the idea took root, a niggling reminder of her promise
to keep and establish Shelby for her parents haunted her. Feeling guilty for even considering deserting her parent's plans, a sob
erupted. She just didn't think she could continue much longer.
What had started as their dream had become a millstone around
Maddy's neck, and the weight of it was drowning her.

No, it was much better to have Daniel take over—for him to
build Shelby into what it should have been. As for Luke, he could

stay on. She would leave him a small amount in trust, perhaps even a modest parcel of land where he could make a life for himself when he was older. Daniel would take care of him, and in time people would forget the stigma of his parentage.

It was for the best.

Thirty-Six

Monday, 20 August 1832—fine day

It was almost a week before Maddy had an opportunity to speak to Daniel about the future of Shelby. *His* future. With Ella. The men had been busy ploughing in preparation for planting maize, Jane and Mary had been busy in the new vegetable garden, and Maddy had ordered fruit trees for an orchard.

The walls of the house were waist high and Maddy had to continuously stamp down the images of Daniel and Ella living in the rooms Mama and Papa had designed. With each new course of stone she knew more clearly that there was no future for her at Shelby. She would never see the house completed.

She gave little thought to how her own life would be if she returned to England, for she'd left few friends, and her life had changed so dramatically Maddy doubted she would be able to tolerate an idle existence. With Grandpapa and the mill gone, there was no place there, and she didn't wish to live in a city—not after living on the river bank. But perhaps she would purchase a small place in the country. With the sale of Shelby, and what remained of Papa's funds, there was no need to decide immediately.

Maddy was sitting on the flat boulder in the glade when she saw Daniel coming down the path. She took advantage of the moment to absorb every detail she could before he noticed her and his guard went up. Concentration was etched on his face and she wondered what he was doing. He was within a hundred or so yards of her when he paused and turned to peer back up the hill. He stepped off the path and took several strides into the trees before again looking towards the yard. Maddy followed the line of his gaze and wondered what he was doing. After a few minutes he dug at the ground with the heel of his boot before re-joining the path and continuing towards her. He still hadn't noticed her.

'Daniel,' Maddy said quietly.

He started and stumbled a little before he spotted her in the dappled sunshine, and with a small wave of his hand he crossed to join her.

'Good morning.'

'Yes, good morning,' Maddy said, and immediately the awkwardness between them sprang up.

'I didn't expect to find you down here,' he said.

'I like it here. It reminds me of the park where my grandpapa used to take me for walks when I was young. Of course this is much smaller, but I like it ...' Maddy faltered. Curse it, why was she blithering on so? Daniel's smile was understanding.

'And you? What brings you down to the glade?'

'I've been thinking of how we could install a horse-driven pump to bring the water up the hill to a tank, instead of filling barrels and hauling them up on the dray from the river. The water is better from the spring.'

'Is it possible?' she asked, frowning as she examined the steepness of the slope.

'I think it could be, but it's just an idea for the moment. It will take a bit more thought before I can determine if there's a way.'

'But you're leaving.' Heat rushed to Maddy's face even as she blurted the words.

He frowned and nodded. 'Yes, but I'll still see if I can install a pump. Before I go.'

Maddy decided to ignore the last, and, grasping for an alternative topic, said, 'It wasn't Papa's greatest inspiration to build Shelby at the top of the hill and so far from the river.' Because although she'd been ruminating on selling Shelby for the best part of a week, now that she had an opportunity, Maddy was reluctant to broach the matter.

'No, but the spring is higher than the water level of the river, and I think if we were to level out that patch of dirt up there,'— he pointed to the place he'd paused to kick the ground beside the footpath—'we could install a horse-works and a pump to the spring.' He glanced at Maddy, his eyes shining with enthusiasm. 'If we build a tank, we can then pump water into it and have a more accessible fresh water supply.'

Maddy squinted up the slope, trying to envision what he described, but, having no capacity for engineering, she could not conceive of it. Which brought her back to the idea that Daniel should have Shelby. She had no doubt that he would bring his idea to fruition, and therefore make the farmyard and house situation superior. Melancholy flooded her; the relief she'd sought and found had been short-lived. There was no getting away from it. Maddy had to take the opportunity and speak to him of her proposal.

'Doesn't it bother you that you have worked so hard here and will leave it all behind?' she asked, keeping her eyes glued to the toes of her boots peeking from beneath the hem of her gown.

'Yes, and no. I have loved my time at Shelby, but it was never mine. And'—he paused, and she felt his stare but didn't look up— 'I'd always intended to have my own place.'

She said it before she lost her courage. 'Daniel, I want to sell Shelby to you. I've given it much thought, and I think I should sell Shelby and return to England. I seem to have lost my …' She paused, unsure what she'd lost. Was it her passion? Her interest? No, it was her heart.

'No, Maddy, you can't sell Shelby.'

She met his gaze and found him much closer than she expected. She took in the lovely blue eyes framed by lashes too long for a man, she saw his full lips were pressed thin and remembered the feel of them. She watched him for a long moment before saying, 'Not to anyone else, Daniel, but you.' She sighed and looked away. 'You and Ella.'

'I couldn't—'

Maddy interrupted him. 'Of course you could, you more than anyone built Shelby to what it is today.' She met his eyes once more. 'You belong here.'

'I had been going to say I couldn't afford to buy Shelby.'

'Oh, I'd not thought of that. But surely Ella—'

'I will not ask Ella for her money,' he snapped.

'But—'

'No, it's not an option.' His expression was closed, and she knew it was useless to try to persuade him.

After a moment he dropped down onto the rock beside her and they sat in silence, lost in their own thoughts.

'I'm sure we could come to some arrangement,' Maddy said eventually, racing through a list of possible scenarios. Now that she'd broached the subject, she wanted it settled.

'I'm not interested in your charity, Miss Barker-Trent.' His voice was suddenly tight.

'It's not charity, it would be a business arrangement of course,' she hurried to assure him. 'I, er, I will return to England, leaving you to run the estate, and you can pay instalments. I'm certain we could find a way.'

'Why?' His anger evaporated.

'I told you I have been thinking about the idea for a while.'

'You still haven't told me why.'

No, she hadn't. And Maddy didn't think she should need to. 'Surely you know how difficult it is for me to see you and Ella together.'

'I see.'

'Do you? I don't think you do. You have made your choice, and I do not condemn you for it, but I can't sit by and watch her have the life I want for myself. I would rather return to England.'

'Ella doesn't wish to stay,' he said quietly.

'Oh.' For some reason Maddy felt miffed by this. That she wanted to go and leave them here was perfectly acceptable, but that they might go and leave her behind was not.

'But what do you want?'

'You have to ask?'

Maddy met his gaze and saw longing and sadness. Tears pricked her eyes. She nodded and struggled to her feet. She had to put some distance between them.

'Perhaps if you speak to Ella about my offer, she might be less inclined to drag you back to England when you have a suitable situation here. The house will ...' Maddy hesitated and gave a humourless laugh. 'Well, no, it won't be built soon, but a start has been made.'

'Maddy, I don't want to be at Shelby without you.'

'And I can't be here without you. Speak to her, please. You love this place as much as I do, so please at least try to convince her. We can draw up manageable terms ...' She stumbled on the words. 'W—when I leave Shelby, there's no one else I'd rather the place belong to.'

They were washing the bedding when Ella Whitfield called. Maddy looked up at the sound of an approaching horse and saw Daniel's betrothed riding Mrs Garrick's brown mare. Why did the ladies of the valley always arrive unannounced when she was up to her elbows in something? As usual, Ella was dressed in another equally elaborate riding habit with matching bonnet, though this one was forest-green rather than peacock-blue. Which reminded Maddy that her own appearance was that of a charwoman rather than a young lady. She might have blushed, but she imagined her face was already beet red from hovering over the steaming cauldron of sheets. She didn't have to do the rough work, but she found it oddly satisfying. And the harder she worked, the more sleep she managed before her swirling thoughts woke her.

'Miss Whitfield.' Maddy crossed the yard with a welcoming smile plastered to her sweating face. 'I'm afraid Mr Coulter isn't here at the moment.' Please let her go now, Maddy silently prayed.

'I'm not here to see Daniel,' Ella said, her eyes looking past Maddy to the fire and the large cast-iron cauldron hanging on a tripod over the flames.

Maddy glanced around to see Jane busy sluicing the laundry, her face every bit as flushed as she imagined her own to be. Mary, Maddy noted, was idling as usual, trying to appear busy by the bench. She sent her a warning look and Mary's face fell, her expression wounded, as if she'd been falsely accused. As this was her usual form of defence when caught dallying, Maddy ignored it and turned back to Ella. 'How can I help you?'

'Can we speak privately?'

Maddy straightened, glancing once again at Jane and Mary.

'Give me a moment to get my bonnet and we can go for a walk.' She looked at the horse. 'There's a mounting block by the yards, and you can tie up at the fence,' she told Ella and turned back to the fire, spitefully hoping none of the men were about to help her.

By the time Maddy returned with a bonnet, and her face considerably dryer, Ella Whitfield had dismounted and secured her mount to the fence of the empty yard where Daniel's mare was usually kept. Having no idea what she could wish to discuss, Maddy hesitated to begin the conversation. Without a word, they began to walk away from the farmyard, along the drive towards the road.

'I came here to ask you to leave Daniel alone.'

Maddy's heart and feet stalled simultaneously. She stared at Ella, wondering if she'd misheard. Surely she'd misheard.

'I beg your pardon?'

Ella stopped to face Maddy.

'Any fool can see he is in love with you, and you with him.'

'Miss Whitfield, I …' She what? She *was* in love with Daniel. 'I assure you, there's nothing between Mr Coulter and I.'

'That *was* what I came here to ask you,'—Ella stopped walking— 'but I have changed my mind.'

Maddy opened her mouth, but no words came.

'Please, let me speak,' Ella said, stalling Maddy's protest. 'It is no secret that I find the colony deplorable. I don't believe I could ever be happy here.' She surveyed the valley. 'I would be miserable living as you do, washing over a fire.' She turned to face Maddy once more. 'You were washing, weren't you?'

Maddy nodded. 'Sheets.'

'If I were to stay, I would only make Daniel as miserable as myself, and if I were to force his hand and make him return to England with me, he would probably do it.'

'He is an honourable man.' Maddy finally found her tongue, but she wondered if Ella was right. He had not given in to such demands to date. Had he told Ella of her offer?

'Yes,' said Ella, lifting her chin. 'And he would be a wretched husk of himself should I take advantage of his decency. I see now I did him a disservice, it was wrong of me.'

Maddy agreed, but didn't say so, for there was little to be gained.

Ella gave her an assessing look and Maddy foundered, did she suspect Maddy and Daniel of —anything?

'There's been nothing between us—no impropriety,' Maddy hurried to reassure her, blushing at the memory of his kisses. It had been only a few moments of silliness; they had been nothing but proper since.

'I've no doubt on that score.' Ella's lips twisted in a bitter smile. 'Perhaps if there had been it would make it easier. If you could ask Daniel to call at Tillington this evening, I shall tell him of my intention to return home to England. That I release him. Beyond this, it's up to you.'

'Please, Miss Whitfield—'

'Maddy, please, surely now you can call me Ella?'

'I'm sorry, Ella, but please, don't be hasty.' What was she saying? Maddy clamped her lips closed. Should she tell Ella of her proposal to sell Shelby?

'Maddy, I have been in New South Wales for four months after a six-month sea journey. I detest the heat, the dust,'—she batted the air—'these awful flies and insects.' Her blue eyes filled with tears and she turned away once more; her lips began to tremble. 'I just want to go home. I thought with Daniel it would be fine, and I would adjust, but his heart is not mine. It never was.' She began to walk once more, and Maddy hastened to follow. Her mind raced as she struggled to take in what Ella had said.

'You will break his heart,' Maddy told her. Why was she doing this? Ever since Maddy had known of Ella's existence she'd longed for her to disappear, and here she was, saying she would return to England without Daniel, and Maddy was trying to convince her to stay? It would be his sister's situation that would concern him, rather than his not marrying Ella.

'I would be doing exactly that if I were to stay, or worse, convince him to leave.'

Maddy took in the perfection of the smooth hair pinned beneath the green of her bonnet, her narrow-waisted riding dress, and then she looked down at her own soiled calico pinafore, dusty boots, and hair she knew had come adrift.

'Look at you,' Ella said, having turned back to face Maddy once again. 'You not only belong, you love it here. I could never learn to make soap and live among the convicts. I don't belong here.'

'Soap-making isn't difficult.'

She snorted a harsh bark of laughter. 'You see, there's the difference—you don't consider the challenges as hardships or the toil as punishment. You belong here. I don't.'

'But you could, if you wanted to.'

'I don't want to.'

But what about the Clintons' financial woes? Maddy didn't ask. How could she? It was hardly something she should know, let alone ask after.

Without any further conversation, they started back to the yard.

'Will you ask Daniel to come and see me?'

'Of course.' Maddy agreed after a small hesitation.

Ella nodded and their eyes met. 'Look after him, he's a good man, a decent man.'

Maddy blinked back sudden tears and nodded, unable to speak.

Thirty-Seven

Tuesday, 28 August 1832—very fine and pleasant

In the week following Ella's visit, nothing changed. She was confused by Daniel's lack of communication, and was surprised when a groom from Tillington arrived one morning with an invitation to visit the following day.

When she arrived at Tillington, Maddy was shocked to find the place in an uproar: trunks, barrels and chests crowded every spare inch of floor space from the door to the sitting room. Maddy was too bewildered to even ask what was going on.

'Oh, Miss Maddy, please excuse the mess.' Cookie hurried from the dining room carrying a pile of silver so high the woman could barely see over it, and if it weren't for her voice, Maddy might not have identified her at all.

'Whatever is happening, Cookie?' Maddy asked.

'We're going back to England,' she said, and at Maddy's gasp, Cookie deposited the silverware onto an already full crate and hurried over. 'I shouldna said that. You best go see the mistress, and she'll explain.'

Maddy stared at her for several heartbeats and nodded. 'Where is she?'

'I believe she and the master are in his office. You go right along: they're expecting you.'

Maddy nodded and returned to the courtyard, the clatter of metal following her as Cookie resumed packing the silver. If they were returning to England Maddy assumed they'd be taking all their valuables with them.

Inside the room was much the same as the hall and what she'd seen of the sitting room. Mrs Garrick had a cloth wrapped around her hair. She and young Bridget were wrapping items in linen and placing them in a chest. Mr Garrick was packing books from the shelves into another smaller crate and was the first to notice Maddy staring at them from the open doorway. He looked haggard and Maddy knew in an instant something terrible had happened.

'Maddy, thank you for coming.' Mrs Garrick glanced around and smiled tiredly. 'You must be wondering what on earth is going on.'

'Well, yes, but Cookie said you are going back to England?'

'Yes, I'm afraid we've had unexpected and awful news.' She glanced at her husband as she spoke, and Maddy was grieved to see Mr Garrick's face crumple a little. Maddy's heartbeat stuttered. Was it one of the children? No, that wouldn't mean they must all return to England.

'Alex, come, let's take a break and get a little fresh air. Bridget, will you ask Cookie to send tea and a light refreshment to the eastern veranda, for three, please?'

'Yes, mistress,' Bridget said and scurried from the room before Mrs Garrick could place the bundle of linen-wrapped ornaments into the chest at her feet.

'Yes,' Mr Garrick agreed, 'tea will hit the spot.'

They walked through the French doors onto a shaded veranda to a cane lounge and small table. It was a pleasant spot, sunny and out of the wind that had sprung up.

'We received a letter from Alex's father. His brother William has been killed in a hunting accident. We've been called home.'

Maddy gasped and turned to Mr Garrick. 'Oh, Mr Garrick, I'm so terribly sorry.' She stopped, unsure what else to say. Of course they would go, but his brother must have died months ago.

'The accident was almost six months since,' Mr Garrick said, confirming her thoughts, 'but my own papa is frail and unable to run the family estate, so it seems as I'm now the heir it falls to me to leave for England as soon as is practicable.'

'I see,' Maddy said and blinked. The ramifications were immense and she felt bewildered.

'Yes, the Clintons have already taken the steamer to Sydney, and we are going to join them as soon as we can. Alex is going to put the estate into the hands of a manager for the time being, and perhaps we will lease Tillington until we decide what to do.'

Maddy nodded and was saved from having to think of a suitable answer or comment when Tida cannoned out of the house.

'Maddy! Did you know we are going on an adventure? But Papa's brother Uncle William has died, and we're terribly sad.' Her eyes were round with sincerity.

'Yes, Tida, your mama has just told me. It is indeed very sad news.'

'But,'—Tida's usual indomitable demeanour reasserted itself—'going on the ship to England will be an adventure. Cookie says she is not looking forward to it, with everyone seasick. But I shall not be sick. I love going on the steamer to Sydney.'

Beth arrived with a tray laden with tea and cake, interrupting Tida's barrage of enthusiasm.

'Give Maddy a kiss and go with Beth and help find Ann and Edwin—you have packing to do.'

'Goodbye, Maddy.' Tida stepped closer to Maddy and offered her cheek to be kissed. 'Perhaps you can come and visit us in England.'

'I may one day,' Maddy told her, blinking back sudden tears. It was bad enough to lose Daniel, but the Garricks as well ... Whatever would she do without these wonderful people? Tida snatched up a biscuit and scampered back into the house. Maddy saw the girl's parents watching her go, indulgence and melancholy etched on both their faces.

'Are the Clintons returning to England as well?' Maddy asked, desperate for a distraction.

Blinking as she refocused, Mrs Garrick turned to her. 'Hasn't Daniel told you?'

'Told me what?'

'That Ella has broken the engagement and they left the valley earlier in the week for Sydney. You wouldn't know this, but Matthew and Charlotte's finances are rather tangled. I shouldn't be telling you, but it might help you understand Charlotte's animosity. I believe she and Matthew hoped a match between Daniel and Ella would, er, solve a great many problems. Ella is from a very wealthy family; new money, but money none the less.'

Maddy started at that and felt heat rush to her cheeks until she knew she must be glowing bright pink. She shook her head. She could never admit Daniel had told her of his brother-in-law's financial indiscretions.

'I've not seen much of Mr Coulter since we, er, since Ella and I escaped the bushrangers.' He'd been around, but they'd managed to avoid each other almost totally since Ella had visited. Whenever she'd come across him, he was always with one of the men.

'Maddy.' Mr Garrick looked at her with such compassion tears sprang to Maddy's eyes. 'Daniel said you offered to sell him Shelby.'

'I thought he and Ella might find it suitable,' Maddy said, hoping he didn't ask for any further details.

'If you do wish to return to England, you would be welcome to sail with us,' Mrs Garrick offered. 'We won't leave for a few weeks yet.'

Her words shook Maddy. It was an opportunity to leave, to have travelling companions—and yet Ella was gone. Did that mean Daniel had changed his mind? Despite the fury burning in her gut she sipped her tea and thanked Mrs Garrick for the offer. Maddy didn't know what the future held, but one thing was certain: she was going to be having a discussion with one Daniel Coulter.

'Daniel Coulter, when were you planning to tell me that Ella and your sister have left the valley?' Maddy slid down from the saddle and, dropping the reins, marched towards Daniel and the men where they were working on the border fence.

Daniel looked up from the fence post he was ramming dirt around with the end of a heavy bar, frowning. He glanced uncomfortably at Joseph, who was holding the post steady, wiped sweat from his eyes with the back of his gloved hand and swallowed as colour stained his neck. His expression was unreadable beneath the shade of his hat, but his mouth thinned into a line. He drew in a breath before words finally came. 'Perhaps we could talk about this later.'

'Yes, yes of course we can.' Maddy spat the words. 'Perhaps we could make an appointment to discuss it some time after Christmas.'

He rammed the bar into the ground beside the post with such force that it sank in a full twelve inches. He strode to her side, wrapped an arm around her shoulders and urged her away from the three men, who stood gaping at the goings-on.

'Maddy, what is the meaning of this? What are you thinking to speak to me like this in front of the men? Have you no thought for your reputation?'

'Reputation?' It struck Maddy then that he must have changed his mind. 'Is that it? My *reputation*? I know well enough how the *genteel* folk of the valley speak of me, but I didn't think you cared about such things.'

'What?' His expression went slack with bewilderment. 'What are you talking about?'

'I know what people are saying about me, living with not only convict servants but with a bastard child, a half-brother.'

'You think I care a jot about that? Those are the exact reasons I love you. Because you don't care about those things nor what people say about you. Don't you think I've gone my own rounds of jeering and scrutiny? I don't care what people say.'

He held both Maddy's arms in his gloved fingers, and she leaned back to peer up at him. She couldn't see his face hidden in the shadow of his hat.

'What?'

'Why didn't you speak to me before now? Ella told me she'd already spoken to you. Why didn't you say anything?'

'Because you didn't,' Maddy told him.

Her cheeks flamed hot and she glanced at the men, who all stood watching. Phil, Joseph and Mick were so entranced that they didn't even pretend not to be listening.

Maddy gazed up at Daniel once more. 'I was afraid.' To her dismay, her lip began to tremble. She bit down on it.

'Afraid of what?' His hands relaxed their grip and began to move gently over the cloth of her sleeves, thrilling and terrifying her at the same time.

'That you didn't love me any more—that you'd had second thoughts and didn't know how to tell me.'

His eyes were still hidden, but his mouth relaxed into a gentle smile, a loving smile. 'Madeleine Barker-Trent, you are a goose. How could I not love you?'

'I wasn't sure.'

'Well, you can be sure—you can always be sure.'

'You must promise to tell me things, everything. I can't stand secrets.'

She knew she'd have to tell him about Luke, and Mama's letter, but there'd be time for that later. It wouldn't matter at all to Daniel. Of that she was certain.

Maddy reached up a hand to push back the brim of his hat and it fell to the ground behind him. His eyes were as bright as she'd ever seen them, and they were smiling every bit as lovingly as his lips. She watched those same lips draw closer as he lowered his head.

A cheer erupted from the men as they stood on the river bank, with the brown ribbon of life-giving water flowing past, taking the fears and secrets away on the current.

Author's Note

The idea for *Daughter of the Hunter Valley* first came to me when a distant relative researching our family tree contacted my father. Finding my ancestry stretched back into the European settlement of the Hunter Valley, and discovering we have a connection with the Assistant Surveyor William Harpur, sent me in search of more information about the early years of agricultural expansion along the Hunter River. The more I read, the more I realised it was often the women who ran these vast estates in their husband's stead, be it due to absence, illness, or death. Brave women, who shot snakes, withstood attacks by bushrangers and battled the elements to shape the countryside into the beautiful and rich farming land it is today. A few miles from William Harpur's property, Oswald, is Dalwood Estate, George Wyndham's vineyard and farm, and when I came across the transcript of his farming journal, I knew I'd happened upon just the thing to give Maddy's farming experience real authenticity.

Acknowledgments

Firstly, I must thank my husband Dave, who grew up farming the rich alluvial soil of the banks of the Hunter River, and was my 'go to' for all farming information and the moods of the Hunter; my friend and accidental mentor, Tea Cooper, who nagged me to rewrite what was initially my practice novel, and who read and reread it and told me all the bits she hated. *Daughter of the Hunter Valley* would not exist without her; and a special thank you to Kate Forsyth, who taught me the value of research.

So many thanks go to my amazing beta readers, Annette Harpur, Gina Radford, Jenni Murrell and Aileen O'Riordan, who all cheered for Maddy when I was struggling to keep her story afloat.

To the amazing team at HarperCollins who have been so patient with my newbie questions and dumb mistakes, particularly Rachael Donovan, Laurie Ormond, and the fabulous editor Kate O'Donnell, who showed me how to shape this story into a beautiful novel.

Daughter of the Hunter Valley is over ten years of research, writing, rewriting and more research. The amount of people who have helped and encouraged me is enormous and I don't think I can ever name them all, but I certainly appreciate you all.

talk about it

Let's talk about books.

Join the conversation:

 facebook.com/romanceanz

 @romanceanz

romance.com.au

If you love reading and want to know about our
authors and titles, then let's talk about it.